Shakar: Blind Ambition
by Chris Godwin

While recovering from major surgery and reading *The Lord of the Rings*, Chris Godwin realized that fantasy novels weren't just for the very young. Out of her newfound interest in writing the first *Shakar* novel was born.

Apart from writing, her interests include travel, painting and playing the saxophone.

Having travelled the world, Chris has now settled down in the Fens with her computer and a cat named Hero for company.

Shakar: Blind Ambition

Shakar: Blind Ambition

Chris Godwin

ISBN 978-1-935786-19-1

Published by
St. Clair Publications
P.O. Box 726
McMinnville, TN 37111-076 USA
http://stan.stclair.net

Contents

Shakar: Blind Ambition

Chapter 1: Contact

Varoi moved along the riverbank with a careful, catlike tread. The path he followed was narrow but well defined. Waving grasses rose hip high, brushing against him as he passed, their drooping heads heavy with sun-ripened seeds ready for release.

Having been sent ahead to scout, Varoi was checking for signs of the enemy, looking for possible clues to their whereabouts. Like a predator seeking prey he moved with a stealthy, feline grace.

He was over seven feet tall and clad in dark leather armour that tended to creak as he moved, which was no hindrance at all to his task.

He was *ananaha*: acutely aware.

In this heightened state his senses were expanded to an infinite degree. All aspects were open to his perception. It was the ultimate protection against unwelcome approach. At the same time, it rendered him vulnerable: pain or pleasure, joy or grief all could be felt with increased sensitivity.

Varoi did not anticipate problems, even so. His sense of hearing was rendered acute, magnified, as were all his other faculties. It was impossible for an enemy to sneak up on him unawares.

He was hunting. And nothing he knew of could distract him from that task.

Except …

She came upon him as a warm breath of wind: a zephyr seeking its origins, touching him, reaching into the secret recesses of his mind, filling him with such a sweet intensity of longing it stole his breath, turning his blood to flame. A living, breathing, profoundly female entity had entered his mind.

The suddenness and subtlety of her arrival took Varoi by surprise. Shattering his concentration, fragmenting his innate ability to remain attuned to his surroundings, leaving him totally at her mercy … and that of any others who might be around.

"Ahhh," Varoi froze in his tracks on a sharp intake of breath, the sigh wrung from him reflexively. Now, after all the long years of searching, when naught save a sinewy, stubborn streak of hope remained, she had reached out and completed the connection. His soulmate had found him … and at the most inopportune time.

Varoi could only pray no one else had heard the sound he had just made. He felt her first as a light brush against his awareness; a feather-light touch that expanded his senses and sent him reeling, but then, departing abruptly, left him desolate, longing for more. Had it happened in the heat of battle he could, quite possibly, have been slain; the momentary distraction of *lossa antario si suve*, first contact between lovers, had a devastating effect on all who were unprepared.

His golden eyes widened in alarm. That she should come to him now, when least expected, was incredibly poor timing. Trembling, he sank to his knees, the blatant candour of her greeting rendering him disarmed; blind to all save her uniquely feminine allure.

That a part of him had been seeking her still amazed him; though, in truth, he should not have been surprised. He was, after all, a full-blooded male in his prime. It was imperative he locate his soulmate in order that they might bond. He had sought her ever since his Quickening, many years having since passed without response. Yet, in some quiet corner of his mind the search, evidently, went on. At last, he had received the long awaited reply.

Instinct compelled him to respond to her wild siren call. Yet when he reached for her again he found her gone, leaving him naught but the mere trace of her presence: a warm glow that infused his being, a faint echo of her seductive caress, which left him bereft and driven wild with desire.

This connection, however ethereal, was just the start of a much longer quest: first the connection, next the finding and then, if the goddess Lecristo was kind, a bonding would take place. Assuming there was no rival ... and if there was? Varoi was under no illusion. It was a sad fact of life. He had less to offer than most.

Varoi's upward-tilted eyes were golden, his overlarge mouth full and wickedly sensual. With his honey-coloured skin, long brown hair and powerful physique he was an impressive figure ... but not handsome, not by any means. It was a fact of which he was abundantly aware; this truth, having been pointed out to him in the cruellest fashion on the same night his sister had died, was something he was hardly inclined to forget.

Varoi came to his senses to find himself crouched, white-knuckled fists clenched and pressed to the hard ground; bracing himself for whatever might come. Hearing the soft footfalls of his cohort approaching from behind he strove to regain his composure, to discover the quarry's whereabouts in the time left available to him.

It was a perilous situation into which he had fallen. There were many places where an enemy might hide. To his right lay fields of barley and wheat, crops ripe and ready for harvest, which grew close alongside the road. To his left reeds and rushes hemmed the muddy riverbank, while leggy trees and overgrown bushes clustered close together like tousled weeds. Each nook and cranny offered a potential hiding place. Even with his *ananaha* gift deployed a minimum of movement was required to attract his attention and warn him someone was close. Thus sight, sound and smell could respond.

He sucked in a breath, releasing it as a soft, ragged sigh. Long had he endured without evidence of his soulmate's existence. To find her now, when he was in no position to pursue, was incredibly poor timing. He was luckier than most: some males never did locate their soulmate; others suffered years of denial before achieving success. He would not forget her existence, not now he knew she was out there, somewhere, waiting for him to appear. Their first contact had been tantalizingly brief, yet undeniably real. Soon, he would begin his search in earnest; but not yet.

Aware that his cohort waited, Varoi turned his unique talents to more appropriate use. He straightened and stood, then pointed at the path ahead.

"They passed this crossroads heading west."

"How long ago?" Commander com 'Dolino asked.

"Not long."

"Then let's waste no more time. With luck we may intercept them before they reach the next village."

After that all conversation ceased. They moved ahead in single file, following Varoi, it being his turn to run in the vanguard. And run he did. But knew better than to outpace his comrades by too great a distance, even so.

The foe they sought was a hostile breed of man. Pulan warriors had invaded the Unclaimed Land before. It was they who had named this land; named it then left it for others to tame. They'd been coming back ever since: first as herdsmen, to that area of swampy grassland abutting the steppes, during the winter months when biting insects were few; later, after the Shakar had arrived, making the fens a more hospitable place to live, the Pulan had returned as raiders, returning more often of late. In years like this, when the harvest was good and the grassy uplands to the south suffered drought, Pulan raiders came in search of whatever they could steal.

10

Men worked these fields and fens but the Fenlanders were a different breed from the Pulan: stockier in build and stubborn by nature, Fenlanders were content to swear fealty to the High Obajan, ruler of all the Shakar, offering allegiance in exchange for protection.

The Shakar called all men breeds and knew each one apart: their customs and allegiances, their weaknesses and strengths. They resembled humans in all respects save one: their eye-teeth were larger, more highly developed than those of men. This was their most distinctive feature. They were taller, too, male and female, though there were some notable exceptions to the rule.

The Shakar, on the other hand, stayed aloof. They were an altogether different race. They were, *Shakar*. And, while humankind might be more numerous, more widely spread and more fecund, the Shakar had come to consider themselves the dominant race; *and*, present conflict aside, more peacefully inclined.

The five-mile tramp to the village passed quickly. Their progress was marked by the rhythmic thud of boots, the dull creak of armour and the occasional chink of swords shifting in sheaths. All other sound was absent. Even the birds were mute, which seemed to signify that their foe was close at hand.

Varoi hoped they would arrive in time, having witnessed at first hand the devastation wrought by Pulan raiders before. In particular were the ones known as Ice Warriors, a group of which they presently pursued. By reputation they were the most ruthless of their kind with regards to their treatment of any who dare oppose them, even when women and innocents were involved. These last risked death or capture and, sometimes, worse.

The distant clamour of conflict having reached him, Varoi slowed. Fifty well-armed Shakar were more than a match for twice that many Pulan; even Ice Warriors treated a Shakar cohort with healthy respect. But the sounds that reached Varoi's ears indicated a far larger number was involved. The expected onslaught was already underway: time to pray the men of this village had been prepared.

Reaching over his left shoulder Varoi eased the bastard sword in its sheath and waited for the rest of his cohort to catch up. This village, like so many in the fens, abutted a riverbank. Without boats, to which the Pulan seemed averse, it could only be reached from three sides.

Commander com 'Dolino considered the situation, then instructed his second-in-command.

"Lieutenant com 'Domicci, I want your section to take the far perimeter. I'll allow you enough time to get into position, but no more. We'll attack the enemy from all sides. That way we'll contrive to pin them down betwixt the village wall and ourselves. Let's pray to the goddess these villagers were ready. The numbers involved may not work in our favour this time."

There was no need to expound further. Varoi replied, "As you command," and turned away. One third of the cohort went with him.

The surrounding terrain was mostly flat, intersected by dykes and shallow ditches that drained into the nearby River Bure. Dry stone walls surrounded the village, creating a boundary that would provide useful cover should the village come under attack.

It was late summer. Most of the harvest was in but some left over stooks of corn remained, while nearby hayfields awaited a second mowing. Varoi took advantage of whatever cover was available, expecting those with him to do the same. Adjacent fields were criss-crossed by a lattice of lanes. Most of the ditches that ran alongside them having run dry, they served Varoi's purpose admirably.

Their attack went roughly according to plan; except for one minor, but all-important detail. Varoi's group was not yet in position when the call to attack came.

Without hesitation Varoi rose from the ditch into which he had just crawled. Drawing his sword he pointed it in the direction he expected his section to run; then raced pell-mell into action. After that he gave no further thought to those following his lead. Each male knew his allotted place in the group's loose configuration. None among them needed reminding of what he had come here to do.

The Pulan were a powerful breed of men, skilled in the military arts. Ferocious and determined, capable of wielding their battle-axes to good effect. Farm implements employed as makeshift halberds and pikes were liable to prove a poor match against such dedicated instruments of slaughter. Apparently the villagers were proving equally determined in their efforts to wreak damage upon their foe. The Pulan force appeared to have suffered a delay. Held at bay they were unprepared for a surprise attack from their rear and the speed with which Varoi's cohort descended upon their ranks.

Varoi had no qualms about taking out his first two opponents from behind. They would attack him in like fashion if they had the chance. One spun about in time to snarl defiantly into Varoi's face before he went down.

The next Pulan was a mountain of a man. Varoi bared his teeth in a fearsome grimace that was meant to intimidate. It worked on some more than others. This man returned the menacing grin with one of his own. His opponent was all muscle and bone; hair the colour of bleached barley straggled from beneath a dented helm; his sole objective seemed to hack and hew. There was no skill involved in his onslaught, just belligerent brawn.

The first blow Varoi sought to parry sent recurrent shock waves travelling down his arm. He blocked two more in quick succession, while seeking a chance to respond. The next strike smashed past his guard, denting his helm and tilting it awry. Varoi staggered back from the blow, the harsh din of hammer and anvil reverberating around his skull.

Retreating one step, then another, Varoi placed a safe distance between himself and his perilous foe, giving himself time in which to gather his wits and clear the haze that mazed his vision. One thing he now knew for certain: his adversary's aim was all-out attack; his defensive ploys were virtually nil. Having already learnt this much, Varoi resolved to find the required opening and put an end to this skirmish forthwith; else create an opening where none existed, if needs must.

With this in mind his next few moves were purely diversional. They served a worthwhile purpose, even so. Then, employing a quick feint as a distraction, Varoi stepped inside his opponent's guard. One quick upward thrust to the groin served his purpose, cutting through chain mail links. The brutal blade sank home.

He'd misjudged. His adversary's axe swung back, catching him a hefty whack to the ribs with the weapon's haft. A reflexive act or pure inspiration, Varoi had no way of knowing. As a result his helm went flying, while the strength of the blow knocked him clean off his feet. Varoi scrambled quickly erect, prepared to defend. But the giant was down on his knees and groaning.

Determined to thwart any further attack, Varoi leapt on his enemy's back and drove his blade home with savage efficiency, severing steel links, scraping bone and damaging soft tissue and vital organs in the process.

There was no time to retrieve his lost helm for his next opponent was already upon him. If there was one thing Varoi knew: this new foe would *not* grant him the courtesy of waiting while he hunted up his missing helm. Varoi was lucky the man hadn't come upon him while he was still down.

Varoi had no choice but to begin this next skirmish on the downed giant's back, a less than stable platform on which to perform. His new opponent appeared to have a worrying penchant for hewing at knees. And, since Varoi's stance was now of a height to assist in such an attack, he soon found cause to rue his elevated position. Whereas his last foe had sought to decapitate him, this next was equally determined to cut his legs from under him.

But his rival's skill soon proved to be all fancy footwork with no finesse. Varoi countered this with some fancy footwork of his own, not nearly so nimble, but effective enough. The end result was conclusive and, as the Pulan's eyes went wide with shock and pain, Varoi leapt down and ventured a quick look round. But there was no time now to reclaim his helm as another adversary homed in.

Beyond that he became too busy: keeping his feet under him on blood-slicked soil; preventing his hands and head from being lopped off.

Hours passed; and the action wound down. When a quick glance round revealed no Pulan in any condition to continue Varoi felt himself sag at the knees. He was sweat soaked and worn to the bone. Still, he could not resist an insolent jibe. "Is there no one left to fight?" he complained.

A wry chuckle to his left, followed by "There speaks a true Shakar," drew his attention that way. The male who'd spoken looked every bit as tired as he felt. Varoi summoned up an insouciant grin and slapped his comrade on the shoulder, before turning away and going in search of his helm.

A thin trickle of blood tickled along the inside of Varoi's ear, a bothersome irritation that could have been worse. He spared a glance back at the village, where all was now silent. There was a disturbing lack of bodies in front of the boundary wall. Did that mean that their aid had arrived too late? Having witnessed the distress caused by other Pulan raids, Varoi was not looking forward to what they might find.

Chapter 2: Reunion

Varoi had his back turned as the first heads cautiously peered over the crown of the boundary wall. He was preoccupied, discovering which members of his section were among those fallen, and so failed to notice when the gate in the wall swung ajar.

"Here they come," someone said, causing Varoi to glance over his shoulder as a small group of people appeared bearing a motley collection of arms. They were led by a sturdy man with a plumed helm rakishly perched atop his head.

His cohort advanced to meet them, anxious to learn how the village had fared, with Commander com 'Dolino striding foremost in the van. Turning back, Varoi bent to straighten the limbs of one of their fallen, before reaching to recover his helm.

"Diabolon's eyes, I don't believe it! Varoi com 'Domicci is that you?"

Varoi straightened from what he'd been doing and spun. His face lit with a grin of sheer pleasure when he saw who it was that spoke.

"Borit Grosgrain, fancy meeting you." Detaching himself from his contingent Varoi strode forward to greet his friend.

Borit laughed, delighted to see again the young male he'd befriended some years before. "You've filled out considerably," he said.

"Well then, just look at you," Varoi retorted in kind. "You've put on muscle and height besides. How fare you these days?"

"Well enough," Borit replied. "I'm a journeyman blacksmith now, I'll have you know."

"Which is why you happen to be here?" Varoi guessed. Giving him a genial nudge, he said, "Nice to see you, Borit. Time we caught up with our news."

"Indeed it is."

A mournful mewing somewhere overhead caused Varoi to look up to see in the distance a lone buzzard riding the thermals. Further off other carrion birds were homing in, ghoulish diners assembling to feast.

"Are you coming, Lieutenant com 'Domicci?" Commander com 'Dolino called, and Varoi's attention snapped back to find his officer waiting for his and Borit's conversation to end. Everyone was staring at them. It seemed not only were they were the subject of overt conjecture but also the unintentional cause of delay.

"Yes, Commander," he said, before wrapping one arm about Borit's shoulder and accompanying him and the rest of the cohort through a gap in the wall. Expecting the worst, he braced for the drama to come.

At first glance the scene of slaughter appeared chaotic. Yet, it was an orderly chaos that prevailed. Bodies were being loaded on to handcarts. These, though, were the bodies of Pulan, many of whom displayed horrendous injuries. Another handcart, placed nearby, groaned under the weight of a different kind of cargo. The bodies of the Pulan dead had been relieved of weapons and armour before being thrown on the handcart ready for consignment to the traditional pyre. While it might be deemed a useful expedient, such practice had never been witnessed before.

The Shakar commander pulled up short in surprise, at which Varoi recalled the equally incongruous sight of the village headsman in his ill-fitting helm. A second glance revealed the item to be of Pulan origin and, therefore, a trophy confiscated from among the dead. That it was adorned by a tatty tuft of white horsehair proved it had once belonged to a warrior of rank.

Some of the community were busy repairing damaged sections of wall, while others stood guard or oversaw its reconstruction. Those few places where the walls had been breached showed a greater concentration of dead. While this was not altogether surprising, Varoi was relieved to find most of these dead were Pulan.

Seeing no evidence of women or children among those who had fallen, Varoi dared to hope they'd escaped persecution this time.

Hearing the commander's surprised exclamation the headsman was quick to explain.

"Having had enough of being caught out by Pulan raiders in the past we resolved to take matters into our own hands. And so, when the blacksmith arrived to mend our tools, we advised him his services would be put to an alternative use: providing weapons we could use against the foe. You may not approve of our methods but you must agree that they worked. We had a plan; one we were not averse to implementing."

"What plan?" Commander com 'Dolino enquired.

Varoi listened with intense curiosity to what the headsman had to say.

"Those men you see loading bodies on to carts were supplied with crudely-made swords, the blacksmith having made good use of whatever materials came to hand. The rest of us armed ourselves with sharpened farm implements that had been converted into halberds and pikes, which is normal practice during such times. The swords are a recent innovation. Doubtless, we shall do this again."

Hearing this, Varoi beckoned one of the swordsmen over, relieving him of his blade. Hefting it he then awarded the sword a more than cursory inspection before handing it back with a satisfied nod. Borit, being far too absorbed in the conversation now taking place, paid no attention to what Varoi did.

Varoi's commander queried, "You say your swordsmen were effective. How so, when they have not been trained? I've no wish to cast doubt on your achievements. I just find them hard to believe."

The headsman dipped his head in tacit acknowledgement of this established fact.

"Our swordsmen lack the necessary skill, tis true. Nor was there was time to practise, other than to learn the fundamentals. And, as I said, their weapons are crude. However ..."

The headsman lifted his chin in a defiant pose, eyes gleaming, enjoying his brief moment of victory.

"On this occasion we felt no need. You see, we chose those men to whom we gave swords with especial care. With strict emphasis on certain ... criteria, I should say."

Varoi saw wolfish grins break out on the faces of those villagers lingering nearby. Only the swordsmen looked grim.

"These ... criteria ... you mention," Commander com 'Dolino said. "What might they be? And how, precisely, were they applied?"

Varoi found himself leaning forward, anxious not to miss the answer to this obviously-loaded question.

"Don't worry, Commander, I'm sure you'll approve. We chose our strongest, fittest men: those who were willing, those with wives and daughters to protect, and reminded them of the usual Pulan attitude towards any innocents they take unawares. As expected, their attack on any warrior who successfully penetrated our guard was merciless in the extreme."

"So, all who managed to climb over the wall died?"

"Oh no, Commander, not quite all. *One* was allowed to survive."

"But why? Surely it goes against all common sense."

"We disabled him first, ensuring he was in no condition to continue the fight. Then, having disarmed him, we handed all responsibility for his welfare to our resident physician. But not before he'd enjoyed a ringside view, a sampling of what his friends endured."

"But that is barbaric."

"True ..." The word was drawn out and there was a degree of truculence now evident in the headsman's tone. "But then, you must agree, it should prove effective. Besides, I'm given to understand the Shakar view all men as essentially barbaric. How could we bear to disabuse you of such a strongly held belief? You'll understand our reasoning soon enough, I promise. But now," the headsman waved an indolent hand, "permit me to show you our ballista."

Varoi turned to stare at Borit. *Ballista?* He mouthed the word, his expression one of stunned surprise and scepticism.

"None of my doing," Borit informed him, taking instant delight in Varoi's incredulity. "The carpenter came up with a plan and things developed from there. These villagers are typical of most. They hate being pushed around by Pulan."

Varoi's expression was pained. "We do our best."

"Mayhap you do, but still you can't be everywhere."

Which wasn't the point and Varoi knew it. It was also a matter of stubborn Fenlander pride.

Thinking it prudent to change the subject, Varoi said, "So, Borit, does this mean you plan on becoming an armourer then?"

The look of amazement Borit returned was rewarding enough. But then he said, "Perhaps I may. I hadn't considered the idea before. I must admit it does appeal."

If Borit was surprised by his suggestion, Varoi was more so by the reaction it received.

They walked in silence for a while, until Borit said, "You're wounded Varoi. You should get that seen to."

"'Tis nothing," Varoi said, reaching up to find one side of his head sticky and sore. Hiding a flinch, he shrugged Borit's concern aside. Wanting to make light of what was, after all, a minor injury, he quipped, "The man who did this looks worse."

"I can imagine. Even so ..."

"It's just a scratch. No point in making a fuss." But Borit would not be satisfied and before Varoi knew where he was they'd entered the healer's tent.

"All that blood," the healer said. "Makes things look worse than they are."

"I said that, didn't I?" Varoi pointed out with smug satisfaction.

"I'll clean it up. It should heal of its own accord after that."

Varoi submitted, without protest but with no real enthusiasm, to the healer's careful ministrations.

Dusk was falling fast by the time Commander com 'Dolino completed his routine inspection, having assured himself that the villagers' defence was more than adequate, compelling the Shakar to abandon their plan to resume pursuit of any remaining Pulan and stay in the village overnight. This pleased Varoi, since it allowed more time for him and Borit to become reacquainted.

Further upstream, a full day's march overland, the town of Tenbay occupied a strategic position, where a wide bend in the river formed a natural harbour suitable for the unloading of ships carrying a wide variety of merchandise. Its stout watchtowers and crenulated battlements, constructed of pale stone, rose in tall, protective ramparts, forming a well-known landmark that was clearly visible for miles around. It was home to a permanent garrison of five hundred Shakar. While it had never yet come under attack it was not invulnerable. Should the Pulan abandon their usual custom of invading only in small groups, their combined numbers could create a large enough force to threaten Tenbay itself. A settlement had been established barely a stone's throw beyond its outer walls, which was home to a large number of Shakar civilians.

Commander com 'Dolino had planned to reach Tenbay before dusk that same day but the Pulan attack on the village had caused a delay. With luck, Tenbay's garrison commander would work to ensure that all necessary precautions were being carried out. There was nothing that could be done this late in the day. The risk of an ambush was far too great. Any Pulan that had escaped might be lying in wait.

Daybreak would be a prudent time to resume their journey. The village headsman had promised a sumptuous feast with which to celebrate their victory and a safe place wherein they might rest for the night. It would be churlish to refuse so generous an offer, although the cohort planned to depart by dawn the next day.

Their decision made and the offer of sustenance gratefully accepted the Shakar warriors and the village delegation repaired to the longhouse, where celebratory meals were traditionally served.

The mood inside the longhouse was convivial. The gathering was seated upon narrow benches set out on either side of two long tables. The polished wood was of ironbark oak, which shone mellowly in the soft light of lantern and tallow dip. The walls had been whitewashed and left unadorned. The window shutters had been closed for the night.

At the far end of the room a small side door led into what was apparently a kitchen. From this quarter delicious and mouth-watering aromas wafted forth and the blithe chatter of women engaged in culinary pursuits could plainly be heard.

Varoi, seated across from Borit and close to the outside door, raised his eyebrows questioningly. "Prepare to be royally served," Borit said.

Varoi glanced round as a large stone flagon was passed along the table from his left, accompanied by a tray of mismatched pewter mugs.

"Help yourself," Borit urged. "No one need stand on ceremony here."

Varoi poured a measure of liquor before passing the flagon across. "What does it taste like?" he wondered aloud, viewing the contents askance.

"Try it and see," Borit challenged.

Varoi did. Tasting a sip, he found it good. Downing the rest with one long swallow, he reached for the flagon, eager for a second sampling.

Borit laughed, pleased to see his friend relax in the friendly atmosphere that pervaded the longhouse.

"This is the first pressing of the fruit," he explained, "before it is set aside to ferment and turn into pure alcohol. It has all the pleasure but none of the pain. This I promise. There'll be no thick heads or hangovers come morning."

"Why do we not get this in the city?" Varoi asked, appreciatively licking his lips and wondering dare he pour another draught.

"There, my friend, you have me at a loss. You're asking the wrong person, it seems. Apparently your noble hierarchy consider this to be an ignoble brew and, therefore, unworthy of their consideration. Look on the bright side, Varoi. Their loss is our gain. I, for one, cannot complain. Drink up. There's plenty more where this came from."

A mug clanged loudly against another, somewhere to his right. Varoi glanced in that direction to find the village headsman rising to his feet.

"A toast: to all those brave Shakar gathered under our roof this night."

Other villagers were getting to their feet.

"A toast!" they loudly exclaimed.

The Shakar commander responded in kind.

"To our indomitable hosts, who showed courage and fortitude despite facing impossible odds, thereby achieving the seemingly impossible."

Varoi stood, along with his cohort, pleased to be part of the celebration. They had seldom found cause to celebrate during an invasion before.

When he resumed his seat Borit lowered his voice to a murmur and said, "So tell me, Varoi, what news? As I recall, when last we spoke you'd just signed up with the military, your prime objective being to gain sufficient experience in order to avenge your sister's death. I can't believe Schezan would submit without a fight. Yet I see no sign of grievous damage having been done to your person. What happened? Don't tell me your grief has now abated and Bayritz's death is but a distant memory. Have you forgotten the vow of vengeance you made that night?"

Varoi glanced down at his hands and, unaware of what he was doing, started to chew on a torn fingernail. This had the effect of making him appear thoughtful, which, in fact, he was.

"How can I forget? I feel responsible for what happened. If not for me Bayritz might not have been there. Twas an ill-omened night all round; a night when the moon goddess Lecristo turned her blind eye to the nefarious doings of all ne'er-do-wells and others of their ilk.

"And no, I haven't yet found occasion to confront Schezan. Our paths have not crossed since that night."

"Do you think he's avoiding you?"

"Mayhap he is. If so, I'm bound to catch up with him sooner or later; and when I do ..." Varoi smacked his fist down hard on the table, making the cutlery jump and earning himself more than a few startled looks into the bargain.

Borit laughed, making the sound a more hearty chuckle than necessary in a bid to draw interest away from Varoi and, by so doing, distract attention from his friend's evident annoyance and carefully controlled grief. Tears swam in Varoi's golden eyes, and, though he held them back, the effort it took was plainly visible.

"Then you'll not let matters rest?" questioned Borit, once interest in Varoi's behaviour had started to wane.

"How can I? Schezan showed no remorse; nor did he offer to atone for any part he had in that fell deed. We were grieving, while he moved on as though nothing untoward had taken place. Furthermore, the crime he committed that night was not just against Bayritz but against the Shakar nation as a whole. Our females are precious and few."

Borit straightened in his seat. "No less than ours, Varoi."

"Perhaps so; but in your case there is a solution to potential dearth. If you cannot find a woman to wed, and your need for one to maintain your breed is great, you can send to the next town, the next city, the next nation if need be." Varoi made an expansive gesture with his hands. "Humanity's hoard is great, compared to ours. What you see of us is all there is. As a species we are unique."
Seeing Borit's pensive frown, Varoi could not help but add, "Unless you know different."

Borit shook his head. "I know nothing more than you. I was just recalling the tale of how your people first arrived on the Dragon Coast. None like you had ever been seen before."

"And none shall, so far as I know. Now do you begin to understand why I cannot let this matter rest. Bayritz said something revealing that night. She said Schezan was to be her Chosen, which meant they would pledge. I think that is what their quarrel was about. I'd like to believe Schezan deprived himself of a mate when he

26

blithely shoved my sister off that precipice. I'd like to believe that but I cannot. I hope Schezan never finds a mate. It would be a fitting punishment for what he did."

"You don't know that he will."

"I know there will always be females attracted to who he is and what he will, one day, become. His father, recall, is High Obajan." The last was said with a certain asperity.

There was no answer to that and Borit, wisely, didn't offer one.

"What about you, Varoi? Have you found your mate?"

"In a manner of speaking, I have."

"Then, let's drink to that and be damned to the rest."

"Aya," said Varoi, as, with a grin of approval, he reached for his mug. Borit wondered, seeing that grin: though he smiled more often than when first they'd met, there was still sadness apparent in Varoi's glance. What might it take to make that sadness go away?

Before they succeeded in raising a toast the door alongside them flew wide. A grey-haired man stood on the threshold, wearing an air of wearied resignation. "May I come in?"

The headsman rose, beckoning the newcomer forward. "Shalwar, please do. You know you are more than welcome at any such gathering."

"In view of what I'm about to report, others present may disagree."

"Nonetheless," the headsman half turned, waving his hands in an encouraging gesture. "Make room please. Allow the physician to sit." Those seated alongside him shuffled further along on the bench. "Shalwar, join us if you please. I'm sure the Shakar commander is as anxious as I to discover news of your patients' condition."

"And, of course," Shalwar responded, his tenor tart, "the Pulan prisoner would just happen to be high on his list of priorities."

"Naturally," the headsman agreed, unperturbed by Shalwar's caustic tone. He gestured toward the vacant space alongside. Grudgingly, the physician complied.

Varoi was puzzled by the physician's apparent reluctance. Something about his manner seemed strained, as though his behaviour were part of an elaborate charade enacted for the benefit of those assembled. Varoi was forced to wonder why. Reaching for the bread he tore off a chunk, pretending to concentrate on his meal. But his attention was otherwise engaged and, at first, he failed to do the food justice.

Shalwar spoke and, while his voice was low, his words carried, as they were, undoubtedly, meant to do. "A couple of men, those among the most seriously injured, have since died. Others respond well to treatment."

"Go on," the village headsman urged. "What of the prisoner? How fares he?"

It was at this precise moment that Varoi became aware of a growing tension pervading the room. The ear of everyone present was so attuned to this particular conversation that all noise in the longhouse had ceased, as though all present held their breath in anticipation of the physician's response.

Into the resultant silence, Shalwar announced, "He has escaped."

The room exploded into uproar. Varoi noticed, with some surprise, that it wasn't the villagers making the most din. Despite the fact that it was their prisoner who had gone missing, their initial reaction appeared curiously restrained. He turned his attention back to Borit, seeking a likely explanation, to find his friend sitting bolt upright, apparently engrossed in the surrounding conversation, his arms crossed on his chest.

28

"Borit," he hissed. "What *is* going on?"

"Wait and see," was Borit's advice. Varoi guessed he would have to be content, for now. The physician, it seemed, had not yet finished his report. "It should be interesting to observe the headsman's reaction," Borit added. With a discreet toss of his head, he directed Varoi's attention that way.

The village headsman raised a silencing hand, then glanced about. "Please," he said. "Let Shalwar finish. Questions and accusations can wait. I would know exactly how this escape was managed." Silence descended as all present turned their glance back to Shalwar. "Be so good as to inform us of what occurred."

With a brusque nod from the headsman Shalwar rose, stepped clear of the table and looked around, taking in his audience at a glance. "My apologies to all who thought to keep the Pulan prisoner. He is gone. I for one do not regret his absence."

At a fresh outburst from those Shakar present the physician held up a hand. When peace returned he resumed speaking. "I shall explain as best I can. Those present must judge as they see fit. I pray you have a thought for my position. It was not easy dealing with the situation that arose." Shalwar gave a satisfied nod, acknowledging the restraint applied on the part of those present, as they kept silent in order that he might continue without interruption.

His glance transfixed by the headsman's apparently jovial countenance, Varoi harboured a nasty suspicion of what the physician was about to divulge.

"As most of those present will be aware, two guards remained in attendance during my treatment of those injured. Their express orders were to ensure the prisoner did not escape."

Guards? Varoi thought. The guards employed must have been villagers rather than Shakar, since neither he nor any of his comrades had been thus disposed.

"The Pulan prisoner was given only a mild soporific since he had suffered a considerable loss of blood. This was administered primarily in order to reduce his resistance, enabling me to carry out treatment of his wounds. Since one hand had been removed below the elbow, rendering him partially disabled, I did not anticipate problems. This, together with another wound to his thigh, caused me to assume it unlikely he would attempt an escape for some time. Even so, his guards were not lax.

"It was another patient who created unforeseen trouble when he succumbed to an apoplectic fit. I was unable to restrain him and administer the medication at the same time. Naturally, I called on one of the guards for assistance. All should have been well but, alas, Lavoy is exceptionally strong. You recall to whom it is I refer?"

The headsman gave a dismissive wave, exhorting the physician to continue.

"One man's help proved insufficient. It required *two* strong men to keep Lavoy still long enough for me to pour a strong soporific down his throat and a few minutes more while we waited for it to take effect. When we looked up from our task we found the prisoner gone. 'He cannot have got far.' I assured my assistants, though they seemed doubtful, I will admit. Just the same, I instigated a thorough search.

"I cannot believe he had sufficient wits, let alone the strength required. He had already imbibed a fairly powerful soporific and should have been well under its influence by then, never mind his already-mentioned limiting disabilities. Who would have thought he possessed the necessary resilience to overcome all that?"

"Who indeed," was Varoi's tartly murmured aside. His gaze focused upon the headsman, who seemed surprisingly unperturbed by Shalwar's admission.

"You made a serious but understandable error in underestimating the prisoner's ability to escape," Commander com 'Dolino began.

"Not at all," the headsman promptly disagreed. "Shalwar was unaware of certain decisions our elders had already made. This was no mistake, Commander, I can assure you. We rather hoped events would turn out this way."

"To what purpose, may I enquire?" There was an acerbic note of censure in the commander's tone.

"Give me a moment and I shall explain."

"Then your explanation had better be good," Commander com 'Dolino said, seeming less than pleased by the headsman's admission.

"It will be," the headsman reassured. "The prisoner has escaped; tis true. The infirmary lies alongside the riverbank. It was arranged thus in order that its occupants might benefit from any cool breeze. The escaped prisoner is bound to have taken full advantage of the ample cover available in that vicinity, although, no doubt, it will take some time before he rejoins his fellows. But when he does he'll have a gruesome tale to tell: of bloodthirsty farmers who offer no quarter to those who undertake an unprovoked attack; a tale where none escaped save he; a tale to chill the blood and leave them quaking in their boots …"

"A tale to rouse them to savage anger and a desire to settle their grievance."

The village headsman looked unconvinced. "I don't think so."

"But I do," Commander com 'Dolino said. "You plot and plan as a civilian does, while I, as a warrior, speak from bitter experience and not just for myself but for every

31

Shakar present. Fear might indeed raise its head at this grisly tale but only briefly. Unless the Pulan have more important plans, ones they intend putting into immediate effect, by your actions you run the risk of a vicious reprisal."

"He will report what he sees to his fellow warriors and they will know in future to leave us alone."

"Perhaps. You had best pray they do. We cannot remain in this vicinity in order to save you from the results of your ignorance."

"We had no intention of asking you to stay here and hold our hands. We are not children to be treated thus." The headsman seemed equally annoyed at such a suggestion. The heated exchange was escalating with no sign of compromise in sight.

"Excuse me, please." All eyes turned to the physician, who remained the centre of growing discord. "You may wish to know that, before the prisoner rudely departed, I managed to extract some information, which comprised a rather garbled threat, it seemed to me."

The commander's attention promptly returned to Shalwar. "Say on."

"In truth, he said little and most of what he uttered I failed to comprehend. He did, however, mention a name, Baltor, which I confess means nothing to me. His attitude towards those trying to render him aid was truculent to say the least. Tenbay was mentioned and another, oft-repeated word was 'niscee'. Does this mean anything, Commander?"

The commander's features froze in alarm. Varoi, who understood only a little of the Pulan tongue, still recognised the likely import behind those few words. His glance slid sideways to encounter Borit's, which appeared perplexed. Seeing this, Varoi hastened to confer the benefit of his greater understanding. "Tenbay is the town to which

32

we were heading before we became involved in the conflict here, a conflict that caused us delay."

"So?"

"Patience, Borit, let me finish. Baltor is a warlord of some repute, known for his bitter hatred of all Shakar. A large number of Shakar civilians inhabit a settlement adjacent to Tenbay. The word 'niscee' refers to a number: ten hundred, if my memory serves me right. Think of it, Borit: ten hundred Pulan heading their way. The Shakar of Tenbay won't stand a chance if we fail to provide warning in time."

"I see."

"Do you, Borit? Do you realise the conflict in which we took part today may represent a calculated ploy? How can we hope to reach Tenbay in time to prevent a massacre? What your village swordsmen accomplished against the Pulan was commendable. Unfortunately, this delay may have unforeseen consequences. It may have made an already bad situation worse."

Varoi's voice had risen in volume as the enormity of the position sank in. Not till he finished speaking was he aware that all attention now rested on him; not till his commander's voice cut in. "That seems a fair assessment of our predicament, Lieutenant com 'Domicci. Any further insights you might wish to impart?"

Varoi flushed a bright crimson. Embarrassed by the unsought attention, he hastened to say, "No, Commander, I think, perhaps, I've said enough."

One of the delegation raised his hand. "If I may interrupt? There is a faster means of travel than going overland; one you don't seem to have considered. You could sail upriver. It permits a fast passage and, if your assistance here has caused adverse delay, I think we owe you appropriate recompense for your plight."

"Yes, yes," other villagers were swift to commend their colleague's idea.

"This offers you an excellent solution, Commander com 'Dolino. Please. I do insist you avail yourself of our aid," the village headsman said.

The commander's voice was icily polite. "I have not the slightest intention of refusing your offer. But, if we *are* to arrange matters thus and without delay, would it not be best if we finished our meal."

"Of course, Commander, whatever you say." If the headsman was perturbed he failed to acknowledge the fact. "After all," he said, "this meal is meant as a celebration of our mutual triumph this day. Let's not spoil the occasion by paying less than close attention to what our womenfolk have worked so hard to provide."

The commander nodded, mollified. Whatever his thoughts on the matter, and Varoi could hazard a guess, there was nothing to be gained by endless recrimination. Varoi returned his attention to the meal, as the conversation of those present became restricted to social niceties.

By the time the meal was finished and cleared away the following day's arrangements had been finalised. The villagers helped to prepare the longhouse so that the Shakar could settle down for the night. The long tables at which they had eaten were pushed back against the walls and the benches set atop, allowing ample space for the warriors to bed down. Since none in the village would rest easy in their bed until the Pulan had been sent back across the border the headsman went to organise the overnight change of guard, while other members of the delegation supplied the Shakar with whatever bedding could be spared.

Varoi bade his friend a reluctant goodnight and prepared to retire. He and Borit had become close since their initial meeting, when Borit had inadvertently chanced upon the event that had cost Bayritz her life. They would always stay in touch, not least because Varoi felt he owed his friend a debt. There was no doubt in Varoi's mind that

Borit had saved his life that night and for that he would always be grateful. Tomorrow they would go their separate ways.

Varoi chose a position close to the outer door. Tomorrow night he would able to sleep further in. It was customary among the warriors for each to take their turn on guard.

Removing his leather armour Varoi set it aside, placing his bastard sword conveniently close to hand. Stripped down to his padded gambeson and soft leather wrap he stretched out on the rough pallet provided, pulled his blanket across and settled down. Sleep was seldom slow in coming. A warrior learnt to snatch rest where he could, even catnapping on his feet if the occasion required.

One shielded lantern remained lit, hung a little way back from the door, its wick turned down so that its faint glimmer cast tenebrous shadows across his comrades' resting forms. Soon only the steady sound of breathing could be heard. Tonight, it seemed, would be different; Varoi could not get to sleep.

Varoi closed his eyes, casting his mind back over the day's events, examining each detail in turn, recalling the sad occasion on which he and Borit had first met and the more uplifting occurrences they'd shared since. If anything good had come of the tragic events surrounding Bayritz's death it had to be the rare friendship he'd found with Borit that still endured.

Varoi flung up one arm to cover his eyes and blot out the light from an overhead lamp, allowing painful memories to fade. Briefly he allowed his *ananaha* gift to surface and unfold; extending his heightened faculties into the night, listening in briefly to muted conversations, then racing past. This was no time to indulge in idle curiosity. If danger lurked nearby it was within his ability to seek it out and identify its source. He found none, and, finding nothing, allowed his untoward concern to ease.

Another incident had occurred earlier that same day, overshadowed, till now, by other, more recent events. Varoi latched on to this singular occurrence: the instant when *lossa antario* had finally proved its worth, by allowing him to connect with his intended mate. Therein lay his hope for the future: a matter of far greater import than revenge, at least for now.

He latched on to the one elusive detail. It raised all manner of questions: who was she, and where might she be found? Snuggling down beneath his blanket, Varoi reached deep inside, allowing that lax tendril of enquiry, which *lossa antario* comprised, to unfurl and drift free, seeking, finding her where he hardly dare hope she might be.

Chapter 3: Speculation

"Ahhh." The soft, drawn-out sigh was barely audible in the pitch-black darkness of the sleeping chamber. Ayesha had been verging on sleep when the sensation swept through her frame, at once vibrant, yet warmly sensual. Now she was fully awake and wondering. *Who?*

One thing she knew for certain: whoever it might be was a full-blooded male, alert, awake and fully aware of what he was about, as he now proceeded to demonstrate to considerable effect.

She recalled something her mother had once said: a warning, for so it had seemed to her at the time. "*Lossa antario* has a devastating effect when it takes you unawares." *Lossa antario si suve*: first contact between lovers was the correct translation from Darubi to the Common Tongue. The words seemed to require capitals when uttered in conjunction. Only now did Ayesha begin to understand why.

She lay back, closing her eyes, waiting to discover what would happen next. No words were spoken, no explanation offered, when he reached for her again. Perhaps, she reflected, he lacked the necessary wherewithal to accomplish such refinement. She would wait to see where this initial contact led.

His mind touch was deeply sensual, provoking a strong wave of arousal that coursed through her body, setting every one of her senses aflame and leaving her shuddering and breathless in its wake, astounded by the strength of his sending.

Abruptly the sensation changed, became subtle, a gentle caress that felt almost constrained, like the tentative touch of fingers that sought only to please. Was he shy, she wondered, or merely cautious. Then those questing fingers touched her in a way she did not expect.

Her lips parted as she sucked in a breath, her heart sped and her shy blush brought a glow to her cheeks. *Who are you?* she enquired, unable to resist the question that begged to be answered. Something entered her mind: a living presence, with, as yet, no name attached. Peeved by his impertinence she tried again, her voice a sly castigation of his incautious presumption. *I don't believe we've been properly introduced.* A hint of amusement accompanied by distinctly male laughter echoed through the hallways of her mind. He had no right to use her this way without permission.

And yet ...

To establish *lossa antario* required that he possess a fair degree of shamanic power; power to which she had limited access of her own. Was it possible she could augment her inadequate abilities by tapping into his and thereby respond in kind? The thought offered unimaginable appeal.

Throwing off all previous constraint she flung the bedclothes aside; after all, they were of no hindrance at all to his sending. She might as well lie here naked for all the difference they made. Slowly she raised her hands. And then, with eyes tight closed, applied her mind to the problem at hand and encountered ... living flesh!

With gentle fingers she traced the firm contours of his well-developed pectoral muscles, following each well-defined line and curve, before proceeding to his flanks. Cautiously she allowed one small hand to stray from there across to his belly, where she encountered a narrow ribbon of hairs leading down. She traced this with equal curiosity. Her touch delicate, she felt his stomach muscles tense beneath questing fingertips and found ...

"O," the small sound of surprise escaped before she had a chance to think of its arrest. She hesitated, but not for long. Laughing softly, seductively she gave one quick upward flick with her finger and withdrew.

Make what you will of that. Lowering her hands to her sides, she awaited his inevitable response.

Nothing happened.

She wondered whether she had gone too far.

She had no way of knowing whether or not he was a stranger or someone with whom she was already acquainted. In truth, that possibility hadn't occurred to her, until now. She hadn't awarded it much consideration. When she did she found it most disturbing.

His touch returned: still tender, still circumspect. It was almost as though he understood and would make no more of her audacious act than she intended. For that she felt extremely grateful. But the warmth that next consumed her body had nothing whatever to do with gratitude. His tactile enquiries now pursued a different objective. At her shiver of uncontrolled delight she felt his instinctive reaction. And then, abruptly, and without prior warning, all contact ceased.

Ayesha waited, convinced he would return. But it seemed the answer to her question, was an unequivocal: *No.*

She sucked in a calming breath, releasing it with a long, shuddering sigh. Her body felt strange, different, in a way she could not define. It was definitely aroused. Yet, denied a satisfactory conclusion, she felt bereft, wanting him to reach out and touch her once again. She drew in another slow breath and wondered, *Would he return? If not this night, at some other time?* Then her mother's advice returned to haunt her and two crucial words sprang to mind: first and future contact. Which meant: *There must* be *more to such a liaison than this.*

Releasing her breath with a slow, deliberate sigh, Ayesha rolled over and gave herself up to sleep.

Varoi hauled the blanket over his head, then gave vent to a low, despairing moan. Merci's breath, he wanted his hands on her again. He'd thought it impossible to feel like this after so brief an encounter. No one had seen fit to warn him just how strong a reaction *lossa antario* could produce. Parts of him ached with the strain of denial. He felt a fierce yearning to reach for her again. He dare not. It was too soon, too early in their relationship. That was, if it could be described as such. And might she not already regret their shared intimacy? He knew only one sure way of finding out. But, not yet, he reminded himself; not just yet.

There is a saying among the Shakar: 'If the breath of the goddess Merci steals across you whilst you sleep you will find yourself a thousand times blessed.' Varoi didn't believe in the remote likelihood of such an auspicious event but, in common with most Shakar, he called on the goddess frequently. That he did so now was more by way of frustration than any expectation of a likely response.

He had learnt a little during the brief dalliance he and Ayesha had enjoyed; and he had been acutely aware of her shy, maidenly blush. But her playful response to his evident arousal had stolen his breath. He had known then that it was time he broke contact. Yet it had proved a difficult decision to enact, for the desire to complete their union was intense.

Varoi fidgeted beneath the blanket, aware that he risked waking those sleeping alongside. His breath came in harsh, sonorous gasps. In desperation he rolled on to his stomach, clenched hard the rough edge of his mattress with two fists and pressed his cheek to the coarse, feather ticking as he fought the urge for much needed release. *Merci's breath, would their encounters always leave him thus?*

Now fully awake and unsatisfied, besides having been denied much needed rest, he went over in his mind his most recent, and least expected, encounters. The wick in the solitary lantern burned down, shedding a warm amber glow throughout the longhouse, while it lasted. Those of his comrades who'd survived the day's conflict slept. All looked much as it had, but something within him had changed.

Revealed by the faint radiance of lamplight his grin flashed wolfishly white, as two canines winked into view. *What was it Borit had once said?* 'Those eye teeth look almost sensual to me.' As to that, there were some truths he would not reveal.

Rising from his pallet just before dawn, Varoi pulled on his boots, tucked his sword into its leather baldric and stepped outside. The cool air was bracing and he stretched his arms wide, drawing in a deep breath of chill air. He needed to bathe; and this was the best time of day for ablutions, before his comrades became fully awake.

Some of those villagers on guard waved him a greeting. Varoi waved in return and continued on his way, pleased to see them taking their duties seriously. There was still a chance the Pulan might return. The vigilance of these men was paramount, since it ensured an early warning should the need arise.

Reaching the riverbank he removed his weapon, placing it within easy reach, before removing clothes and boots and diving in head first. He was a strong swimmer, though he still recalled a time when this had not been the case.

The water was deep, the current swift, and the channel about three miles wide and navigable for a considerable distance upstream. Varoi kept his ablutions simple and discreet. His task complete he rose from the water and perched on the bottommost step, wavelets lapping about his shins. Having wrung as much water out of his hair as he could, he proceeded to rub himself dry, before running long supple fingers through the wet tangled strands of his hair, tying it back with a leather thong. This done he strapped his knee-length leather wrap in place before shrugging his way into the felted gambeson.

Tugging his boots on he caught hold of his sheathed sword and started to stand, then paused, lost in thought.

What was she doing, this lovely sprite who had found him at last, thereby awakening all his previously repressed lustful urges? Might he, perhaps, find her asleep? That prospect alone proved disturbing. More importantly, would she welcome his return? Would she readily submit to a renewal of his advances or offer, instead, a sharp rebuff? He knew only one way of finding out.

Eyes closed he reached for her again ... to encounter silky hair, satin-soft skin and the rhythmic breathing of sound sleep. In haste he withdrew, not wishing to wake her and give her a fright. Merci's breath, why had his search for her taken so long? Still, he felt utmost relief, knowing he could find her again whenever he chose, whenever the need for her arose.

Grabbing his sword and sliding it into its scabbard he strode back to the longhouse, whistling a tune. The sky overhead grew pale, birds twittered in the nearby undergrowth. With his fortunes now on the rise; Varoi could not help but rejoice.

Ayesha awoke with a start, to the distinct impression she was not alone. Opening her eyes she pushed aside a thick tangle of tawny hair that partly obscured her vision. Outside, the first pallid fingers of dawn fractured the margins of the night sky: insufficient light by which to erase the tenebrous shadows that yet lingered in her sleeping chamber, where wooden shutters at her window stood firm guard against approaching day. But as her eyes adjusted she saw that she was, alas, alone.

At least, so it appeared on the surface. Yet, she knew different. That she remained aware of his presence erased all other details from her mind. The presence that had invaded her privacy had a familiar feel: at once vibrant and warmly sensual. She resisted the urge to reach out, to touch him again. Who knew where such casual intimacy might lead?

Ayesha lay back on her pillows, allowing herself to reflect on what had occurred, to speculate on the specific details brought to mind. Shamans who could accomplish so strong a contact were, to her knowledge, few; for one thing their shamanic force must be extremely potent. There was one male with whom she was familiar who possessed such innate ability: none other than Schezan com 'Varicci. But he always arrived in the flesh and was either ingratiatingly suave or obnoxiously demanding. And, if it were not Schezan, there could well be trouble ahead. He was certain to react badly to any prospect of a potential rival. And, if it were not Schezan to whom she was promised, who might this turn out to be?

She had speculated, often, on what manner of lover her future Chosen might be. She knew exactly what she required of such an alliance: something akin to what her parents enjoyed, the loving respect of a mate fully committed to a life shared. Some might ask what more she could want. But she had ambitions too, certain goals beyond this. These last had driven her decisions so far.

As daughter to a chief she had her sights set on a higher rung up the ladder and knew it to be well within her reach since becoming formally pledged to the heir of the High Obajan. She had made her promise. That should suffice.

Except for one thing …

Now there was a complication: one that offered something else, something more desirable, if less easily defined. If this contact through *lossa antario* were in no wise connected with Schezan there would be consequences involved. The thought entranced: Merci's breath, what a sweet and delicious dilemma.

The villagers had left a blue flag fluttering on the mooring post overnight as a signal to any passing vessels that prompt assistance was required. This assistance could take many forms. On this occasion the aid requested was passage upstream for Commander com 'Dolino and his cohort of warriors.

Varoi was part way through breaking his fast when the message arrived informing their commander that a vessel had been sighted and would shortly berth. By the time the cohort had finished their meal and assembled on the wooden decking of the wharf the ship was safely tied up and not a single mariner was in sight.

"Where's the captain?" Commander com 'Dolino said, as he studied the ship's graceful lines. No one answered. No one seemed to know. The sails were all neatly furled, while the only sound was of water slapping against the boat's hull.

"Shall I go aboard, Commander, and find out?" Varoi enquired.

"Best not. Some mariners have definite ideas about whom they invite aboard and whom they do not. And we don't yet know if this vessel is manned by Shakar."

For a while they formed a disconcerted group, chattering amongst themselves. No one yet knew whether or not the request for passage had been passed on and, if it had, whether or not it had been approved. The ship currently tied up alongside the wharf was known as a packet or courier vessel. Its primary use was as a fast means of delivering mail. Although it had been known to transport passengers as well, it had never had so large a number as now waiting to board.

When Borit appeared, sauntering along the narrow planking that comprised the wharf with large a bundle hoisted over one shoulder, Varoi saw his arrival as yet another complication. It wasn't that he was displeased to see his friend; he simply didn't see how there could be enough room for all present. He didn't get the chance to voice his doubts as a booming voice called out, "What's all this?" Apparently, the ship's master had just come on deck.

As the commander stepped forward, prepared to clarify the situation, the boards underfoot started to bounce to a different tread. "Allow me, Commander," the village headsman said. "Captai, I can explain."

All present turned to look at a short and sturdy man whose tousled appearance implied he had just that second tumbled out of bed. His hair was a nest of tangles, he sported a day's growth of beard and his clothes were decidedly messy. He was still pulling them straight as he arrived, though that did not mean he lacked the requisite air of authority. However harassed he might seem, still he commanded the necessary respect.

Climbing aboard the vessel he proceeded to put matters straight. After a hurried explanation, which appeared to involve a certain amount of money changing hands, the captain spoke.

"Commander com 'Dolino, I shall be happy to transport your cohort. I must add, however, that they cannot all be accommodated at the same time. This vessel is just too small to carry an entire cohort. Quite apart from the risk of capsizing, it is built for speed rather than comfort. Too many passengers will slow us down, besides compromising the safety of all those aboard. Borit Grosgrain, come ahead. You're welcome aboard anytime. Commander: a quick word if I may?"

Varoi watched with interest as Borit stepped on to the deck and moved away to one side. Far from proving a problem, Borit, it seemed, was accepted, which was interesting considering these sailors were Shakar. Apparently Borit had managed to endear himself to their captain, to the point where he received preferential treatment.

When the commander returned he split the cohort roughly in half: those who would travel to Tenbay on the first voyage and those who would stay behind. Varoi was glad to be going with the first group, since those who remained had been ordered to make themselves useful until the vessel's return.

It was a fine, crisp morning. The scent of autumn hung heavy in the air, with a stiff breeze to lift the mist and speed them along, as the sleek little craft got underway. So far as Varoi could see she was an excellent example, all graceful lines and neatly stowed gear. The Shakar manning her took obvious pride in how she handled, displaying a commensurate degree of proficiency for their task.

Commander com 'Dolino and most of those with him went below, crowding the tiny cabins and companionways. Varoi and a few others, Borit included, stayed on deck. It was necessary that they be thus deployed, else the tiny vessel would be top heavy and would wallow like a lazy, overstuffed sow.

Sails slapped overhead as the ship cast off and set sail. Then the sails bellied out to an accompanying shout, and sheets and stays were trapped, then hauled tight, and tied off to the nearest cleat. For Varoi it was a familiar sight, one guaranteed to stir old memories. Like his comrades he did his best to stay low, well clear of the main boom lest it swing about and crack an unwary head or sweep a body overboard.

Varoi closed his eyes, hugging himself tight. His left side ached abominably, thanks to the giant of a man slamming into him with the haft of his axe. Nothing was broken, Varoi was convinced. One or two ribs might be cracked; still he could live with that. But he was a mass of bruises, which inclined him to act protectively. Not that he cared to admit that fact.

With his eyes now shut Varoi recalled how, during earlier years, he and his friends had enjoyed their spells

46

aboard such craft. Bayritz, like the rest, had revelled in the freedom of sailing. In his mind's eye he saw her again, running barefoot across spray-drenched planks, brown hair streaming behind her like a glossy flag. He found such memories bitter-sweet, and hot tears of regret pricked the inside of his eyelids.

Varoi ended the recollection on that note, allowing his eyes to drift open to find Borit watching him curiously, from a short distance away. Deliberately, he turned his face away, not liking the idea that his emotions had betrayed him yet again. Even Borit, who knew and understood the cause, was excluded now from too close an inspection.

Varoi's gaze settled upon the far bank, over a mile distant, where reedy shallows and willow hemmed the water's edge. As the water glided past, gleaming ripples curled out from beneath the prow and an occasional plume of spray flew inboard, to grant all within reach a soaking. The calming effect worked.

It was just shy of noon by the time the boat tied up at its allocated moorings in Tenbay harbour. Past pain and old enmity forgot, Varoi seized Borit's wrist in a farewell clasp, arranging for them to meet later, duty permitting.

Having stepped ashore, Varoi took a quick look round. The port of Tenbay, which nestled into a horseshoe-shaped bend on the River Bure, had something of an industrial feel. Varoi studied the fortified harbour, with its curtain walls, high buttresses and crenulated, round towers that rose up on three sides of its four boundaries. It was the port area that interested him most.

The Shakar were a trading nation and nowhere was proof of that more evident than here. Merchant ships from farther down-coast plied their wares; the Cessarii were foremost among them but others also travelled this far. A Cessarii vessel was busy unloading and her decks were awash with bales of merchandise, no doubt gleaned from more than one nation. Not all had ready access to their own shipping or ports.

Varoi's gaze grew unfocused. Distracted, he stared about him with unseeing eyes. Something else was drawing his attention. She was close, closer than she had been so far.

"Lieutenant com 'Domicci!"

Brought back to his immediate surroundings by the sound of his name, Varoi realised it was not the first time he had been called.

"If you're back with us again, Lieutenant, I trust you're not just daydreaming the time away but paying close attention to relevant detail."

The question was implied, if not expressed. Chastened but unrepentant, Varoi felt compelled to recount some of the facts he had so far absorbed. Eventually, he fell silent, signalling his accounting to be at an end.

"Well then," Commander com 'Dolino said, "time to discover for ourselves what sort of facilities the resident garrison can provide."

Commander com 'Tovari was uncooperative. "I'm sorry, Commander com 'Dolino, but I really cannot see the need for such precautions. You said it yourself: '*If* the Pulan forces were coming they should be here by now.' Why concern ourselves with wild rumour and vague speculation?"

"Because, personally, I don't think we dare risk the possibility, however vague such rumour might be," replied com 'Dolino. "Better yet, I believe, to assume they still *are* on their way. Any delay they may have suffered should work in our favour. Let's not forget that. Besides, if that should be the case, the sooner we start evacuation procedures, the better it seems to me. We *must* get our people safely settled within these walls; all of them, not just a select few. That action is imperative in my view.

"There's something else you may wish to consider. Each clan raiding party numbers between fifty and a hundred well-armed men. The Pulan could, quite possibly, muster an army that is ten hundred warriors strong."

"But Tenbay's garrison numbers only five hundred in all," protested Commander com 'Tovari.

"My point precisely: the settlement must be evacuated. It's the only way to guarantee the safety of all involved."

"Why doesn't Commander com 'Dolino just take charge?" Varoi turned to his fellow warrior, Sverig. "After all, if the resident garrison commander has decamped down river to Nai Hai du Veral, doesn't it make sense for the most senior ranking officer to step forward and assume command?"

"Perhaps it would be wise not to judge this officer too harshly. He seems to have inherited an unusual problem. Who says we would do better given the choice?" Sverig quietly replied.

"All I can see is precious time a-wasting," Varoi muttered under his breath.

"Maybe …"

"Look sharp," someone hissed. Varoi stiffened to attention at his superior's approach.

"Right," their commander began. "We have less than an hour in which to down a quick meal, then make our way to an agreed meeting place, which I'm told lies just outside the fortress walls." Pushing wide the door he waited for his junior ranks to follow. Varoi's soft profanity, expressing delight that the situation was about to be resolved, was barely masked by the loud bang of the closing door.

The commander's eyebrows rose in instant rebuke. "What's this Varoi? Did you honestly think I might be dissuaded from my affirmed course of action? You should know me better by now. This young officer has been placed in an impossible position. His commanding officer is absent at a crucial time, leaving him to cope alone with what can best be described as a delicate situation."

"Poor timing," Varoi said. "Leaving your second officer in charge just as the Pulan decide to descend en masse. No wonder he's out of his depth."

"And you would cope with the present situation a whole lot better, would you, Lieutenant?"

"I didn't say that."

"No. But you implied as much."

"Perhaps, but what I meant was, why can't you take charge? At least, until this emergency is past."

"And how would that look, do you suppose, to you, to him, to those over whom he has command? Put it this way. How would you feel if I fell in battle and was dead or too seriously wounded to carry on, so that, as my second, you took charge of the cohort, as is your right? How might you react if someone like Commander com 'Tovari came along and seized command, on the grounds that he was senior and therefore better suited to the role?"

Varoi scowled at the thought. "If that happened I should be decidedly miffed."

"That's putting it mildly, if I know you. You're a first-class frontline warrior. It's why you were chosen for this role in the first place. It's what you do best. It's what I do best, as well. Commander com 'Tovari, on the other hand, is an experienced garrison commander. Our roles are different. I've no intention of usurping him; but I'm willing to offer what advice I can, to add my not inconsiderable weight to any tough decisions he may be forced to make. Any onerous tasks he has to undertake will be borne upon my shoulders as well as his.

"You would do well, Lieutenant com 'Domicci, to watch and learn. Take my advice. Don't judge; lest you be found wanting in return."

50

A prolonged silence ensued, during which Varoi thought long and hard on what had just been said, before nodding his head in agreement. "I'll do my best to remember that."

"Let's hope that you do."

Chapter 4: Ayesha

Varoi looked around. He could see, half hidden through a narrow break in the trees, the outline of roofs. He tried to imagine how this place might suffer from attack by a hostile army of Pulan … and found the thought profoundly troubling.

A scolding squirrel in nearby trees both amused and entertained as it pelted the waiting warriors with acorns, annoyed by their invasion of its territory. A pity the Pulan could not be so easily repelled. He was wholly absorbed by the squirrel's actions, until a noise from behind caused him to turn.

Varoi knew at once he would never forget his first sight of his soulmate, as she strolled toward him across the grassy clearing, which bordered the settlement. The male alongside her was also impressive; tall and well built and, despite the obvious signs of aging, all muscle with no sign of flab. Varoi diverted his attention momentarily in that direction but not for long.

Returning his focus to rest on the female he took rather more time to peruse her obvious attributes, of which she had more than her fair share. Long tawny hair hung loose, its ends floating on a chill autumn breeze. Her mouth, he saw, was full and softly sensual, just begging to be kissed. But it was her eyes that most drew his attention: set wide in a lovely face, they were a startling viridian; not dark, but palest blue green.

She was quite the beauty and the urge to touch, to confirm her reality, was overpowering. But he would not touch her, not yet, since, quite apart from anything else, it would be rude. After all, they had not even been introduced.

She glanced up, and, in doing so, caught his gaze upon her. The mutual shock of recognition showed in her face. Just for an instant Varoi thought she might acknowledge him, though that vain hope was promptly quashed when Ayesha deliberately turned her glance aside.

There was an air of calm assurance about her that seemed strangely at odds with the encounter they had both enjoyed courtesy of *lossa antario*. Plainly there was so much more to her than met the eye. Varoi could not wait for the chance to become better acquainted. To rediscover the pert and, hopefully, passionate nature lurking just beneath the surface of that cool exterior, was a more exciting prospect than ever he would have believed.

It required a real effort of will to turn his attention back to where it belonged, and yet, he had to. In order, at the very least, to learn her name, Varoi had to concentrate on what was being said.

As he listened in to the introductions being made, Varoi waited patiently, as befitted a warrior of lower rank. Offering the appropriate deference due to Chief lo 'Savoi and his daughter, Ayesha, Varoi raised his head in time to catch the princess's eye, and saw that her gaze was every bit as striking as it appeared at first glance. Then, to his dismay, she turned her head aside, choosing to ignore him, as though offering him a silent rebuke.

Varoi guessed he was meant to feel put out by such behaviour, but, instead, he felt mildly amused. She appeared far more interested in discovering the purpose of this meeting between her father and the two commanders. And she was evidently prepared to dig in her heels in order to become involved in whatever discussion took place.

"Ayesha," her father said. "Now that the introductions are complete and you have satisfied your boundless curiosity, might I suggest you return to the settlement?"

"Why can I not stay? I shall not interfere with your business nor offer any form of argument concerning the matter in hand."

"Nevertheless ..."

Ayesha stamped her foot in a fit of pique, which made Varoi's golden eyes gleam with appreciation. She had a temper and was not ashamed to show it. That should enliven his day: never knowing when lightening might strike would add spice to their relationship. How long had he hoped for such a female as this? Ever since losing his sister, Bayritz, it seemed. And here she was, a female with spirit who wasn't afraid to allow it full rein. Varoi couldn't wait to know her better; if he could but think of some way to get her alone.

As he listened in to the ensuing conversation, an idea occurred to him. It was only vague, and he could see many cracks and loopholes through which Ayesha might slip, but it was worth the effort of posing, even so.

"Father, please."

"No, Ayesha. My mind is made up. Much though your presence would be appreciated, the discussion that is about to take place is deadly serious. Your pretty face would prove too much of a distraction, I fear. And so, I must insist."

Now those lush lips pouted provocatively. Varoi felt the overwhelming urge to kiss her and vowed to pursue that objective at the first given opportunity.

"Excuse me, please, if I might make a suggestion?" All eyes turned towards him; Ayesha's were heated, while others held a speculative gleam.

"Well, Lieutenant, and what might your suggestion be?"

Varoi drew in a breath and began. "Perhaps the Princess would consent to show me those parts of town and its inner fortifications that will most likely be affected during the coming attack. I promise to be a polite companion, while using my eyes and ears to good effect in order to augment our present information."

"That sounds like the ideal solution to me," Commander com 'Dolino said, providing, of course, that her father agrees."

Commander com 'Tovari, acting garrison commander, chose this moment to intervene. "Surely, Commander, my experience can better provide you with …"

"… much useful information," Varoi's superior hastened to add. "Doubtless you can. However, if Lieutenant com 'Domicci, as my trusted second, can add a fresh perspective to the problem we face, what harm can it do? Should the Pulan arrive in full force we'll need whatever advantage can be found. Would you not concur?"

The expected answer came. "I suppose I'm inclined to agree."

"If Princess Ayesha feels inclined to assist us, I can think of no better way." Commander com 'Dolino addressed his next enquiry elsewhere. "Chief lo 'Savoi, what are your thoughts on this matter?"

"Let him do as he suggests. Just be sure no harm comes to my daughter." "None shall," Varoi hastened to reassure. "In this respect I believe our interest to be mutual."

If Ayesha looked less than pleased by this, Varoi, at least, enjoyed a brief hint of success. Ayesha's retort brought him up sharp.

"What about me? Have I no say in this matter?"

While Varoi wondered how best to respond, it was Chief lo 'Savoi who intervened. "You, Ayesha, will do as I say. Let that be an end to the matter."

As Varoi and Ayesha started away Commander com 'Dolino called after. "Varoi! I wish you to pay especial attention to the harbour and its surrounds. I suspect that to be where the greatest weakness in Tenbay's defence now lies."

Varoi offered a smart salute. "Consider it done."

Varoi did his best to moderate his long, masculine stride in an effort to accommodate Ayesha's more demure pace. Though they walked side by side, he could not fail to notice the gulf separating them. Ayesha, for her part, appeared to be in an inordinate hurry, as though this were an onerous duty she would soon see dismissed.

The silence between them stretched overlong. Varoi waited until they were well out of sight and hearing of the settlement before attempting to confirm his suspicions that it was Ayesha who had made contact with him, although the mutual shock of shared recognition and the thrill of excitement it aroused were confirmation enough where he was concerned.

"Princess Ayesha, forgive my impertinence but … you *do* know who I am?"

"Since we have just been introduced, I trust you'll not insult me by implying my memory is defective? Because, let me assure you, it is not."

"That is not what I meant. We have met before, and recently at that. Surely you recall the occasion?"

"When was this?" She demanded, keeping her gaze directed straight ahead, refusing to make eye contact with him.

Varoi, convinced she was being deliberately obtuse, wondered what she hoped to gain by her attitude. He could not be mistaken. Having acknowledged the spark of recognition that had passed between them he had no intention of being spurned. He tried again. "Last night, sometime betwixt midnight and dawn, I made contact with my future mate."

"How nice for you." Her acid tone was not lost on him. Varoi wondered why she chose to pretend indifference. "Still, I fail to see what relation this has to me, warrior com 'Domicci."

"Lieutenant," Varoi corrected, automatically. If she was intent on offering him insult she might as well get it right.

They walked a short distance in silence, with Ayesha's pace quickening. Eventually, Varoi could no longer stand her outright denial. Three long strides brought him ahead of her, placing him directly in her path. They were almost within hailing distance of Tenbay's battlements. If Ayesha wished to cry out for assistance, she could.

"Ayesha." He tried her name on his tongue and found it pleasing, and if her reaction was less so he could live with that. The desire to touch her had him reaching out, to trail one long finger down across her cheek in a slow caress. For an instant she appeared to relax. It was risky, what he did. She was a princess and far above him in social rank, but the desire to have her admit the truth made him bold, bolder than he might otherwise have been. His voice softened as he strove to convince her that what he asserted was actually true. "Ayesha, my contact through *lossa antario* was with you. Please don't refute this, for I know it to be so."

"Even if it were I should be forced to deny it, since, for your information, I am already pledged." This was not the answer Varoi had hoped for. Still, it did not mean there was no hope of his achieving a reversal of any such promise.

"So, I have a rival for your affections. Am I permitted to know whom?"

She assumed a pose, arms folded defensively. "You must know him, or know of him. Schezan com 'Varicci is his name; he's the garrison commander here. He's away at present. But, either way, he would not approve of your familiarity."

Schezan! Unable to meet her gaze, Varoi glanced up, past her shoulder, his glance settling upon a long line of trees that hid the settlement from view. What cruel irony was this? He wanted to curse and lash out, to rail aloud at the goddess Lecristo, whose notoriously malicious sense of humour took perverse pleasure in spoiling things by putting yet another vicious twist in his destiny. First his sister, Bayritz, for whose death he still held Schezan responsible, had been taken. Now Ayesha had given her pledge, prematurely, and Schezan was the one to profit by that.

The bitter words slipped out against his will. "Not again."

"What?"

Varoi fought to control the bright pulse of anger that flared, willing himself to appear calm and rational. She was not to blame.

Lowering his gaze to meet hers, he said, "If you were already pledged, what made you reach out and create the connection that *lossa antario* alone permits. Who were you seeking?"

"I thought …" She seemed perplexed by his question. "I expected the person I touched would be Schezan."

"Do you understand the secret of *lossa antario*? How it works? What it means when you touch someone that way?"

So few did, it seemed, females anyway. Males were made aware at the earliest opportunity, during the Quickening. Even then some males forewent the pleasure, assuming there were more certain ways of finding a mate. Schezan included, or so it seemed.

"What difference does it make? It was not my intention to lead you on. Well, not you specifically. I made a mistake. Best we forget it ever happened. I've already made my pledge."

If only it were that simple.

"Then unmake it."

He saw a flash of anger in those pale, viridian eyes.

"I will not."

"Then grant me the right to try and persuade you otherwise."

"And why should I do that?"

Varoi smiled. Perhaps, after all, he stood a chance.

"Because, according to custom, *lossa antario* grants lovers their first glimpse of what shall be; and, since it brought you to me, I think you owe me that much, at least."

Ayesha tossed her head.

"I'll think about it."

Apparently, Varoi would have to be satisfied with that. At least it left him room to manoeuvre. And he had no intention of ceding Schezan so momentous a victory as this. He would fight, tooth and nail, to make Ayesha his. However things turned out, none would say he hadn't tried his best.

While Varoi yet pondered on future possibility, Ayesha stepped round his now less dominating form to resume her interrupted course.

"Are you coming, Lieutenant com 'Domicci? I don't have all day."

Aroused from his reverie Varoi turned on his heel and hastened to catch up. More than anything he longed to halt Ayesha in her tracks: to seize fast hold of her shoulders and spin her about, to place his mouth against hers and savour the long awaited response.

He didn't dare.

Acutely aware they drew nearer, with every pace, to the outer walls, Varoi kept his impulsive nature in check. They were close enough to be well scrutinised by those standing guard atop its ramparts, whose curiosity must, by now, be fully alert.

Tenbay was a man-made town, constructed centuries before the arrival of any Shakar. If its strongly constructed keep and inner fortifications lacked the typical finesse and grandiose splendour of the more elegantly engineered Shakar citadels, it lacked nothing in the way of apparent impregnability.

Tenbay's battlements had been arranged in order to withstand a vehement frontal assault; whereas, by contrast, the citadel of Nai Hai du Veral comprised an altogether more subtle form of strength. Varoi, while possessing scant knowledge concerning the customary disposal of such well-appointed bastions of power, inevitably found his curiosity piqued.

As he set foot upon the drawbridge his glance swept up and out across the surrounding terrain, noticing, as he did, certain intriguing anomalies. The fortress was surrounded by a moat, which, for some unaccountable reason, was currently dry. How strange, he thought, when there was adequate water available in the nearby tidal river with which to ensure it remained full. He strode across the sturdy wooden slats of the drawbridge, ears pricked, listening to the resounding echo of footfalls as they rebounded from off the fortress walls.

"Princess Ayesha, might I suggest that we stop a moment to take in the view?"

"Really, Lieutenant, what is the point?"

Varoi released an eloquent sigh, before doing his best to explain.

"Because I ask it; is that not reason enough? And because, this is an integral part of Tenbay's defence with which I wish to become better acquainted. And, I would prefer that you call me Varoi."

"Very well, I shall do as you request, providing you also forego the honorific by addressing me as Ayesha."

She stopped in the centre of the bridge, waiting for him to come alongside.

"Ayesha," Varoi allowed the word to roll off his tongue, tasting its ineffable sweetness. Then he stepped up beside her and stood looking down.

They stood at the centre of the drawbridge, the pivotal point of Tenbay's outer defence. Below them, a trench several paces wide and many paces deep had been carved out of malleable clay and puddle firm. It ran the entire length of the curtain wall; before ending in a high-sided, gate-like structure that fronted the riverbank itself. Varoi had no understanding of how this last system worked, but he fully understood the purpose of moats and knew they were meant to be filled. The mystery remained as to why this particular one was dry. Still there were no cracks apparent through which water might drain.

The curtain wall was mainly constructed of shaped granite blocks. These outer battlements rose many ells high, topped off by broad, crenulated ramparts. The moat had been created in a manner that provided steep scarps along either bank. When full it would be at least two fathoms deep. Varoi guessed the scarps would be hideously difficult to climb and, when filled with water, an even greater hindrance to those planning any assault. Aside from these difficulties any potential foe must run the gauntlet of whatever missiles might be brought to bear. There would be numerous additional hazards ranged against those enemies trying to gain access to the fortified town, once the portcullis had been lowered and the drawbridge had been raised.

The technicalities of these operations were of scant interest to him at this time, however. What continued to astound was the fact that the moat was dry.

"This below, I see, is a moat," Varoi began, seeking to draw her into conversation and hoping for some useful information besides. "Tell me, Ayesha, why is it not kept flooded? I assume there to be a reasonable motive for this lack."

"Of course there is. Don't be tempted to assume the inhabitants of Tenbay are all complete buffoons. And, I assure you, should Tenbay ever come under attack it would not remain empty long."

"Why not fill it now? Be prepared for attack rather than acting with hindsight. With so much water at Tenbay's disposal it makes no sense to delay."

"I assure you, it makes perfect sense, once you understand the reason."

Varoi tilted his head in tacit enquiry, waiting for Ayesha to explain.

"If the enemy bring up ballista they'll be able to bombard our outer walls and may manage to breach our defences in other places besides. We too have ballista, as yet only one, and that situated atop the main keep. Still, it will give them something else to worry about when the time comes that they decide to invade our outer ward."

She pointed a finger directing his attention back the way they had just come.

"To landward of this man-made dyke is a steep incline, known as the counterscarp, down which the enemy must run full pelt, clad in armour, weapons already in hand or strapped to their backs and belts, bringing with them scaling ladders and any other means by which they intend climbing those outer walls, which, believe me, are stout. It is to be expected they will come in a swarm, their numbers too great to repel. *Then,* when the moat is full of pushing, striving, flailing bodies, those gates will be raised …" Ayesha paused for effect.

Varoi queried, "Gates? What manner of gates would any defender dare raise?"

"Sluice gates, Varoi!" Pale green eyes sparkled with malicious merriment. "Imagine it, if you will: at first a trickle; then a flood. Long before there is any chance of the alarm being raised, a wall of water several ells high will race in to fill the void, created with one specific purpose in mind. Those at the moat's centre will surely drown if they cannot swim. With all that armour, not to mention the additional weight of weapons, any attempt at swimming would likely avail them naught, only serving to delay the inevitable for a short time. Those caught in the process of climbing the scarp would find themselves sucked under by the surging tide. The two opposing waves would converge, to meet with a vigorous rush hurling up a wave so huge it would wash away any left clinging nearby. The resultant loss and reduction in numbers might well prove decisive." She waved her hands with an eloquent gesture as though describing the cumulative effect. "At the very least our foe will suffer a disabling blow."

Varoi pronounced himself appalled.

"Really, Lieutenant, why so squeamish? I thought the prospect of wiping out half your enemy at one blow would please you."

Ayesha cast him a sideways glance, intrigued by his reaction. In truth, she had been no less dismayed when Schezan had taken immense pleasure in informing her of this ruse. It seemed Varoi had certain scruples, despite his trade involving death.

"Perhaps it is just that I find this a dishonourable means to an end; not at all what I would choose to visit upon any foe."

In truth, Varoi was not squeamish. It wasn't the idea of wholesale slaughter being accomplished in this fashion that disturbed him, so much as Ayesha's blasé attitude.

"The Pulan do not seem quite so principled. The way they treat women and innocents, when they come across them, should appal."

"Is that any excuse for us to behave likewise?" Varoi protested.

Ayesha ignored him, hurrying on. "Don't sound so disapproving. Some would survive the setback, enough that your efforts would still be required. We must hope their numbers are few. A horrible death? Yes maybe. A swift and terrible one? Tis true, but one without significant loss to either our allies or ourselves. Personally, I see much to commend it whatever you say."

Granting him no time for further argument she turned away.

"Varoi," she said, as he caught up. "I know little of military tactics or similar niceties. But, it seems to me that in battle, any kind of battle, the main objective is to win, by any means possible. Does that sound an apt definition?"

"Yes, Ayesha, in this I must agree."

"Good, I'm glad that's settled. Now, let me show you our other defences. Just don't expect me to be quite so knowledgeable on all matters."

They passed beneath the portcullis and into the wide passage beyond, where small cubicles had been let into the walls on either side, providing a discreet hiding place for those guarding the entrance to the barbican. Varoi ventured a quick upward glance, viewing the sundry murder holes that pierced the ceiling above his head, through which boiling oil or burning pitch could be poured on invaders who succeeded in breaching these first defences before becoming trapped between portcullis and gate. His flesh prickled at the thought that such barbaric measures might be required. His pace quickened at the realisation of so grisly a fate. Personally, he would much prefer to face death courtesy of a sharp blade. Even the prospect of a swift beheading seemed preferable to what awaited unwelcome intruders here.

Once through the barbican they emerged into the full glare of sunlight. Varoi heaved a soft sigh of relief, then slowed his pace in order to study the killing ground.

"The outer ward or bailey," Ayesha announced, waving her arms in an expansive gesture, "though you would name it something different, no doubt. Something, I dare say, that is far more barbaric." She showed her teeth in a bizarre grimace as though taunting Varoi to attempted denial. Varoi gave her a disapproving glance then looked away.

He knew full well to what she referred. To him this broad swathe of grass that encircled the fortress between inner and outer walls was commonly known as the killing ground; and with good reason. Should any assailants pass beyond the outer ramparts this was where they might be trapped and overcome, where the majority of Tenbay's defenders would be required to make a determined stand.

Ayesha had no idea what sort of bloody spectacle that conflict might become. Knowing the truth, Varoi deemed it best to refrain from comment, especially since, should the worst happen, there were good prospects to indicate that many of Ayesha's own people would be involved.

They passed through the inner gates to where the town of Tenbay, having expanded over recent years, had encroached to fill most of what would have once formed the inner bailey. The keep itself rose several spans higher than the outer walls and atop this stood a lone ballista. All he could see of its structure from ground level were the upper storeys, the lower portions having become completely surrounded and submerged beneath an abundance of other buildings.

Finding himself hemmed in by tall tenements and graceful town houses, plus the attendant profusion of shops, kiosks, booths and covered arcades, Varoi took time to take them all in. Stalls and commercial emporiums were crammed close together and inserted between the high ramparts of the keep and the looming battlements of the inner bailey, all serving to make the keep appear overwhelmed.

There were markets, each devoted to related wares, while others displayed a complete hotchpotch of goods: anything from buckles to besoms, reed baskets to pegs and songbirds in cages. Whatever the customer desired might be obtained here. It was hardly any wonder, with merchant ships regularly returning from visits to far distant, exotic shores, eager to supply all manner of foreign delights alongside the familiar or mundane and all divided by streets awash with humanity's tide.

It was a noisy, hectic, confusing throng, through which Ayesha wove her way with the poise and elegance of an accomplished dancer. Varoi followed close on her heels, a hound pursuing the inevitable hare, temptation luring him on with every stride. Being head and shoulders taller than the average man offered some small advantage, ensuring that Varoi had no problem keeping his quarry in sight. He took time to appreciate the sensual sway of her hips, as well as her lissom, sinuous grace, which brought appreciative glances from other passing males. Varoi's warning growl ensured that none displayed too serious an interest. Ayesha might not be his as yet, but he felt no less protective of her person for all that.

Varoi was equally nimble in his pursuit. His lithe assurance was more suggestive of a caged panther than anything else, a dangerous grace that earnt him respect. As a rule, it took scant effort on his part to clear any obstruction. The broad, toothy grin of a full-blooded male Shakar normally proved menacing enough to deter all but the most persistent offender. Varoi used this ruse sparingly, even so. He was rather amused that so artless a ploy should remained effective when employed against any breed of men, especially Fenlanders, who really should, by now, be well aware of its strict limitations.

No Shakar would ever, knowingly, reveal the truth: that these fearsome canines, which had long been the subject of folklore and myth, came into their own after dark. None save Shakar had ever borne witness to their actual usage, which, in truth, was of a wholly sexual nature.

Occasionally Ayesha called back over her shoulder, pointing out various establishments of interest: here a draper's, where the finest silks and brocades might be bought; there the most reliable cobbler in town; over there a street of ironmongers and weapons smiths; or this, a place where any manner of provisions might be obtained. Saddlers, chandlers, haberdashery stores; the list of establishments seemed endless. Varoi recognised each by its attendant sight and smell besides its traditional signage. But, instead of calling a halt to Ayesha's cheerful chatter he just bestowed his fearsome grin on yet another innocent bystander, watched yet another obstructive tradesman's unctuous smile shrivel, heard the inevitable persuasive patter fade away.

Not all vendors annoyed him. Some did so mainly because he had no wish to lose sight of Ayesha's beguiling form. She seemed amazingly accomplished at avoiding those same pitfalls and snares that regularly beset Varoi. How she managed he had yet to discover, but watching her sylph-like figure proved a more enjoyable pastime than any previous quandary so far contrived.

A young woman stepped forward, blocking his path. She was bearing a large tray on which an array of sweetmeats was displayed. Varoi paused, hungry enough to partake. He selected three, happy to pay the few copper coins she asked.

He stuffed one into his mouth whole, savouring the light and crumbly texture of the pastry and the creamy centre that melted on his tongue. Contentment. Bliss. Varoi closed his eyes the better to enjoy.

When he opened them next, Ayesha was gone. *Vanished!* Somehow she had disappeared, as if into thin air.

Varoi hurried on, head swivelling from side to side, desperate to discover her whereabouts. He was supposed to keep her under his eye at all times. He was her escort for the goddess's sake. How could he have lost her so soon?

The one female he could not live without. It was unforgivable; and *maddening*.

He wanted to howl aloud his dismay.

"Yoo-hoo, Varoi! Over here!" Varoi whirled round, his face a mask of utmost concern … to see her beckoning from an open doorway. He hurried toward her, ruthlessly thrusting aside those few people who dared step into his path. He should chastise her, he supposed. Instead, he was only too relieved to have found her again; and so very pleased to be addressed with such unexpected familiarity.

"Varoi," she said, as he drew near. "I thought some light refreshment might be enjoyable at this time of day." The prospect did have a certain appeal.

It was delightfully cool inside the shop, cool and dim after the harsh glare of day. There were delicious aromas to be enjoyed. Varoi sniffed appreciatively, allowing his senses to absorb the quieter, more restful ambience after the lively bustle he had just escaped, while allowing himself to be shown to a small table occupying a far corner of the room.

"Demoiselle," Ayesha called, as soon as they were seated. "Would you bring us a slate with this day's menu thereon?"

"Certainly, Princess."

Varoi had not noticed the woman before; and, as soon as she stepped out from behind the huge counter that dominated one corner of the room, he understood why.

Demoiselle was of diminutive stature. Her curly brown hair, liberally laced with traces of grey, was drawn back and confined in a tight coil at the nape of her neck. Her dress was of an indeterminate hue, consisting of indigo shot through with rich shades of purple and grey. Around her waist was a white apron with lacy trim.

Demoiselle delivered the slate into Ayesha's hands, offering a deft courtesy before slipping away.

Ayesha perused the menu with a nonchalant air. "What will you try, Lieutenant? Will you take some chocola with me?"

Varoi was nonplussed. Never having heard of such a thing, he had no idea whether it was something he might eat or some sort of drink. Ayesha, seeming to discern the cause of his hesitation, made the choice for him.

"Chocola for us both, I think. It is a new drink," she went on to explain, "just imported from Kapagai. I thoroughly commend it. Now, what shall we have to go with?" She bowed her head over the slate in silent contemplation. The possibilities seemed to be vast. Finally, she passed it across to Varoi.

"You choose."

Varoi said. "Princess, I shall be happy to take chocola with you, but do we have time for anything more?"

"Of course we have time, Lieutenant. How long can it take? Now, do hurry up and decide."

Varoi studied the slate and chose to play safe, requesting a selection of what was available. It seemed to be the wisest option.

Despite the fact that Ayesha continued talking, Varoi found his interest diverted, to some degree, by Demoiselle's activities. First a red lacquered tray appeared atop the counter, to which was added a collection of porcelain cups, saucers and plates, neatly stacked. Next was added a platter upon which a selection of delicacies was arranged. Then came a jug and two small pots, complete with lids; and, lastly, a larger pot, complete with handle and spout, which she dosed with a generous measure of something very dark.

Demoiselle lifted the kettle from the stove and started to pour ...

Ayesha glanced down at her hands; then up, surprised to discover that Varoi's interest had strayed. Not that she minded since it afforded her the perfect opportunity to study him.

For years now she'd been content as Schezan's Chosen, an arrangement that suited them both. Certainly there had been no complaints on either side. She recalled Schezan's arrival in Tenbay harbour. He'd looked magnificent in the black leather armour that proclaimed him Konicci, the red crest of commander adorning his helm. She had decided there and then he would be her mate and had wasted no time in making her interest known. If Schezan had been surprised by her forward behaviour he had hidden it well. Three years ago their pledge had been made and, while their official joining had yet to take place, she had no reason to regret her original choice of mate.

Once, her mother had mentioned the secret rite of *lossa antario*. Ayesha had thought it a far-fetched tale. A mind touch that could have such devastating effects ought to be outlawed. Despite recent events her opinion remained largely unchanged. She wondered, had her mother engaged in such sensual pursuits? *Surely not!* The very idea was outrageous. Scandalised, she thrust that thought aside.

Yet, she knew little enough about Schezan. He was the epitome of arrogance: male conceit personified and little else to recommend him. Sometimes she wondered how their promise endured. They spent scant time in each other's company. When they did their assignations were brief and focused mainly around Schezan's needs.

And then came Varoi, tiptoeing into her private reaches, touching her intimately, setting her passion aflame. The thought of Varoi's large hands executing such soft and tender caresses was enough to trigger unexpected sensations, to send them rippling, unasked, throughout her frame. And, to have the cause of that torment here, in the flesh, was something she could not have envisioned, until now. *How dare he?*

Yet he had dared, which was more than could be said for some. True, she had once thought Schezan superbly restrained; what other excuse could there be for his singular lack of interest in close intimacy? There was passion, but it was strictly controlled. Not that she minded; she preferred things that way.

Varoi and Schezan: her Chosen and the one who sought to claim her as soulmate by right. They were different in other ways: Schezan, with his supreme air of self-importance, his black leather armour always burnished to an incredible sheen, as he strutted atop the parapet seeking constant approbation; while Varoi ...

Varoi wore armour that was an ordinary brown and, if it shone, it was more likely as a result of honest sweat and toil, the sort that came from weapons practice or the heat of battle. And it was stained, perhaps with Varoi's blood; there were enough nicks and scratches to offer potential proof. Varoi's armour had definitely seen much wear and better days; yet he wore it with a quiet confidence. Indeed, he wore it like a second skin.

That thought alone gave Ayesha pause. She had touched Varoi's flesh, but briefly; all too briefly, but long enough. She had found then the hard evidence of his arousal. A thrill shivered its way down her spine at the significance of that realisation. Though she sought to deny her instinctive reaction, she could not ignore the liquid heat that pooled lower down. Such a surprise! To find the idea of touching of Varoi could produce so strong an effect.

Almost, she felt annoyed. How *dare* he invade first her mind and now her life? How *dare* he cause such seething turmoil, such a wealth of lustful emotion? How *dare* he? And how could she reconcile the fact that she welcomed his ardent attentions? For she did. There was no denying that fact.

And now, here they sat. And he was not even paying her proper attention!

71

After all the trouble he had caused he had eyes only for what Demoiselle was about.

"Varoi! Have you heard a single word I've been saying?"

Startled, he turned his golden glance her way and her irritation gave way to wry amusement, even as her insides began to melt beneath that earnest gaze. How could she blame him for what she herself was prone to do?

Then, Varoi smiled. His change in aspect was there and quickly gone; yet it left Ayesha stunned, surprised to find it was a trick she longed to see repeated. That a face so ordinary could, in the blink of an eye, transform into one so startlingly handsome.

And then, as he leant across the table, hands outstretched, amber gaze intense, as he focused entirely upon her and sought to offer an abject apology, she knew. She could so easily succumb to his masculine allure, could get swallowed up in the sublime intensity of his gaze. Smiling she sought to divert his attention. Not until Demoiselle spoke again did she realise that she, herself, had become mesmerised.

"Varoi! Have you listened to a single word I've said?"

His eyes darted back to Ayesha's face. Guiltily, he began to explain. "I heard most of what you said, about the harbour. I confess, I was distracted for a time."

Ayesha gave a tinkling laugh. "I will admit, I too derive great pleasure from watching Demoiselle work."

Her voice dropped to a conspiratorial whisper. "I also confess, when I come here alone, providing no one else is about, I sometimes assist Demoiselle with her task." She gazed at him, pale green eyes sparkling with impish glee. "Are you shocked, Lieutenant? That I have friends amongst humankind?"

Varoi knew he had no right to condemn her, although, admittedly, he *was* amazed by her admission.

"I see that you are," she continued. "Well, now that I've let you into my secret, you know something else you might find of good use."

There was a defiant tilt to her chin as she finished speaking, one Varoi was pleased to approve. He wondered what other disclosures she vhave up her sleeve.

Demoiselle reappeared at his elbow, red lacquered tray in hand. "If you permit."

Only now did Varoi become aware that in his earnest attempt to apologise he had leant right across the table, both hands imploringly outstretched.

Ayesha surprised him further when she said. "Demoiselle, why don't you fetch a cup and join us? Then I can introduce you properly."

Demoiselle smiled a brief flash of even white teeth. "I should be happy to, Princess. But I think, perhaps, the male would like you all to himself." The grin flashed again, and Ayesha laughed, amused by Varoi's nonplussed expression.

He wondered, was his interest so plain?

Ayesha announced, "Now, I shall pour a small helping of chocola and, if you do not agree it tastes absolutely delicious, why I shall have no other recourse but to drink it all by myself."

He watched Ayesha lift the pot to pour some of the dark, aromatic brew into each of their cups, as she did, seizing the chance, to study her further. She was simply dressed in a short-sleeved, linen shift of a pale apricot colour, cinched at the waist with a broad, satin band. Her attire suited her admirably, the colour setting off her bronze skin and long, tawny hair to perfection. On her left upper arm was the heavy gold torc of high rank.

Smiling, Ayesha passed the cup across. "You may wish to add honey, but I suggest that you try it first. Be careful, it's quite hot."

Varoi raised the cup to his lips, then breathed deep of its fragrance before trying a sip.

"What do you think?"

He savoured the taste. "I think shall forego the honey."

"Wise choice; somehow I thought you might. I, however, possess a sweet tooth." Adding a teaspoon of honey to her cup she began to stir. "You cannot forego the cream. It is an essential ingredient if you wish to get the most enjoyment."

Turning a small spoon upside down over the liquid she poured a full measure on to the spoon. To Varoi's profound amazement, cream and chocola did not mingle. Instead, the cream floated on top.

Ayesha watched with interest as Varoi tried yet another small sip. Varoi raised his head and smiled before pronouncing, "Delicious." Then he felt rather nonplussed as Ayesha erupted into giggles.

"What is it? What did I do wrong?"

"Nothing," Ayesha assured, trying, but failing, to keep a straight face.
The sight of Demoiselle doing her best to smother a laugh did nothing to reassure him. "Ayesha?" he growled, warningly.

"I'm sorry, Varoi. Forgive me. I must say, you look absurd when wearing a moustache. It really doesn't suit you."

With these words, she ran one finger across Varoi's top lip, then brought it back to her mouth so she might lick the cream from her finger, unaware how seductive an action this might be.

Varoi laughed, certain she was flirting with him; then watched with interest as one delicate forefinger caressed the rim of her cup. He wondered whether she was aware of what she did or how it might be perceived.

Ayesha flicked out her tongue to moisten her full lower lip, green eyes alight with mischief.

On impulse he leant forward, determined to press his advantage while he could. Cups rattled against saucers, spoons chimed and Varoi heard the gentle slosh of liquid. Loudest of all was his heart, pounding away in his chest, as, leaning across the table, he cupped her chin in one sword-calloused hand and raised her face for his kiss.

Varoi kept the gesture light, no more than a brush of his lips against hers. Then, lifting his head, he flicked out his tongue, licking her lips in a languid caress that was meant to tease.

"Mmmm, you taste good."

Her jade eyes glinted back. Varoi discerned tiny blue sparks in their midst: moonbeams or daggers, he wasn't sure which. What did it matter? He had stolen his first kiss and felt sure there was more and better to come.

Playfully she pushed him away. "Lieutenant, you go too far. You'll rumple my clothes."

"Nothing could ruin your appearance, Ayesha. Not from where I sit."

"Varoi, you are incorrigible. Don't you think so, Demoiselle?"

Demoiselle would not be drawn, though there was a twinkle in her eye. "I but serve. It is not for me to offer opinions"

"Oh, faugh! You're a spoilsport. You could agree if you so wished."

"Very well, then, here's what I think. I think the young male is smitten."

Ayesha glanced at Varoi, who was, by now, studiously engaged in removing some imaginary fluff from his sleeve.

"Did you hear what she said Varoi? I've told you I'm already promised. You must seek for entertainment elsewhere."

Varoi gave her a mischievous grin. "I heard you, Ayesha, but, like it or not, I've no intention of looking elsewhere."

Straightening the cups in their saucers he poured some more chocola and passed it across. Ayesha lifted the cup to her lips and made a moue of her expression.

"Oh, faugh! You forgot the cream."

"Sorry, Ayesha, you wish me to correct my mistake?"

She felt sure she espied a wicked glint in his eye as he went on.

"I would happily remove any surplus from your lips should you so wish."

"I think, perhaps, I like it as it is."

Varoi peered artfully over the rim of his cup, daring Ayesha to catch his eye. Oh, but that kiss had been sweet. He relished the prospect of future opportunities.

They were soon obliged to return to the hectic bustle of busy streets, as they made their way down to the harbour to discover what harbour defences might already have been put in place.

"Tenbay," Varoi explained, "is of great strategic importance. Should the Pulan ever succeed in conquering Tenbay, they could paralyse our trade routes and dominate our inland waterways. The consequences then would be dire."

Having absorbed what he could of the harbour layout Varoi turned away, starting back towards the centre of town. He hadn't gone far before a voice hailed him from the doorway of a nearby tavern. His head swung in that direction, a smile already in place.

"Borit! And how are your newly acquired skills being received?"

"Well enough. What about you? Do things also go well?"

"Well enough. Allow me to introduce Princess Ayesha lo 'Savoi."

With the introductions complete, Borit observed, "I saw you studying the harbour. Any particular reason why?"

"Our defences, Borit. I need to find out what arrangements have been made in order to provide a satisfactory report. The layout seems far from straightforward and, I confess, I'm at something of a loss."

"I can find that out for you, if you wish."

"You're a stranger here, like me. Locals can be rather clannish, I've found."

"Leave it with me, Varoi. I'll discover what I can and report back. Meet me here around sundown. I can let you know what I've managed to discover."

"Here?" Varoi said, in a dubious tone.

Borit grinned. "Yes, here. Afterwards, I promise to escort you safely home."

Varoi growled, unamused. "That isn't funny, Borit."

"It wasn't meant to be. Do you trust me to acquire the information or not?"

"Very well," Varoi reluctantly agreed. "And I'll meet you here as arranged. Just you make sure you arrive on time. I've no intention of hanging about."

By the time they returned to the settlement the evacuation had already begun. Nearing the entrance to the settlement, Varoi grew aware that a heated argument was in progress. Seeing his commander involved, along with Ayesha's father, Chief lo 'Savoi, Varoi could not help but wonder what the problem was. He paused, torn between duty and desire. In the end personal issues won out.

Striding ahead, Varoi stepped into Ayesha's path, bringing Ayesha up short, determined to keep their parting as private as possible. Seeing her father some distance ahead, Ayesha stopped and held out her hand, hoping Varoi would take it, hoping to thereby bring this pleasant interlude to an end.

Keeping her gaze discreetly lowered, she said, "It was nice meeting you, Lieutenant. Perhaps we can do this again."

Because she was not looking at him she failed to see the blank look of dismay cross Varoi's face, to be quickly replaced by one of resolute intractability.

"It's taken me years to find you, Ayesha. Do not think to get rid of me so easily."

Her breath hitched in her throat and her heart skipped a beat. Such sweet constancy was meant to be cherished. She could not speak, would not meet his gaze, lest it undo all her hard-won determination. For the first time that she could recall, Ayesha knew real regret that it was to Schezan she was promised.

A brief flirtation was all she'd had in mind at the start. What harm could it do? More harm than she would have thought, in truth. She'd encouraged Varoi enough already, and would not encourage him further for fear of what might result.

She knew Schezan, knew well that he had a vile temper and had witnessed its effect a time or two, although never had it been directed at her. And Schezan was Konicci: one of an elite group of warriors who had undergone an extreme course of weapons training. None succeeded to that title without having risked death at the hands of an equal in that art. Furthermore, she felt sure that Schezan would not relish the prospect of having a rival for her affections, save that it gave him good cause to demonstrate his prowess with a blade.

However determined, however courageous Varoi was, in any such contest he would not stand a chance. She would not visit such wrath on Varoi. He didn't deserve that.

She had glimpsed a trace of sadness in his eyes and, besides that, a swift glimmer of hope. Hope that she had somehow brought about. Much as she hated dashing that hope to oblivion, she must. And so she stood firm, waving her hand at him in hopes he would simply take it and take this parting as final.

To her relief, Varoi did. But instead of grasping her hand briefly, as she'd expected, he raised it up to the moist warmth of his mouth. Then he reached a hand to tilt her chin. As her eyes again met his, the depth of feeling she saw reflected therein stole her breath, vanquishing all resolve.

As Varoi lowered his mouth to hers for one last, parting kiss, Ayesha knew it was already too late to undo the bond formed through *lossa antario's* gift. Such close intimacy could not be denied.

"You are meant to be mine, Ayesha, however you choose to pretend otherwise."

With his mouth so close that she could already savour its sweetness, a brusque voice from behind gave her a last chance of escape.

"There you are, Varoi. I thought you'd got lost. Tell me later how things went and what you've learnt. Right now, there's a task to which I want you assigned."

"Commander."

Varoi watched as Ayesha slipped away, knowing then, at that precise moment, that his heart went with her. Varoi made himself a solemn vow. Schezan should not have her. Somehow he would win Ayesha. *He must.*

Varoi was busy; busy and glad of it. It helped to keep his mind from desolate thoughts. Yet, however hard he sought for distraction, his thoughts always returned to that dilemma. So far he'd failed to convince Ayesha of his sincerity. What chance did he have if he couldn't accomplish that?   The garrison commander had reluctantly agreed to surrender his well-furnished quarters to Chief lo 'Savoi and his immediate family. No sooner was most of his military paraphernalia removed than the new residents prepared to move in.

Varoi was now prowling the many passages connecting the various chambers, large and small, destined to provide temporary accommodation for those Shakar who had been forced to relocate to a safer environment. That was his role. And, it must be said, a grand opportunity it was proving in which to familiarise himself with the layout of the fortress's interior.

Turning a corner, Varoi was brought to an abrupt halt by the sight he now beheld. If he was honest, it was no mere chance that brought him here. For there she was: the primary object of his interest. And, what was more, she was apparently in dire need of assistance.

Ayesha was forging ahead, regardless of the fact that the bundle she carried was firmly wedged in the doorway behind. Naturally, he felt compelled to intervene, to offer his particular expertise in solving the problem, though in this case it appeared to require more in the way of brute force than military finesse.

It was the obvious question and one he could not resist. "Can I help?"

"Really, Lieutenant, there's no need," Ayesha protested, as two strong arms enveloped her body and two sword-calloused hands set themselves to either side of the unwieldy pack. "I can manage perfectly well on my own."

"So I see," still he kept a firm hold. "What have you got in here anyway?"

"Just clothes, boots, a few basic necessities."

"And that's all?" Varoi's amazement was profound.

"Yes, *really*. Now, will you just step aside?"

Of course, he had no intention of doing so. Having come upon the perfect opportunity Varoi had no intention whatever of passing it by.

When he did not immediately respond she let go of her bundle and turned.

"Varoi?"

The bundle stayed put, which, thought Varoi, in its way, proved his point.

"Yes?" he glanced down. Her head was level with his chest, her silky hair brushing his chin. She looked up and he caught the full force of her gaze; her green, luminous eyes seemed incredibly large. Having found the chance to cage her in, Varoi wasted no further time.

"Princess," he breathed, unable to resist such ripe temptation. His lips hovered a hair's breadth above hers.

He took in a breath and, before his nerve failed, seized the chance. His mouth descended upon lush lips, to taste, perhaps to savour. Her pale viridian eyes offered a challenge; then dark lashes swept down, obscuring his view. Varoi had no way of knowing what she thought; what mattered most was that she responded in kind.

Letting go of the bundle, Varoi slipped strong hands about Ayesha's waist, wrapping her up in his fond embrace. As the kiss deepened, sweeping all caution aside, so hunger emerged from its hiding place and Varoi's passion took firm charge.

"Varoi! What are you about?" Commander com 'Dolino's enquiry sounded unusually sharp.

Raising his head, Varoi looked round; lowering his hands, he caught hold of the recalcitrant pack and gave it a determined shake. Something inside rattled alarmingly and Ayesha's eyes flew wide with shock. He mouthed the word *Sorry* at Ayesha even as he half turned to explain.

"I'm trying to shift this awkward fardle, which seems to be jammed. Princess Ayesha requested my aid."

Turning back he glanced down, amber eyes begging that she collude in his deception.

Ayesha confirmed, "I was trying to explain how the task might be managed."

Silently, Varoi mouthed his gratitude. Smiling up at him she wagged an admonishing finger as if to say *Don't do that again.* He quirked one dark brow in mild surprise, but she turned aside as though she were unmoved, as though she thought to dismiss him easily.

Varoi suppressed a satisfied smile. He was not fooled. He had felt then the true ardour of her response. There was hope still in pursuing his course.

Behind him his commander piped up again. "Then be quick about it, Varoi. I have other tasks lined up in urgent need of your attention."

Ayesha stood at the centre of her new domicile, hands fisted on hips, a disparaging sneer curling her lip. "And this is what we must put up with? This is where they expect us to live? Well, it might suit you, Papa, for five of us to be cooped up in this rabbit hutch but it does not suit me. I need some measure of privacy."

She stepped to the door of the apartment and flung it wide. "You there," she said, crooking her finger at one of the warriors who had just helped install their personal effects. "I demand that you fetch the commander right away."

"Which one?" enquired the unfortunate person thus summoned.

"What does it matter which one? Either one of them will do. Don't waste my time with stupid questions. Go, fetch him, at once."

"Yes, Princess," he hurried away, leaving his comrade to gape in dismay.

"What are you gawping at? Have you not seen a female before?"

Annoyed at this disrespectful behaviour the warrior
spun on his heel and strode away. Behind him the door
slammed shut.

"Now let's see if they can do any better," Ayesha
said.

"Ayesha, really! We all must manage as best we
may in difficult circumstances," her mother said, doing her
best to soothe.

"You may have to, Mama, but I take exception to
the circumstances they expect us to endure. Who knows
how long we may be here. A little privacy is all I ask.
Surely that's not too much to expect. Let's wait and see
whether they can do better."

She had not long to wait for her answer. A slight
scratching at the door heralded the appearance of
Commander com 'Dolino. He was alone. Ayesha invited
him in.

"You did not say what it was you wanted, Princess.
I assumed the matter was private. How may I help?"

Ayesha spread her hands wide, indicating her
immediate surroundings. "What do you think of our
quarters, Commander?"

"Is that all you wanted to ask? If so, I find no
reason why it could not have waited until another time. I
am busy you know."

"It ... Could ... Not ... Wait," Ayesha cried,
stamping her foot. "This will not do: not for my parents,
not for my brothers and not for me."

"Sorry, Princess, but I fail to perceive the problem.
Your quarters are a trifle cramped, I agree, but other than
that, I don't see ..."

"No, you don't, do you?" Ayesha interrupted, flying
into a rage. "There is no privacy here, Commander. Can
you still not comprehend the problem?"

"Ah, I think I do now. You desire quarters of your
own."

"My parents, too, deserve some degree of solitude. Don't you agree?"

"I'll see what can be done. I warn you not to expect much."

Without another word he stepped to the door. Opening it and leaning out he called, "Are there you are, Lieutenant com 'Domicci, the very person I need?" Then he abruptly vanished, closing the door behind.

"Ayesha, that was ill done," her father softly rebuked.

"Do I care? No, I do not. Let us hope the Commander has a suitable solution to our predicament."

Again there came a scrabbling at the door. This time when Ayesha flung it wide *two* male Shakar hovered outside. "Well. Come in."

Commander com 'Dolino was quick to explain. "There is scant room to spare, Princess. But, with regards your brothers, Lieutenant com 'Domicci has a possible plan."

Ayesha pouted before standing aside as Varoi beckoned the two boys forward. Dropping to his haunches he began a quiet conversation with both of them. Ayesha stifled mounting frustration, annoyed by the fact she was unable to eavesdrop without drawing attention to the fact.

After a while Varoi raised his head and spoke. "Chief lo 'Savoi, would you object if your sons, who will one day make fine young warriors, were to sleep with myself and the other warriors in the main dormatorium?"

The chief appeared somewhat nonplussed by this suggestion, which was clearly not at all what he'd expected by way of a solution. Seeing his hesitation, Varoi made haste to allay his concern.

"I have enquired of your sons their understanding with regards to certain rules concerning the use of another male's sword. They seem remarkably well acquainted with those rules in respect of how they are implemented and equally aware it is forbidden to touch another male's weapon without his express permission. I think you need have no fears on this account. As to all else: I promise to ensure their good behaviour and guarantee someone will keep close watch over them at all times."

The chief gave a brisk nod of agreement. "On one condition: they return here if they cannot behave."

The two young males, having already begun to rejoice at the prospect, let rip with a loud shout of glee.

Ayesha waited for the ruckus to die down before asking, "And what about me?"

Varoi, having settled back on his heels to enjoy her brothers' elation, studied her from beneath hooded eyes.

His commander proceeded to explain. "There is a small room next door that might be put to a different use. Normally it is used for storage but there is adequate space for a small truckle bed and, mayhap, a cupboard or two."

"Show me," Ayesha demanded. Turning about, the commander led her away.

As the door closed behind them, Varoi rose to his feet. "If your sons would collect their bedding, I can escort them to the dormatorium and settle them down. We are a friendly crowd. They should fit right in."

"Thank you, Lieutenant com 'Domicci. It is good of you and the commander to put yourselves out. Ayesha has something of a temper, I'm afraid."

"There's no need to apologize. I had a sister once who was much like she."

"Had, Lieutenant? May I ask what happened to her?"

"She drowned."

"How very sad."

"Yes, it was. If your sons are ready, with your permission I'll take my leave."

The chief nodded. Varoi, seeing Sami and Toku already chafing at the leash, left without another word.

"Strange," said the chief as the door closed behind Varoi. "From his behaviour I'm inclined to suspect there was more to his sister's death than he wished to reveal."

"In that you might be right," agreed his spouse. "And, unless I'm mistaken, he also displays more than a passing interest in our daughter."

"You noticed that too?"

"It was impossible to miss."

When Ayesha returned a few minutes later her mother was quick to ask. "Well, Ayesha, do you finally have what you want?"

Ayesha favoured her mother with a dazzling smile. "It is small but it will serve well enough. Most importantly, it affords me privacy, such privacy as would have been lacking had we been forced to share."

"Then it is to be hoped that Sami and Toku feel much the same."

"If their reaction to the lieutenant's suggestion is a reliable guide, I imagine them to be as delighted. So much jubilation; could there be any doubt?"

"And you, Ayesha? Are you satisfied with your lot in life?"

Ayesha subjected her mother to a quizzical stare. "What do you mean?" "I mean, is Schezan still your Chosen? Or have you now changed your mind?"

"I gave my word. I made my promise. Can there be any doubt?"

"This is not what I asked."

"Maybe not; but I think, perhaps, that is what you mean."

"Not necessarily."

"Then perhaps you should make yourself plain."

"We are neither of us blind," her father interrupted. "It is clear to us both that Lieutenant com 'Domicci finds you attractive."

86

"So what if he does? Is that any fault of mine? I have made him aware of the situation. Can I help it if he decides to persist?"

"If he's that determined, why not give him a chance?"

"Papa, I gave my pledge. Would you suggest I go back on my word?"

"Tradition says that *is* the female's prerogative in life: to change her mind whenever she chooses. Why not give the lieutenant a chance, providing you are interested. Let him and Schezan vie for your affection as tradition demands."

"He has a name, Papa, why not use it?"

"Ah, now I see which way the wind blows."

"Do you? Then perhaps you should explain what you mean?"

"It means: I believe you are already enamoured of the lieutenant."

"Papa, really!"

"All I suggest is that you give him a chance in order that you may make a more considered choice. What harm can it do? If Schezan is serious he will welcome the challenge as he should. He's had no competition worthy of notice before this."

"I shall give your words consideration, though do not forget, my pledge has been made."

Varoi found a space at the table. Swinging his long legs across the bench, he seated himself at the common board. Then he reached for a bowl and began helping himself to some pottage. It was an aromatic stew, rich and savoury, with an abundance of the essential ingredients necessary to satisfy a healthy male appetite. Further down the table the lo 'Savoi siblings, Sami and Toku, were engaged in animated conversation with Sverig and one other male. He gave them a friendly wave and went back to his meal. After the excitement earlier, he was famished.

Two of the garrison's warriors moved to occupy a seat on either side. Varoi knew them, slightly, although they seemed friendly enough. Their names, he recalled, were Che and Bigli. They exchanged a greeting as he passed them the kettle of stew.

Moments later they tried to engage him in conversation. Varoi, with his mind elsewhere, did not at first comprehend where this particular conversation was leading. When he did, he perceived that he was being warned off; to what purpose he was not quite sure. Was this friendly advice, or was a more sinister motive involved?

Varoi began paying close heed to what Bigli was trying to say.

"Look, Varoi, I think the Princess should have told you by now. But, since she apparently has not, someone else must; in which case, I'll take it upon myself to see you informed."

Varoi tilted his head in silent enquiry and Bigli went on. "The Princess is promised, Varoi."

"You're telling me I have a rival. This much I already know."

"But do you know who?"

"Schezan com 'Varicci was the name mentioned, as I recall."

"And have you any idea what sort of rival he will turn out to be?"

"I believe I do. I have met Schezan com 'Varicci before. And that once left behind an indelible impression."

"If it left you with that much of an impression I assume you know how dangerous he's liable to be. He has a violent temper."

"I know this too."

88

"Varoi, be warned, he will not take kindly to your having any sort of association with Princess Ayesha. And if he finds out what has happened ..."

Varoi assumed an innocent air, waving his spoon with casual aplomb. "And what do *you* think has happened so far?"

Bigli gave vent to an exasperated snort. "You kissed her. Don't bother denying it. I saw. I was not fooled, even if your commander apparently was."

Varoi ventured an insouciant grin. "And, as I recall, she kissed me back."

Che gave Bigli a meaningful stare. "I said so, didn't I, but you refused to believe." To Varoi he said, "Wipe that silly grin off your face. You're in more trouble than you know. If Schezan finds out, if he even suspects, he'll cut off your bollocks and use them to polish his boots."

Varoi's grin vanished in an instant. "I should like to see him try."

Bigli threw both hands in the air. "It's hopeless. He's just arrived and already he's messing with Schezan's Chosen. He must have some kind of death wish, is all I can say."

"No," Varoi corrected, his words accompanied by a furious scowl. "*He* is messing with *mine*."

They stared at him. "What are you saying Varoi?"

"I am saying: Ayesha and I first made contact courtesy of *lossa antario*."

"This cannot be true."

"Ah, but I assure you, it is. And, believe me; I have every intention of rectifying the sorry situation given time. For now, I ask that you repeat nothing of what I've just said."

"Well, Varoi, it would be nice if we three could become friends. I must confess I quite like you. Sharing the same rank we appear to have something in common.

But I freely admit to some trepidation. You swim in dangerous waters, it seems to me."

"Too perilous, then, for you?" There was a steely glint in Varoi's golden eyes. It gave his fellow warriors pause.

"Perhaps too close an association could turn out to be a mistake. Even so, we shall not reveal your secret. For now, let's just see if we can become friends."

Varoi grinned. In his profession friendship was a rare and valued commodity. "That would please me immensely."

Chapter 5: A Foretelling

Varoi was searching for somewhere to sleep and the dormatorium seemed his best bet at this time of day. One person was there already, snoring softly in a corner of the room. Varoi found a space far enough from his sleeping comrade to catch a couple of hours' rest. Split duties always left him fatigued.

Settling back, he tucked both hands behind his head, crossed his legs at the ankles and fell to contemplating the ceiling; more specifically, that part where an enterprising spider had spun her web, to the detriment of passing flies.

Varoi wondered: dare he risk all? Dare he risk telling Ayesha about Bayritz? Should he take the chance to issue a warning? Should he tell Ayesha that beneath Schezan's handsome veneer lurked a cold heart and an equally cruel streak of malice? If he did, might she then assume his apparent concern to be purely a matter of sour grapes? Might he risk more than he was prepared to lose?

He could, of course, use shamanic ability in order to convince Ayesha he was the more suitable mate. But Ayesha would know and, doubtless, despise him for it; which, in the end, left him only one choice. In truth, it was the one he favoured most, a course that required careful consideration. How might such subtle influence be applied? What did he know about the female of their species that was useful in attracting a mate?

He wasn't handsome. Not by even the wildest stretch of the imagination could he be thus described. He had been told that once, in the cruellest of terms, and had seen his reflection often enough to know it was true. Still, he must possess some redeeming qualities, some less obvious attributes that would serve to recommend him as a potential mate. Surely Fate was not so incredibly perverse that, having brought them together, she now sought to deny him the prize. So, he thought, closing his eyes, what did he know …?

A low hum made Varoi open his eyes. Above his head early blossom hung from the lichen-encrusted boughs. A familiar noise had disturbed his reverie. Numerous small, furry insects collected pollen, taking it back to their hive.

Once, the sight of so many foraging bees would have scared him witless; but not since his mother had seen fit to ensure he was properly introduced. After that he never had a problem, often choosing to visit the hive alone.

Varoi decided it was time to visit the bees again. Approaching the hive, he lifted the lid to peer inside. The last time he'd come here was the day after Bayritz died.

Amazingly, that visit had comforted him, as, sitting cross-legged upon the ground, he'd poured out his thoughts, his woes, his all-consuming regrets, not to mention his seething animosity towards Schezan.

A feeling of languor pervaded the air, an aspect he did not readily equate with so much industry. Lifting the lid, he peeked inside. The interior was as black as ebony, liquid obsidian that glittered ominously … with no apparent sign of bees.

Varoi sank to his knees on the grassy sward. Then, placing both hands on the rim, he moved closer to peer in. Something within that inky darkness stirred.

Varoi gaped aghast as silvery ripples spread, as though the interior contained a watery pool. Slowly the disturbance subsided; then, like a mirror reflecting an image, a face appeared; one that was pale and ghostly … and, obviously, not his.

At first he failed to comprehend, since it was not his reflection but that of another; one he failed, at first, to recognise. Varoi gasped as the vision grew more distinct. Then he loosed an astonished cry.

"Bayritz! How came you here?"

"I've always been here. Twas you that brought me long ago."

"I did?"

"Yes. Varoi, you must recall. It has been long since your last visit. Where have you been? I miss you terribly."

"And I miss you. But tis long and long since last I saw your face. Nor did I expect to find you here."

"I know this well." Bayritz's voice lowered in volume, taking on a confidential tone. "Come close, Varoi, and listen well to what I say."

Varoi leant forward, creeping as close as he dare to the hive's dark, mysterious interior.

"What is it, Bayritz? What would you have me know?"

"First, make sure to keep both wits and weapons sharp and go well armed."

Varoi gave a wry chuckle. "As though I would dare to do different! I'm a warrior now, I'll have you know, not the gangly fledgling you recall from long ago."

"Nevertheless ..."

Faint ripples began muddling the surface, causing his sister's reflection to oscillate. Her voice, too, was becoming faint.

"Bayritz, you must speak up." In desperation Varoi leant closer, until it seemed he might fall in.

Bayritz's voice was reduced to a hollow echo.

"Remember this: what once was shall be again."

Frantic to prolong the exchange, Varoi cried out his sister's name.

"Bayritz!"

Pool and reflection were gone, only her words lingered on. "Remember this ... it's most important."

A prophecy, Varoi thought. It had to be. What else was important enough to drag her back from the past, when she might otherwise rest in peace? And there were

93

questions, too, in sore need of answers; answers she alone might provide. Like ... what actually happened the night she died?

Frilly ripples frayed the surface of what should have been a hive, leaving Varoi to wonder what other revelations he might have missed.

"Bayritz!"

The door opened and Demoiselle looked up, alerted by the jangling of a bell. Varoi stood on the threshold looking distracted and at something of a loss; a male she recalled seeing before.

Demoiselle asked, "Can I help you, Lieutenant?"

Varoi paused, uncertain of his welcome. It was one thing to come here as escort to a princess; quite another to arrive unannounced and alone.

"Is Ayesha here?"

Ah, that explains it, Demoiselle thought. She returned to her task, cleaning up after the mid-morning rush. "No, Lieutenant. I'm afraid you just missed her."

"How long since she left?" Varoi took a step further into the room. The door behind him clicked shut, with yet another musical jangle.

Surprised, Demoiselle again glanced up, "It is not an hour since she declared it was time she returned to her room," though, as she recalled, Ayesha had chosen a somewhat pithier phrase to describe her present abode. No doubt she would return via the docks, having availed herself of a draught of fresh air; if the air at the harbour could be fairly described as fresh.

"Then I'm safe for the moment," Varoi declared, sighing and moving still further into the room.

"Slumming, Lieutenant?" She hadn't intended her tone to be tart. But it was rare for a Shakar, let alone an adult male, to linger long in her emporium. One look at

94

what was plainly the haunt of humanity usually sufficed to make them turn tail and run.

"If I'm unwelcome, you just have to say."

Driving potential clientele away would be foolish. "Not at all, Lieutenant," she hastened to reassure. "I'm just surprised you should wish to stay."

Assuming he wasn't planning to sit at a table and while away his time, Demoiselle brought out a small lacquer tray and prepared to attend to Varoi's needs.

"Chocola, Lieutenant?"

"That would be nice. And some advice, if you're willing to give it."

"Advice is free, on the house. Chocola comes at the usual rate."

"I'm a bit burdened down. Can I put these somewhere out of the way?"

Demoiselle glanced up from ladling water into a vessel and saw that Varoi's hands were full. Setting the kettle atop the stove, she stepped round the counter to help him. Most items he held were wrapped in tissue paper; some were tied with colourful ribbon, besides.

"Gifts, Lieutenant?" she dared to ask, hoping to put him at ease.

"A few items I thought Ayesha might appreciate, to brighten up her dingy room. Perhaps I shouldn't say that," he chided himself.

In truth, Demoiselle thought, Ayesha had said much worse. Having helped him to unload the items and settled him into a booth, she went back to her task. When she returned, tray in hand, Varoi stood. Relieving her of her burden, he asked, "Won't you join me, Demoiselle?"

Surprised, she tilted her head questioningly. Seeing Varoi was serious, she said, "I'd be delighted, Lieutenant. It's about time I took the weight off my feet."

When she came back with a fresh cup and saucer, Varoi passed her the one he'd just poured and smiled disarmingly. "If we're going to be informal, I much prefer that you call me Varoi."

Demoiselle swallowed the tart response that rose to her lips. It was rare, in her experience, for any Shakar to make such a concession. This male was different from the one Ayesha had brought here before. That one had been Garrison Commander Schezan com 'Varicci and Ayesha's Chosen. Arrogant and domineering, he had gone to immense trouble to ensure Demoiselle remembered her place. This male was an entirely different character, one of whom she could approve. Demoiselle relaxed, prepared to offer whatever advice she could.

Ayesha perched on the edge of her seat, intrigued. The hard bench was set to one side of the practice arena, an area of the inner ward that had been set aside for this precise purpose. It was a place where members of the garrison could practise the martial arts. At this hour of the day it was especially busy as those warriors not on duty went through their various routines.

She had chosen a place sheltered from the overhead sun. Toku, her eldest and favourite brother, was perched alongside, paying keen attention to all that took place. They were engaged in watching the newly-arrived warriors. Toku was volubly expounding, at length, on the various merits of specific techniques, while extolling the innumerable ways in which particular warriors put their unique virtues to use. It was a pastime that had him much enthused.

"What about him?" Ayesha said, indicating one warrior who had just entered the arena. As with all other warriors practising alone, he wore only the requisite leather wrap and boots. His thick mane of glossy brown hair was drawn back into a tail, while the long hilt of his hand-and-a-half sword protruded above one shoulder.

"You mean Varoi," Toku mused, following the direction his sister indicated. "Varoi's fast, Ayesha, very fast. His best asset in any form of combat is speed."

"You mean he lacks patience?" Ayesha queried, deliberately pretending to misunderstand, curious to know how much her brother had learnt. Besides which ... an impatient lover would be hard to handle, impossible to command.

"Not that I am aware, Ayesha," Toku was quick to refute any such suggestion. "At times he seems the epitome of patience, when occasion demands."

So Varoi had plenty of patience, did he? That was just as well, since she planned on putting it to the test. Aware that Toku had not finished speaking, she turned her attention back to what was being said.

"... Varoi is quick to seize any advantage; a useful trait in any warrior from what I hear tell."

Ayesha continued her observation as Varoi went through his paces alone.

It was pleasing to hear him described as patient. If he *was* determined to pursue his courtship of her, despite her already being pledged, Ayesha had not the slightest intention of making things easy on him. The final decision would always be hers: to continue as she was or apply to Schezan for formal release.

The sun was high by the time Varoi completed his routine. Sweat trickled between his shoulderblades; his face and neck were drenched in perspiration. Sheathing his sword, he wiped his brow with the back of one hand. Where tendrils of hair had come loose during practice, they clung to his face in damp curls. His boots were covered in a fine film of dust.

Others beside him had finished practice. Together they made their way to the communal baths: the best place to wind down, relax and get scrupulously clean. It was a pleasurable experience and one to which he looked

97

forward; a chance to share in the usual gossip peculiar to male Shakar.

He'd hardly gone a few paces when a shout rang out from behind, causing him to turn. Toku was running toward him with Ayesha sauntering behind. Varoi could not have been more pleased or surprised by this unforeseen encounter.

Toku soon outpaced his sister, though he was not fully grown and would not attain his full height yet awhile. Varoi, noticing the difference in length between Toku's and Ayesha's limbs, could not help but wonder: what might it be like having Ayesha's legs wrapped around his? He felt his body harden with urgent need.

Varoi, halting, bent to scoop Toku up and, to Toku's delight, plant him astride his broad shoulders.

Toku whispered, confidingly, "She likes you, Varoi, a lot."

Varoi, having stopped to allow Ayesha to catch up, did his best to conceal his surprise at this statement. "How can you tell?"

Toku, grinning, tapped one finger against his nose. "She's my sister. Trust me. I know."

"Hmm …" thought Varoi, *If only that were true.* He was not convinced it was.

As Ayesha drew abreast, Varoi fell into step alongside. "Ayesha," he said, "Toku and his brother have settled in well. I thought you might like to know."

"So he informs me," Ayesha said, contriving to sound off-hand.

"How are your quarters?" Varoi persisted. "Have you everything you need?"

Ayesha slowed. Placing one hand on her hip and looking up at him for the first time she said, "Thank you for asking, Varoi. Apart from my parents, you're the first to bother putting that question. Yes, the room will do fine. After all, it's not as though I expect to be there long. It isn't like home, I will admit. There are many small comforts I miss. Then again, I have my privacy and on the whole I'm satisfied. I should like to thank your commander for that, if I but had the chance. Perhaps you could pass my message on?"

"I shall be happy to do so. Why not tell him yourself? He *is* approachable, you know."

"I intend doing so at the earliest opportunity but he must be busy right now."

Varoi nodded. "As you wish."

Ayesha did her best to ignore the fact that, after several hours of strenuous exercise, the honey gold skin of Varoi's torso glowed with a light sheen of sweat. Soft skin and hard muscle made an irresistible combination, one she was just aching to touch. Had he any idea how profoundly attractive he was? Varoi's gaze, so intense and golden, locked with hers. It was almost as though he could read her thoughts. Ayesha did her best to appear immune, which wasn't easy when he stood so close.

"Now, froglet," Varoi said, lifting his gaze to address Ayesha's brother. "Unless you fancy joining me in the bath, it's time to get down."

Toku screwed up his face in distaste and alarm. Twisting about he appealed for support.

"I don't need a bath, do I, Ayesha?" Slowly she shook her head, "No."

Varoi could not resist pointing out the obvious. "Froglets are supposed to like water."

"Not this froglet," Toku disagreed, before turning to face his sister again. "Can I watch Varoi bathe? *Please.*"

"You're a strange little fellow," Ayesha said, reaching up to tweak his nose. "I've no objections, providing Varoi doesn't mind."

Varoi shook his head. Setting his passenger down, Varoi took hold of Toku's hand and led him into the cool, airy chamber that fronted the baths.

Ayesha found herself staring at their departing backs, surprised by Varoi's relaxed attitude towards Toku, which she felt sure was not the least bit feigned. Toku might be young but he was too astute to allow a friendship to flourish if it didn't suit.

She wondered, too, what it might be like to watch, as Toku planned to watch, while Varoi bathed. The very idea of seeing Varoi naked sent a ripple of pleasure through her frame, to coil in her gut like molten honey. How had her awareness of him changed in so short a time? It seemed unlikely; still, it had. He was working his way under her skin in a way she found disconcerting.

Halfway down the tunnel Toku turned to give his sister a farewell wave, only to find her already gone. The main baths of the fortress had been set aside for the exclusive use of its five-hundred-strong garrison of Shakar. The building was divided into three sections: outer, wet room and garb. Varoi entered the outer chamber, doffing his clothes as he went, leaving weapons, belt and boots where they could be reclaimed on the way out. Toku swaggered alongside.

Varoi, glancing down, suggested, "Why not join me, froglet?"

Toku shook his head vigorously. "I don't want to get in your way."

The answer surprised Varoi into suspecting a less obvious cause for Toku's reluctance to bathe. "What makes you think you will? I'd hardly suggest it if I thought you would. Or is there another reason you're unwilling to disclose?"

Toku continued shaking his head. "I'm not like you and the other warriors. They're all full-blooded males, whereas I'm still small." Toku sounded wistful as he spoke these last words.

"And you think that is a problem?" Varoi asked. "Toku, if I considered that any kind of difficulty, I never

100

would suggest the idea. Do you think I would want to see you embarrassed? Do you not trust me enough?"

"I trust you." Toku's amber eyes were large and round with concern.

"Then why so reluctant, froglet? Could it be you don't enjoy getting wet?"

Toku glanced up, his expression grave. "I'm not big and muscular like you."

"And you think that matters?"

"I don't like being the odd one out."

"No one does, froglet. And you won't be, just as long as you're naked like everyone else. But walk in there fully clothed and they'll assume you have something to hide, something of which you're ashamed. I know different and so do you. But ..." Varoi let his statement hang.

Toku, grimacing, reluctantly agreed. "I'll do as you say. Then, if they get nasty, I'll just lay the blame on you."

"Fair enough. Now, hurry and get undressed. I'm getting cold hanging about while you make up your mind."

Toku vanished, to re-emerge stripped to the skin.

"Now," said Varoi. "Let's have some fun," and with that he started to run. Toku was at first left behind, though, having ensured he did not go too fast, Varoi was unsurprised when Toku passed him.

"Hey there, froglet, wait for me!"

Toku's giggles echoed back down the tunnel. "No fear. Like you said, it's too bloody cold."

Varoi put on a spurt and soon caught up. Entering the wet room together they skidded to an abrupt halt. The place was packed, with no room left for either one of them to wriggle between.

The one main feature of the wet room stretched the entire length of the vast space: it was three paces wide, over an ell deep, twenty paces long and, right now, brimful with hot sudsy water. The bath itself was an amazing sight when stuffed to the gunnels with full-blooded, naked males. And not just any male Shakar but warriors: each one tall and powerfully built, many sporting battle scars that gave clear evidence of the conflicts in which each individual had been involved. To Varoi this was a familiar sight but not so for Toku. Toku's time in the dormatorium had helped familiarise him with some aspects of close camaraderie but nothing had quite prepared him for this glorious melee.

Crouching down, Varoi brought his mouth close to Toku's ear, where he could whisper without fear of being overheard. "This inconsiderate lot have taken up all available space. Why don't you go ahead and make some room?"

Toku brought his face close and, in awed tones, enquired, "How?"

Varoi showed him a toothy grin, one designed to instil confidence in his diminutive friend.

"There's one sure way I know. It involves a small, would-be warrior achieving the impossible. Are you game?"

Hands resting on Toku's shoulders, he spun him about. "They're packed as tight as herrings in a crate: should be easy for one as nimble as you. Take a running jump and then use them as stepping-stones till you reach the end. If that doesn't make room, nothing will. The trick is to not get caught. What say you? Can you manage it?"

Toku assumed a pose of quiet deliberation, hands on hips. Then, his decision made, nodded once. Varoi straightened, his features a mask of satisfaction. The challenge had been laid down. Toku had swept up the gauntlet with casual aplomb. All he need do now was wait to see how events panned out.

Toku stepped back, gave himself room, and then started his run, to finish it with a flying leap. The bath erupted, a seething, thrashing turmoil of wet, slippery bodies. Toku's feet hardly touched down between one leap and the next. Everyone yelled encouragement as they followed his progress across the heaving throng.

Varoi grinned, pleased with the success of his strategy. By the time Toku arrived at the bath's end all sign of nerves had vanished as though they had never been. Coming to the climax of his run Toku bounced once, turning in mid-air, arms held aloft in a gesture of sheer exultation. Upon landing he slipped, to land with a whump on his rump, driving all air from the lungs of the unfortunate male into whose lap he fell. The resulting maelstrom of turbid water sloshed up on all sides. The cheer that met his exuberant display was deafening.

At the far end of the bath Che ruefully studied his newly arrived bath-mate. "Are you, then, a warrior full-grown, Toku? Here, let me count the hairs on your chest. One ... two ... three. I'm not sure you qualify. Perhaps I should throw you back."

Varoi, glancing down the length of the baths to where Toku lay inelegantly sprawled, answered Toku's cheeky grin with one of his own. Laughing, he clambered into the bath and sat. It was a squeeze but there was room enough ... just.

"Budge up there. How's a fellow meant to get clean with you lot taking up all the room like fat hogs in a wallow?" Sponges were lobbed in Varoi's direction at that rude remark. Varoi, laughing, snagged one in midair, putting it to good use.

Varoi stared across the harbour, to where three ships, having just weighed anchor, were sailing out of the bay. A remaining two were still being unloaded by bustling dockers and lighter-men.

For some reason he could not explain, the apparent tranquillity of this scene caused him rather more than momentary concern. The harbour master's lack of interest served only to heighten his sense of frustration. He was meant to devise some suitable means of making the harbour area more secure. So far nothing useful had come to mind and the harbour master's air of complacency was proving tedious, to say the least. Varoi was obliged to come up with answers of his own, which seemed a far from satisfactory state of affairs.

Turning his back on the scene, Varoi stomped off in search of Borit, intent on learning what his friend had managed to glean. He found Borit easily enough, led by the strident clangour of a blacksmith's hammer, which fractured the calm of the morning air, announcing to all that Borit the blacksmith was hard at work. Varoi strode into the smithy's back room, where the heat of the forge was suffocating in its intensity. Catching Borit's eye he gave an authoritative jerk of his head, then vanished the way he'd just come.

Outside the air was cooler and an overhanging canopy kept off rain and sun while he waited. When Borit emerged from the smithy he wore a disgruntled frown.

"What happened to last night's meeting? I waited over an hour before anyone bothered to turn up and inform me you were otherwise detained."

"I'm sorry for that, Borit, but I was assigned to guard duty when another Shakar fell ill. I'm afraid I just assumed you would receive my message in good time."

Borit shook his head. "Never mind. I just wish I'd known sooner, that's all. What's this about? It had better be important, I'm in the middle of a rushed order right now." Glancing over his shoulder, he said, "You do pick you moments, Varoi."

"I need to know whether you learnt anything useful as regards to the harbour's defence. I've learnt nothing from the harbour master, who treats me like some sort of imbecile. If my timing is off I apologise but the harbour's defence is crucial, as I'm sure you appreciate. I'm desperate for information. So, what do you know?"

"Ah, well," said Borit, wiping his hands on a damp, oily rag. "My employer did suggest I might take an early lunch."

"In which case, allow me to buy you a meal in humble recompense for last night's prolonged wait."

Borit seemed pleased with the suggestion. By the time he had chomped his way through two hot meat pies and a couple of porters of watered down wine he was in a more congenial mood. "Had he felt so inclined, the harbour master could have informed you the harbour already has sufficient safeguards in place. Anything else?" Borit brushed himself down, "Only, I've plenty of work on my hands."

"Nothing that cannot wait."

Borit nodded, then strode away.

Returning to the harbour Varoi established a fresh perspective on its surrounds. The steep walls of the town's escarpment jutted far out into the bay, continuing the curtain wall. It was in these areas that a strong undertow prevailed. The innocent seeming sandbars, fronting the far shore, indicated where quicksands were known to exist. These, together with fast flowing currents and steep crumbling banks, were among a number of natural and man-made hazards any enemy would be forced to negotiate. Last, but by no means least, was the row of rotting hulks moored far out in the bay; distant enough from the docks to present no hazard to shipping, yet close enough to be easily set on fire. It seemed the harbour master had just cause to feel so complacent.

Varoi was on his way back to the fortress, heading for the main part of town, when a ruckus down by the wharf drew his attention that way.

Having extricated the young urchin, who'd proven to be the main source of disruption, Varoi took pains to assure the harbour master that a higher authority would deal with the difficulty. If the scamp involved suffered qualms, he gave no sign.

Commander com 'Dolino was not as amenable as Varoi had initially hoped.

"What means this intrusion?" the commander bawled. "I issued strict instructions that Commander com 'Tovari and I should not be disturbed. By what right do you presume to overrule those orders?"

Varoi remained stiffly erect until the tirade ground to a halt. "Forgive me, Commander. This lad has information that I thought you should hear."

"So you say." Though he still seemed disgruntled, Varoi fancied there was a softening to the commander's terse tone.

Despite his superior officer's annoyance, Varoi maintained a firm stance. Having learnt much from the small intruder during their walk through town, he was convinced the boy had crucial information to impart that would bear heavily on their imminent encounter with the Pulan.

"He tells me he's rowed the best part of the night to get here," Varoi began. "Won't you listen to what he has come to say?"

Varoi strengthened his grip on the small boy's shoulders, easing him further into the room. The problem was, they were not alone. A delegation of townsfolk was also present, which no doubt explained his sharp dressing down.

Someone gave a dismissive snort. "Rowed through the night? A likely story!" Varoi glanced round to see one of the town's burgesses glaring at the boy.

"I did so!" The boy was indignant.

"All night? Without stopping? Really, boy, do you take us for fools?"

"I may have stopped once or twice. That's all and only when needful."

"Aha!"

Varoi couldn't help wondering why the burgess should be so dismissive of this tale. He couldn't resist a sneaking admiration for the small boy's gritty resolve in face of such blatant disbelief. No one had forced him to come here and be insulted. Well … except for him.

"I had to, when I had no other choice. Only to catch my breath or take a quick piss over the side. It's hard on a body to keep on rowing when your bladder's close to bursting, with all that water sloshing noisily about. I dare any one of you to give it a try."

Varoi managed to suppress a sly smile at the small scamp's outrageous remark

The plump burgess was unimpressed. "I don't think your bodily functions a suitable topic of conversation. Commander, might I suggest we resume the discussion that was under way at the time your warrior and this rude boy intervened? It is of vital importance, as I'm sure you'll agree."

"I do, indeed, consider our discussion to be vital. However, I feel bound to admit an interest in what the boy might reveal. As unlikely a messenger though this young rogue appears, I feel obliged to listen, especially since my lieutenant considers the information pertinent to the task in hand. In view of this I feel it best we terminate our meeting and reconvene at a later date: say tomorrow, noon. Is that agreeable?"

Despite their annoyance, the town's dignitaries wisely acquiesced. A face-saving reversal seemed prudent to all concerned. Rising from their seats they prepared to take their leave with as much aplomb as could be managed. Varoi kept both hands clamped to the boy's shoulders, lest his charge lose his nerve and attempt an escape.

"Varoi, be so kind as to show these honourable gentlemen out."

Varoi backed towards the door. Releasing his grip on the young urchin he offered a smart salute. The boy, turning, made a grab for Varoi's sleeve.

"Don't leave me here. He may decide to eat me if he doesn't like what I have to say."

Varoi glanced down and then back up, clearly nonplussed by this bizarre suggestion, and caught the amused glint in his officer's eye. Commander com 'Tovari also struggled to hide a wry smile. Unlikely as it might seem, the Shakar's fearsome reputation had not diminished in any respect. Varoi's attention returned to the small boy, whose dark eyes had grown surprisingly large in his pale, pinched face.

"You have naught to fear, providing you stick to the truth," Varoi assured.

"You think?"

Uncaring that he risked disapproval, Varoi dropped to his haunches, confronting the boy eye to eye. "I am certain. Now, make your report and I shall see you later." With these few words Varoi rose, spun on his heel and strode away.

Out in the corridor, he found the burgesses waiting. Flushed with irritation, they made no attempt to hide their curiosity. Varoi considered it was not his duty to enlighten them in any regards concerning the small boy's news.

Signalling those warriors on duty outside the room to provide them with escort, he simply said, "Gentlemen, if you would follow me."

With those few words Varoi led the dignitaries along the corridor and out through the keep's main door. Listening to the conversation around him, he discovered some interesting facts of his own: this fortress apparently predated Shakar occupation of the Unclaimed Land, which meant it must have been built by men, although what breed of man remained a mystery. It was definitely not the Pulan, whose construction methods were unreliable and crude. This fortress revealed evidence of a stronger, more pragmatic breed of man. Varoi wondered whether it was possible that Fenlanders, now a sparse and scattered breed, had once been in the ascendance here. If so, perhaps that explained Borit's marshal tendencies, his keenness that men should be allowed to train as warriors to protect their land. If such a situation should come about, what might its future implications be?

Hardly had he returned to the room in which the meeting had been convened when the door ahead of him swung wide.

"Ah, Varoi. Just in time. This young man tells me he's had access to neither food nor drink since first he took to his boat. Perhaps you would escort him to the kitchens and see if they can rustle up something appropriate to assuage his appetite. Then hurry back here, if you please."

Varoi stole a quick glance at his commander before leading the boy away, but saw nothing to signify the gravity of the message received. He had some idea what the small boy might have said but his knowledge was limited unless he could pry loose the boy's tongue by means of judicious questioning.

Varoi, deciding he had nothing to lose, asked. "So, what did my commander say?"

The boy gave him a quizzical stare. "My grandsire warned me against talking to strangers." Then he asked, "What sort of food will the kitchens have on offer?"

Varoi stifled a sigh of vexation. The young scamp seemed more interested in filling his belly than anything else.

"Bread, cheese, fruit and cold meats; whatever comes most readily to hand. You'll be well taken care of. Have no fear."

109

"Good." The boy glanced up. "May I know your name?"

"Lieutenant com 'Domicci is how I'm known. You can call me Lieutenant."

Relenting a little, the boy then said, "I told your commander what I told you. Large numbers of Pulan are moving through Greenbeg Fen. There's not much else I can add other than to relate my family's sorry fate. I doubt you're interested in that."

Varoi couldn't help but express surprise at this sudden loosening of the boy's tongue. "I thought you didn't believe in talking to strangers?"

"I don't, as a rule. But I know your name and consider you friend enough to trust. You certainly told that horrible man down at the harbour where to get off."

Varoi gave a snort of amusement. "Well enough. Since you know my name, perhaps you'd oblige me by revealing yours. I can't keep calling you 'boy'."

The small lad peered up through a curtain of hair and ventured a mischievous grin. "Horace Wimpole, that's my name; just like my pa. Horace to you. There's a favour I should like to ask, if I may."

"And that is?"

"If your commander plans to send warriors to Greenbeg Fen, then I want to go with them, providing no one objects. My grandsire is injured and in sore need of aid."

Varoi considered the request before making his reply. "Well, Horace," he said, at length, "let's first see what the commander decides. After that I'll see what can be done to accommodate your petition."

"I suppose that will have to suffice. But you'll need to be quick now that the Pulan are moving. They won't hang about while you make up your mind."

Varoi nodded, then pushed the kitchen door wide. The warm smell of baking issued forth, causing Horace to pause and sniff appreciatively.

Having urged the cook to do what she could to satisfy Horace's hunger Varoi headed back. He was anxious to know what had been learnt. His commander had given every indication he wanted the boy kept confined to the keep, which implied there was more to discover. By the time he returned to the garrison commander's office, others from among the garrison had started to arrive. On entry he found the table set about with chairs and a number of scrolls laid out and weighted down.

It was Commander com 'Tovari who addressed them first.

"Be seated, all of you. There is an important development we must discuss."

Varoi seated himself at the table and waited to hear what would be said. Whatever information Horace had divulged appeared to comprise only a small part of events.

"As some of you know, a small boy arrived today, bringing us warning of the latest deployment of Pulan. The tale sounds a trifle far-fetched but we're inclined to give it credence just the same. Whatever we decide has to be done soon. This meeting has been convened in order to set certain events in motion.

"It seems that a large force of Pulan are on the move, heading toward Nai Hai du Veral. Hard as it is to believe, I think we must act fast to avert the risk of such an attack taking place. This garrison should enable a large enough force to be dispatched in order to intercept and dissuade them of their mistake. I feel ..." he cast a sideways glance towards his counterpart, "... we both feel that it's imperative we at least try.

"Of course, the essential truth of this statement has yet to be confirmed but, if true, it explains a few things. Like why the Pulan force that was expected to attack

111

Tenbay has not yet arrived. Perhaps they never intended such an attack. Either way, it seems expedient to reduce their numbers; now we know where they may be found."

With careful deliberation, Commander com 'Dolino unrolled one of the maps, weighting it down at the corners as he proceeded to explain.

"The boy says his parents' small farm was overrun, that he and his grandsire were the only ones to escape alive. This attack took place on the easterly border of Pennyblack Fen. It seems obvious, from what the boy says he overheard, that the Pulan target is the Shakar capital."

Bigli, who had been studying the map, chose to interrupt. "Excuse me, Commander, but if the attack took place close to the border, between Pennyblack and Greenbeg Fen, is it not also likely the Pulan might go either way?"

"You think the boy may be lying? But why?"

Varoi spoke up in Horace's defence. "I don't think the boy would deliberately lie. If what the lieutenant says is true, consider this. Might he have misunderstood what he overheard?"

"You think that possible, Lieutenant com 'Domicci?"

"I believe so. If he was in hiding, how could he have overheard unless he was dangerously close? Perhaps he misheard or, even, assumed?"

Commander com 'Tovari drew his dark brows down in a scowl. "You think he might be sending us on a wild goose chase? If so, that would be a perilous ploy."

"Dangerous for him, maybe. I think his primary concern right now is saving his grandsire's life. Perhaps I'm reading more into the situation than is right, but still …"

"You think we may be walking into a trap if we go ahead with this plan?"

"If not a trap, then a situation where we'll find ourselves outnumbered. The boy is desperate to save his grandsire, don't forget."

"You think this may be a ruse?"

"Perhaps a ruse, but if so, then one devised by a child; a child at the end of his tether. He can't help those who died, so he's focused on the sole relative who survived."

"We need to find out. Can you do that, Varoi? Without frightening the boy unduly, I mean. He's been through enough already, it seems."

Varoi said, "I'm willing to try."

"In that case, I give you leave."

Varoi rose, preparing to depart. Commander com 'Dolino spoke again.

"While you're about it, it would seem prudent that you take a look from the roof of the keep. Try to discern in which direction the Pulan are heading. It could save us valuable time."

Varoi nodded his understanding. "Consider it done."

Varoi's original questioning of Horace had been prompted by nothing more than idle curiosity, whereas his commander's interest lay with matters concerning the Pulan. Neither of them had paid more than passing heed to the plight of the small boy's grandsire. Yet Horace claimed they had both escaped alive. If that were the case, Varoi wondered, why had his grandsire not accompanied Horace to Tenbay? If he were too seriously injured it would make sense. The answer to that question might reveal much.

Varoi climbed to the top of the keep, intent on carrying out his task. A chill breeze plucked at his clothing, as he stood scanning the countryside for miles around. There was a limit to his ability, but one thing was soon apparent. If the Pulan were closer than ten miles distant they were either in small groups or were well concealed. Varoi had no doubt regarding their ability to remain hidden, however many their number.

Varoi adjusted his visual senses, tuning them to a fine degree. Not for nothing was he described as *ananaha*. Among the Shakar few existed whose vestigial senses were especially acute and only when enhanced by the *ananaha* gift. Varoi was one. As such he was highly valued, especially among the military. Varoi closed his eyes, oblivious to external influence, and prepared to allow his unique faculties free reign.

Opening his eyes he scanned various points of the compass in turn. Not until he sent his talent ranging due east did he discover the Pulan horde. It seemed Horace had not lied. Then again, neither had he offered the complete truth. There was, indeed, a large army of Pulan on the move. They *were* currently marching through Greenbeg Fen. But they were heading due west rather than east, converging not upon Nai Hai du Veral but upon Tenbay.

Varoi managed a quick assessment of overall numbers, then snapped his thread of focus down tight. Opening his eyes he gazed into the distance. Now that he knew whereabouts they could be found it was easy to do so again. At this distance they were no more than a dark smear on the landscape, a slow moving smudge, but a smudge all the same. In two days' time, by his estimation, they would be encamped outside of Tenbay's walls. Then the battle for Tenbay's survival would begin.

The kitchen was swarming with people by the time Varoi returned, most of the activity to do with the preparation of the evening meal. A few servants were busy laying out a midday repast. Varoi snatched a thick hunk of bread and a huge wedge of cheese as he made his way to where the cook, Mistress Bardol, presided, her podgy hands plunged into a bowl of flour.

"Where is he, Mistress?" Varoi began. "Where is the boy I brought in earlier?"

She gave a sharp order to one of the scullions before deigning to offer reply. "I did as you bade me, Lieutenant. I fed him, then found him a bed. Don't say you're going to disturb him already. The poor mite appears quite worn out."

"So, where might I find him?" Varoi persisted, snagging two apples from the pile while her attention was directed elsewhere.

"Abed and asleep, I should imagine. Why do you ask?"

"I have cause to speak with him again. Take me to him now."

"*Now!*" she complained. "Poor wee mite. He has hardly set his head on the pillow. Why such disagreeable haste?"

Varoi made an impatient gesture with his hand. He had no time to waste and no wish to discuss such matters here, not with so many ears bending his way and so many tongues ready to wag. Rumours ran rife in any small community and the kitchen was a virulent hotbed of gossip. She caught his meaning and lifted her hands from the bowl. Wiping them clean on a towel kept tucked into her apron, she led him to a small door that opened on to a narrow, draughty passage.

At the far end she stopped before a closed door. Pulling herself up to her full height she endeavoured to look him straight in the eye.

"I put him in here, thinking he would remain undisturbed. I hope you have good cause for waking him so soon."

He glanced down at her as she stood, one hand resting idle on the latch. "I can't say he lied to me, Mistress, but still, he did not tell my commander the whole truth. I'm making it my personal business to find out why."

"What harm in a lie if tis only a small one?"

"This one could cost lives, not to mention leaving your fine town of Tenbay seriously undermanned with an enemy army on the way."

"Then, I take your point." Grudgingly, she lifted the latch. "Just go easy on the lad. I'm sure he had sound reason for saying whatever he did."

"As you suggest," Varoi gave no more reassurance than that. Stepping through the door he turned swiftly, barring her entry. "Return to your duties, Mistress. Whatever he says, I'll not harm the boy."

She sniffed loudly, pursing her lips in plain displeasure at his curt attitude, then started away. Over her shoulder she offered some parting advice.

"See that you don't hurt him, Lieutenant; since, if you do, you shall answer to me."

Varoi stood, one hand on the latch, watching her retreat. Then, closing the door behind him with a soft click, he uttered a quick incantation, setting a small spell of coverture in place, before moving to where the boy, Horace, lay. Gazing down at the small, recumbent figure, Varoi felt reluctant to wake him at first. Someone had helped him undress down to his small clothes. His garments lay neatly folded and set in a pile alongside the straw pallet that served for a bed. His pale face was grubby and tearstained. Even in sleep, it seemed, he did not rest. The hand that lay on his pillow twitched spasmodically. And, as Varoi watched, a single tear escaped from beneath a dark fan of lashes to trickle down one dirty cheek.

Remorse was an icy lump in Varoi's breast but he hardened his heart, prepared for what he must do next. Horace may not have meant to mislead, but mislead them he had. It was imperative the truth be found out. Still, he resolved to wake the boy gently, if he could.

"Horace," Varoi said, keeping his voice soft. At first he saw no reaction. Varoi persisted. "Horace. Wake up," he laid one hand gently upon the boy's arm.

The effect was immediate and startling. Horace shot up in bed, feet kicking the blankets aside, fists clenched as they prepared to defend against an imaginary foe. Varoi spoke again, his voice reassuring.

"Relax, Horace. You're safe."

The boy's eyes were wide with alarm, pupils dark and dilated from unshed sleep. "Get away. Begone. It's not safe," Horace hissed, the urgency in his tone and fear in his voice tugging at Varoi's heartstrings.

Still, Varoi resisted the impulse to gather the child close, knowing, intuitively, this would not help and might even succeed in compounding the boy's fears. Instead, he waited patiently for the small child's sleep-befuddled brain to clear, for Horace to focus on his surroundings and realise that what Varoi told him was, indeed, true. He was safe and there was nothing he need fear.

Understanding arrived with a rush and the clenched fists and tense muscles relaxed. "I thought I was someplace else," Horace explained, shamefaced.

"Evidently," Varoi said, then waited patiently for the child to regain his composure before revealing the reason for his unexpected presence.

"You lied to us, Horace. I'm disappointed that you should consider it necessary and, while I'm sure you had good reason, still, you lied."

Varoi watched as Horace, again, grew tense, seeming to expect some form of punishment. Varoi kept his manner calm as he resumed speaking. "Are you ready to reveal the truth of what you know and, perhaps, explain the reason behind your apparent deception?"

To his surprise Horace screwed up his fists and stuck out his chin in a brave gesture of defiance. "If you know so much, why don't *you* tell *me*?"

117

Varoi fought the urge to grin. He tried to be angry at this response, to find a means by which he might prompt Horace to reveal the relevant facts without causing harm, but he could not. Instead, he felt a sneaking respect for the child facing him. Horace was trapped with no means of escape or evasion. His lies had brought him to this pass. Yet, he prepared to face his accuser with what courage he possessed.

"All right," said Varoi, sensing that there was nothing to be gained by further prevarication. "Since you ask it, I'll tell you what I have just learnt. Perhaps, then, you'll oblige me by filling what gaps in my knowledge remain. Does that seem fair?"

The boy offered a slow nod of assent.

Varoi settled himself on the end of the pallet, wanting to bring himself down to the child's level so they could view each other eye to eye, while offering no obvious threat. He spoke softly, keeping his demeanour calm. He already sensed that the boy's ordeal had been worse than hitherto revealed.

"Horace, I am *ananaha*. Do you know what that means?"

"That you can see farther and hear better than anyone else."

Varoi managed a small grin. "Something like that. There is more to it besides, but nothing that need concern you now. Horace, I have seen this army of Pulan, the ones you say are marching through Greenbeg Fen."

"And?"

"As to that, you did not lie. They are, indeed, marching through Greenbeg Fen."

Horace made a sharp dismissive gesture, as if to say *I told you so*. Varoi acknowledged this and then went on.

"They *are* marching across Greenbeg Fen, but *not* toward Nai Hai du Veral. Instead, they are heading towards Tenbay fortress."

118

"You saw that?" The boy's expression was one of pure disbelief. "How could you see their direction from so great a distance?"

Varoi said nothing to that at first. Then he saw the boy start in alarm as another thought occurred.

"Are they that close?"

"Not so close," Varoi assured. "Two days distant, maybe more. The fact remains, you lied. Why bother? What did you hope to gain?"

The boy lowered his gaze, gave his thin shoulders a negligent shrug and muttered something caustic under his breath.

Varoi said, "Tell me, Horace. Help me understand."

Horace lifted his head. "I seek vengeance for those I have lost, by any means possible: I want to wipe my feet on their faces once they lie dead. I would kick them as they lay dying. I would grind them into the dirt. I would ..."

Varoi raised a silencing hand. "Enough, Horace; I get the picture. I take it we're meant to be your means of revenge? But that doesn't explain the need to lie."

"For family, Shakar; for those who offered no form of resistance but were slain where they stood, just the same." Varoi tilted his head in silent enquiry. "And because my grandsire needs your assistance. If I don't return soon it will be too late."

Horace's voice broke on a swelling tide of emotion. With some difficulty he resumed. "I was the only one to recognise the danger. I saw a huge force of Pulan coming towards me across the fen. I called a warning, then ran and hid. There were many more than usual. By my cowardice I am proven unworthy of my father's name. There! Are you satisfied?"

Varoi saw the boy's defiance crumble, saw tears well unbidden in his eyes.

119

Varoi said, "There is one thing I don't understand. You say your grandsire escaped. How can this be? Injured or no, he could have accompanied you."

"He did not escape unscathed. They wounded him badly, left him for dead. Not until dusk did I dare creep past their campfires to investigate and discover what fate had befallen my family. My parents and baby sister were slain but my grandsire yet lived. I managed to help him to my hiding place but he was too weak then to go further. Leaving him hidden, I took to my boat and rowed through the night, seeking aid. Revenge may have been uppermost in my mind by the time I arrived but it was my grandsire's need of healing that brought me this far. And now, because I offered you a falsehood, you will do nothing and my grandsire will die. I think my behaviour fully justified but understand you may not see things my way."

Varoi grew quiet, dwelling on the wider implications of what he had learnt.

Varoi knew it was common practice among farmers to offer no resistance when faced by a hostile group of Pulan. By this means their losses remained minimal, an irritation but little else. The Pulan followed an unwritten code that allowed any such farmer and his family to go unharmed. That such behaviour had been altered showed a marked change in conduct, and a worrying one at that.

It was adult males who traditionally invaded the Unclaimed Land, each clan group consisting of between thirty and a hundred warriors, each determined to do battle on his clan's behalf and return home with whatever booty he managed to purloin. These groups did not normally combine; yet even small groups were too great in number for one farmer to withstand, especially when encumbered with young.

So what had gone wrong? Why needlessly slaughter helpless people? Unless, of course, there was good reason. Was it possible, in this case, that a change in strategy had been prompted by the need for secrecy? The desire to ensure none learnt of the army being formed? Varoi felt sure he saw a pattern emerging and decided to question Horace further. The boy was holding up well under duress.

"These warriors, you say there were more than usual. How many more?"

Horace gave his shoulders a disconsolate shrug. "How can I say? Do you think I took time to stop and count? My grandsire seemed amazed by their greater number. I heard him say as much, even as I ran. He made no attempt to stop me, nor call me back. I wish I'd had the courage to stand firm."

"Had you done so, you might also be dead."

"And yet, because of me, he may well die."

"What makes you so sure of that?"

"He will die because I lied and so failed to bring the help I promised."

"Perhaps in that you are wrong."

Varoi couldn't help but sympathise with Horace, whose sad misfortune meant he and his family had been in the wrong place at the wrong time. At least he and his grandsire had survived, though small consolation, that, if the one surviving member of his family later died of his wounds. Right then, Varoi made up his mind to do whatever he could to help put matters right.

"I shall help as best I can. But only if we do things my way."

Hope kindled in the small boy's eyes. "You mean that?"

"I make no promises, but I will try. In exchange, I expect complete honesty."

"I shall be truthful. On that you have my oath."

Varoi required no such affirmation, but chose to accept it, just the same for appearance's sake and in hopes of offering Horace some form of surety.

"First, I require my commanding officer's agreement. Until then, I can give no firm undertaking. You will just have to trust me when I say, I shall try."

"That's better than I hoped for moments ago," Horace confessed. "What must I do now?"

"Dress quickly and we will go to inform the commander." While he spoke Varoi deposited one of the apples he had filched atop Horace's bed: a peace offering, if such were required.

Horace stopped him at the door. "May I know your given name?" Horace, having picked up the apple, asked with an insouciant grin. Varoi recognised both question and action as measures of trust. He matched Horace's grin with one of his own, allowing two large canines to slip into view. To his credit Horace barely flinched. Varoi proffered the desired information before closing the door behind them.

"Commander, I think I have ..." Varoi froze in mid-sentence. ... *The information you need* ... he had been about to say but the anger evident in his commander's glance warned him to silence. Commander com 'Dolino had been in the act of conferring with the garrison's temporary commander before his untimely interruption.

Varoi began backing away, dragging the small boy, Horace. "Forgive the intrusion, Commander. I shall return at a more convenient time."

Horace tugged urgently at his sleeve. "I thought you were going to ..."

"Hush," Varoi hissed. "Later, you heard me say." Varoi's hand found the latch and he started to turn away.

"Wait!" Varoi was brought to an abrupt halt by the gruff voice of authority. "Since you've already intruded and your message would seem urgent, I prefer that you stay and apprise us of its content. That is, if Commander com 'Tovari has no objection. Have you any objection, Tovari?

No? Well then, in that case, Varoi, close the door. The boy stays, since I assume this matter in some way concerns him."

As Varoi did so, a sharp prickle of Power brushed his awareness. His commander was putting a spell of coverture in place. Then the latch was snatched from his grasp, the door slammed and the latch came down with an audible clang. Varoi flinched. Had he dare look he felt sure a dark, angry weal would be seen crossing his palm. Not because the latch had been plucked from his grasp. No. Rather he had felt the deft flick of magic: a controlled but summary reprimand. It was small compared to what might still lie in store.

He would be lucky to escape with no more than a dozen lashes and three days detention after what he'd just done. Perhaps the commander would hold his punishment in abeyance, at least until the boy's grandsire had been located and the Pulan army put to rout. Perhaps. Varoi didn't hold out much hope.

Varoi waited in silence, unwilling to aggravate the situation more than he already had. Commander com 'Dolino gave a small but satisfied nod. "You may proceed."

Varoi drew a deep calming breath and began. "Commander, as requested I have questioned the boy extensively ..."

"Horace, my name is Horace," hissed an irate voice alongside. Varoi patted the boy's head and continued, with one small amendment.

"I have questioned the boy ... *Horace* ... and believe I have a better grasp of the situation than before." Varoi hesitated, unsure how best to proceed.

"Go on. If you think this relevant, then I want to hear."

"Horace tells me that most of his family were wiped out when their farm was overrun by the Pulan. The boy hid, which is how he managed to survive. Later, when it was dark, with the Pulan encamped all around, he slipped past their guard to learn what fate had befallen his kin. All save his grandsire were dead. Presumably the Pulan thought him also dead. The boy rescued his grandsire, spiriting him away to a place of safety but was unable to bring him here. Following that the boy ..."

Varoi heard again the soft hiss of displeasure and sought belatedly to amend his manners, thereby avoiding further interruption. "Horace took to his boat, intent upon rowing upstream, hoping to find help for his grandsire and provide those he met with whatever warning he could.

"The thing is," Varoi went on, "as I'm sure you're aware, the Pulan usually leave farmers alone. They may indeed harry their livestock for sport and take whatever food they require but provided no resistance is offered they generally leave the farmers unharmed. This time, things were different. Despite no opposition being shown, the Pulan wasted no time in ensuring that all the residents on the farm were killed. The fact they failed in this instance doesn't mean it hasn't happened before. It may have and us none the wiser.

"What is significant, I believe, is their unprovoked change in tactics. I think I may understand why." Varoi paused. He was taking a chance in what he was about to surmise. He could be wrong.

Commander com 'Dolino gave a peremptory wave. "You have our undivided attention, Lieutenant. Finish what you came here to say."

"In the past, the Pulan have always attacked in small tribal groups. This time the clans have combined. They have come together with one specific purpose in mind. They mean to wage war, and what better place to begin than right here? Tenbay is a fortress, but it is also of strategic importance to the success of their overall plan. Seize Tenbay and they have a base from which to ravage the countryside around, a base within easy striking distance of the capital. This, I think, is their true objective and they are ready to kill any who might warn us of their intent, any who might seek to interfere with their plan. We are about to engage in all-out war, Commander, not a series of minor skirmishes. The prize, should they succeed, is the Unclaimed Land."

"Would they do that?" Commander com 'Tovari sounded appalled at Varoi's suggestion. Varoi fell silent, one hand resting on his informant's shoulder.

"Oh, I think, quite possibly, yes. If they thought it in their best interest." Varoi's commander wore a pensive frown.

"But why? What could they hope to gain?"

"I think all here know the answer to that. They wish to take back that which they once gave away."

"I hardly think abandonment could be described as giving away?" 'Tovari queried.

"When the Pulan first removed themselves to the steppes," explained the commander, "they saw only limited value in this region. That is why they disparagingly named it the Unclaimed Land. It was, you recall, unwholesome, virulent marsh and quagmire, a boggy wilderness wherein little of any real merit grew. It was forever accursed by pestilence and plague. Who could blame them? Only social outcasts and misfits, plus a few robust individuals with little to lose, saw fit to remain.

"The land has been much improved, thanks to Shakar ingenuity. They hate that we succeeded where they made no attempt. What better revenge could they hope for than reclaiming that which they once viewed as a common commodity? Yes, I understand to what Varoi refers. You did well, Lieutenant com 'Domicci. If this *is* their intention then, for now, while it *is* supposition, we would be wise to ensure their intention fails." He tilted his head in a questioning pose. "Was that all?"

"Commander," Varoi said. "The boy Horace has done us a great service by making us aware of the potential risk. Might I request permission to return the favour by finding his grandsire and bringing him here, where he can receive aid?"

"How many warriors will you need to assist in this task?"

Varoi, hearing the note of caution in his commander's voice, hastened to explain. "None save myself and a friend, who is human. This is all the assistance I expect to need. And, of course, Horace, since he alone knows where we must go."

"And this friend ... can he be trusted?"

"So I believe."

"Well then, since I see no reason to refuse, permission granted. I assume you intend leaving soon."

"If it can be arranged. The rescue will take place today under cover of night."

"Then see to it, Lieutenant." Varoi saluted and began backing toward the door. "One moment, please. I cannot risk this boy revealing what has just been discussed."

"Oh, I won't," cried Horace, horrified, "I promise, I won't."

"Be that as it may, I wish to be sure. You, Horace, will give me your oath." From a pouch at his belt the commander produced a small ivory carving, pressing it into Horace's right palm. "Your oath, Horace. Repeat the pledge after me."

Horace's voice dropped to an awed whisper as he uttered the words he was required to say. Varoi knew, as Horace did not, that the fragment of carving was imbued with magical power ensuring that Horace kept his word under pain of death. Horace, having finished the oath, paused to study the ornament before passing it back, as if bemused by what had occurred.

The commander gave a satisfied nod, certain their secret would now remain safe. "I shall speak to you later, Lieutenant, regarding what it is you intend."

Grabbing Horace by the hand, Varoi offered a smart salute and left. He stepped out of the keep's main entrance and on to the broad, sunlit street. As was usual at this time of day, the town thoroughfare was crowded. Without prior warning or explanation he reached down and scooped Horace up. Lifting him high and whirling him about, he set the boy astride his broad shoulders. Having felt the boy stiffen in alarm when first he'd grabbed him, Varoi was pleased when Horace settled back and relaxed. "If you want my help, you must learn to trust me," was all he said, before moving his hands to the boy's upper thighs, where he ensured the boy's utmost safety. If Horace suffered any more reservations, wisely he chose not to air them aloud.

Varoi and Horace had shared an impromptu repast prior to leaving. Despite the noise and bustle of their surroundings he was unsurprised when two small hands settled atop his head as the child's body grew increasingly lax. Rather than disturb his young companion Varoi retained a firm hold, confident that, should Horace fall asleep and start to topple, he could remedy the situation speedily enough. Above his head, Horace grew drowsy, beginning to nod.

It took Varoi the best part of an hour to negotiate his way through the teeming populace. By the time he arrived at the smithy where Borit toiled it was well past noon and Horace was slumped overhead, his short arms wrapped tightly about Varoi's neck. Even so, Varoi was reluctant to wake him. Letting Horace sleep on, he ducked under the smithy's low entrance and looked around. Taking in his surroundings at a glance he saw no visible sign of his friend. Borit, he reasoned, must be labouring somewhere within. The loud, incessant clang of hammers, two of them working in unison, rang out from the furnace

127

room beyond. Reaching up, Varoi laid a protective hand over the small boy's crown and ducked through the second entrance.

Within the forge the furnace was working at full blast. Met by a searing wave of heat, Varoi halted in mid-stride. The air alone was hot enough to broil a body alive. He wondered how anyone could manage to tolerate such working conditions; that two men did was cause for amazement. The verve and vigour they displayed, coupled with the intensity of their concentration, was sufficient to make Varoi gape.

He sensed a disturbance in his young charge's posture and guessed, rightly, that Horace was now awake. Varoi wondered what Horace would make of his changed situation. To his surprise, Horace made no noticeable sound. Perhaps he, too, was stunned to silence.

It took some little time before Borit grew aware of their presence, during which Varoi took scant note of his surroundings but considerable note of Borit. While he did he remained constantly aware of the heat blasting forth from the furnace and the abundance of raw energy with which master and skilled apprentice toiled.

Borit was clad in similar clothes to his companion. Boots, trews and a long leather apron protected vulnerable parts of his anatomy. Apart from the apron, neither shirt nor tunic covered his upper half, but stout, leather bracers protected each wrist from the worst of the sparks that flew. His two-coloured hair was dark with sweat and slicked close to his head, while the powerful muscles of shoulders and arms flexed and rippled beneath a light sheen of sweat that, in turn, caused his trews to cling like a second skin to his lithe, sturdy frame. Varoi could not help but marvel that any man could tolerate such conditions. Any such man deserved his utmost respect.

"Varoi." Borit did not look up from his task while acknowledging his friend. "I trust your errand to be of the utmost importance since, as you see, I'm fully occupied with the task at hand and have no time to spare for idle chat."

And not much breath either, thought Varoi, though he kept that observation to himself. "I'm afraid it is," he said.

"Then wait outside if you would and I'll try and find time. We should finish this task ere long."

There was nothing else to do but comply. Borit was, after all, subject to his master's command. Varoi ducked back out through the door and thence to the partly covered yard that fronted the smithy. The sun's burgeoning heat seemed a welcome respite from the roasting inside. Making his way to the wooden bench set against one wall Varoi lifted Horace from his perch and set him down alongside.

Horace studied Varoi with a quizzical frown. "That man called you by your given name. Does that make him your friend?"

"I believe him to be one of the best friends I've ever possessed, the best and truest. Why do you ask?"

"I'm just curious, that's all. My grandsire believes men and Shakar can never be friends. He says they have nothing whatsoever in common."

"And is that *your* belief, Horace?"

"How can I say? You're the first Shakar I've ever had a chance to know."

"Ah well," said Varoi, adopting a philosophical tone, "plenty of time yet in which to form an opinion."

"Why are we here?" Horace asked, wisely changing the topic of conversation.

"Because I intend asking my friend, Borit, for assistance."

"You mean he might be able to help save my grandsire?"

"That is what I'm hoping, yes. Let's just wait and see if he agrees."

By the time Borit strolled out through the smithy's main entrance, Horace had, once again, fallen asleep. Varoi hadn't the heart to wake him, knowing how tired he must be. Borit's pale brows climbed to his hairline at the sight of the shabbily dressed boy, his tousled head casually resting upon Varoi's knee. Borit studied Varoi with a pensive expression. This was a side to his friend that seemed rather at odds with his otherwise lethal persona … and yet, in a way, it quite suited him.

Varoi, grinning, patted the bench alongside, inviting Borit to join him. Instead, the young blacksmith strolled to a water barrel, helping himself to a drink before refilling the ladle and pouring cool water over his head, letting it run down over his shoulders and back. Then he strode to the bench and plonked himself down.

"What is it you want, Varoi? I don't have long, so this had best be quick, whatever it is." Water dribbled down his face in sultry rivulets, as Borit wiped strong, calloused fingers on an oily rag.

Varoi made haste to explain, providing only the essential details while omitting those that served as unnecessary embellishments of Horace's tale.

"So you see, Borit," he finished, "if no one helps him he'll have lost his entire family through no fault of his own. I cannot let that happen."

"Then this, here, is the lad of whom you speak?"

"It is."

"And you need me to help you perform this rescue mission?"

"If you would."

"Will he accept my aid?"

"If he accepts mine, surely that tells you how desperate he is."

130

Borit grimaced, guessing how sad that must make Varoi feel. "Quite."

"So you'll do it, then? Help us, I mean."

"I'll do it because you ask, Varoi, if for no other reason. As you rightly say, it would be a shame if Horace were to lose his entire family to the Pulan. When were you thinking of leaving?"

"Today, Borit, later, before dusk maybe. I can't risk us being caught by the Pulan; nor can I leave it too long. The grandsire's condition may well be dire."

"Make your arrangements and let me know the details. I'll explain to my master, make him understand. Natu's a reasonable man; I'll have no problems there."

Varoi rose to his feet, hoisting Horace into his arms and draping his drowsy head across his shoulders. "I'll leave you to it," he said, even as Borit's employer appeared in the doorway. "You don't need me to complicate matters. I'll see you later, Borit." With a nod of his head he ducked through the entry of the smithy and into the street beyond. Varoi had a shrewd idea how the rescue might be accomplished, provided things went according to plan and Borit could indeed persuade his employer to agree.

It was just past noon and the harbour was bustling. The two ships he had noticed earlier had now finished unloading and were taking on water and stores, while their holds were being filled with grain for transporting downriver. Varoi wondered what possibilities resided there.

He sought out the harbour master first and, with the minimum degree of fuss, confided his needs, confident the man would come up with answers. If nothing else, he must know where Horace's boat had been moored.

The harbour master, Janus Vanlow, was a square man, short of stature and broad of beam. His close cropped, silvery hair and neatly trimmed spade beard merely served to enhance the overall impression. He was definitely square.

Varoi approached him with all the due deference, while leaving Janus in no doubt whatever about what was required. Janus responded in typical fashion, by drawing himself up to full height and trying in vain to stare down his nose at the tall Shakar warrior who had the temerity to assume that what transpired in this harbour was any business of his.

Varoi waited for the expected explosion. It never came.

"Varoi," murmured a small, sleepy voice. "When are we going to rescue my grandsire?"

Varoi gave no immediate reply. Instead, he raised one dark eyebrow in unspoken query, while fixing the harbour master with a quizzical glance.

Janus Vanlow sagged at the seams, all bluff and bluster promptly dispelled by one small boy's sorry plight.

"I'll see what can be done," was all he said, before striding away.

Chapter 6: Solitude

Varoi shifted the load in his arms, trying to find a more comfortable position. He wanted a hand free to open doors. So far it had not been necessary; someone had always been around to offer assistance. But not now.

He contrived a different arrangement, one less secure. Being precariously balanced, it posed other difficulties. Still, it freed two fingers with which he might manipulate a latch. It would have to suffice.

Solitude, thought Ayesha, as she lay on her hard, narrow cot; the one thing she had earnestly craved, until now. Now she had rather more of it than she could reasonably stand. And where was Varoi?

If he *was* so intent on wooing her, on persuading her to change her mind about tying herself to a life with Schezan, why did he not contrive to contact her more often? Even their connection through *lossa antario* seemed to have been set in abeyance. Or was that just a figment of her imagination? Had it happened at all?

Truth to tell, she was beginning to doubt. And now, just to make matters worse, she was homesick. She was missing her own cosy bedchamber back in the settlement.

A light scratching at her door drew her attention that way. *A mouse? Surely not! Not at this time of day.* Hope rose in her breast. Visitors of any kind would be welcome. Perhaps Toku had become bored with the company of older males.

Scrubbing the heel of one hand across her face in a hasty attempt to banish those tears that had managed to creep past her guard, she swung her legs over the side of the bed and stood. Thanks to her fidgeting, the carefully-made bedding was now reduced to a mess of wrinkles, her room hardly fit to entertain guests.

"Come," she called, keeping her tone light as she turned her attention to removing tell-tale folds.

Varoi applied two fingers to the latch, then stepped inside, surprised to find how small the chamber actually was. His attention was held by Ayesha's lithe form as she bent over the narrow bed, busily straightening crinkled bedding.

Ayesha's eyes remained on the task in hand, not yet ready to face her visitor, whoever he might be. Certainly it was neither one of her two brothers. This male was too tall, besides which, his lower half was clad in warrior's garb, which left his knees bare. "Yes. What is it?" she asked thankful her voice remained calm.

"I have brought a few things I thought you might find useful, Princess."

A formal enough response, yet she felt sure the voice belonged to Varoi. She had no wish for *him* to see her looking like this. "There is a table over against the wall. If you put them down there, I can attend to them later. I am somewhat busy right now."

Such unfortunate timing he had, for a potential mate. She'd looked forward to seeing Varoi again, certain the encounter would lift her flagging spirits; just not when she had dishevelled clothing and tear-stained cheeks.

Behind her she heard the door shut with a decisive click and was dismayed to discover that he was still there. Ayesha scrubbed angrily at her face, anxious to erase all evidence of recent distress. Straightening, she turned to confront him, rewarding his continued presence with an angry glare. *How dare he invade her privacy at such an inopportune time?* The fact that, only moments ago, she had bemoaned his lack of appearance was forgotten now that he was actually here.

Varoi, who had been busy admiring Ayesha's trim waist and well-rounded hips, abruptly finding himself confronted by a furious female with red-rimmed eyes and flushed cheeks, had the courtesy and good sense to keep his counsel regarding her distraught appearance.

"Sorry to disturb you, Princess," Varoi began. "If you'll take a look at what I've managed to obtain you can decide for yourself which items might be of some use."

Ayesha's fraught glance strayed to the bundle Varoi held in his arms, then back to his face. If her present demeanour betrayed evidence of earlier distress, he gave no sign. Softening her tone and allowing herself to relax Ayesha stepped forward to see what it was he had brought.

"You found these, where?" she ventured to enquire, as with careful hands she lifted the first small packet from atop the pile. Ayesha noted with some surprise that it had been lovingly wrapped in tissue and tied with a satin bow.

Varoi gave a flippant wave of one hand, as though dismissing his efforts as trivial. "Oh, they were just lying about and nobody had laid claim to them at all."

A likely story! thought Ayesha, as she placed the first item on her bed and went back to the pile. Things discarded seldom came wrapped in tissue and tied with a green satin bow. Still, she would permit Varoi his small deception, for now; or until such time as he gave her cause to query his good intentions. The next few items did not come wrapped. There were bars of soap and beeswax candles, variously scented: one each of violet, honeysuckle and rose; none of which had been previously used. There was also a small crystal vase, minus water, which held wild roses and a few sprigs of lavender. None of these were come by through chance, although it was possible the two brass candleholders next revealed might, perhaps, have been left lying around unclaimed. She set these last aside on the table, having enjoyed a long inhalation of the soap's distinctive and heady aroma.

She hadn't anticipated such thoughtful behaviour from a potential mate. Varoi was proving to be a constant surprise. She studied him now from beneath a thick fan of lashes and found his expression to be intense.

Curiosity drew her back to the bed and the tissue wrapped packet, which was flat, oblong and curiously shaped, suggesting a selection of interesting possibilities. Childlike, she held it up to her ear and gave it a shake, although what she expected to hear was difficult to tell. No muted rattle greeted her burgeoning curiosity.

The next minute she was ripping into the wrapping paper with feverish haste, anxious to have the puzzle solved. The object revealed was a silver-backed mirror, ornately embellished and set with sparkling diamante, few of which were thought to exist outside the Shakar capital of Nai Hai du Veral. Certainly, this was the first Ayesha had ever laid hands on.

She stared at it for a long thoughtful moment, viewing her reflection for the first time that day. She was definitely not looking her best. Her long tawny hair was a riotous nest of tangles, her cheeks were pale and her pert nose was decidedly pink. Anger warred with rising chagrin. He could have warned her. Could have given some indication of how unkempt she actually appeared. Instead …

Varoi wasn't sure, even now, whether or not this had been such a good idea. He was beginning to wonder what it might take to please Ayesha. Females were such contrary creatures in his experience: buy them something pretty and they were liable to burst into tears; whereas something practical in nature provoked the reverse effect; pretty and practical, such as these items he had taken pains to provide, could result in a totally confusing response. They might even prove tantamount to ruining his chance with Ayesha once and for all.

"Varoi." Ayesha's voice was ominously quiet as she stood clasping the mirror close to her breast. "I don't believe you found *this* just lying around," she challenged.

136

Varoi opened his mouth to respond but she forestalled him, wagging an admonishing finger in front of his face. "And another thing, while I'm about it. You could have told me I look an absolute mess. It would have been courteous, to say the least."

How could he explain that he found her most appealing in her present guise? Exactly how he hoped she might look after a long night of hot, steamy love-making.

"Ayesha," he spoke her name softly as though it were a caress. "To me you could not appear lovelier. And now you have the means of knowing what others see."

"Liar! Cheat! You deceived me, let me believe I looked presentable."

"You do," Varoi's mien was one of frank admiration, which was hard to resist.

"Do not! And there is no further point in continuing the subterfuge."

Varoi chose to disagree. "You will always attract me in any guise. Whether you were eight months gone with child and waddling like a duck or bedraggled as a hen caught out in a thunderstorm; you could never be anything less to me. As your mate, I see what lies beneath the surface, what others fail to appreciate."

"You paint a most unflattering picture," she stifled a laugh, trying but failing to be angry with him.

"Don't argue, Ayesha. Just accept. This is how things are meant to be."

As fresh tears prickled the backs of her eyes, she glanced aside, determined to hide the effect he had on her carefully-maintained poise

"Well. I have nowhere suitable to keep it here, save on this table. And tis such an expensive item, I should hate for it to get damaged in any way."

"Then place it on the table for now, until somewhere safer can be found."

She did as Varoi suggested. One more item remained clasped in his arms. He held it out to her as she turned.

"There is still this."

Ayesha gazed at the plump bundle, wondering. "Hold it up that I may see."

Varoi did as she asked, wearing an optimistic smile. "I hope you like it. I recall your saying how much you missed your own room and bed and, though this is but poor consolation, I hoped it would cheer you even so."

Ayesha stared in confusion at the quilted comforter Varoi held, which was woven in her favourite colours of apricot and leaf green and richly embroidered with cloth-of-gold thread.

"It's lovely," she breathed, fighting back tears as she smoothed the soft, velvety folds. How could she have thought him uncaring? Impulsively she twitched aside the coarse, woven blanket with which she had been supplied. "I cannot thank you enough." In truth, words did not suffice.

"There is no need." Varoi stood above her gazing down. An engaging smile tugged the corners of his mouth as he recalled what he had come here hoping to do. He longed to draw Ayesha close: to run sensitive fingers across honey-gold skin in a lingering caress. To explore: to follow every line and curve of her luscious body until he knew it intimately, to discover those secret places, those hidden treasures reserved for him alone, to kiss every inch of satin-soft skin, starting with her delectable mouth. To awaken her most passionate response and then …

"Varoi, why are you looking at me that way?"

The fool male had a lopsided grin plastered across his face. Ayesha wasn't sure she wanted to know what thoughts held sway behind that absurd mask but felt obliged to enquire.

138

Varoi, startled at her words, had been unaware how foolish his expression was until she spoke. Quickly he removed the inane grin, assuming, instead, a benign innocence.

Looking her straight in the eye, he said, "I don't know what you mean?" For good measure he lifted one brow in a demonstration of mild surprise.

What could she say? Almost, she wanted to laugh. Almost. In any case he had cheered her up no end.

"Thank you for the gifts, Varoi. They were most thoughtful," she smiled up at him, half hoping, half expecting a token kiss.

Varoi raised a hand to her face, gentle fingers cupping her chin as he rubbed the firm pad of his thumb along the lush curve of her lower lip. Merci's breath, he wished he had more time. Wished he were not due back on duty. There was never enough time for what he wanted to do. What little he had spare was already spent.

It had taken an age locating the appropriate shops, with the precise choice of merchandise required in order to please Ayesha's every need. She would never learn how long it had taken to find and acquire a quilt in those particular colours and in fine enough material to suit her exacting needs. That it had been worth it in the end he had no doubt. Her evident delight at what he had brought her was reward enough. He lowered his mouth to hers for the briefest kiss. It was tantalising being this close.

After a moment he raised his head. "I must be going. I have duties to attend to."

She stepped back, disappointed by his decision to depart while refusing to acknowledge that fact.

"Then, please, don't let me keep you. And thank you for all you've done. This room looks so much brighter than before."

139

Ayesha took another step back … and realised that somehow their positions had been reversed. She was now much closer to the door.

"Princess?" Glancing up, she was suddenly struck by the warmth in his golden gaze. He filled the entire room with his presence. He was so tall, so virile and so unmistakably male. Yet, there was nothing menacing about him. She was surrounded, wrapped in an aura of warmth and gentleness.

She reached back, one hand groping for the latch. "Best I don't keep you."

With two swift strides he reached her. Ayesha was taken by surprise as he set his palms against the wall, one on either side of her head. Then, lowering his mouth to hers, took total possession.

There was something exciting about being this close but barely touching, sharing their body heat while only their mouths made contact, something exquisitely erotic. Varoi fought to stifle the inevitable moan that threatened to escape.

Ayesha leant close, seeking to become a part of him. She wanted him in ways she had never dreamt possible: moth attracted to candle flame. It had been apparent after only a short time that if she were the flame then he was the moth, unable to resist, constant. At least, that was how the attraction had first seemed. Now she was no longer sure which role was hers. And did it matter?

When, at last, Varoi drew back, he did not, at once, release her. Instead, he stood a moment gazing down, amber eyes intense. She realised she was breathing hard, and yet was hardly out of breath, Hot blood was singing in her veins. Was this what was meant by physical attraction? Slowly, Varoi lowered his hands.

"I should go."

"Aya."

Still neither one of them moved. Candle and flame: a constant, yet potentially fatal attraction.

Ayesha didn't know how she came to be on the battlements but she was there now, gazing out across the surrounding land. The sun shone bright overhead but a chill wind swept the parapet making her shiver. She wished she had worn a cloak, one of the soft, woollen ones she had brought from the settlement. But she had not; too late now to regret the lack.

She had time on her hands, too much time in which to think. Her thoughts were not always conducive to a serene frame of mind. Varoi entangled her thoughts too frequently of late. Not intentionally, she was certain of that. But his mere presence in her immediate vicinity had a disruptive effect. He persisted in proclaiming her to be his soulmate. That claim alone had her thoughts in turmoil. Just today he had said something to that effect. *'Eight months gone with child or looking like a drowned hen, you would still look lovely to me.'*

With child! Parenthood was one thing she could never associate with Schezan com 'Varicci, no matter how hard she tried. But Varoi was an altogether different prospect. With him? Yes, with him! And that discovery alone sufficed to fluster her, to upset any well-nurtured vestige of calm rationality, to set flame within.

In truth, he disturbed her: with his gentle persistence and his thoughtful manner. He was quite different from what she had first supposed, in ways she would not have dreamt possible. And there was something else, something more disturbing: an underlying current of tension she longed to unearth. She wanted to know what it might take to unleash the passion that lurked beneath the surface of him?

Ayesha leant forward, pressing her body against one of the merlons, raising both hands to her cheeks, certain

141

they must be every bit as red and heated as they felt. How could she be so on fire with desire for a male she barely knew, yet not reveal evidence of her salacious thoughts? Softly she moaned the litany with which she was becoming increasingly familiar: *Varoi, how could you* do *this to me?* Thank the goddess Merci none was close enough to hear.

She was a pool of molten honey inside. Only the cold stone of the parapet kept her from falling to her knees. Lowering both hands she placed them atop the merlon, feeling the reality of rough stone beneath her palms and using the distraction as a means to control her innermost yearning. *Concentrate. Think other thoughts.*

Sometimes it worked; but not today. Today Varoi was ever present: a tangible thread of awareness that bound her tight, as though, even now, she was trapped within the close confines of his embrace. He haunted her dreams without let; now he had taken to haunting her waking moments as well, a poignant, sweetly provocative spectre who was fast becoming an integral part of her. Would she ever break free of his influence? In truth, did she actually crave such release?

"Have a care, Princess. Tis a long way down." Startled, Ayesha half turned and recognised the male as one of Tenbay's garrison.

"I was just looking."

"There's no need to explain, Princess. I just thought it prudent to warn you, that's all. You seemed a mite distracted, if you don't mind my saying."

She managed a reassuring smile.

"I was, just a little, I fear. Bigli? It is Bigli, isn't it?" Sometimes she remembered their names wrong. There were over five hundred Shakar warriors permanently attached to the garrison, plus those of the cohort who'd recently arrived. She wondered whether this would be enough should the Pulan appear in force.

"Yes, Princess." He seemed pleased she recalled his name.

Ayesha smiled. "I think I had best leave the battlements to those who belong here. These are troubling times for a visit but I wanted to see."

She pushed herself back from the merlon, without another word passing between them, and walked away. Bigli offered a respectful nod, then returned to patrolling the heights.

What to do next? Ayesha required some form of useful distraction. It was hard being at a loose end. Always, in the settlement there were tasks to attend. Perhaps the healer would welcome assistance. Mayhap the infirmary was a good place to start.

Shoes scraped against worn stone as she wound her way down the barbican stairs. Outside, in the bailey, the brisk wind that beset the parapet was a less intrusive force. Ayesha assumed a purposeful air. A brief visit with Demoiselle seemed in order. Some chocola would cheer her no end. First she would present herself to the Shakar healer, Soleil. Let Varoi com 'Domicci and his haunting presence go hang!

Hours passed before Varoi returned to report. When he did there was a slight hesitation in him as he approached the door leading to the office. Despite ensuring that no spells of coverture were in place, he felt a twinge of trepidation as he raised one fist to give a single sharp rap.

The door flew wide with unexpected alacrity, as though the person within awaited him with growing impatience. Varoi was relieved to find his commander alone. If punishment were about to be dealt he would as soon receive it without benefit of an interested witness.

As he stepped past the threshold the door closed behind him with an audible click. He felt a brief prickle of Power as spells of coverture were woven in place.

"Commander?" he ventured, unsure what form of welcome he might expect.

"Sit down, Lieutenant. There is something important I wish to say."

Varoi did so and then waited for his commander to do likewise; but instead his officer chose to hover a pace to his rear. Varoi tried to appear unperturbed.

"Earlier, when you so rudely interrupted the meeting I'd arranged, I was most annoyed. Since then I have given deliberate consideration to the various means by which I might teach you better manners ..."

"Commander, I sincerely regret ..."

"There you go again!" Commander com 'Dolino huffed, "always interrupting. A far from satisfactory state of affairs. Yet I find, however regrettable your attitude appears, that you seldom interrupt without good cause."

Varoi swivelled in his seat.

"Face front!"

This reprimand had the desired effect. If punishment were about to be served, it would doubtless come in an unexpected form, which proved no reassurance.

"This time, Lieutenant, I find it necessary to commend your diligence in pursuing the truth. Your abrupt entrance may have been annoying but the information thus gained has the undoubted potential to save lives. This fact alone forces me to be lenient."

Varoi itched to confront his commander face on. He settled, instead, for turning sideways in his seat, determined to remain silent, if only to prove he could.

"Commander com 'Tovari and I were in the process of planning a punitive strike against the gathering Pulan force, with the express purpose of reducing their numbers and, hopefully, sending them running for home. Instead, we risked losing what minor advantage we had. Horace has unwittingly supplied information that allows us to act more prudently. Not that I knew this. Not till you succeeded in extracting that same pertinent information and adding it to what you'd previously unearthed, drawing an accurate conclusion in the process. I should, by rights, issue a reprimand for your precipitate behaviour. And would, were I not indebted to your inborn acuity.

"I should like to commend you for your promptness. At the same time I have no other choice than to place you under severe reprimand. You *must* learn to exercise better control, Lieutenant. If not, your impulsive behaviour will land you in trouble ere long. Now, I've no wish to impede the rescue, so tell me. What are your plans?"

Varoi explained as briefly as he could. Once he was done, and the commander had offered his final approval, Varoi felt compelled to enquire, "You didn't say what form my punishment would take."

"Did I not? How very remiss of me. It must have slipped my mind. Well, there's no time to discuss it now. If I'm not mistaken you have little enough time in which to catch the late tide. Be off with you, Lieutenant, before I change my mind."

Varoi rose and, turning smartly about, gave his officer a snappy salute and left.

Outside he stood in confusion, unsure how things now stood between himself and Commander com 'Dolino. He vowed to keep his own counsel and reduce interruptions to a minimum from then on. Perhaps, in hindsight, that had been the commander's intention all along.

The sun was barely skimming the far horizon as Varoi and his charge made their way up the narrow gangplank, which connected ship to shore. Borit was already aboard. *The Gull*'s crew were ready to cast off and a line to starboard was securely attached to the dinghy Horace had brought upstream.

The harbour master had done as requested in smoothing the way for Varoi's rescue mission to succeed.

"Tis woeful tidings from what I hear," the ship's master declared. "Never have I heard the like regarding Pulan treatment of farmers before."

"Captain com 'Binaro," Varoi said. "I regret it seems all too true."

"A new pattern in Pulan hostility, do you suppose?"

Varoi nodded. "Let's just pray that it proves to be short-lived."

"Indeed so. If you'll excuse me I have matters to attend to."

Varoi dipped his head in a show of respect then strode aft to where Borit and the boy leant against the ship's rail.

"The ship will soon be getting under way. Best we keep out from underfoot," Varoi said, promptly suiting action to words by seating himself atop a closed hatch cover, indicating that his companions should join him there.

Above their heads loosed sails slapped lazily in an offshore breeze as *The Gull* eased its way out of the harbour, past smaller boats that bobbed restlessly in her wake. Long sweeps drove her forward as she was deftly manoeuvred clear of the docks and out into the steady flow of midstream. The creak of the ship's main boom as it pressed against taut rigging and the occasional slap of sails overhead formed a soothing background to the sailors' shouts and the pound of a drum beating out a steady rhythm for those plying the oars.

Varoi lay back, allowing himself to be lulled by the ship's motion. It would be time soon enough for him and Borit to go into action. For now he resolved to grab a few hours' welcome sleep. Beside him Horace stared aloft, watching the billowing sails. The ship had been brought into midstream, its oars had been shipped and the sails had been set; by the time a sailor arrived to check on the passengers, he found Varoi fast asleep.

146

Lossa antario, Varoi reflected, could be considered both blessing and curse. It was at once a gift of the gods and an eternal torment; a glimpse of a future as yet denied. Nor could he explore its unique possibilities to their fullest extent. Since Ayesha was already pledged to Schezan and no joining between them could yet take place, he must refuse the temptation on offer.

Oh but then, if he might not plunge into the depths, still he might dabble; although, not unless he could do so in the flesh. And, for that he required Ayesha's willing consent.

He yearned: to touch; to taste; to fully explore. Most of all, he wanted her under him. That prospect alone caused his body to stir, so much so that Varoi groaned. Turning, he found himself not on his pallet as he supposed but on a moving deck. The sharp rap of approaching boot-heels caused him to struggle erect.

"Borit?"

"The same."

The sound of sails slapping idly in the offshore breeze turned Varoi's attention aloft, where smothering darkness hid all save the faintest glimmer of light. If the sails were backing and the ship seemed to be losing way that could only mean one thing.   "Are we there?"

"So the boy, Horace, would have us believe."

"Then we'd best get to our stations right away. The ship's master won't want to hang about here for long."

Borit turned without another word, leading the way to where a thick length of rope dangled over the side. Horace, it seemed, was already aboard his little craft, which could just be seen dancing merrily on the ship's wake. A shudder of ship's timbers underfoot informed Varoi that the stern anchor had caught.

With a quick word of thanks to the ship's master, Varoi swung himself over the rail. Soon after, his boots touched down on the transom of Horace's dinghy. Finding his balance Varoi moved forward to take up position on the forward thwart, then took up an oar in preparation for Borit coming aboard. Seconds later they were rowing away from the ship's side.

Horace directed their passage, aiming the boat unerringly toward that section of the near bank where a dyke fed tributary drained into the river. Soon they were obliged to ship oars as the boat proceeded to nose its way along a weedy stretch of the dyke, which fed the nearby River Bure with water drained from Greenbeg Fen.

Varoi set one oar abaft the stern then began to scull. They were hemmed in by rustling reeds and tall rushes. Water glistened like a black oily slick in their wake, ripples fanning out to lap the bank and water slapping gently against the hull to provide a constant accompaniment to their progress. It occurred to Varoi how trying a task this journey must be for Horace, returning to a place he knew as home, a place that should represent safety, a place where his family had been recently slaughtered. How must it feel knowing there was nothing that could be done to put matters right?

From time to time Varoi ceased rowing, allowing the boat to drift, *ananaha* senses highly attuned to their surroundings. All he heard, all any of them heard, was the lapping of water against wooden hull and sundry other sounds common to night in the fens. There was no danger they needed fear, other than men; and the Pulan, it appeared, were no longer in the vicinity. Still it paid to remain wary, it being less than a day since Horace had last been here. If any Pulan yet remained, their lives would almost certainly be forfeit if caught.

Easing his oar back into the water Varoi resumed sculling upstream. Not a word had passed between them since entering the dyke. Silence and darkness were their best allies on this trip.

They took a while in finding a place where the dinghy could be tied to a solitary post hidden deep in a stand of reeds. Varoi insisted on being first ashore. Crawling to top of a steep embankment, he lay full length on the ground, searching for any evidence of Pulan forces. Finding none he beckoned his companions ashore.

"Horace," he whispered. "When you're ready, lead the way; you alone know which direction to take."

Horace turned, dark eyes glinting. "The farm is not far. My family are there. All now dead, save for my grandsire, should he still survive."

Rising swiftly to his feet Horace led them along a track that took them deeper into Greenbeg Fen. Before long they sighted the outline of a barn. Approaching its main doors they crept cautiously inside. The reek of stale urine and the sweet scent of hay was redolent of livestock; a smell now overlaid by the rank stench of death.

"They slaughtered all our herd," Horace sadly explained, before proceeding towards a vacant stall where he hauled aside a large bale of straw, revealing the vague outline of a hatch.

"Here. Wait here," he advised. "I'll bring my grandsire out."

Horace stepped forward, disappearing into the hole. Minutes later he reappeared.

"I can't wake him." There was a shrill hint of panic evident in the small boy's tone as he spoke.

"Shush," Varoi warned. "Not so loud; we may be overheard."

Turning to Borit he said. "Will you see what can be done? I want to check the buildings, just to make sure we *are* alone. There may still be Pulan present in this vicinity." He left unsaid the problems such an eventuality might pose.

Horace crawled out of his hiding place.

"It's all my fault," he whined. "I should never have left him, save that he insisted I go."

Borit sent a meaningful glance in Varoi's direction.

"Do what you must," he said. Then, as Varoi moved away, Borit turned his attention back to Horace.

"Show me," he said. With those few words he followed Horace into the dark and dingy cellar.

Varoi was on his way back from the house, having found no evidence of Pulan, when he stumbled upon the bodies. Death was an inevitable part of life, all warriors learnt to accept that. But cold-blooded killing, such as this, was something Varoi would never get used to. Nor did he wish to try.

In his case, at least, he'd been in a position to tackle the person he held responsible for Bayritz's death. Not that his efforts had done much good. That villain still walked the earth.

Seeing Horace's family trapped in the rigours of death made it somehow more real and brought home to Varoi the enormity of this brutal act. Someone had closed their lids: Horace or his grandsire? Varoi pictured a dying man somehow contriving to crawl the distance in order to perform that rite, and felt his heart cramp in his chest. The growl that escaped his lips was menacing in the extreme.

On closer inspection, Varoi was surprised to find that a knife had been used to slit mother and small daughter's throat, which meant this was a close quarters killing, a more personal act than most. These people had looked into the eyes of their executioner knowing they were helpless. How cruel was that?

The father lay a short distance apart, the blade there having pierced his heart. Had he lived long enough to see what was done to his wife and child? How come the old man had survived such efficient butchery?

Varoi straightened from his ghoulish discovery. There was nothing to be done for these people now, save find them a suitable place to rest until a burial could be arranged. The small stone building he'd found in back of the barn could be used for that.

He wondered then. *Had Horace heard their pleas, their screams, their last cries for mercy?* It beggared belief that he'd had sense enough to stay hidden throughout that … or perhaps he was just frozen with fear. No shame in that, if so. He'd been surrounded and grossly outnumbered by hostile Pulan. What good would it have done the boy then if he'd shown his face?

By the time he returned to the barn and slipped inside Borit had already emerged with the body of an older man draped across one broad shoulder.

"He isn't dead yet but his pulse is weak," he informed Varoi. "He's lost too much blood. Do you know anything about healing? I'm not sure if he'll survive without help."

Varoi edged closer and bent to examine the body, which was ice cold.

"He's in shock. If I'm going to do anything here, I need light by which to see." No sooner had he spoken the words than Horace arrived with a lantern. Once it was lit Horace did his best to hold it steady, despite the shock of seeing his grandsire lying so still, his pallid flesh almost transparent.

Borit leant close to whisper, "He's quite a mess." Then he reached to rip open the blood-drenched tunic, so that Varoi might know with what he must deal. Varoi sucked in his breath, stunned to see how bad the situation was. Judging by the number of deep cuts and lacerations to both hands and arms, this man had fought. The evidence was plain. Varoi wondered, *Could that be why he still survived? If his efforts had caused the fatal blow to pass wide of the mark, might it not have provided him with a fighting chance?*

Producing a small leather pouch from the belt at his waist, Varoi set to work. Field dressings were something all warriors habitually carried. Having packed and strapped the worst of the old man's wounds, he left Borit to finish dressing the others while he went outside to move the bodies.   Aware that Horace had followed Varoi explained, "I know you would wish for better. But we must get your grandsire proper aid if he's to have any chance of survival."

On their return to the barn they found the farmer wrapped in a blanket to keep out the cold. Varoi lifted the farmer's limp form, finding that, while Horace's grandsire might be lean and scrawny, in his present state he was almost a deadweight.

Bleached grasses brushed against them in passing and a solitary owl ghosted low overhead as they made their way back to where the boat was moored. A fulgent moon rode low overhead and a chill breeze ruffled the waters of the bay, turning its surface to frilly wavelets as they nosed the dinghy past the floating hulks that ringed the harbour's outermost perimeter. All seemed peaceful enough, until Horace leapt ashore and began tying up the boat.

Two men suddenly loomed out of the darkness, each with a cudgel in hand. Varoi stood up in the boat's stern, making his presence obvious. His leather armour creaked ominously as he moved. The sight of his sword hilt protruding above his left shoulder seemed sufficient to convince those on guard that he was Shakar and a member of the town's garrison. Even so, wisely, they challenged him. Varoi commended their vigilance and stated his business, after which each tugged at his forelock in a show of respect, dipping his head before melting back into the shadows.

"They could have offered to help," Horace grumbled.

"That is not their job," Varoi explained, ruffling the boy's hair affectionately. "They need no distraction from those duties to which they must attend. Be grateful they remain alert. Hold the boat steady, Borit, while I check on the farmer."

After a moment Varoi stood erect. Hefting the lax form across one broad shoulder, he stepped ashore.

"Is he alive?"

Varoi, recognising the plaintive note, responded accordingly. "Yes, Horace, he lives. We must make haste and find a healer, even so."

Varoi listened attentively as the healer explained those problems attendant on the old man's condition. Some hours had passed since they had brought him ashore and not only was he responding well to treatment but he was also in and out of wakefulness. Today, it seemed, he was more lucid than had been expected.

Horace's grandsire had the pale translucent look of an alabaster statue, an image that was rather spoilt by both hands and arms being swathed in dressings. His grizzled hair stood at shocked attention and he sported several days' growth of beard. Apart from that he was remarkably feisty for such a seriously injured old man.

"You helped my lad when he needed someone to listen and I thank you for that," he began.

Varoi inclined his head in a polite show of respect. "It was no hardship."

"Just don't expect me to feel grateful for everything you've done."

Thinking that he understood, Varoi said, "I am sorry for your loss, old man."

"And why should *you* be sorry? What inconvenience is it to you *Shakar*?"

"I ..."

"Your people are safely tucked up inside this fortress. They do not risk their livelihood as do we of the fens. You protect those living in town and village but give no thought to how we farmers fare. Now my family has perished, what shall I do? Do you even care? I think you do not."

"Not true. We do what we can to offer assistance where it is most required. But the farms are widely scattered, the distance between them too far. We replace stolen grain and livestock whenever we can once the danger is past."

The old man gave his head a scornful toss. "Too little too late and never like for like is not good enough," the old man complained. "You cannot replace what it has taken generations of hard work and selective breeding to acquire. To *you* a cow is just another beast. A snap of your fingers and it can be replaced. *You* do not have to stand aside and watch the livestock you've raised butchered to fill the enemies' belly. *Your* pride is not so sorely abused. The Pulan have slaughtered an entire generation of my family. How shall you replace *them*? What will you do when there are no farmers left alive to work the land? Will you then train slaves to perform that role?"

Varoi could only stare in blank amazement. "That would not happen."

"But you'll do nothing about the Pulan until it's too late. You accept our fealty in return for aid. We deserve better protection, do we not?"

"What would you suggest?"

The old man shook his head. "I'm a farmer, not a politician. But something must be done. You have a voice. Why not speak up, use it in our behalf?"

"If only it were that simple."

"You are one of many; I am one of few. Yet if you, as one of the many, speak up in our defence, perhaps those who matter will pay close heed."

Varoi found the idea thought-provoking. In the meantime, he simply said, "You *shall* return to your farm. The Pulan *will* be driven away. As for the rest ..." Varoi gave an expressive shrug. "I know of nothing I can say or do that will change things now. If the goddess is kind I may find a way."

Varoi lowered his hands and took a swift step back. He had hoped for a meaningful conversation with Ayesha, alone. Yet within seconds of entering her tiny chamber he was reduced to monosyllabic statements. He should have known better, should have guessed that without others in attendance his passion would interfere.

So, why had he come? The answer was plain, even to a love-struck fool. He could not stay away. Restraint was a condition Varoi found well-nigh impossible to maintain in this situation, though he did his best. The urge to touch, to taste, was a living entity that threatened what small control he had. He stretched forth a hand to run strong fingers down a fall of silken hair. Pale viridian eyes glinted back. He fancied he caught a faint glimmer of consent within their luminous depths. Sometimes Ayesha seemed distant, self-contained. He longed to rip off her clothing, casting aside all constraint; to clasp her tight against him, flesh to flesh.

His hand slipped lower, cupping her chin. He *could* wait, let her come to him. But sometimes waiting was as hard as going without. In any case, he was well past waiting. Their first kiss had set spark to the fire within. Banked embers required scant encouragement to ignite into roaring conflagration.

Ayesha tilted her head up, lips parted, permitting a brief glimpse of white teeth. Like him, she possessed prominent canines, though not as large, more in keeping with female grace. That brief glimpse sufficed to put fire in his loins. Varoi forgot all his good intentions, drawing her close, moulding her body against his. His mouth was on hers, hot and demanding. When would she accept the truth?

A bell tolling the quarter hour brought Varoi back to his senses. He had just time enough to make his way to the watchtower where he was due on guard. Reluctantly he raised his head.

"Ayesha." His voice sounded harsh to his ears. She was a temptress and he, given the chance, would be her willing slave. But how was he to make her recognise that fact? He tried again.

"Ayesha. You *are* my Chosen. No matter how you seek to reject that truth there is an attraction between us that cannot be denied. I will not force you. I ask only that you give me leave to prove myself worthy of your regard."

Into the following pause, she spoke, "Yes." Her voice was so soft he barely heard.

"You are my soulmate; destiny decrees that we join. Will you at least give me a chance?"

Ayesha tilted her head askance, peering up at him with sly mischief evident in her glance.

"I said *'yes'*. How many times must I repeat myself?"

Varoi stared, confounded and confused, unable to believe her words. Then, a slow smile lit his face. Trapped by that smouldering amber gaze, Ayesha let herself be caught up in his embrace. And when his lips came down upon hers, hard and hungry, she allowed him to feast, until a bell tolling the midnight hour intruded.

"Must dash," Varoi said, his voice husky with barely suppressed emotion. Plonking her unceremoniously down on the bed, he opened the door and slipped away.

Ayesha stared at the door, left half ajar in his haste to depart. *Well, really!* A bemused smile quirked up the corners of her mouth.

Chapter 7: Preparation

Varoi was on his way from the dormatorium to the stairs and the next level down, where the first meal of the day was already being served, when he felt a slight tug at his sleeve. Knowing who must be accosting him, since it was her door he had just passed, he did not react as he might otherwise have done.

"Princess?" he said, as he turned to face her.

"Then it is you, Varoi. I was hoping it might be. Would you consider doing me a favour?"

"That depends on what it is," he answered warily.

"Let's not discuss it now. Come with me and find out what I have in mind." Intrigued, despite his reservations, Varoi consented to her request, following Ayesha a few paces further down the corridor. Ayesha stopped at her parents' door. When permission to enter came, she stepped boldly inside, dragging Varoi with her.

Her parents were still in their night attire. Her mother lay propped against the pillows, while her father was seated on a canvas stool in his nightshirt, paring his fingernails.

"Ayesha," her father began without looking up. "I told you before: I will not countenance such stupidity."

"Papa, this is important."

"You wish to visit your garden, to check that all is well and see how your plants have grown during your absence. In your opinion this may seem important, but not to me."

The Shakar chief finished what he was doing and glanced up. A look of consternation flitted across his face at the sight of Varoi. It soon vanished, to be replaced by one of frustrated chagrin.

"So, you think to enlist an ally in this idiocy. I see. Do not for one moment imagine this changes anything. It does not."

"Papa, please."

"I have told you before …"

"Papa, allow me to explain. You would not listen yesterday. Give me leave to help you understand."

"Very well, but do not be surprised if I still refuse you permission."

"That is your prerogative. Still, I hope to make you see the sense of what I propose. The healer is running out of herbs. Her store is seriously depleted and there is nowhere within the town's confines that she can gather more. Her garden must be visited too. I'm sure you'll agree it is imperative she has sufficient to carry out her role during what lies ahead."

"Then let her go to the market and purchase whatever she needs with the money I have already supplied."

"There is nothing suitable. The herbs she requires must be gathered fresh. During the early part of the day is best, before the harsh rays of the sun cause essential oils to evaporate. If there *is* going to be a battle, and it would seem that there is, an abundant supply of salves and unguents must be available. Essential oils require time to distil. We must be prepared. Please, father, say that I may visit the gardens."

"If the healer needs these things let her go and collect them herself. I will speak to the garrison commander and arrange an escort. There. Does that not seem reasonable to you?"

"Papa, you are not listening. The healer is too busy to go herself. I have volunteered. There is little else I can do. Permit me this, at least."

An irritated growl was her only answer. Then the chief fixed his gaze on Varoi.

"What about you, Lieutenant com 'Domicci? You seem to have been dragged into this argument. What is your opinion? Should I allow Ayesha to go? And, if I do, will you go with her? Will you act as escort and ensure her safety?"

"I knew nothing of Ayesha's plan. She asked a favour without revealing what was involved."

"So, what do you think?"

"I can see why this might be important."

"You think I should agree to her request?"

"I think you should give it serious consideration, yes."

"Faugh!" Ayesha stamped her foot in a fine display of temper, green eyes ablaze. "What a pair of weak-kneed pansies you both are. There is no time left for contemplation. This problem must be dealt with *now*."

"Ayesha, mind your manners."

"This minute, papa. I insist."

"Varoi?" said Chief lo 'Savoi. Varoi was too busy gazing at Ayesha to pay her father any heed. Merci's breath, she was magnificent when roused.

"Varoi!"

"I think, perhaps, on this occasion you would be wise to concede."

"And that is your considered opinion?"

"For what it's worth, yes."

"Very well, if it must be. Will you arrange a suitable escort?"

"No, papa, I shall go alone; although I should be pleased if Varoi were to consider accompanying me."

"It is unsafe."

Ayesha said, "What Varoi suggests would be quicker and more discreet than arranging an entire cohort as escort, which is what you expect."

"Lieutenant, can you make her see sense?"

"To be honest, Chief lo 'Savoi, I can see her point."

"At last!" Ayesha exclaimed.

"Be still, Ayesha, let him finish."

Before Ayesha's father could forbid her from venturing forth alone, Varoi spoke up in her defence.

"Ayesha is right in one respect. A large party as escort would draw attention. I believe it safe enough for now that we keep numbers small. I offer my personal protection, if that will suffice to reach agreement between you." Varoi knew better than most, he had more to lose should Ayesha come to any harm.

He went on, "In tactical terms, let me put it like this. Two people visiting the settlement may pass unobserved, for a short while at least – long enough to achieve what Ayesha has in mind – whereas a troop of warriors is far less likely to escape notice. Some would be killed during the inevitable skirmish that would ensue should the Pulan be close enough to react. If the worst happens and Ayesha and I are slain during this expedition, there would be one less warrior and one less civilian, hardly enough to affect the numbers when it comes to battle. Let us go, Chief. I promise to keep your precious daughter safe."

"And these are your thoughts on the matter, Varoi?"

"They are."

"Then perhaps you know best. But be sure of one thing. Should you return without my daughter by your side your life will be held forfeit."

Varoi bowed his head in tacit agreement. "I would expect nothing less."

"Very well, Ayesha. You have my permission Do not tarry overlong."

"No, papa. Two hours at most is all I shall need, with Varoi's assistance."

"Then let it be done."

It took Varoi rather longer to convince his commanding officer that the sortie was, indeed, essential, but at last he received the permission he required.

The healer's garden was alive with insects when they arrived, most of them sipping at nectar or gathering pollen.

"I shall take only what I deem necessary," Ayesha explained. "It is always wise to leave some for the bees. Will you place the cut herbs in my basket while I move on?"

Varoi did so, savouring the sweet scented blossoms along with the pungent reek of less fragrant herbs. There was comfrey, self-heal and wormwood as well as lavender, rosemary and sage. Some he felt were best added to food but he made no comment regarding her choice of herbs. Ayesha knew best what was required.

Soon enough they moved on to Ayesha's small and secluded garden. Here all was a riot of colour, with plants intermingled and overgrown.

"Varoi, would you mind giving me a hand?"

He was supposed to remain alert and on guard, still he found it hard to refuse. She was delving in a sunlit corner where prickly thickets of rose and lavender bloomed. Her body was bent over as she worked at her task. What was it about the female form viewed from behind that was so alluring, making him sexually aroused? Valiantly, Varoi struggled to ignore the soft growl rising in his throat, the wild surging of blood through his veins. Instead, he reached to hold aside the offending thorny stems.

Released from the prickly predicament into which she had carelessly forced her slender frame, Ayesha backed up and straightened with a sigh, inadvertently brushing her body against Varoi in the process. For once he felt grateful for his customary encasing of heavy leather armour, relieved she would not be aware of his instinctive reaction to her touch.

"I think I shall need rather more in the way of assistance, Varoi."

Turning, she found him blocking her path.

161

"And you cannot possibly do as I require when hampered like this."

So saying she set both hands to the buckles of his armour.

"This has to come off. Don't argue. I insist."

Insist she might but Varoi had other ideas and they in no wise conformed to hers. She wasted no time in suiting words to action. He was already bareheaded, having set his helm aside, but the thought of going unarmed and unarmoured was unthinkable. Still, she divested him of pauldrons and curiass with summary ease. But when she started in upon the buckle of the zone to which his lambrequins were attached, he did raise protest.

"How can I protect you, Ayesha, if you persist?"

It did him no good. Before he could stop her the buckle gave way to her skilled manipulation.

"Oh, I see," was all she said.

Heat rose in his face. He felt it, but could do nothing to hide its effects as a fierce blush swept across his face and neck.

Ayesha then made things worse. Though he would not have thought it possible, still she did. Raising one small hand to his chest, she trailed her fingers downward in a long, languid caress that caused his heart and whole body to leap in immediate response.

Varoi clenched his teeth, certain he would have no wits left and no further will to resist if she did not soon cease her flagrant temptation. Her downward journey ceased at the hard thrust of his arousal. Varoi closed his eyes. Unable to bear what she might seek to do next, he waited.

Ayesha let fall her hand. "Such a fine looking, upright male should never be ashamed of his body."

His eyes flew open in surprise at this unexpected comment to find her turning away.

"Come, Varoi, we have much still to do."

He let out his breath with a slow, considering sigh. She was full of surprises. He could never hope to comprehend her actions, not when this was how she behaved. Grabbing hold of his armour he drew it back on, fastening it in place, settling baldric and sword across his shoulder. Whatever she said or thought, he had a responsibility to uphold, one he could not fulfil if inadequately garbed.

With the necessary herbs gathered and laid in the basket, then covered with a thin layer of muslin, Varoi thought it time to depart. Ayesha, however, had different ideas, deciding there was time enough for her to visit the bees. Varoi's meaningful glance at the sky could not change that decision once made.

"How long before the enemy arrives do you think?"

Varoi's reply was succinct. "About midday."

"Then we still have time, Varoi, so stop fussing. You wear sword and armour so are well prepared and none could approach without your being aware. Is that not true?"

Reluctantly, he admitted it was. There was, as yet, no sign of the enemy, only the sound of birdsong and the soft soughing of wind through trees. It was autumn and leaves were on the turn, vibrant red and gold intermingling with the green; but it did not mean he should be any less vigilant.

Ayesha kept her visit brief. All seemed well within the hive and with its resident colony. Varoi led the way to the bench where lay his helm. As he reached for it Ayesha set a restraining hand on his arm. He glanced round to find her smiling up at him.

"Before you do that there is something I wish to say and one extra task I wish you to perform."

Varoi tilted his head in silent enquiry and Ayesha went on. "I have thought long and hard about what you have said."

163

She turned aside and, without thought, he followed, on to the close-clipped lawn.

"And?" He wasn't sure to what she referred but could think of only one matter of any real significance to him.

"I have reached a decision of sorts," Ayesha turned, eyes demurely downcast, as thought intent on studying the grass at her feet. No longer spangled with overnight dew it seemed to hold some fascination for her, since she spent several moments contemplating its neatly manicured sward.

Varoi waited. Impatience would serve no useful purpose now.

"I have decided that you and Schezan may vie for my favours. Later, I will choose which one I want. If that is agreeable, then you may kiss me to seal the bargain thus made."

Slowly Ayesha raised her eyes. Varoi hesitated. She offered him a chance previously denied. *What* did *it take to please him?* Then with two swift strides he reached her and swept her up in his arms.   Startled by his action Ayesha cried out in alarm. "Varoi! I did not say you are Chosen, only that you might vie with Schezan."

Laughing he set her back down.   "Forgive me, Princess," he murmured. Then leaning down he claimed his kiss. Her arms entwined about his neck as the kiss deepened. He was overwhelmed by the warmth of her response; thrusting caution aside he sank to the ground, taking her with him. His senses expanded and took in the mingled aroma of lavender and musk rose, contrasted now with the sharp, astringent scent of apples. The lawn on which they lay was chamomile.

Varoi gave his unique talent free rein, his main attention on their immediate surroundings. As expected there was no indication of the Pulan being anywhere near.

Shifting sideways Varoi maintained the kiss, sliding one cautious hand downwards in a slow caress. Soft,

164

supple and infinitely desirable, he felt her moving beneath his weight. Varoi felt his body harden in response.

A rustle behind him was easily dismissed. A thrush seeking worms? Maybe. Nothing more sinister than that.

Instinct said different, though. Instinct made him react. Hissing venomously, he rolled, taking Ayesha with him as he went. He continued to roll until his body, again, lay uppermost.

Swiftly he sprang to his feet, one hand reaching for his sword hilt. He was relieved to have kept weapon and armour strapped to his back. Stepping across Ayesha's prone form, he prepared to confront a deadly foe.

The Pulan grunted with effort, struggling to release the axe buried haft-deep in the lawn, a hair's breadth from where Ayesha's head had recently lain. Varoi paid her no heed as she scrambled safely out of reach. His attention remained riveted. His blade swung down with grievous intent as the Pulan's axe sprang free.

The resounding crash as weapons engaged sent shivers racing along Varoi's arms and echoing chills skating down Ayesha's spine. So close. Disaster had come perilously close.

Varoi was focused as never before. His *ananaha* senses still expanded, he caught every expression on the Ice Warrior's face, every slight nuance that might betray his enemy's fell intent. Where he had moments ago strained to hold passion in check that same intensity lent vehemence to his mood and untold vigour to his sword arm. Temper converted his handsome face to a grim mask of hatred and rage.

Compelled to observe in amazed trepidation, Ayesha stood her ground. She had watched Varoi at weapons practice but this encounter in no way compared. Now every stroke was potentially fatal; every riposte revealed lethal intent; and the smallest mistake might be his last. And yet, she could not help but admire the speed and agility involved.

Varoi knew at once that his opponent was experienced, by the skill with which he counteracted every assault and the brutal strength behind each blow, not to mention the evil grin and nonchalant manner. It pleased Varoi to discover they were well matched. To joust with an inferior adversary was no challenge at all.

Whirling his weapon round and back he applied skill and ingenuity to the task. A fumbled parry allowed the Pulan to smash through his guard. The axe made short work of boiled leather armour. The Pulan blade laid Varoi's shoulder open to the bone. Varoi growled a frustrated denial, gritting his teeth against the pain.

Another vigorous assault sent Varoi crashing to his knees. He turned this drawback to his advantage as, with a deft flick of his wrist, he diverted the next blow, sending it wide. Turning his sword at an acute angle, he thrust with the blade, feeling it bite. He drove home the point with ruthless tenacity and saw the Ice Warrior sag at his knees.

Downward pressure forced Varoi's fist to the ground. But the Bastard sword was now driven deep. Varoi braced his weapon and applied his considerable strength to defeating the enemy. A bubbling sigh told him victory was imminent, even as the Pulan warrior's axe landed alongside, slicing partway through his vambrace.

Varoi felt no pain, though the blade scored a bloody line through mortal flesh. He knew only a deep sense of relief. He'd succeeded in keeping Ayesha safe.

Varoi twisted his arm sideways, toppling the dying Pulan to the ground. One hand still clutched the battle-axe he had wielded with utmost ferocity. Varoi kicked the offending weapon aside; then stooped to wipe clean his sword on the Pulan's clothes. The man was nigh dead. Using his foot he rolled the Pulan face down. No need yet for Ayesha to confront Death's grim countenance. Varoi spun swiftly about.

Ayesha stood as though transfixed, her honey-coloured skin ashen. Sheathing his sword Varoi strode to her side.

"Ayesha," he murmured but she did not respond. Tilting his head he looked into her face, hoping for some kind of reaction. Her eyes jade were enormous in her pale face.

"Ayesha?" he said again, concerned that she seemed too frozen with shock to pay any heed to her surroundings.

Taking both her hands in his he brought them to the warmth of his mouth, planting a soft kiss in the centre of each palm.

"Ayesha, speak to me, Bayshir. Tell me what's wrong. Were you harmed in any way?"

She shook her head and stifled a rebellious sob. "I thought he would kill you, Varoi. You fought so valiantly. But when his battle-axe smashed through your defence, I felt sure the blow must prove mortal."

So that was it! Relief flooded him; followed by a sense of bitter remorse that she should witness his near defeat and be appalled at the prospect. And yet … at least her reaction showed that she cared, if it affected her thus.

"And you promise me you are unharmed?" he asked.

"I am not injured in any way. But," she glanced up, "the same cannot be said of you. You were wounded in my defence and all I can do is stand and stammer. What kind of healer would I make when confronted by the heat of battle?"

She was unlikely to find herself in such a situation but there was no point in telling her that now. They had to get moving in case this Pulan warrior had not come alone. He was probably an advance scout who had seized the opportunity on offer. None could fault him for that. But where one came, others were bound to follow. If more *were* in the vicinity…

"Ayesha, we should leave here. *Now.*" He put urgency into his tone, hoping it would prompt her into action. To Varoi's considerable relief it worked.

While keeping a firm hold of her arm he ran the fingers of his free hand lightly down the side of her cheek in a gentle caress before letting his hand fall away. Then he stooped to pick up the baskets of herbs, holding them out. Threading them on to her arm he turned aside, drawing his weapon with his free hand, determined he would not be taken unawares a second time.

As he started to move away she looked down at the corpse. A small sound of distress caused him to glance her way.

"Why must they do this, Varoi? What can they hope to gain? This man doubtless has family who will grieve without ever knowing his fate."

Mounting pressure to see Ayesha back inside Tenbay's battlements gave Varoi a keen sense of urgency. Still, he chose to answer her question as dispassionately as he could.

"The Pulan named this the Unclaimed Land with good reason. Before our arrival they came here often with their herds. And while their sojourn was always brief, subject to transitory migration, they nevertheless viewed it as their right. They never stayed; only the Fenlanders put down roots. Our arrival changed all that. The Pulan could not believe any race would wish to adopt the Unclaimed Land as its permanent home. When we came this was hardly the best place for settlement, but by then the Shakar were desperate for a place of their own. We did not want to fight our neighbours for land. That was never our intention. Fenlanders were able to accept us and live in peace. The Pulan were not around at the time and showed no interest when we took up residence. Who knows why they should resent us now? Unless it is because we have succeeded in draining the land and unlocking its potential where they could not even be bothered to try."

Hastening his stride he gave voice to his opinions. He would not look at her directly in case he got lost in her gaze. He would not risk her safety through his inattention again. Instead, he kept glancing about, vigilant and ever alert for trouble.

"And now?" questioned Ayesha. "What has changed now? We have put up with minor incursions in the past but nothing like this. Always their forays were brief and unsettling but that was all. Now small war bands gather together; the clans are uniting as they never have before. To what possible purpose, Varoi?"

"Who knows? They don't want it all, Ayesha, only the best part, the driest and most fertile area of land. The part we think of as home; where our capital, Nai Hai du Veral, is situated. That part where Fenlanders lie thick on the ground. The Fenlanders are harried from pillar to post while we do our best to protect that which is theirs, sometimes to no noticeable effect. One thing I do know for certain. They will not find it easy to drive us out."

Ayesha considered Varoi's statement and found much of it made perfect sense. It certainly would explain the changing situation. His comments also revealed a hitherto unknown facet of his character.

She was having real difficulty reconciling two opposing aspects, having seen him change from a sweet, solicitous lover into a cold and calculating killer in less than a heartbeat. Such an experience was bound to raise interesting questions. What concerned her most was how he compared to Schezan. At first glance the comparisons seemed far from complimentary. Closer analysis brought certain anomalies to mind.

That Ayesha was unharmed gave Varoi no real comfort. As her soulmate it was his responsibility to keep her safe. The desire to ensure her safety was inherent in him, an imperative it was impossible to ignore. Keeping his sword at the ready he hustled her swiftly along the path.

The Shakar settlement consisted of a large cluster of houses, hemmed in by tree-lined streets, with gardens and hedges between. It was the ideal site for an ambush: many places where the enemy might lie in wait.

Varoi allowed his *ananaha* senses to expand, to sift through the details he found. But too many obstacles interfered or interrupted his overall view. It was a nightmare situation. He dare not admit to his growing concern. He kept a tight hold of Ayesha's hand, his long fingers gently entwined with hers, while resisting the urge to place a protective arm about her shoulders and draw her close. He dare not falter in his chosen course of action. There was no time left to waste. A swift return to the fortress was essential if Ayesha's safety were to be ensured.

What had she been thinking? Ayesha wondered. In suggesting Varoi vie with Schezan for her favour, she had bought herself a whole barrel load of trouble. There would be nothing to stop him now. Not that he'd required any encouragement in the first place. In that respect he differed greatly from Schezan.

Perhaps she already knew enough about them both to form a useful opinion.

From the first moment they had met she'd been tossing her skirts at Schezan. Any ruse she could contrive by way of encouragement she had tried. And for why? Because Schezan was undoubtedly the handsomest full-blooded male she had encountered so far. That was why.

Reflecting on her first meeting with Schezan, she tried to recall what it was about him that impressed her most. He was tall and muscular, with attractive features, broad shoulders and a proud carriage. In fact, he displayed an exceedingly healthy dose of male arrogance. And who could fault him for that? He was Konicci. More than that.

He had passed that qualification at the highest degree, meaning he was not only entitled to wear the close-fitting black armour of a Konicci trained warrior but also the red plumes of the elite.

She slid a sideways glance at Varoi and noted that he too held himself with a prideful air. But whereas Schezan's armour was black and immaculately maintained Varoi's was an oft-mended brown that had been heavily scuffed by hard usage even before his recent skirmish with the Pulan.

There was something distinctly dangerous about Varoi's demeanour now. The way he held himself, the way he moved, like a hungry panther stalking its prey. His lethal air was manifestly feline: a dappled Saarcat, stealthy denizen of the Molukai Range; or a Shadow Panther, if such did still exist. Varoi's relaxed, rangy stride and rippling muscles hinted at something similar to that ilk. She for one would not wish to cross him, though there was scant chance he would ever seek to harm her.

So, little distinction between them there. But they did differ in some ways.

She knew Schezan's arrogance invariably took the form of cruel indifference; she had often endured personal experience of that. She noticed no such characteristic in Varoi. Furthermore, she had seen at first hand the way Schezan behaved towards those he considered "inferior". These last included Toku and Demoiselle. She was acutely aware that not all Shakar felt kindly disposed towards Fenlanders. Many considered them an inferior breed, but Schezan in particular had proved unpleasant in his dealings with them. Sometimes his behaviour made her cringe. Toku was another case entirely. Toku possessed an irrepressible good humour it was nigh impossible to quash. Yet, somehow, Schezan had managed the impossible. Few ever found cause to berate Toku for his lively loquaciousness. But there again Schezan had succeeded in

171

quelling the spate. What was it about fledglings that aggravated Schezan? She had no idea. Varoi's easy acceptance of her relationship with Demoiselle and equally friendly attitude to Toku had restored her belief that not all male Shakar behaved thus.

There *was* a significant difference between them after all. She risked another furtive glance at Varoi. He might not be as tall or as handsome as Schezan, but there was an aura of confidence about him that made him every bit as imposing. How could she have cozened herself into believing Schezan the soulmate of her dreams? He was naught but a pale imitation of what every true soulmate should be.

Varoi stole a sideways glance at Ayesha, hoping she understood his sense of urgency. Hoping she realised that in their present situation speed was paramount. He was determined to reach the fortress as fast as her legs would allow. He would carry her if necessary in order to ensure they were safe inside its walls before any more Pulan warriors appeared.

By the time they arrived at the edge of the moat Ayesha had calmed. She no longer trembled beneath the steadying hand he laid on her shoulder and her footsteps had grown increasingly assured.

Sheathing his weapon, Varoi reached into his belt pouch and drew forth a wadded length of cloth. Ayesha glanced at it curiously, but said not one word.

Raising his arms, Varoi gave a series of hand signals, hopeful that whoever was posted on guard remained vigilant, and would understand his message and pass on the word. The straggling line of trees marking the settlement's boundary was too close for comfort. He could but hope that, should the Pulan be present, they had not been followed. Lastly, he unfolded the pennant, a white boar on a field of green, his particular cohort's flag, and held it aloft two-handed so that all on the battlements might see and be aware who it was that required entry.

It seemed an age before Varoi heard the reassuring rumble of well-oiled gears informing him that the drawbridge was being lowered. Even then he kept the pennant high. With the drawbridge almost settled on the moat's embankment, Varoi set one hand to his sword hilt and the other to the curve of Ayesha's waist, urging her forward. Halfway across he raised his sword hand and gave yet another signal, one he hoped would be fast acted upon.

Hardly had they gone a few more paces forward than the structure beneath their feet began to shudder. Ayesha gasped and looked up at Varoi, her emerald eyes wide with alarm.

"What's happening, Varoi? The ridge has never felt unstable before."

His arm about her waist grew tense and he gave her a comforting squeeze.

"Have no fear, Ayesha. Tis just a precaution. I have commanded the drawbridge to be raised. We will reach the far side very soon."

"But the portcullis remains down. We shall be trapped between that and the bridge."

"The guard will raise the portcullis as soon as it is safe. Trust me, you will come to no harm."

The tension he felt in her body did not diminish despite his reassurance. Varoi, however, remained confident that whoever was in charge of the gatehouse would see to it that their safety was ensured.

As the bridge slowly rose off the ground, a distinct incline became evident. At first this caused no real problem, but the gradient grew noticeably steep. Ayesha's panic began to show. Varoi wondered, might she appear this fearful if she were alone? Perhaps she welcomed his attentions. But then he reminded himself what had just occurred. The incident involving the Pulan scout would suffice to confound the most hardened nerves.

"Don't worry, Ayesha. I shall ensure that you neither trip nor fall."

Glancing up she ventured a wan smile.

"Are you sure?"

"Even if we both should slip we have not far to fall. Look, Ayesha, we have almost reached the end."

It was true. Even as he spoke, Varoi heard a series of clanks and rattles as the mechanism controlling the portcullis was set in motion. Slowly the huge iron grid that formed it began rising in its grooves. By the time he stepped off the bridge it had already risen chest high. Varoi ducked under the lower edge, drawing Ayesha with him. Then they stood watching as the bridge and portcullis were locked back into position. It would be a while before anyone left Tenbay that way again. At least, not until after the Pulan had been safely driven from the lands.

Varoi's gaze swung back to Ayesha, who released a profound sigh of relief as she set down her basket of herbs. "I should thank you for saving my life."

Varoi shook his head. "Think nothing of it, Princess Ayesha. It was my duty and an honour to ensure your safety."

Once more you become formal, thought Ayesha with a certain chagrin. But then she recalled the gatehouse guards and realised that Varoi was intent on protecting her reputation. What would her father think of the incident with the Pulan should he find out? "Promise you'll not say a word to papa."

"What could I say, Princess? We collected herbs for the healer, as was promised. You checked on your hives while we were there. Nothing of special import in that, so far as I can see."

He was protecting her, yet again, by evading the issue. She met his gaze, calm now she was on safe ground.

174

"Thank you, Varoi. Will you assist me in taking these to the healer?"

She was pleased when he agreed to accompany her. Removing his gauntlets, tucking them behind his belt, Varoi accepted one of the baskets and fell into step alongside her. Ayesha mused on how much she enjoyed having him around.

They hadn't far to go in order to reach the infirmary, a low building situated near the entrance to the inner bailey, conveniently close to the practice arena itself. While few injuries occurred during practice there was always one or two. It was ideally situated for those warriors manning the battlements. Although, should the Pulan manage to breach the curtain wall and enter the outer bailey swift evacuation of its personnel would become a high priority.

Ayesha recognised this fact as well as any trained officer might. Just for a moment she considered withdrawing her offer of assistance, made to the resident healer on an earlier visit. The incident with the axe-wielding Pulan had left her shaken. But she had given her word to do what she could. Maybe it was just as well she had viewed death at close quarters, even though she hadn't exactly stared it in the face. Perhaps it would help her remain firm when the attack on the fortress began. After all, what made adult males assume that they alone were capable of coping with such stressful situations?

Ayesha resolved to discuss the matter later, though not with Varoi. It was enough that he be aware how nervous she had been. The healer would be just as understanding as Varoi. Besides which, she was female. Surely she would offer a few suggestions regarding the best means of helping her cope.

So absorbed was Ayesha in her deliberations it took her a while to realise Varoi had spoken.

"I'm sorry, Varoi. What was it you said?"

175

"I suggested you might wish to share some chocola with me. It might help settle your nerves."

Ayesha's sharp intake of breath and glance of annoyance forced Varoi to moderate his words.

"I meant no offence. I hear tell the beverage has a soothing effect. It was just an idea, assuming you have nothing more important to attend."

He left his suggestion hanging in mid-air as, reaching the infirmary door, he took hold of the handle and swung it wide. Then, with a crisp curtsey, he ushered her inside.

Plonking her basket on one end of the long wooden bench that served as preparation table and workbench, Ayesha indicated that Varoi should do likewise. Then she went in search of the resident healer and physician. Varoi cleared a space wherein to set the baskets of herbs and appropriated a three-legged stool. It was not the most comfortable seat but he felt inclined to assume that the two high-backed chairs, with their torn leather upholstery, were not meant for the likes of him.

Ayesha returned with the healer, Soleil com 'Vasain, following close at her heels. Soleil was a Shakar in her middle years, her brown hair loosely tied back from her face. Her skin was paler than Ayesha's, almost creamy in hue, and she had a long nose that seemed to dominate her face, though her amber eyes were bright with intelligence and laughter lines creased the corners of those same eyes. She could in no way be considered beautiful, but Varoi liked her straight away. Perhaps because she reminded him of a favourite aunt. Either way her friendly manner put him at ease.

"So, you are the warrior who helped Ayesha collect these precious herbs. Thank you so much for all you have done. These supplies will make a great deal of difference to what I can lay in store. I must be ready for when the

Pulan attack. It would not do to be caught low on essentials."

Varoi nodded his understanding and started to rise.

"Of course, no one hopes more than I that my skills will not be required", Soleil went on. "But then, you can never be too sure."

Varoi hesitated, prepared to leave but not certain whether he should. He had no wish to appear rude.

"Would you both like some tea? We could chat perhaps, get to know each other better.?" Soleil inclined her head in silent enquiry. "Unless, of course, you have better things to do."

Ayesha glanced at Varoi. "I'm afraid I have something I must attend. Perhaps later?"

Soleil nodded, absently rummaging through a basket of herbs. "Later will do just fine."

Bidding Soleil farewell, they stepped outside, Varoi infinitely relieved to be back in the fresh morning air. The smell in the workshop made him want to gag. What was she brewing in there? And if Ayesha had something more important to do there was no chance she would take him up on his offer. Sadly, he prepared to take his leave.

But Ayesha, it seemed, had something on her mind. Her hand on his arm bade him linger. Gazing down into luminous green eyes he fought a rising desire to draw her close.

"Varoi, there is a question I've been meaning to ask. Goddess knows why I haven't brought it up before, but still ..."

"What is it, Ayesha? As long as it doesn't pertain to military matters, I'll do my best to reply."

"It's nothing military on which I desire your opinion, Varoi. I just want to know ..." she shook her head and scowled as though admonishing herself for a foolish thought. Varoi wondered what question could be so difficult to ask. "I need you to explain what it means for you to find your soulmate. There. That is all."

Varoi studied her, considering how best to explain. Ayesha lifted her chin in a defiant tilt, a warning glint in her eyes. Did she think he might make fun of her for asking? Nothing could be further from the truth. Taking both her hands in his, he gazed deep into her eyes, his attention riveted. She had asked a most important question, second only to "will you consent to be mine?" Why would he belittle her for that? He had no intention of being anything other than deeply serious.

"Ayesha, I would kiss you here and now if I thought that might help you understand. But I see that my actions alone are insufficient confirmation of what I claim. We are two separate halves of the same whole. Apart we exist, but cannot thrive, can never be truly content. At least, for me that holds true. Together and joined we become complete as nature intends, that is what it means. Soulmates need each other for completion. Completion, the joining of our bodies, makes us one. It is a confirmation of our pledge and a declaration of total commitment to one another. That is what being soulmates means."

"I see." She said that, but did she truly understand?

"Do you?" Varoi wondered, tempted to risk her wrath in a desperate attempt at provocation. "If you do, then I trust you understand what makes you so important in my eyes. Why I refuse to give up my pursuit, however long it takes me to persuade you that you are destined to become mine."

"Yes." Again the shy tilt of her head. "Varoi, will you do something for me if I ask it?"

He wondered what she might request, hoping it would prove neither foolish nor suicidal. Either way he felt obliged to agree.

"Tell me what you would have in mind."

Her lips curved in a shy smile, one he found utterly beguiling.

"Kiss me."

Varoi studied her a moment longer, certain there must be a catch. She tilted her chin, raising her face to his, making the invitation plain. Slowly he lowered his head, intent on taking possession of her mouth. Their lips met in an eruption of volcanic passion that sent hot blood coursing through his veins and heat pooling low in his loins. Purposely, he touched only her lips. Determined to let his mouth affirm all that was left unsaid.

Varoi heard a soft moan, hers not his, confirmation his message was getting through and, reacting instinctively, deepened the kiss. Reaching, she twined her arms about his neck, taking a firm grip on his hair, no easy matter considering it was tied back in a warrior's tail. His tongue slid across her lips, demanding entry ... and Varoi knew a swift surge of unbearable pleasure when her lips parted, allowing him in.

He was nothing if not thorough, making Ayesha aware he would take full advantage...providing she granted permission.

The scent of him, an awareness of his body heat, his physical presence, his sheer male intensity was such that she felt ready to capitulate then and there.

As the urge to go further intervened with Varoi's erotic investigations he drew back, no easy task while Ayesha retained a firm grasp of his hair. Ayesha, sighing, raised slumberous eyes.
I think, perhaps, I understand. Any chance you might repeat the demonstration?"

She watched him from beneath a fan of dark lashes; a speculative glint to her smile suggesting other delights yet to materialize.

Varoi, shook his head. "Not here and now; but maybe some other time?"

"Oh?" Ayesha sounded peeved by his resolute stance, but only mildly so.

"Besides, as I recall, you informed Soleil there was something you had to do."

"There is."

"Well then. Best I don't keep you if that is the case."

"But I thought you intended partaking of some chocola too?"

"I did …" Realisation of what she inferred took him by surprise. "Was that the something else to which you referred?"

"Of course. Then again, if you've changed your mind and would rather not?"

"Yes. I mean. No, of course. I should be delighted to share your company." Varoi reached out a hand; smiling coyly, she placed her hand within his.

Chapter 8: Arrivals

It was the fifth hour of the night, although the full hour had not yet been rung. Varoi stood atop the parapet looking out across the countryside beyond. It was the dark of the moon, that particular night in each moon cycle when Lecristo, Goddess of the Moon, turned her blind eye towards all manner of crime and indiscretion. There was little to be seen, even *with* his *ananaha* skills fully deployed.

The air was still and cool against his skin. Not a breath of wind stirred among the grim stones of the battlements at this early hour. With the town's fires damped down for the night the air smelt remarkably fresh and clean. More of the land than the nearby river; the latter a sour reek redolent of slimy mud and all things piscine.

Another aroma assailed his nostrils now, the slightest hint and nothing more. With his senses expanded Varoi caught a strong whiff and instinctively bristled. One minute his stance was relaxed yet alert, the next it was tense with foreboding. Something distant stirred, something even his keen eyesight could not clearly discern, though he knew at once what it must be.

Someone took a step forward. A tall shape emerged from the surrounding gloom, resolving itself into another Shakar.

"What is it, Varoi? What can you see?"

Varoi laughed, a low humourless chuckle devoid of mirth. "Even my eyes cannot see far in this murk."

"Sorry, I spoke without thinking. But there is something of which you're aware; or am I mistaken?"

"There is indeed. And if you draw in a good breath of air tis possible you too will recognise its essence."

Bigli did as Varoi advised, then gave vent to an eloquent moan. "Sorry friend, the smells are too muddled for me. Tell me to what it is you refer; then, perhaps, I shall know its identity."

"The rank stench of stale sweat and unwashed bodies have combined to create a distinctive aroma. Can you recognise it now?"

Varoi caught a glimpse of white as Bigli's eyes widened in comprehension. "You mean the Pulan are already here, camped on our doorstep. How did they arrive unseen?"

Varoi's reply was typically droll. "I imagine it was never a part of their strategy to draw attention to their arrival. And they are not quite on our doorstep, but camped a few miles distant from here. Even so, they are close enough."

"How far away are they now?"

"Not far at all, Bigli, two or three miles at most. It's a wonder we cannot see their cook-fires from here. We must assume they have none lit. In which case their arrival would come as a complete surprise. I assume overrunning the Shakar settlement to be their primary objective. If so, they will find nothing of value there."

"Which is all to the good. Goddess be praised, the boy Horace brought us fair warning."

"Yes, indeed." Varoi, too, felt immeasurable gratitude for that piece of good fortune. Somewhere within the town walls a bell began chiming the hour.

"Varoi, if they attack in force do you think there is a chance we can win?"

"Has Tenbay ever come under attack before?"

"Not to my knowledge and certainly not during the years I've been here. The settlement may have experienced the occasional assault, but the Pulan were always repelled. The enemy have never come in such numbers before."

"You may be wrong in one respect. I think their numbers have always been sufficient to form an army. It's just that the clans have never joined forces until now."

"Why now? What has changed that they decide to form an army now?"

"Who can say? My guess would be that they covet the land on which we have settled. They mean to dispense with the Shakar."

"Do you believe they have any chance of success?"

"I think it all hinges on us. If Tenbay as a whole stands firm and we win the coming battle, then perhaps we may banish them for good."

"I suppose all we can cling to now is hope and conjecture."

"Until the numbers ranged against us are fully revealed, there is little else."

"And if we *are* seriously outnumbered? Do you believe there still is a chance we can win?"

"We must do our best, Bigli. It's all we can do."

"Then I hope my best will be good enough. I have never been in this situation before."

"You have not fought in battle, Bigli? Have no prior experience of what is entailed?" Varoi could not hide the depth of his surprise. He thought all Shakar warriors had spent some time on the front line. To find Bigli had not was a matter of some concern.

"No, Varoi, nor am I the only one of rank in this situation."

"So how did you come by your rank without proving yourself thus?"

Bigli loosed a wry chuckle at Varoi's apparent incredulity. "You'll never believe this, Varoi, but I was among the group that helped put down a rebellion among slaves in Nai Hai du Veral."

"Unarmed slaves launched an attack on Nai Hai du Veral?"

"They were not unarmed and the attack came from within the High Citadel."

"Indeed?"

Bigli caught the implicit question, which Varoi hesitated to voice, and gave an explicit reply.

"It was an especially bloody conflict; few slaves survived to tell the tale. Those who did were executed soon after the skirmish was brought to a close. I felt no particular credit was due for my part in the conflict. Some, apparently, thought otherwise. Thus was I raised to the rank of lieutenant, along with one other. After which I was assigned here. Far enough from the scene of conflict that news could be stifled without further protest from us."

"The other warrior of rank that you mention, may I enquire his name?"

"No doubt you've guessed it already. It was Che."

Varoi shook his head in disbelief, a slight movement, which, in the darkness, passed almost unseen. In the near distance the last chime of a bell marking the hour died away.

"You will do well," he said. "You and Che. If you could keep your head in such a situation as the one just described you will manage well enough now."

"You believe that?"

Varoi made his voice firm, injecting as much conviction as he could into his following statement. Che and Bigli deserved all the encouragement he could give.

"I do indeed. But now," he said, looking around, "if my relief has arrived, I intend grabbing what rest I can while I still have the chance."

"I'm here!" said a cheerful voice behind as another tall figure detached itself from the prevailing gloom.

Varoi acknowledged the new arrival with a quick nod of satisfaction. "In that case I shall away and get what sleep I can before the dawn watch is called."

"Or you could stay and keep us company," Bigli quipped.

"Not I," Varoi growled. Turning he strode swiftly away.

184

Soleil glanced up and smiled as the door opened and Ayesha entered the room. "You've come," she said, sounding rather surprised.

"I said that I would. Did you think I'd forget or find something more entertaining to do?"

"Of course not. It's just that the duty you've agreed to assume must seem a tad daunting in prospect."

"Because I'm a princess, is that what you mean to infer?"

Ayesha felt annoyed to find herself discomposed by Soleil's concerned attitude but knew getting prickly about it was no solution.

"I'm sorry, Soleil," she apologised. "I seem to be all on edge."

"You have every right to be nervous. And no. I didn't say that because you are a princess. Rather, I said it because you are young, with no obvious link to those who must man the battlements."

"I have my reasons."

Soleil tilted her head in silent enquiry. Ayesha pretended not to notice her interest. Picking up a discarded smock that lay across one of the chairs she pulled it on; then took a quick look around.

"What must I do?"

Soleil sighed in resignation. She knew Ayesha was troubled about something. All she could do was wait until her friend was prepared to talk. By all indications that wouldn't happen any time soon.

She decided to suggest a suitable distraction. "Have you broken your fast?"

Ayesha shook her head. "I couldn't stomach a heavy meal. Not today."

Soleil offered her most reassuring smile. "I understand perfectly. But you'll need something inside before you start your day. I cannot have you fainting on your feet. Where would we be if that should happen; with those presumptuous males eager for any excuse to exclude us from the battle zone. Then, who would tend their hurts and woes and see them amply fed?"

"I imagine they would cope somehow," Ayesha grumbled, running distracted fingers through long, tawny hair.

"No doubt they would, were we not around to help. But is that fair? We are not allowed to participate in the conflict. The least we can do is see that they're well cared for when the need *does* arise."

Soleil set the kettle she had just filled on top of the stove to boil, then began laying out a light repast.

"You will eat some of this, Ayesha, if not much. Please don't argue, I've made up my mind."

"Don't worry, Soleil. I've no intention of arguing. But there must be things I can do. Some sort of preparation you wish carried out." She looked around the room, seeking a worthwhile diversion.

Soleil watching, sighed. It was going to be a long and irksome day.

"There is little that needs doing at present, since my preparations are well in hand. Sit down, Ayesha. Tell me what troubles you so."

Ayesha let out her breath in a long, despondent moan. "I don't think sharing my problems with you will diminish them in any way, Soleil. This is something I must deal with alone. I just wish I could see a way out of my present predicament"

"Nevertheless, they do say a problem shared is a problem halved. By talking it over with a friend you might see things more clearly. I might even be able to suggest a possible solution. I can keep a confidence if that's what's worrying you."

Ayesha gave a disconsolate shrug. What had she got to lose?

"It's Varoi. It is always Varoi of late."

"The young male who helped you gather my herbs?" Ayesha nodded, her expression glum. "But he seemed so solicitous to me."

"And he is. But that's just the trouble, he ought not to be. He claims the right of soulmate, Soleil. I've told him about my promise to Schezan, but he remains insistent. In a moment of weakness I granted him permission to vie with Schezan. I cannot imagine what will happen when Schezan discovers what I have done. Or rather, I can and that's what worries me."

Soleil was silent while she considered the likely repercussions of Ayesha's actions. Busying herself with filling the pot and steeping the leaves, she wondered whether the soothing brew would prove sufficiently potent. This done she dropped a knob of butter on to a heated griddle and, when it started to sizzle, poured spoonfuls of batter into the heated pan. She managed all this with one eye for the task in hand, the other on Ayesha; who twirled elegant fingers through a long strand of tawny hair, twisting and untangling the glossy strands in a distracted fashion.

Still with her mind on the pancakes, Soleil enquired, "What frightens you most Ayesha? Schezan finding out what you've done or Varoi proving he truly is your mate?"

Ayesha lifted her head in surprise. She had not viewed her problem in quite this way. But instead of answering Soleil's question she posed one of her own.

"Varoi is gentle and considerate, qualities I find attractive in a male but not ones I normally associate with Schezan. I have to ask myself: what is it I want most? Schezan can offer me a better future than Varoi. As potential heir to the High Obajan he stands to inherit position and power."

"And is that what you consider most important in a potential spouse?" Ayesha, bristling with indignant affront, said. "You sound just like Varoi. Except he did not use quite the same words."

"What answer did you give; might I ask?"

"I cannot recall my exact words. I know I was most annoyed that he should have the temerity to pose such a question in the first place."

"Perchance, do you object most to his question or the sly inference thus made.

"Both, I think."

"If he claims you as soulmate I assume he has already made an approach by using *lossa antario?*"

Soleil tilted her head questioningly. She knew this was the crucial question. *Suve si lossa antario* roughly translated as "right of first contact" in the Common Tongue: the acknowledged means by which any full-blooded Shakar male possessing shamanic power could claim his soulmate. If Varoi had contacted Ayesha by this means his claim on her as Chosen was indisputable. In which case his display of patience was beyond reproach.

Soleil had not yet found her soulmate. She was young, though, and still had hope.

Ayesha studied Soleil through narrowed eyes. Such provocative questions she was plying her with, what potential conclusion might they imply? Had she, mayhap, overlooked some important detail? "You think I have my priorities all wrong. Is that what you're trying to suggest?"

"It seems you had your future all mapped out until Varoi appeared on the scene. His arrival – or was it *lossa antario?* – proved an unforeseen hitch in those plans. Mayhap a review of those tactics would not go amiss. So tell me. Have you been privileged to enjoy *lossa antario* with your intended mate? Is it all that is claimed?"

"For me, it is. Soleil, what would you advise I should do?"

"It seems you have reached a decision, with scant interference from me."

"If only it were that simple."

"Which brings me back to another question, one I posed earlier. What, or rather who, is it you most fear?"

"If I'm honest, Schezan finding out what I've done. He has a temper that once inflamed is hard to douse."

"Now that is a serious problem. Even so, until your choice is announced he must remain mindful: it is your undisputed right to choose. No male can force you to a decision. Give yourself ample time, Ayesha, and make a considered choice."

"That then is your advice?"

"It is my opinion, for what it is worth." Soleil set a large platter of steaming pancakes down atop the table. "Now eat! There's butter, honey, cream and conserves to go with these; no need to stint ourselves just yet. Trouble always seems less on a full stomach and we've a long day ahead. No excuses now, Ayesha. Tuck in."

Ayesha shook her head in silent denial. Her appetite was well and truly quenched, until the mouth-watering aroma of freshly cooked pancake reached her nostrils, tempting her to try a small bite. Once the taste of warm bannock slathered in honey and butter all but melted on her tongue, she found her waning appetite revived.

Varoi bounded up the steps of the barbican two at a time. The air around him felt chill. Breath rose in a cloud of vapour before his face. If anything, it seemed colder than before.

Reaching the top of the stairs he pushed open the door, which hit the wall alongside with a dull clunk, then strode to the edge of the parapet and looked around. The merlons of the crenulated battlements were almost as tall as a man but, being Shakar, he stood head and shoulders above them all.

Staring out across the surrounding countryside he drew in a steadying breath. He was ahead of time in

189

arriving on duty, he knew, but he felt drawn here inexorably. The coming conflict represented a new experience for him and he was eager to embrace it wholeheartedly. But not yet: the enemy he sought were still not in evidence ... or if they were their presence was screened in some way. The land that encompassed the fortress of Tenbay was hidden beneath an impenetrable rolling bank of fog, which shrouded the vicinity for several miles in all directions.

That the Pulan army were now massing and on the move he had no doubt, yet barely a whisper of sound reached his ears. And with the thickness of the vaporous screen he could almost be blind. He must wait a while yet before the size of this army would be revealed.

Varoi stifled his frustration and turned back to the stairs. Others were now arriving on duty, the noisy clatter of their footsteps sounding harsh on the still morning air.

Varoi, recognising some of their number, waved a greeting before returning to his appointed task, his *ananaha* skills now fully deployed.

The sun had risen, dark and ominous, shedding its ruby light across the land, a crimson glow that touched the vaporous blanket, turning it into a bloody shroud. Had the Shakar been superstitious, they might have viewed this as portentous. That they did not was in no way remarkable, since they were not that way inclined. Besides, it was the Pulan and not they who were trapped beneath that same bloodied shroud.

Varoi stood with narrowed eyes, seeking the smallest indication that the enemy was near. In this he was not alone. There were others stationed up on the battlements who possessed the abilities of an *ananaha*, though few among them were as practised or more skilled. Nor was Varoi the only one among his cohort, but he was the best of those three and the one on whom his commander most relied. All now employed their unique talent in a broad scan of the surrounding area, each hoping for first sight, if not first kill.

Varoi tugged irritably at the shortened hair of his warrior's tail. Since losing part of its length to an Ice Warrior's blade during his recent skirmish with a Pulan scout it frequently worked loose from its bindings.

It was a matter of pride and long held tradition that those Shakar who served in this manner should wear a warrior's tail. A few others who served in high places were also permitted the tail, provided they had served their time as warriors. Mostly, the right was reserved for warriors alone.

To have his tail thus shortened was therefore more than a mere annoyance to Varoi; it was a blight on his overall appearance he could well do without. Worse still, at a time that required full concentration for his given task, it reminded him of other things. Mostly, it reminded him of Ayesha.

Varoi was aware he could never completely exclude Ayesha from his thoughts, however hard he tried. She was a part of him and always would be. *Lossa antario* had awoken a longing within, a fierce hunger that could never be assuaged. Not even their joining and ultimate completion could change that. This was the way of things when soulmates were involved and he would not have wanted things any other way.

Something black rose from the surrounding murk and flew swiftly overhead. Instinctively Varoi ducked, then glanced up. A bird, most likely a crow, had been disturbed. A slight eddy caught at the ruby-tinted mist, flurried briefly, then stilled. "Did you see that?" whispered a voice alongside.

"Yes," said Varoi, straightening again to stand alert.

"Do you think it means their scouts are moving in?"

"No," said Varoi. "Their vanguard, perhaps, or even the main force, but not their scouts. Trust me, the scouts are already here."

Varoi chose not to explain how he knew this, having already informed both commanders about the incident with the advance scout at the settlement. If they chose to inform others it was not up to him to decide who. It had been necessary to share that information. If nothing else, it explained his shortened tail. That he altered certain details in the telling to protect Ayesha's reputation was for him to know and no one else. He would not compromise Ayesha in their eyes. The entire debacle was down to him.

Remembrance of his commanders tart comment, "you should have been on guard, Varoi, not too busy smelling the roses," brought forth a wry grin. He wondered what else Commander com 'Dolino might have said had he known the true facts. Just as well he did not!

A light breath of wind swept the parapet, raising the dust at his feet. A loose tendril of hair brushed his cheek. A stiff breeze was just what they needed to lift the fog and drive it away. Then they might see how large an army they must confront.

Swirls and eddies began moving across the surface of the all-concealing mist. He saw movement underneath. If he could see it, others would too. He heard their low murmurs of speculation, as with narrowed eyes they sought to pierce the gloomy shroud beneath which all knew the Pulan hid.

It was a full hour past dawn but the sun had not yet gathered enough heat with which to banish the lingering brume. A dark speck appeared in the distance, too far, too indistinct to really be seen. Then it vanished instantly, swallowed up by a thick bank of fog.

Varoi cursed eloquently under his breath, now certain what he thought he had seen. He narrowed his perspective to a finite degree, concentrating all efforts on identifying the thing.

Minutes ticked by unheeded. Somewhere in the city a cocked crowed. Belatedly a bell tolled the hour. Whatever was happening within the fortress held no present interest for him. Let others concern themselves thus. He hardly dare blink for fear he might miss what he next expected to see.

He caught a glimpse, no more than that. A brief sight of something menacing, something large and looming, before it was again obscured. Yet, this sighting sufficed to identify the threat.

"Ballista," Varoi's voice emerged as a harsh croak. He swallowed past the lump in his throat, then spoke again. "They have ballista, at least one I have seen so far. Will someone pass that information on?"

It was not Varoi's task to deliver messages of that import. This role was assigned to others who were not *ananaha*.

Varoi rubbed his eyes in a vain attempt to relieve a growing discomfort. They were sore and gritty after several hours of scouring the area around. He hoped the fog would soon lift in order that all might know precisely what manner of threat the Ice Warriors posed.

Away to his left something moved, close enough that even those not gifted *ananaha* could see. With his acute eyesight and narrowed perspective, Varoi identified it easily. "Wolf clan, pack leader, man of rank," he listed the information carefully, seeking to clarify details where necessary.

"How can you know all that?" enquired a voice at his elbow.

Varoi turned his head slightly that way, his attention still keenly focused where it needed to be.

"Hello, Bigli, you decided to join us then?"

"You haven't answered my question, Varoi."

193

Smiling, Varoi gave the requested information. "I caught a glimpse of shoulders and helm, Bigli."

"And you can tell all that from only a glimpse? Tell me, how you can be so accurate? If you've no objection, that is."

"It was easy enough to determine," Varoi said, doing his best not to preen but failing miserably. "His helm is grey, as was the tuft of coarse hair rising above it. A dead giveaway in that it tells me to which clan he belongs and that he holds rank. I glimpsed a gold torc round his neck, which confirms him as pack leader, although that was much harder to see."

"Amazing. And do you know all their clans by sight?"

"I can identify most, especially those encountered during battle. Ice Warriors will be here too. And, if Wolf are present, then, no doubt, also Eagle and Bear. We must wait and see what others will honour us with their presence this day."

Bigli nodded as though in silent satisfaction at his comrade's observation and Varoi returned his full attention to the task in hand. The eddying vapour hinted at many things and Varoi was convinced it hid far more than had so far been revealed.

A sudden chilly blast caught him, whipping his clothes about and trying to knock him off his feet, but Varoi was planted four-square upon the parapet and was too sturdy an obstacle to shift. Leaning into the wind, Varoi scented the air, hoping that it would prove a useful ally by blowing away the fog obstructing his view and that the heat of the sun's rays would burn off any lingering vapour. This fog was a serious impediment to his abilities. He wanted desperately to know the true magnitude of the army they were forced to confront.

194

How could they successfully defeat the Pulan if the numbers involved should prove overwhelming? It was a question he had avoided until now.

A glistening black helm, to which a disembodied head was attached, arose out of the mist in front of him. So. Bear clan were, indeed, here. Varoi called out the clan name, even as the warrior himself disappeared. Were the enemy maintaining a low profile in order that their positions could not be espied? It seemed more than likely they were, for surely the fog was at last beginning to thin.

The sun rose higher in the sky, warming the stones of the battlements hardly at all. It was too bleak to have any effect, and the wind was becoming blustery. It rose with a shrill, mournful wail and, gradually, the chill vapour began to lift.

More disembodied heads appeared.

Varoi was quick to identify those clans he recognised: Ice warriors were no surprise, neither were Wolf or Bear; Eagle materialised eventually, as did Raven, Saarcat, Helvan, Wolverine and Wild Boar. Most appeared to be here. There were others, too, not so readily recognized. Varoi left that task for those who could.

Varoi settled down, instead, to absorbing the sheer volume in numbers of Pulan ranging outwards across the fen. It appeared as though a plague of showy locusts had descended, intent on one thing only: annihilating all opposition. It was a daunting spectacle, even for one as inured to conflict as he.

Varoi wondered how Tenbay's inhabitants might view this imminent threat, were they ever to view it clearly as did he from atop the curtain wall. There seemed little likelihood of such an event occurring. That didn't mean they had no useful role.

They now knew the answer to one crucial question. It would take some time in bringing this battle to a close.

Varoi pushed the door to the dining hall open, then held it wide as his companions filed through. One in five of those who had been stationed atop the battlements since before dawn had been ordered to stand down and break their fast while they had the chance. This number included all who were *ananaha*, their skills being no longer required now that the threat to Tenbay was visible to all.

They had clattered their way down the steep stairs of the barbican and across the outer ward, more than a little surprised by the number of goats tethered within those looming walls. Apparently these last were a new addition to the fortress's inhabitants, having just recently been installed. They would be removed to safer quarters once the fighting got underway. Meantime they enjoyed the freedom to roam between the walls and their slit-eyed stare followed the Shakar with rapt curiosity.

Once within the keep's confines a babble of conversation arose. They had maintained a discreet silence before, unwilling to divulge what they now knew for fear those listening to such information might repeat what was overheard, and thereby create panic among the populace as a whole, once news the Pulan were encamped in huge numbers outside their walls became general knowledge. The inhabitants would learn soon enough what they were up against. For now the Shakar had been warned to maintain a discreet silence. Once within the keep's confines, however, their tongues could be loosed.

Closer to the dining hall, silence resumed. The kitchen lay conveniently to hand and all warriors knew that the kitchen staff would be all ears, agog to catch the smallest morsel of interesting news and only too willing to pass on idle gossip. Each retelling would be awarded detailed and lurid embellishment.

Cook arrived first with a number of serving maids in tow, each encumbered with heavy pots and heated cauldrons of food. These were quickly set upon the table and Cook prepared to take her leave. But not before she had a word from those present.

"Enjoy your meal and eat your fill. There are no short rations for now. I fully expect to find these dishes empty upon my return." She made a quick gesture with her hands that signified she expected them to tuck in. "There are more victuals available should any among you not be satisfied."

They thanked her by acknowledging her efforts on their behalf, then waited a full minute after the door closed before resuming their interrupted conversation. Varoi had already set a spell of coverture in place, lest any be tempted to listen in outside the door in hopes of obtaining useful information.

Varoi ladled a good portion of porridge into his bowl before helping himself to honey.

"At least we know why there are goats grazing the outer bailey," he remarked, as he proceeded to pour from the jug of warm, frothy milk. Passing the pot of steaming porridge, he began stirring honey into his meal. There were ample portions of everything on offer. Enough to go round twice should they have time, which he doubted. He poured tea, which was hot, black and strong enough to stand his spoon up in, lacing it liberally with honey, certain he would need all the energy this meal promised if he was to survive the next few days. And he intended surviving, any way he could.

"I heard you naming the various clans, Varoi," said a younger member of the garrison named Aheb. "Would you mind repeating that list for me now? I had no chance to absorb it properly at the time."

Varoi peered over the rim of his cup, certain there was more to the enquiry than this, yet willing enough to oblige. When Varoi had finished speaking, Aheb fixed him with a quizzical grin.

"I admit, when I first heard you name the different clans I was struck by one peculiarity. Perhaps you would care to explain?"

Varoi tilted his head in enquiry as Aheb went on.

"Call it idle curiosity, but I cannot help wondering why all clans bar one are named after either animal or bird, the exception being *Ice* Warriors. What makes them different?"

"Ice Warriors are no different, in truth. They, too, are named after an animal; in this case it is the Ice Bear. Ice is their clan title as opposed to that of Bear, which, you may recall, is another clan entirely."

Aheb gave a satisfied nod. Instead of returning to his meal, Varoi surprised his audience by launching into a brief monologue regarding the main difference between Ice Warriors and other clans.

"I know I don't need to remind you that among our near neighbours the most hostile towards us are the Pulan or that, even among the Pulan, Ice Warriors have a fiercesome reputation, one gained in battle against other clans. Their bloody exploits and rampant killing sprees are legend. Not for nothing are they known among their own kind as Southern Wolverine.

Around the table several heads began to nod in silent agreement. But Varoi had not yet finished what he had to say. He swept the table with a considering glance, ensuring he had their undivided attention. Gesticulating vigorously with his spoon, he waxed eloquent.

"What few know, because it never was recorded, was the unprecedented change in Ice Bear attitude, which prevailed among some members of the clan for a very short while." Varoi noted, with some satisfaction, he definitely had their attention now. "It is several decades past, as I understand, but still the tale is handed down, of the time when Ice Warriors traded with our southernmost towns."

198

"Traded! You surely are mistaken, Varoi." He caught the note of startled disbelief and was unsurprised that this news should be questioned.

"No, I am not. The trading lasted for half a century or more, as I heard tell. Most surprising was the reason for this change."

Varoi plainly relished his role of storyteller as he went on.

"According to my information, the change in attitude was brought about by a woman. A beautiful woman by all accounts, one of their Taken."

"I've heard that name applied before, Varoi, but never understood its meaning. Care to explain?" Che had almost finished his meal, whereas Varoi had barely begun.

Varoi took another mouthful of porridge before clarifying his statement.

"You all know that when a village is overrun by the Pulan some warriors prefer to take captives. Of the women, those not employed as slaves but chosen as mates are called Taken. It is considered a title of honour, although some might disagree. This particular Taken chose her moment well when it came time to escape and return to her own breed. In doing so, she left behind a son. He was too young to be parted from his mother but, nonetheless, she refused to acknowledge him as her own. Her Pulan mate, when he returned from raiding the Unclaimed Land, vowed he would find and take her back. The unlikely means he chose for his purpose was trade. He did succeed in locating her, and he *did* persuade her to return with him, but her condition for this agreement was unequivocal. He must give up all raiding and embark on a non-violent path of trading. Not just him, but all other members of his clan.

"It seems he was desperate enough to have her back, for he agreed toher terms. Thus began a long period of peaceful contact. It could not last, though. Eventually the Ice Warriors returned to their old ways.

199

"Still, it's amazing the power of persuasion one woman managed to apply. It makes you think."

Varoi dipped his head, returning his attention to his unfinished meal. Time was short. He hoped they would not ask him any more questions.

Varoi had just pushed his empty bowl aside and cut himself a thick wedge of crusty bread when Aheb raised another interesting point. Despite the desire to get as much nourishment into his stomach as possible before their brief respite came to an end, Varoi again found himself caught up in the conversation.

Aheb glanced around the table before saying, "That's all very well, Varoi, but it still doesn't explain the Pulan's abrupt change in tactics after all these years. Why does an army now stand before our gates? Why are they so keen to drive us from our homeland?"

Varoi suppressed a frustrated sigh, declining to answer until he had spread the bread in his hand with an ample amount of butter.

Further along the table Che took up the dropped thread of their conversation. "Aheb," he chided. "You know as well as anyone present: the Pulan have always called this the Unclaimed Land with good reason. It is common knowledge, they were nowhere in evidence at the time of our arrival simply because it was their custom to spend spring and summer upon the bare waste of the southern steppes. You must also be aware that the Fenlanders' acceptance of our continued presence has long been a bone of contention among the Pulan. What else is there to know? However …" Che fixed Varoi with a pensive frown. "I *should* like to know who built this fortress. Was it in fact the Pulan, or earlier occupants of this land? What do you think, Varoi?"

Varoi had managed to make some inroads into the wedge of bread now clasped in his hand. He took yet another mouthful before attempting to reply, still hopeful another would answer for him. Plainly, this was not to be the case. Cutting himself some more bread, he proceeded to offer his personal opinion on the subject.

"It cannot have been the Pulan who built Tenbay's sturdy fortress walls and high battlements. That must be the work of another breed of man. Fenlanders maybe, I don't know. The Pulan erect nothing more substantial than yurts, even in the more established encampments. Stone and mortar are unfamiliar materials where they are concerned."

"And what basis do you have for that assumption?" wondered Che.

Varoi shook his head in weary frustration; would he ever be allowed to eat his fill? "Have you seen one of their permanent camps? Their method is simplicity itself – a willow frame covered with skins – effective, but primitive in the extreme. Even Ice Warriors, who inhabit the glacial coastline furthest south, are satisfied with this form of residence, or so it seems. I don't believe any Pulan have ever built anything approaching the size of this fortress. Never would they consider the need. Does that answer your question? Only, if it please you, I should like to finish my meal."

His comrades gave considering nods. Relief evident, Varoi helped himself to another cup of steaming beverage.

As those around him made as though to leave, Varoi decided to make one further contribution to their education. He had noticed how tense some of the younger, less experienced warriors appeared and chose this moment to offer pertinent advice.

"One more thing ... I'm aware the situation with the Pulan army is unusual so you might wish to consider this: they are, as you know, a belligerent breed. The force ranged against us is excessive, making them well placed to win this battle. But first they must breach the ramparts, which, let me assure you, will be no easy matter. Next they must overcome our defence and, remember, we are taller on average, affording us a longer reach and providing some advantage in hand-to-hand combat, even against men wielding so brutal a weapon as they."

Varoi considered each one of them in turn through narrowed eyes, then added his final thought. "Lastly, consider this: they too are mortal, just like us. They can be killed. They have been defeated before. Just because they have never come against us in such numbers does not make them invincible." Varoi finished his speech with a dismissive wave of his hand, downed the last of his drink with one long swallow, and then rose to his feet, prepared to return to his post on the parapet.

Others had already risen, preceding Varoi along the stone-lined passage that led to the outer ward. Their quiet voices drifted back to him as they stole across the bailey where goats now chewed their way through mounds of hay and straw. The animals watched with the same slit-eyed curiosity they had shown before.

Ayesha glanced up as the door swung open for the umpteenth time, then returned to her designated task upon seeing a female head peering around the frame.

"Ready yet?" The question was always the same, voiced with varying degrees of optimism.

Soleil answered for them both. "Almost done." That answer too was roughly similar. "Have the trestles, pallets and stools I asked for been taken across?"

"Yes, and they've all been set up, just as you require. We are waiting on you."

"In that case, you may as well begin lugging some of these packs over. The piles of clean linen go first. I'll keep back enough for our needs here, just in case the battlements should get overrun and we have cause to leave

202

in a hurry, in which case I shall want an ample supply for when we return."

The head disappeared with its accustomed alacrity and Ayesha heard the sound of muffled conversation taking place. Moments later two male and one female shaman strode into the room and began removing those items Soleil pointed out.

She and Ayesha were last to leave the workshop, each carrying a useful selection of salves and soporifics, sufficient supplies to see them through the day. There was no point, as Soleil pointed out, in taking too extensive an amount, just in case they were forced to arrange a hasty retreat.

They hurried in the wake of the three shaman healers, who, despite being burdened, set a surprisingly brisk pace.

"Nervous?" asked Soleil, keeping her voice discreetly soft so that none around them might hear.

Ayesha shook her head, unwilling to admit to her true feelings in the face of Soleil's demeanour of calm assurance.

"That's good," said Soleil with the faintest of grins. "Since, if I'm being honest, I'm absolutely petrified by what we might be required to deal with during the coming days."

"You are?" Ayesha could not keep her disbelief from creeping into her voice. Soleil seemed so firmly in control of her emotions.

"Yes. And I'm more than amazed you don't feel the same."

Ayesha said, "I am frightened at the thought of what we'll be required to do. I wonder whether I'm really up to the task. I was just too ashamed to admit it."

"There's no harm in confessing to a healthy dose of fear, Ayesha. It's what keeps us alive at times like this. If we're lucky, this first day won't be all that bad."

"It won't?"

"Hopefully not. But who can say what this day will bring?"

They hurried across the broad, grassy expanse of the outer bailey, their progress marked by the inquisitive gaze of a small flock of goats.

"Where did they come from?" Ayesha enquired. No one chose to offer reply. They certainly hadn't been there the previous day when she and Varoi had returned from the settlement.

Varoi kept low as he approached the crenulated wall of the battlements. He knew what he expected to see and was well prepared.

A large army of Pulan swarmed across the land that fronted the steep curtain wall, approaching almost to the edge of the scarp that rose sharply along each bank of the dry moat. How long before that teeming hoard dared the moat and attempted to climb this very same wall?

Before they did, something else would have to happen. Something for which the garrison had just been prepared. He, along with several other warriors, those possessing sufficient shamanic power, had been assigned a most daunting task. Daunting, because if they failed, as fail eventually they must, it would herald the demolishment of certain parts of the wall. When that happened the battle for Tenbay would begin in earnest.

Along with others he was required to devise an adequate shield with which to protect the ramparts. That way, when the ballista began the bombardment, which was certain to happen very soon, some form of protection would keep at bay whatever missiles might be launched.

Varoi's prime point of guard lay to the right of the barbican. The shaman given that particular assignment was strong in the Power but young. Too young and inexperienced, in Varoi's opinion, to be trusted with so

204

important and onerous a task. But it was not he who had made this decision. All he could do was ensure that his own responsibility was adequately carried out.

None of those given this role had been required to assume such an undertaking before; and their brief practice session, carried out in the topmost room of the barbican, had highlighted a disturbing number of inadequacies among those present, together with certain disparities in skill.

Between them they possessed sufficient Power to perform as required. But Varoi harboured serious doubts that some of those nominated to crucial positions would perform as desired. It remained to be seen whether he was proved right.

"Husband your Powers," Varoi advised, as the small contingent of which he was part clattered its way back up the stairs. "Remember, we may have to last out not just this day but long into the night as well."

Some listened, nodding their agreement. But there were others less astute who turned on him with disparaging sneers. They said nothing, offered no opposing views. But their expressions said enough.

Varoi kept further thoughts and comments to himself. He would play his part in this defensive action. It was up to others to see they played theirs.

Five ballista confronted the fortress walls, close enough to do considerable damage without a shielding spell in place. Four were positioned opposite each of the long walls that stretched between the guard towers, while one monster opposed the barbican itself. This sight alone sufficed to raise the hairs on his neck.

Varoi steeled himself for the assault to come and turned his attention to the warrior alongside him. They were working in pairs, the better to combat fatigue in either partner. Varoi hoped this precaution would suffice to stave off disaster.

"Remember what I just said. Always keep something in reserve."

Aheb nodded his agreement. At least this youngster had sense enough to listen to well-meant advice. A pity others were less willing.

Varoi wondered when the Pulan ballista might be brought into action. For now it was mainly a war of nerves. But he could see men working on the huge machines and knew it could be only a matter of time. The waiting would be over soon enough.

A rustling behind drew his attention back to the activity of some fellow Shakar. Warriors had begun removing heavy tarps used to drape over some form of equipment. Varoi had paid scant heed to these items before. Now he wondered what it was that had been hidden there, its lower half screened behind battle-scarred walls. A brief glimpse of what appeared to be scaffolding served him no useful clue.

Curiosity piqued, he asked Aheb, "What is that? What are they doing there?"

Aheb's grin grew incandescent, his huge canines lending a wolfish expression to his face.

"Shall I make you guess, Lieutenant?" Varoi noticed how the young warrior reverted to a formal mode of address now their two commanders were in attendance.

Varoi gave a negligent shrug. "Please yourself, Aheb. It makes no difference since I truly do not have a clue."

The grin remained, evidence of Aheb's smug satisfaction. Aheb's golden eyes glinted with sly amusement.

"The Pulan think us unprepared for this engagement, an assumption of which they are about to be rudely disabused. Let them see that we, too, possess the ability to respond in kind, to create equal havoc and commotion."

Varoi lifted his brows in querulous frustration.

"Can you imagine?" Aheb expounded. "Surely you must recall: Tenbay has its own ballista?"

"Atop the keep? This I already know. It's too far distant to aid us now."

"Atop the ramparts as well. And, should the battlements be overrun, we have the means by which to disable them swiftly to prevent them being turned on our fleeing garrison.

Varoi glanced behind to find one of the siege engines already revealed.

"I had no idea. Still, huge rocks will make minimal impression against an army of this size."

"Not large boulders, but small. Small and deadly, as Commander com 'Varicci likes to say. And you'll find we have an ample supply of ammunition in store."

Varoi wished that Aheb had kept his rival's name out of their discussion, but could not deny the ballista should make a useful addition to those weapons available. And a considerable impact once the conflict got under way, provided they performed as required.

He now recalled the pile of pebbles, smooth and round, plus the equally large mound of water-worn gravel piled up on the quay and stacked in each corner atop the keep. And realised too their intended usage: small and deadly did indeed describe their purpose well.

Varoi braced himself, trickling the necessary amount of Power into his shield as yet another huge boulder headed his way. For now he was taking the brunt of this assault, with Aheb holding his strength in reserve. The younger Shakar was contributing as necessary from time to time, and the arrangement was working well so far.

The barrage had begun early and it was now late afternoon. Varoi wondered how long the Pulan planned to continue.

Each contact with the protective shield produce a flare of rainbow luminescence the like of which Varoi had never before witnessed, accompanied by a corresponding jar of pain. The pain was bearable but weakening; nothing he could not withstand, for now.

He wondered how the other teams of shaman fared, faced with such stressful conditions. It was the continual drain on Power that troubled him most, not for himself so much as for those of less experience. So far he had managed to ensure that Aheb did not suffer similar debilitating effects. He expected there to be problems soon, though. The bombardment was ceaseless. No sooner had one boulder been catapulted away than the teams manning the ballista had them cranked down, refilled and yet another missile launched on its way.

The main force of attacking Pulan seemed none too pleased to find their assault delayed by magical means. Their early demeanour of arrogant assurance had soured. The first shouts of derision had died away to an angry murmur that was almost a growl. Varoi could see how this delay had spoilt their plans, but could find no measure of sympathy for their plight; only sad recognition that, however determined, none of the shamans involved in this defence could endure indefinitely.

The ballista atop the ramparts remained idle. They would not be brought into action until the assault proper was well under way.

A slight tug at his sleeve proved a welcome distraction. Varoi focused his attention there, allowing his Power to be concentrated into the shield even as he turned away. To his surprise he became immediately aware of Aheb taking up the reins and, with a swift nod of gratitude, allowed his control to slip away. He was still there to be called on if necessary, but it gave him welcome respite and a good chance for Aheb to prove his ability.

He was confronted by a wide and confident grin.

"Froglet!" he cried in dismayed alarm. "What are you doing here? It is unsafe."

Toku's ebullient grin faded to a rare scowl. "Don't you dare tell me what I can do, Varoi. I may not yet be a full-blooded male but I am old enough to bear weapons in defence and, should the need arise, that is exactly what I would do. If I am old enough to die, then I am old enough to fight, to stand second in the line of defence behind my sire and the other males. So, don't you *dare* deny my right …"

Varoi raised a placating hand. "Enough, Froglet; I am suitably reminded. That still doesn't explain why you are here now."

Toku's unrepentant grin returned. "I bring refreshment for you and the other warriors. I and those others in my group."

"What others?" wondered Varoi doubtfully, his suspicions aroused by Toku's relaxed attitude, whatever he might wish to imply to the contrary.

"My brother Sami and three others have permission from our sires and both commanders, so any protest you might seek to make is already overruled."

Varoi managed a wan smile as he accepted the brass cup full of water Toku offered. He now noticed the large water skin slung about Toku's shoulders and the leather harness that draped his chest on which similar vessels were hung. There was immense pride in the youngling's stance. Pride that he had been permitted to assume this role. Varoi had not the heart to deny him that right.

"Have a care, Froglet." There was affection in his glance even as he started to turn away, prepared to resume the task that Aheb had so readily assumed.

"Ayesha also does her duty this day."

Varoi stilled, chilled to the marrow by a swift stab of dread as that last comment sank in.

209

Slowly he turned back. Certain he had heard correctly, still he felt compelled to ask, "Ayesha? In what way does your sister give aid?"

"She assists the healers. She is not alone. Still, I thought you should know."

"You did? I assume you refer to her work in the infirmary, which is situated a safe distance from here."

"If you think that, you don't know my sister all that well."

Varoi's sharp glance was a warning of which Toku took prompt heed. Moderating his tone, he proceeded to explain.

"The healers have set themselves up in the lower level of the barbican, the better to give aid when the fighting begins. I have words with her occasionally. Is there a message you would like delivered?"

It was all he could do not to growl. Did he have a message? Yes he had a message. Just not one *she* would want to hear.

He wanted her safe. As far from this conflict as possible. But she was not safe at all ... and neither were Toku ... or Sami. It made him despair. *All three precious eggs in one basket: how long before the handle broke?*

Chapter 9: Impact

Varoi raised both hands to his temples, knowing his concentration was frayed. It wasn't just that his reserves of Power were diminishing; some other anomaly was involved. Nowhere along the length of the ramparts did the individual shields meet. Each pair of shamans played their part, but independently of those stationed alongside. How long before the Pulan noticed this discrepancy? They had not done so thus far. How long before a slight change in trajectory or a potential near miss found the inevitable weakness.

It was a question to which he hoped both commanders were applying their minds. They too possessed shamanic Power, unlike the Pulan. The deficiency must be visible to others not required to maintain the shield.

Another boulder drove with a whump into the magical barrier. Energy dissipated outwards across the shield as the stone tumbled downwards into the moat.

Slowly a mound was beginning to form where it landed atop the pile. Varoi believed this, too, was cause for concern. Might it not aid the Pulan later, once the wall had finally been breached? He had no way of knowing, but still found it a worrying thought.

To his left the magical barrier protecting the barbican pulsed gently. Too much power was being employed there. Yet another cause for concern.

It was not quite twilight. One more hour before the sun went down and still no sign of let-up in the barrage. Carts heavy laden with boulders were still arrayed alongside each ballista.

And *still* the Pulan army waited, silent now as they had not been before. They too must realise it was just a matter of time before the heavy bombardment had some effect. It worried him.

Varoi raised his head. Feeling his partner tire, Aheb had seized the reins. Smoothly, he maintained the shield, and, despite his lapsed concentration, Varoi could tell that Aheb was well in command; and he didn't waste effort, as others plainly did.

Varoi's attention strayed to the two shaman protecting the barbican. Their contribution was vital to the overall success of this ruse. That pair had competed, each determined to outdo his partner, since this task began. Varoi took in their condition at a glance. Their situation had changed. Their stance was unnatural. Something was horribly wrong.

Next he glanced to his right, where the adjoining shield was still in place. No longer did it pulsate with vibrant energy. Instead, it flickered and dimmed.

A chance movement caught his eye and he jerked his head back that way, feeling his helmet drift askew and cursing his reduced warrior's tail, which was responsible for that situation. It bothered him, but not nearly as much as the huge missile that had just been loosed.

It was larger and heavier than most; that much was apparent at a glance. But something else was different, too. Those men in charge of that ballista had changed trajectory. Worse! The shield at which they now aimed had not the strength to stop a child's fist, let alone a massive boulder.

There was no time in which to amend matters. Beside him, Aheb stood firm. All he could do was act on instinct. Varoi ran, ignoring the angry bellow from behind. He did not stop or look round, but quickened his pace.

Varoi slowed to a stop before the door to the barbican, which was flung wide. Gripping the frame with his fists, he leant forward as far as he dare. Bracing himself, he yelled a command.

There was urgency evident in his tone, a strong surge of compulsion attached.

They had to get out of there: *now!*

He heard a thump as the huge rock clouted the barbican, causing its structure to shake. Sharp movement underfoot sufficed to make his balance shift.

Holding on by his fingernails was not enough. Varoi, slipping, lost his grip. Then, as the ground rose to meet him, he plummeted feet first. He just had time in which to realise, before darkness swept all further thought aside, *it was too late.*

His efforts had all been in vain.

Ayesha was bored. She couldn't believe how bored she'd become. She had expected action, a chance to play her part by rendering aid to those injured in the fighting. Instead, she sat here twiddling her thumbs. She might as well have brought her weaving or her embroidery frame. She could have sat here like some old crone waiting for the end.

It made her want to grind her teeth with frustration, this extended lack of purpose. But she could not. That was a male means of expressing irritation. How she hated hearing that sound. She refused to show vexation in that way.

"You wait, Ayesha," Soleil's voice was reassuringly bright and enthusiastic. "Tomorrow, when all hell breaks loose and you're surrounded by spilt blood and broken bones, you'll recall this peace and long for it again."

"That I shall not," Ayesha ground out the words between clenched teeth. "I just wish there was something useful I could do."

"I'll put the kettle on. At least we can enjoy an uninterrupted brew."

"Not more tea," Ayesha moaned. "My innards are already awash."

The trouble was, they had nothing better to do. All five of them sat like tailor's dummies, in various poses of ennui, waiting for duty to call.

And then, without prior intent, for some reason she could not explain, Ayesha rose from her seat and headed for the outer door.

A voice echoed down the stairwell. She paid it no particular heed. Instead, she and all others present, hastened to leave.

How strange!

Ayesha stopped and stamped her foot in a fit of pique. She was *not* an automaton. She refused to mindlessly react like those others around. Slowly she started to turn.

Ayesha felt, rather than heard, the impact, but guessed at once what it must mean. Beneath her feet foundations shuddered. The sturdy iron braced door creaked in its frame. Trestles and pallets shifted sideways even as she reached out a hand to steady herself against the nearest wall. A shower of coarse dust and grit pattered down upon those pallets ranged along one outer wall.

The neatly-folded packs of sterile instruments jiggled, while baskets full of potions skittered sideways. Three precious jars of ointment, resting atop the nearest trestle, slid sideways across freshly scrubbed boards, to teeter precariously before starting their fall.

Ayesha flung out an intervening hand, catching one as the others escaped her grasp. They fell to the ground with a tinkling crash, which set her teeth on edge. Another discordant sound reached her ears.

Something heavy was coming down the stairwell.

Something that bounced solidly against wall and door.

Something that would not be stopped until it reached the bottom.

Instinctively, she ducked and covered her head. A stunned silence enveloped the room. Ayesha rose to her feet and looked round, expecting the worst.

214

Soleil also stood, looking down, at the shattered mess of glass shards and salve near her feet, the remains of a useful emollient that could never now be put to good use.

"Oh bother," she said. "After all our effort. Still, Ayesha, at least one jar is saved. And there *are* others."

Soleil stopped speaking, aware that Ayesha's attention was focused elsewhere. Her lucent green eyes were wide with horror, and there was a stricken expression on her face. She was staring aghast past Soleil's shoulder, mouth open, bereft of speech. Slowly, Soleil turned round.

Ayesha could not tear her glance away from the tall male who had just arrived at the foot of the stairs. His body lay slumped, his limbs entangled and his dark head impossibly askew. He looked dead.

"Oh, poor thing," Soleil, glancing back at Ayesha, saw she had not moved. "Come, Ayesha, let's see what can be done."

Still Ayesha did not twitch a muscle but, instead, stood as though transfixed.

Signs of impending disaster: the rapid pounding of boots coming down the stairwell, harassed shouting somewhere overhead, even the swirling eddies of choking dust, which threatened to obscure her view, could not distract from Soleil's focused intent. One of the male healers, prepared to assist, started to brush past. Soleil raised a restraining hand, waving him impatiently away. This would not do.

Once again she tried to gain Ayesha's attention. Hearing approaching footsteps on the stairs, and concerned as to what other disaster might be heading their way, she took a firm grip of Ayesha's shoulders and gave her a vigorous shake, to no avail.

The footsteps halted one floor up and she heard muffled voices overhead. In desperation Soleil drew back her hand and let fly.

The stinging slap to her face brought Ayesha out of her trance. Green eyes blazed with righteous indignation as she raised one hand to her cheek. Soleil gave her no time in which to offer protest.

"Snap out of it, child. This is no time to indulge your finer tendencies. This male is in urgent need of aid. And that *is* what you are here to provide."

"But he looks dead," wailed Ayesha. "It looks as if ..."

"... his neck is broken? Yes. I can see *that* for myself. But looks are no indication of his actual condition, child; as you should know well enough by now. Either way, he cannot stay there long. Come, Ayesha. Let's see what can be done."

If Ayesha moved somewhat reluctantly in the fallen male's direction it was understandable, but at least she moved. The clatter of footsteps coming downstairs galvanised Soleil into action. Grabbing Ayesha by the hand, she dragged her closer to the first injured warrior she was obliged to touch. There could be quite a few more before this day came to a close. Whatever happened, Ayesha needed this initiation, needed to get past the hysteria it had caused.

Dropping to her knees beside the body, Soleil said, "Look here, Ayesha. What can you see?" she directed her friend's attention to the ungainly tangle of limbs.

"Nothing. It's all such a horrible mess."

"Then perhaps you need a closer look, child."

Reluctantly, Ayesha knelt. As she did so she became aware of footsteps on the stairs. She wanted to look up, to look anywhere other than at what she was compelled to see. There was no evidence of blood as yet and for that she felt grateful, but something nagged at the back of her mind. She knew this male. Something about him was vaguely familiar, even though his face was not visible. His head was turned at an impossible angle, the

216

helm tilted sideways on. She refused steadfastly to consider what that might mean. Instead, she concentrated on what Soleil was saying.

Soleil bent closer. "He's still breathing and that's a plus. It gives us hope, at least. We need to disentangle his limbs, to get his helmet off and check his pulse. We'll start at the bottom and work our way up. You go on that side, Ayesha. You know what to do."

Surprisingly, she did. At least, Ayesha hoped she could remember all she'd recently been taught. It was one thing to examine a healthy body, but quite another to check and reorganise limbs that might be damaged in some way.

"What if we harm him?" she wanted to know. "What if I cause him pain?"

"Be very careful and, if in doubt, don't be afraid to speak up. If he cries out in pain that'll be good news."

"In what way good?" Ayesha wanted to know. She was running her hands gently down first one leg and then the other. With his boots on there were limitations to what she could feel.

"Well, for one thing it means he's regaining consciousness and can tell us whereabouts he's hurt. For another it means he has sensation in that limb."

"Oh," said Ayesha, checking his right thigh, relieved to find nothing amiss. Carefully she removed his greave, then straightened his lower limb. Nothing grated and she found no overt sign of damage. Soleil, watching, gave a swift nod of approval before moving on to check his other arm.

Whoever had been pounding down the stairs came to an abrupt halt.

"How is he?"

"We don't yet know," said Soleil, raising her eyes to the questioner's gaze. Seeing the distinctive black armour of a Konicci trained warrior and the red crested helm of rank, she amended her statement slightly. "He's

217

unconscious, Commander com 'Dolino. So far as I can tell, we'll be lucky to find no broken bones, but I live in hope. My greatest concern is his neck, which appears to be twisted. He fell a considerable way and landed badly."

"So I see. Is there anything I can do to assist?"

"Not at the moment, Commander. May I know his name, in case …?" Soleil left the sentence unfinished, certain they both knew what she meant.

His swift sideways glance at Ayesha was thoughtful. "Let's first see how he fares."

How very tactful, thought Soleil. Not many males would understand. But then, perhaps she had developed a rather jaundiced view of male attitudes over the years. After all, she reflected, not all full-blooded males would react the same.

Soleil rocked back on her heels, her part of the examination concluded for now, and watched her student appreciatively. Ayesha completed her task and straightened her back, settling her gaze on Soleil.

"The next part of this operation," said Soleil, "is more delicate and requires considerable care. I feel sure you will manage it perfectly well. Ayesha, I need you to slide your fingers up inside his helm keeping your hands in direct line with his shoulders. I want to know whether his head appears to be twisted in any way."

"Why me?" Ayesha protested. "I've never done anything like this before."

"Then it'll be good experience for you," Soleil replied, tart. "Besides which, your fingers are longer, more slender than mine, and I don't expect there to be much room. Now, when you're ready, do as I direct. I want to know exactly where his ears are placed; hopefully they are still in line with his shoulders."

"His ears?" Ayesha exclaimed.

"Yes, child. Every male has them, I'm reliably assured. Although their ability to listen leaves something to be desired."

A loud snort of masculine laughter caused Soleil to glance up. She locked eyes with the commander still seated a couple of stairs up. Soleil flushed with an acute sense of embarrassment; she had quite forgotten he was there.

"I'm sorry, Commander, I did not mean to infer ..."

He gave a dismissive wave of his hand. "Don't apologise on my account. I often wonder the same when otherwise competent members of my cohort do the exact opposite of what they've been told. Admittedly it doesn't occur often. But still, what you see here is a prime example of what can befall."

Soleil nodded her understanding and watched as Ayesha's slim fingers vanished inside the battered helm.

Consciousness returned to Varoi in stages. At first only muffled conversation penetrated the prevailing gloom. Then other sensations began making themselves felt. It alarmed him somewhat that, despite opening his eyes as wide as he could, he appeared unable to see. What had become of his *ananaha* abilities? A numbing ache in the region of his lower spine caused him concern since he seemed incapable of moving his lower limbs, as though a great weight had settled upon them, holding him down. Worse still was the impression of being stifled. He couldn't get enough air into his lungs, no matter how hard he laboured to draw in a breath.

The touch of cool fingers sliding slowly along the side of his neck felt equally strange. Whose were they and what did they hope to achieve?

Varoi cudgelled his beleaguered brain, desperate to make sense of the situation. What was it that had just happened? He recalled seeing a huge missile aimed directly at one section of wall adjacent to the barbican, an area where the adjoining shields failed to meet. He had taken the risk of warning those on duty in the lower levels of the barbican, knowing that Aheb had their section well warded against attack. In desperation he had included a direct, shamanic imperative along with the command to vacate, not something he would ordinarily do.

His next memory was of a sudden jarring sensation, of losing his balance as everything shifted underfoot. The next instant he was hurtling downstairs and not with any degree of control, feet first until a landing area created an abrupt change in direction, which bounced him off the opposite wall. He remembered being launched head over heels, the rough jouncing that incident incurred bruising more than male dignity. After that he must have passed out, all else being naught but a blur.

He must have arrived at the bottom by now. No wonder everything felt so weird. Instinctively he tried to speak.

"I'm fine."

His voice came out as a muted growl that rumbled around in his brain and seemed hardly adequate for gaining attention. He guessed that someone was trying help him in some way. Those cool fingers sliding delicately across his skin raised goose bumps along his spine. He had to make himself understood. Yet the words he sought failed to emerge.

"Right," said Soleil, now confident their next act would cause no lasting harm. "If his ears are in line, as they ought to be, that implies one of two things." She sucked in a slow, calming breath before proclaiming. "Either his head faces forward as it should and hopefully no damage has occurred or ..." she paused, then went on in a rush, "... his head is twisted back to front, in which case naught can be done."

She allowed the enormity of her statement to wash over her listeners, while she reached back to accept the board that one of the other healers held.

Into the stunned silence that followed, the Commander spoke.

"I sincerely hope he *is* still alive. He's a reliable officer, if a little precipitate at times. But I seldom find fault when sufficient caution is applied. I should hate to lose him."

Soleil could only nod and shrug. "It's in the lap of the Goddess, I'm afraid." Shifting a little sideways she added. "Seeing as you *are* still here, and in the ideal position to assist, I wonder, would you oblige me by supporting his head and shoulders as I slide this stretcher into place? Ayesha, stay exactly as you are," she instructed her protégé. "Don't move a muscle until I say you may."

The Commander said, "I can just see what's left of his warrior's tail. I assume that's a good sign."

"The best, providing it's in the correct position," Soleil confirmed. "Now, let's just get his helmet removed so we can place him on the pallet."

Varoi, hearing her comment, tried again to be heard. "I'm ..." but a sudden movement of his helm caused a distraction and he promptly fell silent as a sideways motion of his headgear smeared the soft part of his nose across his face, restricting his airway even more.

He tried to raise vigorous protest, to get their attention in some way, wanting them to desist. But the uncomfortable tugging continued until something abruptly gave way and his helm was mercifully removed.

Varoi blinked, trying to bring his surroundings back into focus. But his hair had come loose in the struggle and now partially obscured his face. Still, at last he could breathe freely again, despite a considerable weight pressing down on his chest.

Swallowing hard, he sucked in a breath and sought, again, to make himself understood.

"I'm fine." Muffled though it sounded to his ears, at last Varoi managed to make himself heard.

"You're not fine, Lieutenant," said a gruff voice somewhere overhead. "It doesn't take an expert to see that. But by some incredible mischance you do seem very much alive, which means that not only have you survived to plague me, but you still fall under my command. So, until I decree otherwise, you'll stop mumbling protests and do exactly as the healers advise. I trust I make myself abundantly clear. They are here to sort you out and I am present to see that you obey, even if I have to sit on your chest and shove their foul potions down your gullet myself."

"Really, Commander," Soleil objected, "there's no need to be quite so harsh."

Commander com 'Dolino perked his dark brows. "Is there not? Tell me then that he didn't almost succeed in getting himself killed."

Soleil sighed and shook her head in resignation. She found it impossible to wholly understand this male's psyche. One moment he was highly solicitous, the next all rancorous recrimination. What did it take to please him? Glancing up, she caught the commander's eye. Hard to believe, but beneath that darkly ominous scowl she could swear she detected a sly glint of humour. With most of his face concealed behind his helm, Soleil could not quite distinguish the commander's features, but there was no doubting the way his eyes crinkled at the corners. Confirming, he smiled.

Ayesha remained silent as she helped Soleil and Commander com 'Dolino ease the pallet beneath Varoi's prone body, then assisted in carrying him to one of the cots set against the wall. Her mind was a turmoil of powerful emotions: fear, anger and raw grief. They boiled just below the surface waiting to erupt. Hidden behind her façade of outward composure, it was only a matter of time before one or the other broke free.

The commander straightened. "I'm relieved to see my lieutenant is in capable hands. Hopefully he'll recover fast. I must return to my duties. Let me know if he will be incapacitated for long." He wagged an admonishing finger in Varoi's direction. "Do as you're told, Varoi," he warned. With a quick nod of satisfaction he spun on his heel and strode away.

Soleil looked down at her patient to see how that last caution had been received and did her best not to smile at Varoi's rueful grimace.

Glancing up at Ayesha, who still hovered alongside, she said, "We need to remove as much of his armour as possible in order that I can make a proper assessment of his injuries. Let's get that done first."

Ayesha nodded in silent agreement and they set about their task. As they worked, Soleil talked, asking questions of her patient and taking careful note of his replies. Plainly, Varoi thought this procedure needless, yet he tolerated it with stoic acceptance.

Ayesha allowed her fingers to undertake the various tasks with equal poise. None present would be aware of her reaction until the entire situation was satisfactorily resolved.

Soleil carried out the necessary actions, asking Varoi to raise and lower each limb in turn, testing reflexes and checking for injury not so far revealed. Reluctantly, Varoi admitted to a small amount of pain in the lower region of his spine.

"Turn over, Lieutenant."

Varoi did as instructed, laying face down, acutely aware of Ayesha's considering gaze.

Ayesha watched as Soleil gently eased one hand under the thin leather strap that covered his loins ... and

223

felt an unexpected stab of jealousy. She took a swift step back, seeking to distance herself from the cause of this unwelcome emotion.

"Nothing broken, Lieutenant, you'll be pleased to hear. You're just a mite bruised from the lengthy fall. You're lucky. I consider you fit enough to return to duty. Get some rest later if you can. I'll dose you with a mild palliative before you leave. Nothing that will slow or hamper your actions, just enough to ease your various aches and pains." Finished with her patient Soleil turned away. "Help him to dress, Ayesha, if you would."

Slowly, Varoi rolled over and sat up. Ayesha glared at him, unable to hide any longer the strength of her feelings. She curled her hands into fists.

Help him? She wanted to help him to a good swift kick.

Instead, she struggled to master her temper enough for speech.

"Fake!" She hissed the word out from between clenched teeth. "You are a fake, Lieutenant com 'Domicci: an out-and-out fraud. To think you had all these good people worried on your behalf when there was no need, no need whatsoever. They thought your stupid neck broken. Do you realise that? That or something far worse, when there was no likelihood of that at all."

She had been profoundly shocked to discover it was Varoi sprawled helpless at the foot of the stairs, shocked and fearful at first. But then she'd recalled her sudden unexplained urge to rise from her seat and make for the outer door; she and all her companions had been affected the same way. It led to but one conclusion. Varoi had used a spell of compulsion and this enraged her more than anything else. Fear and anger held violent sway over her emotions.

Varoi looked her straight in the eye and lifted his brows in quizzical enquiry.

224

It was just too much.

Ayesha injected her next words with the maximum amount of venom at her command.

"You are too thick skulled, too ridiculously muscle-bound for such misfortune to lay *you* low." Ayesha stopped, drew in a ragged breath and, in a voice so soft it could barely be heard, declared, "I am a fool. To think for just one minute I was beginning to care." She lowered her head to stare at her hands. All anger seemed to have drained out of her with that last admission.

Her declaration was so unexpected it took Varoi completely by surprise. Risking a sharp rebuttal, he asked, "And do you, Ayesha? Do you care?"

"Yes." She sounded angry all over again. Lifting her head she looked him straight in the eye. "More fool me."

He rose to his feet with the lithe, supple grace of a panther. Ayesha began to retreat, to place distance between them, to move safely beyond reach. Varoi took hold of her upper arms, sliding both hands downwards in a slow caress.

Ayesha stilled. Breath caught in her throat. He was all male pride, pure and simple. She could not fault him for that. But she knew if she did not escape him now she never would. Still she hesitated, allowing herself to be lulled.

As he drew her toward him, lowering his head to hers that they might kiss, she slipped both hands under his gambeson, slid them inside the waist of his leather wrap and then ... because she wished him to know she would not be taken for granted and as a timely reminder should such be required that, like the panther, she too possessed teeth and claws ... she bit down on his lower lip and dug her nails into the small pad of flesh on either side of his lower spine.

Carefully, Varoi lifted his head and she let go. Though his golden eyes gleamed, she could tell nothing of his reaction from his expression: his face was closed. He did not smile; nor did he utter one single word of rebuke. If anything, his gaze seemed more intense, fiercer than she had ever seen it before.

Now she would learn what manner of mate he might be. Hopefully ...

Varoi gathered her close, dragging her tight against his hard, muscular frame. His mouth, when it claimed hers, was hot and demanding. There was a rampant ferocity about his kiss that had not been apparent before.

She leaned in close, became soft and pliant as she moulded her supple body to his. Varoi's hands slid lower, pulling her against him, making her abundantly aware of his growing need. A low growl rumbled up from deep within. Ayesha felt it reverberate throughout her entire being; the beast within him wanting to break free. Ayesha allowed him to take charge, to manipulate her however he pleased, raw passion swamping her awareness. She lost all sense of who and where she was.

Ayesha wondered, was this how it felt to be joined as mates? Was this what it meant to be complete?

A discreet cough from behind caused them to spring apart.

Soleil ignored their guilty reaction, instead offering Varoi a small cup of evil smelly brew.

"It smells worse than it tastes, but it will bring you ease."

Varoi accepted the proffered cup and thanked her. He downed the contents with one long swallow and, shuddering, gave a wry grimace of distaste.

"If that, in your opinion, is none too bad, I cannot imagine what worse potions you produce."

Soleil gave a merry laugh.

"Return here in dire need and you may find out."

"Not me. No disrespect, Soleil, but I hope not to need your attentions again."

226

"See that you don't," she warned. Turning away, she left Ayesha to help Varoi don his armour again.

He was remarkably quick about the task, considering the scrapes and bruises he must have suffered during his tumble downstairs. His leather armour had provided ample protection for his upper body, but below his waist those same lambrequins that gave him such freedom of movement on the field of conflict had proved scant protection against stone risers and treads.

As Ayesha handed him the various items of attire, helping to fasten them closed, she felt Varoi's glance upon her often. There was puzzlement in that golden gaze.

As she helped buckle the last items of his harness, he spoke.

"Ayesha, if I have angered you in some way of which I am not aware I wish you would say."

Her hands stilled at their task and she looked up. There was sadness in her voice as she replied, "You set me under a spell of compulsion. Why?"

"I had to, Ayesha. There was no other way to be sure."

"Sure of what, Varoi?"

"I had to be sure of your safety."

"There was no need."

"I thought there was. It was a general command to civilians present in the barbican."

"And you think that makes it better? Because, let me assure you, it does not. Never, and I mean never, set me under a spell of compulsion again."

She fixed him with an adamant gaze that brooked no further argument on his part and saw him nod. Satisfied, she finished her task and tucked the spare leather away.

"Visit me later, Varoi."

If she could be obstinate, so could he.

"I don't know that I can."

Determined, Ayesha caught his eye.

"Not with the mind touch. I want you to come to my room."

Varoi's face showed his understanding; but still he offered excuse.

"I may not be able, Ayesha. I have no way of knowing what duties I'll be assigned. We're under siege. That makes a difference you know."

She nodded and he started to leave. At the foot of the stairwell he spun back.

"I'll try," was all he said, and then he was gone.

Ayesha turned, to find herself the subject of avid curiosity. She threw up her hands.

"Well?"

No answer came. She could guess what they must be thinking. But if they thought she should be contrite they could think again.

Varoi strode out on to the parapet to find that dusk was falling fast. Out on the fen a village of tents had sprung into being, at its centre one larger than all the rest. Two standards fluttered in the chill breeze, atop tall poles erected in the clear space before this pavilion. One depicted a white bear on a field of blue, the other a bird of prey with a lightening bolt grasped in its extended talons.

So, Ice and Helvan commanded this campaign.

"There you are, Varoi, and just in time." His head jerked round in response to his commander's words. "So glad you've decided to join us. As you can see," Commander com 'Dolino flicked a dismissive wave towards the battlements behind, "events have moved on since your unseemly departure."

He paused, waiting for the expected sniggers to die down. Varoi did his best not to grin. More often than not, he was guilty of gallows humour. It made a change for him to bear the brunt.

"Divide into your watches, Shakar. First and third, go for a well-earnt respite. Second, you remain here. Though the ballista are now silent, they may start up again at any time. Shaman, to your respective posts; I'll see you relieved soon."

Varoi went to relieve Aheb, who was part of the first watch. The young warrior looked sorely in need of rest. They exchanged a few brief words before Aheb hastened away. Enough to reassure Varoi that no more missiles had breached their defences during his prolonged absence.

Varoi turned back to the battlements. A light drizzle had started to fall and out on the fens Pulan cook-fires, hundreds it seemed, flared yellow in the fading light.

The land across from the moat was deserted. Apart from a few raised voices, the Pulan were ominously quiet.

What did they plan for the morrow? Varoi would have liked to know, if only so that he might be adequately prepared.

Varoi made as if to stand. Ayesha placed a restraining hand on his arm.

"Don't go."

"I must, Ayesha. I've important duties to attend."

"I'm frightened, Varoi. Don't leave me, not yet."

"Frightened, Princess, what of?"

"What if we don't win? What if the Pulan overrun Tenbay? What then?"

"We will win, Ayesha. I promise you that. We may be outnumbered, but still there is much that remains in our favour. The Pulan will be banished. I and the other Shakar will see to that."

"But what if you fail?"

Varoi felt sure he understood. It was custom among many Pulan to rape any females found amongst their defeated foe. To female Shakar this was a punishment

229

worse than death, especially so when virtue remained intact. The Pulan were not known to differentiate between human and Shakar.

There was but one defence he might employ to aid Ayesha. It would not save her life, but at least her virtue would remain her own, to bestow wheresoever she saw fit. Her choice to whom it would be given. He had tried once to initiate the process to no avail; the hostile attack by a Pulan scout had proved an unwelcome distraction. In order to work it required her complete cooperation.

More important was his lack of knowledge regarding how it might be deployed. The last record of a Shakar shielding was during the Lost Leven wars, when Diabolon and seven lost immortals had rampaged unchecked across the face of Etheria. Driving mortals before them like sheep, they had scarred the land until it was almost unfit for habitation, taking mortals to mate with as they pleased.

It had been a time of widespread devastation, which most humans seemed to forget. But not the Shakar or the Tsaidou, unlikely allies in times of dire adversity. Between them, the shaman of both races had joined ranks and stood firm in the face of iniquitous persecution and had, at the last, prevailed.

There was a saying prevalent among the Shakar: *"ole ve lo sa baram"*, meaning "what once was will be again." Sadly, most human breeds paid scant heed to this prophesy.

Varoi would try to shield Ayesha if that was her desire. He had the necessary Power; it was expertise he lacked. First, he must prepare her, before placing a safe distance between them, keeping her safe from his attentions as well as those of the Pulan. Up close he might be tempted to forget his good intentions. He might lose all self control. Distance would provide the necessary protection for them both.

"We won't fail, Ayesha, you have my word."

She looked away, refusing to meet his gaze.

"Papa thinks I should give you a chance. Allow you and Schezan to vie for my favours in time-honoured fashion by proving yourselves worthy of my regard."

It was what she had told before, but the fact that her sire also believed this to be the right decision was promising.

"And what of you, Ayesha? Is that what you want?"

Her gaze swung back, to lock with amber eyes that glinted warm in the candle-flame's ambient light.

"I think ... I *know* that I want you to stay. If for only a short while. I desire your company. Unless you think that too much trouble."

Varoi let out his breath with a shuddering sigh. What mattered most at this time was Ayesha's need of him.

"If it does, I shall set matters right. Have no fear."

"Then will you please kiss me again?"

Varoi leant forward, gently cupping her face with his hands. Candle flames flickered from sconces on the nearby wall. Reaching up he snuffed out the flames with his fingers, returning his attention to what he had been about to start.

"Bayshir." He breathed, so soft, so sweet the endearment whispered against her skin. He called her "Beloved" and, despite his obvious strength, handled her tenderly. Ayesha marvelled that, in all the time she had known Schezan since declaring him Chosen, not once had he managed so much as this.

Varoi kissed her gently, first on her brow, then on each eyelid in turn, each kiss no more than a feather-light brush. He touched his lips to the tip of her nose, the petal-soft flesh of her cheek and, finally, the tilted corners of her mouth. Each kiss he bestowed merely left her wanting more. Varoi stopped.

Their lips were close, so close that Ayesha felt the moist whisper of air caressing her lips as he breathed. His golden glance was warm, flowing over her like molten honey. Whatever it was Varoi had in mind, she couldn't wait to find out.

Heart beating fast, she rose on tiptoe. At last their lips met. Ayesha pressed her body closer to his. They were already seated side by side on her bed. She wondered, what more encouragement could he possibly need?

Slowly, Varoi moved back, and then stood. Ayesha's eyes flew wide open in surprise. He must not leave her, not like this. But it seemed he had only risen in order to remove his armour. Relief flooded her at this realisation. She had been unaware how much she craved his touch till he seemed about to depart.

Ayesha swung her legs up on to the bed, garbed in nothing more concealing than the flimsy shift she wore to sleep. Impatient, she pulled this over her head and set it aside as Varoi settled back on the bed and then turned to face her.

"Ayesha?"

But she had no desire for further conversation. What she wanted could be better accomplished without words. Raising one hand, she seized fast hold of his warrior's tail, guiding his mouth unerringly down to hers. His kiss began gentle. By contrast, hers was demanding. He must understand the hunger trapped inside.

Passion blossomed unrestrained, as with one hand he supported her head while the other strayed further afield; supplying her body a fond caress, each touch teasing, tantalizing, his actions gentle but sure.

She murmured a soft endearment, intent on that one wandering hand; then knew a brief surge of frustration when that hand stilled. Despite her fierce grasp of his warrior's tail he managed to raise his head.

She drew in a sharp breath to upbraid him. But she stopped as the wandering hand moved lower still, coming to rest atop the slight swell of her belly, fingertips nestling in crisp, silken curls.

"I can afford you protection, Ayesha, if that is what you want. But you must be very sure. Once set in place it cannot be easily removed."

Tears glimmered in her eyes and on her lashes as she nodded acknowledgement of the protection he was willing to confer. It was the chance, should the Pulan succeed in overrunning Tenbay, of denying any one of them sexual intimacy, a cross-species act, which was wholly repugnant to female Shakar. Death was preferable to mutilation and rape. The protection Varoi offered was infinitely better than that.

Her answer came in swift response.

"Yes. Oh yes. Please."

Then her grip on his hair tightened and she drew his mouth back down to hers. Eyes closed in silent surrender, Ayesha opened herself up to him completely, body and soul.

Varoi seized the advantage she offered with a profound sense of gratitude, certain it should take only a little effort to prepare the way. He wanted Ayesha so much he ached with the pain of denial. Yet he dare not abuse her trust. Instead, he must ready her for what he was about to attempt. A little light teasing should suffice to encourage a receptive mood.

Varoi pushed his tongue past Ayesha's lips as she gave herself into his care. Her heartfelt invitation was one he could not misconstrue. Gently he explored the possibilities such access allowed, permitting his tongue to express his heightened desire, even while he sought to satisfy hers. This act in which they now engaged was a preliminary to something far more consequential. The prelude to greater trust and a shared understanding of personal needs.

Tauntingly elusive, his tongue swirled past her teeth, then swept inside; avoiding direct contact with hers even as she pursued.

Ayesha moaned softly into his mouth. He felt the tension within her build. His caress insistent, he loosed a deep growl of satisfaction when she responded favourably to his exploration with slight movements of her hips, one hand holding his, in place encouraging him further, making him aware of her increasing need. Then, as his busy fingers eased her towards climax, he felt the inevitable slow shudder of release ripple its way through Ayesha's slim frame. At last, Varoi gave in to her persistence, allowing their dancing tongues to fully engage.

As Ayesha succumbed to sweet ecstasy, Varoi knew his first objective had been achieved.

Chapter 10: Shield

Ayesha released her grip on his warrior's tail. Lowering his head to the pillows, Varoi grew aware that his breathing came hard and fast, his gnawing hunger barely restrained. What he was primed to do next required trust and commitment on both their parts. Shielding could not be achieved otherwise. He knew *that* for a surety. There was but one means by which it might be applied.

The last time an intimate shielding had been employed was during the Lost Leven wars, at a time when those fallen gods referred to as "Lost" plagued females of every race and breed with their lustful attentions. And it had been considered a useful expedient, a preventative to counteract wanton lust.

Shakar were unique in possessing the ability to shield their females intimately, an act that had not proved wholly effective at first. Some females had succumbed to an Immortal's seduction, to the distress of their mate. Notable among such renegade Immortals were their leader Diabolon and Baylor, his trusted aide. Varoi knew the principles involved. With luck he would succeed in achieving his intended goal.

Varoi's heated gaze drew Ayesha; she saw how his eyes had changed from molten gold to dark, expressive pools. She wondered, did he regret what had just occurred? It had been her decision to accept his offer of magical protection, yet she had given him very little choice. Nor did he give any hint of his particular needs.

She watched with interest as he buckled his armour back in place, slipping his baldric over his head.

"I have to go, Ayesha. There will be trouble if I'm late."

"Go then, but reach for me later if you can. Awake or sleeping, I'll welcome your touch."

"Expect me soon," he murmured, turning to leave. As his hand sought the latch she forestalled him.

"One last kiss before you go. It need only be brief."

Returning swiftly, he leant down. She reached to twine her arms about his neck. His kiss was light, the merest brush, but she drew him close. Then, while he was thus distracted, she slid one hand up his inner thigh and found what she'd hoped to: the hard evidence of his arousal.

Gently removing her hand he stepped back.

"I must go; there's no time left."

He slipped through the door like a wraith, closing it quietly behind him, oblivious of the satisfied smile that crept across Ayesha's face.

Lying back she drifted off to sleep, her curved hip and smooth, silky thigh bathed by the moon's tinselled light. Varoi took note of her pose upon parting, unaware that the sublime, evocative image would lodge fast in his mind's eye.

Varoi strode the length of the corridor before slumping against a convenient wall. He knew that to complete the protective construct a sacrifice was required. That was his responsibility. One distinct option came immediately to mind. Nor did it entail immense effort on his part. That last kiss they'd shared held the pure, sweet taste of innocence on its breath. That, combined with her touch, which had exposed, to the fullest extent, his arousal, had almost seen him undone. He needed release and he needed it now.

Continuing along the corridor, he sought the nearest gardrobe, hoping to find it unoccupied at this late hour. Finding one he slipped inside, driving the bolt home. The unsavoury reek that assailed his nostrils was nauseating. Still, it would serve well for what he had in mind. It offered the required privacy but he must be quick. Turning about he spread-eagled his body upright against the nearest wall. Ayesha had charged him with providing her innocence with a protective shield. In this position his ardour would be suitably constrained. It was a matter of trust, one he dare not abuse. Though, with *lossa antario* deployed, there was always a risk.

Arms outstretched, legs spread, his shamanic powers aligned to encompass the extremity of his resonant ability, Varoi closed his eyes and focused his intent on the mind touch they shared. Determined to complete the task, he reached for Ayesha again. In this position he could perform no action, whether intrusive or invasive, nothing that might shatter her innocence. To do so would be in direct contravention of their accord

She was there, exactly as he'd hoped to find her. Her body was relaxed and receptive to his commands.

First he had to gain access to her female inhibitions; then he had to bind them and lock them up tight, making them secure and impervious to outside interference. Now that the selected construct had been initiated, only Ayesha and a mate of her choosing could be empowered to release those same wards. It would be just too bad if he were not the male in question. But then, such applications seldom proved perfect in any case.

He must stay calm. What he intended was laden with difficulty and risk. Despite the heat, which coiled in his belly like a living serpent, and the way his groin cramped with an unrelenting ache, it was imperative he attempt to relax. It would get worse before it got better. There was no hope for it, certain tasks had to be carried out. Now that the required permissions had been obtained he could proceed.

Closing his eyes he reached for Ayesha again, setting in train the necessary sequence of events. Then, laying all personal imperatives aside, he acknowledged the constraints in order to complete a construct of sufficient potency. The command consisted of a simple directive, one not easily misconstrued. He recited the last words of the incantation aloud.

"Accept me as you would no other. Protect yourself from all who seek to come between."

There. It was done.

Taking a pace back he dropped both arms and spun about. Relief was but an instant away ... and could not come fast enough.

Cursing fluently under his breath, he struggled free of his nether garments and took himself quickly in hand.

Eyes closed, his inner focus grew more intense. Ayesha stayed foremost in his mind's eye. He saw tawny hair spangled by moonlight, a negligent sprawl of lax limbs. Whether the vision were blessing or curse was impossible to say.

Varoi stood a moment looking down, breathing in her essence where it clung to hair and clothes. He savoured her sultry beauty ... and found her nubile repose too beguiling a temptation to resist.

Varoi heaved a heartfelt sigh, accepting the constraints he'd just imposed. Even as his mind furnished him with an image of Ayesha; his hand afforded him the necessary release. Varoi watched as a stream of viscous pink liquid disappeared into the midden below. It grieved him to waste his seed in this fashion, but he had no other choice. It was a torment, wanting her like this.

On the morrow he would learn whether, in fact, he had succeeded in creating the construct. Or maybe not, if the Pulan should breach the wall first.

It seemed that the Goddess Merci was on his side in one way at least.

He strode on to the parapet just as the bell signalling the start of his watch rang.

It was the thirteenth day of Panos, considered auspicious by some, if you believed in superstition, which Varoi did not. The third hour of the second watch was known as the death watch amongst military personnel. That time of night when reserves of energy reach their lowest ebb and vigilance is correspondingly slack.

A light drizzle had begun to fall, reducing visibility to a few paces beyond the curtain wall and adding further to the misery of those on guard. Across the fens the Pulan army slept on. A minimal number of their sentries appeared to be on guard and cook-fires that had flared bright hours earlier were reduced to sullen embers now.

Atop the battlements of Tenbay fortress Shakar warriors prowled, awaiting the dawn, a change of watch and the welcome chance to snatch a few hours' sleep.

Varoi yawned hugely. His back and shoulders felt stiff. His legs ached from the fall. And those scrapes sustained in the process stung mercilessly, courtesy of the ointment Soleil had applied. He reminded himself that it could have been worse. Rotating his shoulders he stretched his mouth wide in yet another yawn.

"Tired, Varoi?"

"Daft question, Che. What do you think?"

Che grinned, "Not long till our relief comes on watch."

"Can't come soon enough for me. My concentration's not what it should be."

"It's the same for us all, Varoi."

"Yes. But you don't have to be ready to throw up a protective shield at the first sign of their ballista coming back into play."

"Would you see that from here?"

"Damn it. No. The night is too obscured by mist and mizzle. Hopefully I would hear something though."

Together they peered out across the moat to the fens beyond, straining their eyes to see what they could make out: to no avail.

There *had* been movement early on, during the later part of the first watch. At a time when there were no *ananaha* gifted shaman to apply their acute powers of observation to the task. Since Varoi had come on duty nothing had stirred. His eyes had grown gritty and sore from his continual efforts to pierce the surrounding gloom.

The moon had been all too frequently obscured by ragged, low flying cloud and its brief appearances shed little light on what was happening below. There was no sign yet of any Pulan attempting to advance under cover of night. Perhaps those who'd reported movement earlier had been mistaken after all. No doubt daylight would reveal the truth of their situation. Varoi cracked his jaw with another vast yawn and rubbed his eyes. Goddess, but he could have done with more sleep.

Varoi stared hard, blinked, rubbed his tired eyes, and blinked again.

Just for a moment he thought he'd seen something move. Hard to make out, with the drizzle becoming heavier, dark against darkness the persistent rain. Away to his right he heard a sound, a sort of crump, then two more crumps soon after.

"What's that?" asked someone standing nearby.

"I can't be sure. There's too much obscuring my view, but I think we're about to …" Something large and pale loomed up out of the gloom.

"Everybody down."

A series of crumps sounded in short succession at the same time as a huge missile homed in on his section of the battlements. Varoi stood firm, determined to display no sign of weakness. Ducking would make no difference if this attack was what he assumed. Two more boulders landed close at hand. The stones under foot shuddered in response. Losing his balance, Varoi stumbled, as a cloud of grit and dust rose above the battlements themselves. A roar of approval rose from the enemy camp. Apparently, not all the Pulan slept.

Varoi had lost the shape of his construct. Quickly he brought his powers back to bear. Even so, he suspected Tenbay's safeguards to be compromised to some degree. His defensive action would come too late to prevent whatever damage had already occurred.

"Anyone hurt?"

Recognising the watch commander's voice, Varoi shook his head. Around him others were regaining their feet. Before he could reform his unravelled construct and set the protective barrier back in place, another boulder landed alongside with a loud thud that sent cracks chasing their way along the base of nearby merlons. Stones toppled and rolled, the low rumbling noise they made sounding a discordant note.

Varoi ignored all such distractions, determined that no more missiles would get through.

"I could use some help here," he complained." Was he the only shaman present to recognise the danger now posed? Two more shields flickered into life on either side of his and Varoi heaved a huge sigh of relief.

He was tired and miserable. Things were not going entirely to plan, either in his personal life or in the task he'd assumed. Perhaps the damage just sustained would not prove too weakening to Tenbay's defence. And perhaps it was just as well he had dared to afford Ayesha protection, for both her sake and his own peace of mind.

To his relief the surprise attack had petered out. No more boulders were hurled at Tenbay's crenulated walls. As the stones under foot settled back into place Varoi relaxed.

The garrison had been taken off-guard. Lulled into a sense of false tranquillity by two nights of relative peace, they had been totally unprepared for this assault. An uneasy silence resumed, broken by the occasional crude joke or wry comment, a little levity applied by some to relieve the deceptive tedium. None on guard would take this nightly respite for granted from now on.

Ayesha stood alone atop the battlements, beneath the pale sky of a brand new day. It was early and, though the moon had long since set, the sun had not risen far into the sky. The air remained frigid and still; few of their enemy appeared to be on the move

The land she overlooked was swathed in a thick blanket of fog. Somewhere away to her right, not more than three ells' distance from where she stood, a thin line of trees marked the western boundary of the Shakar settlement.

It was not this that held her attention now, though. Hidden beneath that dense mantel of vapour an immense army of Pulan were encamped. And there was no sign yet of their resuming their attack. At her back the fortress lay silent as the grave, awaiting the expected call to arms.

Why was she up here alone? She could not imagine a reasonable excuse. Except ... except, mayhap, she expected all she held dear might perish this day.

And where did the enemy lurk? Why did they not show their face? Impatient, she pushed back her hair, which hung in damp tangles about her face. No tears. She would not weep until she knew for whom she must mourn. Until it appeared that all was lost and beyond salvation, she would remain resolute in her defiance.

Peering out across a land swathed two paces deep in misty brume, she thought she saw something move.

Slowly it rose above the pale, floating vapour that wreathed the landscape for miles around. Her eyes beheld a man of extraordinary proportions, taller, more powerful than any male Shakar. He held her unsettled gaze with dark eyes that were gimlet sharp. His whole countenance was menacing in the extreme. A shiver of fear ran the length of her spine and her limbs grew weak. She closed

242

her eyes. Awestruck and unable to move, she gave vent to a faint mewling cry.

Varoi lay perfectly still. He had not expected events to turn out like this.

Once the repercussive echoes of the Pulan attack had died away and the stones of the parapet had stopped vibrating underfoot, his thoughts had travelled a different path. It was inevitable, he supposed. As though the two things were connected, which in a sense they were, his thoughts had strayed to Ayesha.

Which was why, when he came off duty, he'd wound up outside her door.

His quiet rap had elicited no immediate response, so he'd spun on his heel and started away, only to be brought up short when her door cracked ajar and a soft voice called out, "Varoi?"

He'd taken pains to explain his uninvited presence.

"I was worried, Princess. I thought mayhap I had gone too far in my efforts to obtain permission and prepare you for the protection I had in mind. And ... I wanted to be sure you were safe."

Well, of course she was safe, locked up within the fortress walls. Why would she not be? Even to him it seemed a lame excuse. But the need to see her, to speak with her again, however briefly, was a compulsive urge. One he found not easy to ignore.

A quiet word, a moment alone would have sufficed. Instead, she'd offered him more.

Beckoning him inside, she had closed the door. Ayesha explained how, having been woken by the unexpected noise of the Pulan assault, she was now too frightened to fall asleep. Lest in doing so she awake to find the fortress overrun by the enemy.

He had given in to her desperate pleas. Despite serious reservations he had wound up here, in Ayesha's bed, watching over her while she slept.

Not that he considered this any sort of hardship, far from it in fact. Admittedly, he should be sleeping himself. Getting what rest he could while he still had the chance. He badly needed to rest before his next turn on guard. Instead, he lay perfectly still, watching over Ayesha while she slept, relishing the brief opportunity conferred. A more pleasing indulgence he could not have imagined had he tried.

He had wrapped her up in his warm embrace and listened as the pattern of her breathing changed. A couple of hours and he was required back on guard.

And still he had managed not to succumb to his own prurient needs.

He had lain like this for what seemed like hours, although stars still pricked the night sky and dawn remained naught save a pale promise. Had anyone dared to suggest he'd be content simply holding her this way he'd have called the idea absurd.

A flutter of dark lashes and a softly murmured entreaty stirred the blood in his veins, causing the hair on his arms to prickle erect.

"Ayesha?" he whispered in reply.

Opening her eyes she knew at once it was no more than a bad dream. She was not on the parapet alone facing an unseen army and a deadly threat. Instead, she was safely tucked up in bed.

Varoi lay snuggled at her back, one arm draped casually across the generous curve of her breast. As though, even in sleep, he feared she might try to escape. Small chance of that. She could not. The bond between them had already grown too strong. Though she would die first rather than admit it, even to herself.

She felt the hard thrust of him pressed up against her bottom and knew at once he was already aroused. That fact alone brought a satisfied smile to her face. If only he would permit her to offer him some release. But he would not, despite the fact he had once done as much for her.

Beneath the colourful quilted coverlet Varoi had so thoughtfully provided they were sparingly clothed, some semblance of modesty being required. In Varoi's case his night attire consisted of a soft leather wrap that covered his nether regions, while she wore nothing more substantial than a thin, linen shift. It had seemed adequate enough when she had first lain down to sleep. Now, she was made abundantly aware of the steady throb of Varoi's arousal, which made her own pulse leap in response.

Secretly she yearned for the sweet pain of his invasion. Not that she dare admit as much. One day she would submit, but not yet. The waiting would do neither one of them any real harm. On that point she *was* determined.

"Ayesha?"

Hearing the question in his voice, she wriggled backwards, intent on informing Varoi she was awake. Then she began a slow, careful turn.

She was the one lying closest to the wall, which decision ensured there was no likelihood of her falling out of bed. But the cot with which the room had been furnished was of mean proportions, which left Varoi at something of a disadvantage since he'd been the one to insist on sleeping nearest the edge. After various trials, and one or two ludicrous mishaps, they had worked out a way they could share her meagre accommodation without either party coming to grief.

She wondered, had his comrades missed him from the dormatorium? Would he find himself in trouble if they had? It was a question she had not thought to pose.

Ayesha finished rolling over, her head eventually coming to rest against the hard muscles of his chest. She found she could hear the steady pounding of his heart, and wondered, did it beat just a little too fast?

Varoi's chest and belly were covered with a wealth of tight curls, some of which persisted in tickling her nose. She would not giggle. She had promised herself she would not to give in to mirth. Sometimes he failed to appreciate her wry sense of humour. It had seldom been a problem before. Perhaps it was due to the changing circumstance in which they now found themselves.

"Ayesha?"

At last she consented to look him in the eye and, looking up, was swept away by the sheer intensity of his gaze. All thoughts turned to dust and were blown away. His glance was compelling, mesmerizing, sizzling with lust.

He cupped her chin in one sword-calloused hand. Then, as his mouth found hers, she felt her resistance melt from toe to crown like warm honey dripping from the comb. His mouth on hers became hot and demanding. How could she refuse? She sensed again the fierce urgency of his need and it started a fire burning in her belly and loins.

Abruptly he released her and drew back. She thought she understood his problem. It was common belief among the Shakar that any warrior who spilt his seed on the eve of battle would die the next day. Still, she saw no reason why they could not share some small pleasure.

Ayesha raised one hand to stroke the heavy muscles of Varoi's chest. And, when he did not stop her, slipped that hand around to his back and slid her hand downwards in a slow caress. Setting her mouth against the small, hard prominence of his nipple she curled her tongue around to supply him a teasing suckle.

246

She heard Varoi suck in a breath and knew his pleasure had just intensified. Content to continue her manipulations she was unprepared for what he did next.

Varoi was on fire, head to toe, swamped by an overwhelming need; driven to the brink of insanity by a desire that was beyond his ability control. Resistance seemed futile, if indeed he could resist. Temptation caused him to react instinctively.

Gradually he eased his body backwards, inch by inch, moving closer to the edge, making room for what he had planned, while still maintaining the kiss.

Unthinking she followed his lead, determined in her pursuit. Vaguely aware of how close he came to disaster.

"Ayesha," he whispered, a pleading note in the way he said her name.

She glanced up, taken unawares by the desperation she heard in his voice, raising her head from the pillows in response. Before she knew what he had planned, giving her no opportunity to protest, he flipped her over on to her back.

"Varoi?"

"Hush, beloved. You need not fear." In truth she did not fear him at all, not any more, if, indeed, she ever had. Carefully he eased his body atop hers and lay above her looking down, cupping her head in two strong hands.

The intensity of his gaze held her mute and when his mouth closed over hers she was powerless to resist. Slyly his tongue teased until, beneath the gentle pressure of his, her lips parted granting him access. His tongue darted inside, to engage hers in purposeful pursuit. Ayesha sensed it might be up to her what happened next.

Ayesha had fantasized how it might feel, having Varoi's hot, hard, hungry body lying above hers, pinning her down. Now she knew.

Once she had come close to discovering the truth. Then there had been several layers of clothing and the

247

trappings of armour to keep them apart. This was nothing like that. This was like being skin to skin, with nearly nothing in between.

She had thought it might be terrifying, lying here vulnerable and exposed beneath so much heavy muscle. It was anything but.

It was intriguing, intoxicating, exciting, all of those things, and maybe more. Her hormones had gone into overdrive. Her whole system was melting down. She was thrilled to the very core.

Right now she longed to find out how much difference a little friction might make. She had an overwhelming urge to fidget.

So she did.

Varoi felt his libido spiral out of control. Had she any idea what effect her slow, sensuous movements were having on him?

He tossed back a dark tangle of hair. He burned for her. He wanted her more than he would ever have thought possible. And she wanted him ... or so he believed.

Varoi slid lower, using the superior weight of his body to force her thighs apart ... then froze when something landed on the bed ... something miniscule but momentarily distracting.

One swift glance and all thoughts of present conquest fled.

Now he knew the pounding he heard in his head for what it was. He recognised something sinister in that minute grain. A slight vibration in the ceiling overhead saw his worst fears confirmed.

Ayesha stared, confounded, confused. "Varoi?" In the time it took her to draw in a breath he had changed, from gentle lover to dangerous predator. One swift blink and the transformation was complete.

Now he prowled the room like an angry lion, or a hungry Saarcat stalking its prey. Hauling on clothes, buckling up armour, settling his baldric in place. One hand rose to ease his weapon in its sheath. That act alone provided a vital clue to her unanswered query.

The Pulan were poised to invade. How had he known?

His amber gaze connected with hers. She started to speak, then stopped when he raised a silencing hand. "Hear me out first, Ayesha. I beg." How could she refuse? Without waiting for her reply he went ahead. "Don't go to the barbican today. If you must help Soleil, do so from within the inner ward. Tis safer there."

He smothered her protest with one last smouldering kiss. Then he was gone.

Ayesha sat, silent and stunned. Resentful, she felt inclined to disobey. But, sensing his directive was well meant, she chose not to.

The thin drizzle that had fallen overnight had now ceased. Low mist carpeted the ground, filling in pockets and hollows, making the Pulan appear as though they were chopped off at the knees. It might almost have been amusing; under different circumstances it might. Varoi found he was hard pushed to find any humour left in the situation.

Something had changed overnight.

It was as though, up until now, the Pulan had been toying with them, seeking out a chink in their impregnable armour. Now they knew just where it was. They could break through their defences at any time. So it appeared to him.

It made Varoi nervous, wary, ready for anything. And none too happy with the situation. There was tension in the air and he wasn't the only one to feel it.

Sensing movement alongside he glanced round.

"Hello, froglet," he said, catching sight of Ayesha's brother and acknowledging his presence with a friendly grin. He felt something being pressed into his hand and looked down … then up again. "What's this, Toku?"

"Well, food, evidently," came the sarcastic reply. "What does it look like to you, Lieutenant?" That was an unusually formal response considering how friendly they had become.

"Well. Food, as you so rightly point out. I just wondered, how come?"

"Commander's orders, Varoi. You eat on duty from now on. No relief without adequate excuse." Toku moved away, to the next warrior along.

So, their commander had noticed the difference too. Varoi felt the surrounding tension crank up another notch. Around him the air fairly thrummed.

Varoi stared out across the battlements while he ate the food he'd been given, though he tasted nothing of what he ate. His attention focused on just one thing: the grim business of waiting for impending conflict to commence.

The Pulan were ominously quiet. Sunlight glinted on armour and helm and on wicked looking battle-axe blades, as though all had received special attention overnight. Now they waited.

The silence held as the tension grew: along the battlements themselves and down in the grassy confines of the outer bailey, where the reserve forces had recently arrived; in the town behind and out across the rolling countryside beyond. Not a dog barked, not a bell peeled, nary a cock crowed, no hammer on anvil rang.

Silence: as loud as any raucous shout. Fraught. Oppressive. Laden with cruel intent. As though the whole world held its collective breath. Waiting. For this portentous battle of life and death to begin.

Varoi glanced down at the stone parapet alongside, at the newly created maze of tiny cracks that crazed its surface, and wondered. Since their defences were plainly compromised, how much more effort might it take for the

Pulan to demolish one section of wall and barge their way inside? Was that perhaps the Pulan leader's intent? To keep them guessing and so rack up the tension to breaking point. If so, he had made one serious mistake. The defenders had nowhere to run and no intention of giving ground. Win or lose they were in this to the bitter end.

Silence ... which implied something else. If the blacksmiths had completed their assigned task and freed the rusted-up gates, why was the moat not yet filled?

There was a sudden sound, soft yet savage, a slight shifting of stone under foot. Startled, Varoi spun ... and stared in horror as a fissure appeared in the parapet alongside.

Despite the threat, Varoi resumed his allotted task. Perhaps because he focused his attention solely on maintaining his section of the shield, or perhaps because his *ananaha* senses were expanded, he viewed impending events with dispassionate calm.

Subtle changes began taking place. Slow at first they quickly gathered pace: a slight gaping at joints where mortar bound the stones, a grinding screech that grew in volume; an insidious creeping sensation under foot. As though he were moving sideways, closer to the widening crack that yawned wider even while he gazed.

Oblivious to the fact that he now teetered on the very brink of disaster, Varoi could only stand and stare transfixed. How long he tarried he could not say, overlong it appeared to some.

A sudden shift and that part of the parapet alongside crumbled and fell. Those rendered oblivious to their immediate danger went with.

But not Varoi.

As several tons of displaced stone and compacted earth infill plummeted earthwards, taking with it the unwary and ill prepared, a hand shot out to hook itself about Varoi's arm. Varoi gave a startled shout as he felt himself hauled backwards, away from the edge and impending disaster. He did not seem altogether pleased by his rescuer's prompt reaction.

The rumbling roar of displaced stone swallowed all sound save for the startled yell of doomed warriors. And one strident scream abruptly cut off.

Varoi, disgruntled, shook himself free and, standing, turned to confront his saviour. Being hauled backwards on his arse was, in his view, an undignified means of travel, no matter the excuse.

Before he could raise pithy protest, Aheb said, "How long were you planning to stand there, Varoi? Until the wall fell down about your ears? You seemed to view approaching calamity like a man enthralled."

All discomfort was reduced to irrelevance before Aheb's look of sad reproach. Varoi shook his head. Words failed him. An apology seemed more in order than a harsh rebuke. Instead of venting his ire, Varoi turned aside and gazed down into the yawning abyss once occupied by a large section of wall. A few mangled bodies could partly be seen, buried beneath tumbled remains of fallen stone and clods of earth.

"Poor bastards," Varoi murmured, half to himself. "That could have been me."

He turned back to confront the young warrior whose swift reaction had ensured things turned out differently.

"Thanks to you, I was saved."

Aheb just shook his head and grinned. "Think nothing of it, Varoi."

The silence did not last long. While the defenders yet stared in solemn dismay, a roar of triumph swelled to fill the sullied air.

An instant later the first ranks of Pulan were on the move.

No time remained in which to mourn their loss or consider their breached defence: time, instead, to engage the enemy.

Varoi laid a heavy hand on Aheb's shoulder and held Aheb's glance with a steady gaze. It was not his place to assume charge of the situation, but under present circumstances he felt sure few would object.

"Stay here and see the shield maintained. We dare not risk another breach in our defence."

"What about you, Varoi? What will you do now?"

"Exactly as I think fit," he said. Then, without further comment, he spun about and leapt: agile as a mountain goat, he leapt and landed some distance down, then proceeded to bound from boulder to boulder the rest of the way down. During his swift descent he let rip with a fierce yell of defiance that echoed those of the Shakar on the wall as well as those men and Shakar assembled within the outer bailey, who awaited the imminent arrival of the invading horde.

From high above came an authoritative shout.

"Rally our defences, Varoi."

He tipped his commander a brisk salute and looked behind. Already the Pulan were busy scrambling into the moat and running across its muddy bottom. Before long they would arrive at the steep ascent of the scarp, now all the more hazardous thanks to the debris of the partially demolished wall. Behind him rank upon rank of Shakar seethed. Scattered amongst them, a hitherto unfamiliar sight, were small groups and knots of roughly armoured townsfolk, including a liberal sprinkling of beardless youths and stringy old men. Varoi found this last a heartening sight. They might not be as well trained or proficient with weapons as the Shakar, but their commitment and zeal might still turn the tide of battle in Tenbay's favour. Providing their nerve held.

Varoi drew his bastard sword from its sheath and held it aloft, a shining example of what the Pulan army were about to face. He cared not for his enemy's reaction, only for his comrades' enthusiastic response. It came in the form of surging bodies, all eager to reach his side and plug the gaping hole just punched in Tenbay's defence. Varoi uttered one loud rallying cry and turned back. He was no longer alone in the face of enemy attack.

He saw how Ice and Wolverine, Helvan and Boar dominated the Pulan's front ranks. And he grumbled to see the moat, which represented Tenbay's primary defence, noticeably unfilled.

There was no time left to ponder the reason. The Pulan were almost upon them.

Jostled on all sides by keen defenders Varoi awarded his comrades precedence, seeking room, instead, in which to organise a reasonable defence. Varoi itched to become involved but found himself shuffled aside, hemmed about by those Shakar so far denied access to the fight.

While the battlements above had mainly been manned by those shaman powerful enough to maintain a magical shield, other ranks had been forced to seethe in simmering frustration, awaiting their chance to act.

Now was their time. Varoi was not so selfish as to refuse them this right. Stepping back he waited for battle to come to him, knowing it could not be long.

Opportunity came quite soon enough. Thereafter, as fast as one foe was dispatched, another stepped forward to take his place. There was no time for fancy manoeuvres. A vicious melee of stabbing swords and swinging axes forced him to concentrate on just one thing: staying alive. No mean feat with barely room in which to fight.

There was limited room in which to move, limited room in which to make a killing strike. Forced consistently to back up, Varoi kept his weapon in play. A quick parry followed by a vicious upward thrust put an end to one particular threat.

Someone tapped him on the shoulder and Varoi whirled, sword swooping down in a deadly arc. The man behind him ducked aside. Avoiding the killing strike he spun clear, then glanced up.

"You're lethal with that blade," Borit yelled, teeth flashing in an uncivil grin.

"I should hope so," Varoi growled. "I'd not last long otherwise."

"Watch your back," Borit warned and Varoi spun again.

Behind him he felt Borit, almost shoulder high to him. He was aware of his friend's body heat and the protection thus provided as the burly blacksmith aligned with his defence, hard muscles jostling against Varoi's back.

"What are you doing here, Borit?" Varoi wondered, his voice harsh with effort as he countered one Ice Warrior's determined attack.

"Just making myself useful," countered Borit. "You looked as though you could use some help."

"I'm fine," Varoi rumbled, as his blade slid home past his enemy's defence.

With one hand Varoi heaved his blade free. He watched the Pulan stumble to his knees, dismissing the man as a continued threat even as he fell.

Briefly, Varoi raised a hand to straighten his tilted helm. Mayhap a willing ally guarding his back was no bad thing. "Stay if you wish," Varoi amended, as with cold efficiency he confronted his next adversary.

Varoi was unaware how much his expression had changed; that his grin was nasty, vicious even, his focus one of lethal intent. He would not have been surprised ... much. Nor would he have been amazed to learn that his canines were now on prominent view. It was an instinctive reaction amongst the Shakar when any found themselves under threat and was most disconcerting for any sworn enemy.

A series of deft feints and nasty jabs, smart ripostes and swift evasions denied his present foe satisfaction. Varoi sought the required opening with determination and tenacity. Pulan warriors varied in ability and this last was a worthy adversary.

Varoi despatched him at last. But not before the Pulan foe had left his bloody signature on Varoi's thigh and knee. Leather armour was of scant use against a battle-axe blade. Still, a surprised grunt of pain proved just reward for Varoi's gritty effort.

He glanced about. His brief survey of the outer bailey sufficed to convince him how much trouble Tenbay's defenders still were in.

Just then the door to the inner bailey suddenly swung wide to disgorge a motley gang of men, each armed with a deadly blade. The result of Borit's alliance with Tenbay's blacksmith, no doubt.

The door slammed shut with a discordant clang and the sound of heavy bolts being jammed home informed him that these new contenders were here to add strength in numbers if nothing else. Varoi hoped they had some useful skill with a blade. They'd not last long otherwise.

At his back Borit gasped, "They've come at last. There may be more. I hope there's more. Let's pray I'm right. We made enough weapons to equip an entire army. Only time will tell how valiant these men are."

Varoi found he had no breath left to pass comment. Their situation appeared dire.

The Pulan had poured through the gap in the curtain wall like an unrelenting tide. Jammed elbow to elbow there was barely enough room for either side to breathe, let alone swing a blade. A hand-and-a-half sword required room, so also a battle-axe. This fact seemed not to matter much.

Men and Shakar both died. Whether the killing stroke was
swift or slow, clean or messy, the results were the same.

The fiercest fighting occurred near the breach in the
curtain wall and the door to the inner bailey. Somehow
these reinforcements had got through. What more could he
add to Borit's heartfelt plea.

The ground under foot was slippery with blood and
entrails, reduced to a treacherous mire and littered about
with the fallen. Varoi struggled to remain upright amidst
the press of friend and foe.

From up above there came a sudden roar of
approval. Varoi had no time to ponder the cause. His
attention was focused on the foe in front. He shifted his
feet and parried a killing stroke that was meant to cleave
him in twain. As his opponent raised his weapon again
Varoi moved in and took the Pulan through the one opening
provided. Beneath the raised arm was a gap in steel armour
that offered him a swift reprieve. A quick thrust and blood
spurted spattering across Varoi's face. Varoi knew at once
that his blade had found the heart.

With a swiftness that stole breath, sound filled the
surrounding air: a roaring, rushing deluge that defied
description. "What?" he muttered, not really aware he'd
asked the question.

Behind him Borit stirred. Muscles flexed and
strung sinews strained as his blade flew in a murderous arc
that took his opponents head. "Tis the moat," was all he
said.

Varoi felt his own muscles strain with effort as he
caught his opponent's blade in a desperate bind. How
much longer could they hold out against overwhelming
numbers before they were overrun? He barely registered
the import of Borit's words.

Slowly, understanding sank in. Gradually those
around him took heart. The tide of battle was now turning
in favour of those striving to maintain an adequate defence.

Confined to the outer bailey, pinned between two towering walls, the Pulan's one means of retreat was the deep, swirling waters of a moat, or death by the sword. In essence, it was much the same choice. Still they did not abandon the fight.

The closing conflict was bitter and bloody but mercifully brief.

Varoi wiped blood off his weapon and glanced around.

"What now?" asked Borit, doing the same.

"Many Pulan still wait on the far side of the moat," Varoi reminded him.

Chapter 11: New Beginnings

Varoi spun on his heel and started away. "Where are you going?" asked Borit.

Varoi pointed towards the battlements themselves. "Up there is where I shall gain an improved view of our situation and obtain a better idea of what lies ahead. How else can we hope to counter their next attack?"

Reaching the entrance to the barbican Varoi thundered his fist against the heavy, iron-strapped door, demanding entry. Borit shook his head in baffled dismay. Varoi took too much upon himself in assuming such responsibility. No doubt others were already thus engaged. Still, he thought it worth the effort to follow his friend's lead.

Even as he put this thought into action another raucous shout rang out to echo about the slick and gory confines of the outer bailey, where so many Pulan and Shakar had just died. Stopping, he raised his head to listen to what was being said.

Ahead, Borit saw that the door to the barbican had been unbarred. Without hesitation Varoi started to ascend.

Varoi climbed the stairs to the battlements at speed, taking them two steps at a time. Half way up Borit was forced to pause and catch his breath, and could not help but marvel at the Shakar warrior's stamina. After several hours spent fighting to stay alive, he still had energy enough with which to make this climb without pause.

Varoi stalked out on to the parapet to be met by a solid wall of sound, a rowdy, rhythmic chanting that rose from those Pulan still assembled on the far bank.

Then, out of the trees bordering the settlement, the last remnants of morning mist clinging to their clothes, marched a formidable contingent of armed Shakar, each with a weapon in hand. This time it was the turn of the Pulan to find themselves outnumbered.

Just for a heartbeat, all shouting ceased. Nothing moved, on either battlements or fen, as though none present could believe what they saw with their own eyes.

Suddenly the Pulan were running. Running, but not fast enough: if there was one thing Shakar warriors were good at it was running down prey. And these Pulan, lately encamped upon Tenbay's doorstep, had, assuredly, now become prey.

Foremost among the vanguard of those pursuing the Pulan was one who stood out from all the rest. He wasn't just taller than most of his fellows; he was garbed in the distinctive black armour that pronounced him Konicci trained.

Not all commanders were Konicci and not all Konicci attained commander rank. This one had, and more besides, since he not only sported a red-crested helm but the crest was extended, flowing out behind him like an elongated tail. A tail denoted just one thing: this Konicci had excelled at weapons skills; this Konicci was reckoned among the elite.

There were others present on the battlements who knew what that meant … and who this particular Shakar must surely be. They gave loud voice to their belief.

"Com 'Varicci, com 'Varicci, our saviour returns. Com 'Varicci shall banish the Pulan plague. O la, com 'Varicci, see how the Pulan flee. O la, O la, Commander com 'Varicci."

The shouting increased in volume as more and more warriors joined in. Yet, not all those manning the ramparts added their voice to the overall din.

Varoi's lip curled back in a silent snarl. It seemed his rival had finally decided to return … and in force.

Varoi accounted Schezan com 'Varicci his most despised rival and adversary, though few present were aware such enmity existed between the pair. Varoi had entrusted no more than a few with that knowledge. He watched proceedings with interest as, below him on the fen, Schezan com 'Varicci waved his sword aloft in recognition of those among Tenbay's garrison who sought to offer encouragement. Soon the Pulan were no longer bunched together but stretched out over the flat landscape of the fen, heading in haste for the nearest bridge or shallow ford. Varoi neither knew nor cared where or how they crossed the river, just so long as they left and did not return. Somehow he doubted that would be the case.

High up on the parapet all shouting died away.

Then, in a quiet voice, that nonetheless carried, someone declared, "It seems the Unclaimed Land is no longer under immediate threat. The Shakar nation still has a home."

The words were met by a profound silence, none present having anything further to add.

Varoi saw Borit standing a few paces distant, leaning out to study what went on, and wondered what his friend's opinion of the developing situation was. For now he chose to keep his own counsel, waiting to see how others felt.

Che stood nearby and it was he who first ventured a comment. "You don't seem overly impressed, Varoi."

"For what it's worth, I can't say I am. Pray tell, what are your feelings, Che?"

Che gave a disparaging glance towards those Pulan now fleeing across the fen. "It seems wrong to me that we were forced to rely for our defence upon tradesmen, young apprentices and worn-out old men."

"Even so, on the whole, they acquitted themselves well."

"Yes, they did. There's no denying that fact. But they're not trained to use weapons like the Shakar. They lack the strength and skill required to wield these hand-and-a-half blades effectively."

Che fell silent then, as though the thoughts he was about to express might well amount to treason. He spoke softly when next he put his opinions into words. "He should have been here."

Varoi felt bound to agree. "We could have used his expertise in our defence."

"Even so ..."

They fell silent, musing on what had just passed between them.

"Why did they run?" asked Borit, coming up on him from behind and causing Varoi to startle. Borit showed an insouciant grin, amused by his friend's reaction. "I thought they would fight to the bitter end rather than flee in so undignified a fashion."

"A wise leader knows when to fight and when to flee, just as a warrior requires courage enough to stay the course and win. Wisdom and courage don't always walk hand in hand. The Pulan leader seeing, that his men were greatly outnumbered, rather than risk all, chose prudence over audacity. Perhaps they go to lick their wounds or mayhap to arrange a better offensive at some later date."

"You think the Pulan leader will try again to seize the Unclaimed Land?"

"Undoubtedly. What better reason could he have for saving as many warriors as he can?"

Varoi glanced behind to where those who'd survived the day's conflict were busy lifting bodies on to carts: tumbrels for dead Pulan and more respectful transport for those Shakar who were numbered among the fallen. The drawbridge was being lowered into place. Soon a pyre would be built on the plain opposite where the bodies of dead Pulan could be burnt on a pyre. Dead Shakar were destined to receive a more ceremonial passage across Death's Divide.

Dusk was descending by the time the first contingent of pursuing Shakar returned. The elongated

262

shadows of towers and barbican crept outward across the fen. A rosy glow touched the far horizon where the dying sun was sliding to rest.

The main force of Shakar who'd gone in pursuit of the fleeing Pulan would not return to the fortress for quite some time. Not until they had succeeded in driving the Pulan past the low hills, which bordered the Unclaimed Land and on to the grassy uplands where they belonged. Then, and only then, would they return.

Schezan strode at the front of his warriors, head high, his demeanour one of haughty arrogance. The mere sight of him caused Varoi to succumb to a wave of resentment. How many need not have died had Schezan been present from the first?

He moved back from the merlon against which he leant, intent on blending in with those deeper shadows that now clothed large parts of the barbican. He wanted to see for himself how Schezan might behave toward those gathered; those who had fought and suffered loss or injury. Whether or not Schezan had humility enough to acknowledge the effort required to keep Tenbay secure during his absence.

Schezan strode on to the parapet with an assumed air of conceited aplomb, as though expecting, as his rightful due, the adulation with which he was greeted. Varoi all but choked with frustration and rage, biting back bitter words that rose like bile in his throat.

In his view, Schezan had no more right to such respect than any other officer present. He seemed to expect it even so. Varoi bridled with fury at that assumption.

Varoi knew for a fact that Schezan could have reached Tenbay well before the final battle was joined, in sufficient time to offer pertinent advice and assist in organising Tenbay's defence. A message had been sent requesting his urgent return with reinforcements. Why the delay in answering that appeal? Was it possible that

Schezan had chosen to ignore the imperative implied? Had he deliberately delayed? Timed his return just right, in order to accept this accolade?

Varoi knew Schezan com 'Varicci of old; knew well his capacity for cunning duplicity. If Schezan had changed one iota in this respect he saw no clear evidence to prove it.

Varoi growled softly, low in his throat, then ventured aloud the scathing remark he could not contain.

"You took your time, Schezan. What kept you?"

Schezan whirled. Proud posturing and arrogant affront overcame his self-assured demeanour as he spun to confront his impudent accuser head on. An overall expression of haughty disdain served naught to disguise his intense irritation.

"Who among you dares reproach me thus?" Schezan demanded, in a voice grown soft with hidden menace.

Varoi stood. Unfolding his lithe, muscular frame he stepped forth from the gloomy shadows in which he'd been waiting, prepared to face his nemesis once again, certain that this confrontation might well be his last. That nothing would be resolved by his impulsive actions, but willing to chance it nonetheless. At sight of him Schezan froze, momentarily stunned to silence, but not for long.

Varoi knew what he did was risky. Too many among those present might take Schezan's part. But the history of sworn enmity that remained between them urged him on. To bait his rival into taking rash action might be worth the risk if, in so doing, he achieved his ultimate aim: that of bringing Schezan's past deeds to final account. A life was owed: his sister, Bayritz's life at that. Varoi could not forget a debt of such enormity. Nor could he resist this godsent opportunity. Once more that day, rash bravado drove him on toward hell-bent destruction.

Schezan's reaction, how he bristled with malicious intent, simply confirmed for Varoi the true nature of his adversary. He half expected Schezan, faced with such blatant provocation, to draw sword and make a determined attempt to run him through. He was prepared for such eventuality, would pay whatever penalty was demanded in order to extract sweet revenge. In truth, it could not come soon enough.

Some things had changed over the intervening years. No longer was he an untried youth starting out on the ritual path to becoming a full-blooded male. Nor was Schezan a mere common warrior: he was Konicci now and elite, which added yet further complication. Still, Varoi determined to seize this opportunity with both hands.

Yet, even as he squared up to his nemesis, ready to do battle, physical or magical, he didn't care which, another voice rose in angry dissent.

"What are you doing, Lieutenant com 'Domicci?"

This interruption proved just enough to undermine his decision.

Half turning, a fierce scowl of rebuttal fixed in place, he snarled a respectful answer. "What I feel I must, Commander com 'Dolino." Still, he kept one wary eye on Schezan and would not allow his concentration to stray.

Commander com 'Dolino moved forward to place his substantial bulk between the two protagonists, determined no more blood should be spilt that day. If he ever had cause to doubt Varoi's normally pragmatic attitude it was now. Never had he seen his lieutenant quite so incensed. Nor was his second's chosen target any less ready to respond in kind.

He felt like pulling the pair apart, taking them by their ears and banging their hard heads together for good measure. The situation facing him was volatile in the extreme. For all he wished to deal with the matter brutally, to settle the problem in a conclusive fashion, a more rational solution seemed the only way out.

Turning toward Schezan, whom he assumed to be the most stable person present, he said, "Allow me, Commander, to introduce Lieutenant com 'Domicci. The lieutenant is *currently* acting as my second-in-command. I apologise if his attitude appears somewhat offensive. He needs to calm down." There was a bite to the commander's words, a strong hint of asperity in his, otherwise placating, tone. "Don't you, Lieutenant," he added, with a warning frown.

Varoi took the hint. He didn't know why he chose to react favourably to the explicit warning, but he did. "As you say, Commander. Conditions are fraught."

"Indeed."

If Schezan com 'Varicci appeared, however briefly, willing to concede a point, then room remained in which to negotiate. Commander com 'Dolino allowed himself to relax, just a little. Aware that Varoi remained noticeably tense, he invented a suitable errand with which to keep his second officer occupied.

"I need a report on those warriors who have succumbed to injury. Can you see that I receive it soon, Lieutenant?"

Varoi's brows remained tangled in a furious scowl but he gave a curt nod of agreement.

"Then you have my leave to visit the infirmary."

Considering himself dismissed Varoi spun on his heel and started away. No words of objection would salve his troubled conscience. Anger still consumed him. There being no space left for hostile manoeuvring he chose to concede the commander's point with reasonable grace.

Behind him he heard his commander's voice attempting an apology. "I had no idea Varoi harboured such latent animosity towards you. Mind telling me why?"

Once again he was apologising on his lieutenant's behalf, as though there were any real need.

Reaching the entrance to the barbican Varoi paused, hovering just inside the door, interested to learn what form of excuse Schezan might use for his hostility.

Schezan dismissed the apology with an airy wave of one hand, "Tis ancient history. A personal grudge, which Varoi cannot let be."

Varoi sniffed at that gruff comment. There was more to his grudge than Schezan was willing to admit.

"Indeed?" Varoi caught the hint of curiosity in his commander's tone.

"You should ask your lieutenant if you wish to know more. No doubt he will relish the chance of putting his point of view. He is quite unreasonable in this respect, I have found."

"Really?"

Varoi hoped it *was* disbelief he now heard in his officer's voice. Either way he had no alternative other than to accept the situation as it stood, for now. He continued his noisy descent of the barbican stairs.

Varoi's whole body ached, but it was a good ache, the most satisfying kind. The kind that came at the end of conflict, when yet another foe lay undone. The kind of ache he could readily accept. Unlike the dull enduring ache of loss, which had remained long after Bayritz's body had been laid to rest. Her murder was a crime for which Schezan had gone unpunished far too long. And if another chance came to confront his tormentor he might not refrain from finding a pretext of drawing his blade.

Ayesha elbowed the door open and stepped through, then paused as it closed behind her with a decisive click. She eyed the occupants of the first two pallets with wary unease and more than a little contempt. They were both men. Not men of Tenbay – she had no argument with tending any of them. The pair she contemplated were Pulan. Wounded Pulan, but still, they numbered among the hated enemy. She had no doubt whatever that they would show scant mercy were their positions reversed. Yet here they lay, taking their ease, receiving treatment that should be lavished on better men than they.

Why had the Shakar healers seen fit to care for them? Why had they not been put to the sword as befitted any who attacked unprovoked?

Behind her the door again swung open. A small hand was set to the space between her shoulder blades and slight pressure applied.

"This is no time for dithering, Ayesha. Delay long enough and the brew you carry will grow cold. There are more than enough tasks to go round and no time for selfish indulgence." Soleil's remonstrance was gentle but firm.

"But why must we pander to the likes of them?" she hissed, nodding her head in the direction of one Pulan who lay prone on his pallet with a thick wad of bandage covering the shortened stump of one arm.

"That question is not for you to ask, Ayesha. It is our role to deal with injuries and heal the sick, regardless of race or creed. If you cannot act without discrimination I have no use for you. Is it that you tire of your duties? Do you wish to be relieved?"

"Of course not. I just question our priorities. It seems risky to me that such as they should share the same quarters as our most seriously injured."

"Granted they pose a possible risk, which is why we keep them sedated. Now, if you will." Soleil gave her another light shove. This time Ayesha moved.

She wove a well-plotted course between individual pallets, filling cups with the posset supplied and setting them to lips. The soporific was strong enough to keep the worst pain to a bearable level and, more importantly, ensure the Pulan remained sufficiently subdued.

Ayesha had no wish to be removed from duty. To begin with her interest in offering aid had been purely self-indulgent: she had wanted a useful way to help pass the time. Now her reason for being here had become personal: her brother Sami was among those who'd been brought in injured, having fallen down the barbican stairs. Fortunately the fall had occasioned him nothing worse than a broken leg and Toku, at least, had escaped the conflict unharmed. Still, Ayesha felt an added incentive to help out.

The presence of Pulan warriors posed unnecessary risk, it seemed to her. Yet none seemed inclined to take notice of her concerns.

There were guards appointed to the task of watching over these prisoners. That should have eased her anxiety. Still, she could not stop speculating on what might happen should their vigilance prove at all inept.

A soft voice from behind made her turn. "I had hoped I might find you here."

"And so you have, Lieutenant com 'Domicci. Have you some special reason for you seeking me out? Only, as you can see, I am a mite busy right now."

"In truth, it isn't you I seek so much as a useful source of information. Commander com 'Dolino requires a complete list of those wounded and an accurate description of whatever injuries they may have sustained."

"I have only rudimentary knowledge regarding this matter. You'll do better addressing your enquiries to Soleil, who is presently in charge."

It was no more than Varoi had expected. Still, he hesitated before moving on.

"Was there something else?" she asked, tilting her head quizzically.

"You might wish to know … Commander com 'Varicci has just now returned."

"Schezan is here?" Ayesha raised one elegant hand, pushing aside a lock of loose hair, tucking it neatly behind one ear. Varoi might have felt flattered had he not been convinced that this casual act of primping her appearance was done more for Schezan's benefit than his. Grinding his teeth in frustration, he forced down a sarcastic retort. It would do him no good to give in to the sharp spike of jealousy he felt. Ayesha was entitled to know Schezan had arrived back. But her instinctive response to this information made him simmer inside with wounded rage.

"Yes. He is." Varoi politely confirmed. Ignoring the hectic flush, which rose in her cheeks at the news imparted, he went on without pause, "Where is Soleil, by the way? Since she's the one best placed to provide information, I'd best not delay."

Ayesha waved a dismissive hand in the Shakar healer's direction and watched Varoi stride away. He did not seem unduly put out by Schezan's return; or perhaps he was and simply refused to admit it. Either way, she had seen no reaction to her overt display of interest in personal appearance. Her behaviour was merely a ruse aimed at discovering how he might respond. Its effect had not been all she could have hoped. Varoi's calm composure had been disappointing, to say the least. Especially since it provided no useful clue in regards to whether or not his feelings had changed. She would have to wait to see how Schezan behaved when confronted with the news that he now had a rival. Perhaps that reaction would prove satisfying enough.

Varoi was obliged to walk the entire length of the room before locating Soleil, which was just as well since it gave ample time for his temper to cool. She was currently engaged in a heated debate with two fellow healers and, while he hated disturbing her during such consultation, he felt obliged to do so nevertheless. If he *was* to obtain the required information it was better all round that he not delay.

Varoi was convinced he was now in serious disgrace following his ill-timed and apparently unprovoked behaviour towards a superior officer, chiefly because it had occurred in full view of all other's present upon the battlements. Speculation regarding the true likely cause of his animosity would doubtless be rife.

He wondered what form of hostility Schezan might have offered in response had their encounter taken place when they were alone and unobserved. Varoi thought it best not to dwell overlong on that prospect.

The information Soleil provided was edifying enough. Despite the apparent disadvantage of being compelled to engage the enemy in cramped conditions, which worked against them, the Shakar had given good account of themselves. Whatever injuries they'd sustained in the process, while serious enough, were mostly restricted to the lesser effects of a vigorous campaign. Not bad considering the preferred weapon of the Shakar was a hand-and-a-half or bastard blade and far more suited to less restricted situations. But then the Pulan had suffered similar difficulties in confronting the bulk of Tenbay's Shakar garrison in the outer bailey where conditions were such that there was barely room enough in which to swing a blade.

Few among the combined ranks of Shakar and supporting human combatants had suffered the serious wounds more closely associated with the hacking and hewing of a battle-axe blade. Varoi would have preferred to remain in ignorance of how badly those last had been affected, having witnessed first-hand the devastating results.

Thanking Soleil, Varoi turned on his heel and strode briskly away. Nodding an acknowledgement, in passing, to those few injured he recognised he deliberately avoided the chance to observe too closely the severity of their wounds.

Ayesha watched Varoi from under a dark fan of lashes, her head lowered over a wound to which she was busy applying a fresh dressing. He seemed oblivious to her presence. But still, she wondered: did he consider it inappropriate to acknowledge her existence or was he just too absorbed in his duties to pay her close heed?

She could not help but speculate on what manner of reception Schezan had received, from both the Shakar garrison and from his rival Varoi.

And she couldn't wait to find out.

Varoi was relieved to find his superior alone when he arrived with the report he'd managed to compile. It was bad enough that he was due a severe dressing down. He fully expected to be kept standing while his commanding officer fumed. In the end, things didn't turn out quite that way.

Commander com 'Dolino gave the list of dead and wounded no more than a cursory glance before setting the wad of paper aside. Leaning back in his chair, he glanced up at Varoi.

"Relax, Lieutenant, I've no plans to eat you, just yet. Chew on your soft edges a while, mayhap. You must admit you deserve some form of rebuke."

Varoi conceded the point with a resigned nod; then waited to see what else might be said.

"I feel I'm entitled to some sort of an explanation. Your conduct just now was far from normal. If you have a complaint against Commander com 'Varicci, it's best aired in privacy. Most grievances can be dealt with thus. Such outrageous behaviour does not befit a warrior of your rank. But then, you knew that already without being told."

Varoi kept silent, determined to offer no further source of annoyance.

"So tell me, Lieutenant. What is your problem?"

"He should have been here, could have arrived sooner than this."

His commander waved that explanation aside. "Could have, should have ... who is to say whether it would have made any difference? Be grateful Commander com 'Varicci and his reinforcements arrived when they did. Besides, that isn't an answer, just an excuse. Don't trifle with me, Lieutenant. If you wish to keep your present rank, just tell me the truth."

"And what is truth?" Varoi grumbled. "Any one of us might interpret it differently, according to what suits our needs."

His commander fixed him with a steely glare. "It's you that I'm asking. No one else. I'll make this easy so we can get to the facts by the most direct route. Commander com 'Varicci claims there is a history of animosity between you. Ancient history in his terms, but it looked pretty recent to me."

"Six years – I'd hardly call that ancient," Varoi muttered the words under his breath and looked his superior straight in the eye. He wasn't willing to divulge all the details, but a selective description of relevant facts should suffice ... beginning with an apology.

"I'm sorry if my behaviour caused you unnecessary grief, Commander. There is an outstanding dispute, one that has never been satisfactorily resolved, between myself and Schezan ... Commander com 'Varicci. In my opinion, at least.

"Which is?"

Varoi sighed, wishing the details could be kept secret. But it was too late for that. "I hold Schezan com 'Varicci responsible for my sister Bayritz's death."

"That's hardly a matter to be resolved by public confrontation."

"In this instance, having no other choice, I felt my behaviour justified. But, saying that, I should have thought

twice before starting an argument in front of his entire
garrison. If I'm being honest, the sight of Commander com
'Varicci accepting accolades he didn't deserve enraged me
beyond reason."

"So I noticed. But that's no excuse. Why has this
not been brought before the Council? The Elders should
deal with serious accusations such as this."

"Because, Commander, I have no solid proof.
Without proof there is no charge to answer."

"So, why not tell me what took place?"

"You won't be impressed," Varoi promised,
recalling his puny efforts against a larger, more impressive
male. He'd been too late to save his sister, which hadn't
stopped him from seeking revenge.

"Why not let me be the judge of that?"

Varoi's thoughts raced back to that fateful night.
Even as he began his recounting, keeping the details
distinct and concise, the memories rushed in. It was ever
like that. Bitter remorse was set to waylay him whenever
he dare venture along this path.

A black moon had risen, dense shadows clothing
the land. He'd never been scared of the dark, before or
since. That night was different. He'd been offered a
challenge; the first of three he was obliged to attempt, prior
to his Quickening.

Since his sister Bayritz had issued the formal
challenge, she was required, as witness, to attend that
night's event. Without his knowledge or consent, she'd
invited along a guest: Schezan. Dismayed at this
unforeseen development, he'd left them alone to their
lovers' tryst, while he went ahead to complete his task
alone.

The gorge into which he must descend was known
as the Demon's Throat. Its precipitous flanks were many
ells deep. Perilous enough to negotiate during broad
daylight, it was much more so in the dead of night. At its

bottom, the cascades and rapids were reduced, by a long season without rain, to a muted roar.

There was a path, of sorts. But it was incomplete and littered with obstacles Varoi was compelled to find a way past. Intent on accomplishing his given task, he'd given no thought to what was going on between Bayritz and Schezan.

His thoughts leapt ahead to what came next, even while his speaking voice droned on, reducing to soft syllables events that had left behind an indelible scar. Even so, his recounting remained suitably discreet. No point, he thought, in laying bare every nuance of these events. Those facts revealed were chilling enough.

The night was dark, yet black silhouettes stood clearly outlined against an indigo backdrop of star-spangled sky. The occasion was there in his mind. He hadn't quite gained the top of the cliff when Bayritz passed him, going down.

That resurrected yet another frozen moment in that night's events, when Schezan's aggression had achieved new heights. It could have been yesterday. He remembered Schezan grabbing fast hold. The shock of being yanked off his feet. The frightening knowledge that he was perilously close to a fifty-foot drop.

Schezan's breath had been rank on his face. His deep voice was a menacing growl, all the more menacing because it was dark and he couldn't see the look on his opponent's face, could only guess that its expression was hideously grim.

Even now his heartbeat sped, as in his mind's eye he clearly saw: *Schezan leaning forward, shoving his face close, to murmur in mesmerizing tones, "Now, here's an idea. One I quite like. It would make for a cleaner solution all round, if I just let you fall."*

"You wouldn't dare." That was the wrong thing to say, as Varoi knew.

"Don't tempt me."

He preferred not to think about what had happened next; how his struggles had caused the ground to give way, leaving one foot dangling in space. If not for a stranger happening along, he might not have been here to relate his tale.

Never had he felt so frightened or helpless, so hopelessly overwhelmed. One moment he'd been consumed by a savage fury, determined to avenge Bayritz's death; next instant he was fighting for his life.

The emotions he'd felt then lay perilously close to the surface now, leaving him drained. By the time Varoi had finished speaking, his knuckles were clenched white while he remained dry-eyed, his expression a stern mask of impassivity. His commander would find no sign of weakness in him, he vowed.

"I'm telling you this in confidence, Commander. I've no wish for it to become common knowledge."

"Nor shall it," his commander declared. "You have my word on that." He went on. "I take it there's not much chance of you setting personal differences aside."

"I could try. But I couldn't guarantee my success in any such undertaking."

"In which case, you leave me no choice other than to search for another solution."

Varoi tensed as his commander rose to pace. The room seemed too small to contain such restless concern.

"I have no wish to demote you," his commanding officer informed him. "Your actions today cannot be condoned, but you've suffered enough already, it seems to me. In the past you have proved yourself to be rash and impulsive, sometimes morose, inclined to outspokenness at times. But you're also a useful officer with an abundance of sound military acumen and no lack of courage. I shall be sorry to lose you, Lieutenant, but you cannot stay here, where provocation is too great a temptation to bear."

As though resigned as to which course of action he must take, Commander com 'Dolino stopped in front of Varoi.

"I think I have a fair grasp of the situation, Lieutenant. As it seems to you. You realise, of course, it is your word against his? Not that I suspect you of lying, since I know that is not your style. But still ... you can see what kind of predicament you've placed me in?"

Varoi pulled back his shoulders, straightened his back and waited for the hammer blow to fall.

"Some of us," his commander went on, moving to sit behind his desk and lean back in his chair, hands steepled in his lap. "Some get a chance to order the direction in which their life's course will run. Others have no recourse other than to accept what buffets or windfalls life deals out. I suspect you to be in the last group. As I recall, not long back you asked me to put you forward to train as Konicci. I was loath to lose your services at that time. And now ..."

As he spoke, Commander com 'Dolino leant forward to open a draw, producing inkpot, parchment and quill. "It seems you leave me no choice." He pulled out a dagger and began sharpening the quill pen. All the while he studied Varoi, who, profoundly aware of that solemn regard, kept his expression strictly neutral.

His senior officer went on, "There would have been a parting of our ways sooner or later. This way we both get what's best. I've just been informed that a new intake is due to enrol for Konicci training in five days' time. The question is: can you stay out of trouble long enough for me to arrange transport down river?"

Varoi fought to repress a recalcitrant grin. "I'll do my best."

"Then, we'll just have to hope that you succeed. I'm not sure what else I can suggest to keep you out of harm's way."

As reality struck home it was all Varoi could do not to shout aloud his relief and delight. Far from losing out on what promotion he'd so far gained, he was being offered the long awaited chance to build on his military expertise.

"As you say, Commander," was all he managed by way of confirmation.

"Very good, Lieutenant. I was rather hoping you would agree to my suggestion. There's one more duty I require you to carry out on my behalf. Assuming you're amenable, that is. And why wouldn't you be?" he added without pause. "Since you've just been offered a most worthy prize."

Varoi waited to see what task he would be expected to perform. The silence was broken only by the scratching of quill pen on parchment. "This is your letter of introduction to the weapons master at the High Citadel in Nai Hai du Veral. And this," his commander said, indicating the missive he was now in the process of composing, "is a letter explaining that those Pulan under your charge are captives taken during the siege."

"You're putting me in charge of our captives, Commander?"

"A temporary move, I assure you. They are a drain on our depleted resources, both medical supplies and provisions. The best solution is that we rid Tenbay of their presence with all conceivable haste, and offload our responsibility on to the Council of Elders. For that, I have need of a reliable escort to see them safely delivered to Nai Hai du Veral. You seem to be the obvious choice. I take it you have no objections?"

"As you command," Varoi said, indicating his full agreement with a brisk nod of assent.

It hadn't occurred to Varoi during the interview that he was about to depart Tenbay without having assured himself of success where Ayesha was concerned. The fact that Schezan had returned to take up with her where he'd left off would cause him more than a little distress once reality struck home.

Still, there was always *lossa antario* to provide him with access to Ayesha, which was some consolation, assuming she chose to make herself available to him.

"Is there anything else, Lieutenant?" Commander com 'Dolino enquired.

"Nothing of importance, Commander, so far as I'm aware."

"Very well. Return to your duties. I'll let you know as soon as transport has been arranged. Just do your best to stay out of trouble until that time."

Chapter 12: Konicci

Soft rain pattered against his face, unheeded. Brisk gusts of wind slapped at Varoi's head and neck, loosening damp tendrils of hair that alternately clung to his cheek or drifted behind, lashed by a rising gale.

Oblivious to outward distractions, Varoi gazed at the fast dwindling outline of Tenbay, easily distinguished by its flat-topped towers and crenulated battlements. Its bustling quayside and harbour were now diminishing with ever-increasing speed.

He was lost in quiet reflection, adrift on a sea of memories and partly accomplished ambitions. At the heart of those recollections were a few last precious hours spent alone with Ayesha.

In his mind's eye he saw again the tumble of tawny hair trailing across her pillow, her lush mouth and slightly parted lips, her lax limbs, modestly clad in a fine linen shift and something else. Something he had taken immense pains to arrange.

He recalled withdrawing from Ayesha's presence while she slept. And, as he did, saw again the subtle, yet significant, change. Enmeshed in her aura was a soft, ethereal glow. Reaching out he had set a splayed hand atop her lower belly and thighs, had experienced a slight tingling sensation that represented a unique protection of which she was yet unaware.

Varoi allowed himself a secretive smile. He had succeeded. Better than that. If what he believed was actually true, other Shakar male, when they came into close contact with Ayesha, would know at once what had been done. Better still. That included his rival, Schezan. And, while Schezan might not at once recognise its significance, Varoi's signature energy would remain, evident within the construct itself, until such time as it was removed.

Flushed with a sense of accomplishment, Varoi withdrew. He wanted to shout aloud his triumph, but prudently decided against, which fact in no wise diminished the virtue of his achievement.

The rhythmic thud of boots on weathered planking caused Varoi to return his attention to his immediate surroundings; reminding him where he was, compelling him to consider who might be about to intrude upon his solitude and recalling again the reason he had been forced to leave Ayesha behind. The sailors manning the vessel went barefoot, which narrowed the possibilities down, since, apart from Varoi, there were but three others aboard who might be wearing boots.

Varoi turned at the intruder's approach. Then he smiled with relief, on seeing that it was not, as he feared, one of those warriors assigned to guard the Pulan prisoners, but his friend Borit. His friend had elected to accompany him. It was Borit's intention to return to his home village. And since Varoi's father resided in the Shakar settlement, which was situated nearby, Borit had readily agreed to inform Varoi's sire of the Konicci training his son was about to undergo.

"We'll be there in next to no time, judging by the speed this vessel has put on," Borit pointed out, seeing Varoi glance aloft at the sails bellying above his head.

Varoi grunted his agreement and continued to scan the rigging. Moments ago, just before turning back to watch the port of Tenbay vanish behind a fine mist of drizzle, Varoi had stood and observed as the boy Horace swarmed nimbly aloft. Now he searched amongst overhead sails and rigging trying to see where Horace had gone. Varoi found him at last, perched on the topmost boom; his face, reduced by distance, no more than a pale blur. He, too, had been looking back the way they had come.

"Can you see him?" Borit asked. "He'll make a fine sailor from what little I've seen."

"If his grandsire allows," Varoi replied, morose, "which I doubt he will. Not with Horace being his sole remaining heir. Does it seem likely to you that his grandsire will forget all that he came so close to losing, not to mention those family members he actually lost?"

Horace had cadged passage aboard ship upon learning whereabouts Varoi was bound. He would return to Tenbay with the rest of the ship's crew, working his passage and learning the ropes at the same time. Horace was at something of a loose end until his grandfather was fit enough to return to what remained of his farm, which might be some time yet from all accounts. Borit, having suffered only minor injury during the battle of Tenbay, was intent on returning to blacksmithing forthwith.

The boat cut through the water like a knife. Christened the *Falcon Gris* it was currently living up to its name. Built with swift travel, rather than creature comfort, in mind the *Falcon* was suitably equipped for fast passage, for the express purpose of transporting couriers and courtiers alike. It had three cramped but well-appointed cabins, one situated at the bow and two at the stern. The stern cabins were specifically designed for passenger use, which was not to say the forward cabin could not, at a pinch, be similarly utilized. And, just like its namesake, the *Falcon* was capable of an unprecedented turn of speed.

Varoi glanced at the scenery flashing past and felt an unexpected exhilaration. So fast was the boat going, he calculated, that in less than a day he would arrive in Nai Hai du Veral. The prospect of so soon offloading his Pulan prisoners suited him admirably.

A shouted order drew his attention as barefoot crew hastened to adjust rigging and tighten sheets, ensuring that every scrap of available canvas could be employed. Varoi ducked low, avoiding the main boom, as the master brought his vessel about. Then he braced his stance as boards shuddered under foot. The vessel changed tack; then canted to port, catching the wind from a different quarter. It was a salutary example of naval expertise.

Beside him, Borit let out his breath on a windy sigh. "No matter how many times they do that I can't help but admire their skill and proficiency."

Ayesha perched on the edge of her bed contemplating the sorry condition of her hands. Who would have thought that three days of continuous hard usage could have such devastating effects on them? In that short time they had gone from soft and graceful to rough and chapped and anything but presentable. In truth, she would not have minded any other time. Today, though, was different. Different in that she wanted to look her elegant best.

Preparations were well in progress. A special celebration had been planned. The people of Tenbay were keen to show their heartfelt gratitude to those responsible for saving them from the Pulan. Principal among the invited celebrants were those of the garrison. As prominent members of the local Shakar community, Ayesha and her family were also expected to attend. A refusal would be deemed most impolite.

Yet, here she sat staring at her ruined hands, while outside her window night drew in and stars came out. The trouble was that it wasn't just her ruined hands that kept her here. Her skin might be chafed and sore, the nails themselves an eyesore but more than that she felt no urge to venture forth. A sigh escaped her, unremarked.

In all her life she had never failed to find merriment a worthwhile form of recreation. Dancing and feasting and all manner of lively conversation helped to stave off boredom and banish mournful musing. Yet, here she sat on her narrow, little cot, in her equally narrow, meanly furnished room, which Varoi, curse him for his absence, had once cheerfully likened to a broom cupboard, unable and unwilling to join in with the festivities.

Just last night Varoi had stood in this very room explaining, informing her of his intention to travel to the capital of Nai Hai du Veral. There he would embark on a course of training, with the prospect of being declared Konicci should he succeed in passing every test. She had been stunned to silence by the unexpected tidings of his planned departure. She could do no more than nod her acceptance of his glad news.

He had brushed one finger against her cheek and said, "I should go." Without waiting for her to add comment he had lowered his mouth to hers.

He had left soon after, returning, no doubt, to the dormatorium where he planned to take final leave of his friends.

This morning, an hour prior to sailing, Varoi had returned. As she cracked the door ajar in answer to his knock, he'd pushed his way in, a sense of urgency apparent in his demeanour.

Her thoughts still muzzy from a fitful night's rest, she had not been in the best of moods. His words on entering the room and closing the door did not improve her humour.

"I shouldn't be here, Ayesha. You know there'll be trouble if I'm seen."

"Then why bother? I didn't invite you, Varoi. You know that."

"Maybe not, but you wanted me to come."

"How very arrogant of you. How very male. And if I ask you to leave?"

"Then I shall go. But not before explaining a few things."

"Explain away, but make it quick. I have important duties to attend and they won't wait on your convenience."

With that she had turned aside, intent on avoiding his scrutiny. But Varoi had seized hold of her arm and spun her round to face him. Placing both hands on her

284

shoulders he had gazed down at her, a sad expression shadowing his face. She could not help but return that gaze. Angry though she was, she had no wish for him to leave; not yet and maybe not ever, if she had her way. But events had overtaken them both, it seemed. Looking up into his amber eyes she felt exposed, as though the true depth of her emotions was clearly on show. It was an unnerving feeling. Knowing that had not improve her mood one jot.

"As long as I can recall, I have wanted a chance to train as Konicci. It is the pinnacle of achievement towards which all Shakar warriors strain. Not all are granted their wish. To turn down such an opportunity would be foolhardy in the extreme."

"Fine. If it's that important don't let me stand in your way. Go."

She'd waved one hand in the door's direction, willing him to leave. She'd sounded peevish, a veritable shrew, not that she cared. They'd only just met. Within minutes of their first encounter Varoi had declared them to be soulmates. Not that she had agreed. She'd required considerable convincing, in fact. Now, six days later, he was planning to leave and not return for an extensive period of time. She felt entitled to get angry. How inconsiderate of him.

Varoi was not so easily deceived. "I know you're sorry to see me leave, Ayesha. Believe me if there were any other way."

"Don't fool yourself," she'd snapped. "I'm not sorry. I'm pleased. We've known each other a very short time. Not long enough to be truly committed, for which I am grateful. If this is the life you expect me to lead, forget it."

But Varoi wasn't listening.

"I promise to contact you the first chance I get, Ayesha, once I'm alone."

"Don't trouble yourself. I'm perfectly capable of finding amusement elsewhere."

He'd placed one gentle finger against her lips as though intent on softening the sting in her words.

"I mean it, Ayesha. I keep my promises. If I could fly to you, I would."

"Then it's just as well you cannot. I suppose I should be grateful for small mercies."

She wasn't sure what she'd meant by that remark. Either way it hadn't deterred Varoi in the slightest. Lowering his head, he had pressed his lips to hers in the sweetest, gentlest kiss she had ever known.

Cowardly tears had threatened to destroy whatever decorum she retained. Without thought she reached to twine both arms about his neck. She savoured the warm candour of his response as he drew her tight against his chest, felt again the rough bristles of his chin brushing her cheek. Reluctant to let go of him, she clung.

Disentangling himself, Varoi had taken hold of her hands, pressing a kiss to the centre of each palm in turn, whilst capturing her gaze with his.

"Never doubt my commitment, Ayesha. When I say I intend making you mine, I mean it."

His heated glance vouched more than words. In that moment, she had believed every syllable. But now … now she was assailed by doubt. And she knew she must confront Schezan with information he would not want to hear: the fact that he now had a rival in Varoi com 'Domicci.

It was close to dawn when they arrived at their moorings. Sails were slackened to flog lazily overhead, as the master backed his vessel into the wind, losing way and effectively reducing speed. Once again, Varoi and Borit were up on deck, keeping well out of the way as scurrying deckhands hastened to obey orders. In no time at all the sails were safely stowed and the boat rocked gently at her moorings. Low mist hung over the water making the harbour appear a mystical place.

Varoi could not wait to see the fabled skyline of Nai Hai du Veral come to life. Long had he heard of this City of Lights, where every window was reputed to be slanted at an acute angle in order to catch the sun's rays. His one previous visit had coincided with winter's solstice and a brief period when sea fog shrouded the city in its grim and clammy shroud. Today promised quite a different aspect, one to which he looked forward immensely.

Pennants snapped overhead as the wind began to pick up. Soon the sun would rise on a brave new day. The start of a significant change in Varoi's life. He could not help but respond to even the most meagre shift in his surroundings.

"Soon," said Borit, as he leant over the rail watching those hands who had been given the task of lowering the dinghy that would take them ashore.

"Yes," Varoi agreed, his voice clipped. Then he spun on his heel and strode away, intent on organising the removal of his prisoners under guard at the earliest opportunity. There would be time in which to gawp once that task was attended to.

As he turned to leave, a stray beam of sunlight crept over the horizon's rim. Varoi froze in his tracks, taken by surprise as the unequalled splendour of Nai Hai du Veral finally made itself known. For a moment he could only stand and stare.

A thousand lights winked into existence, as though on cue. They glinted back from every canted window in view, a scintillate blaze that brought the city to instant and unimaginable life. Designed with a unique objective, those panes had been angled in order to perform a specific task: to remind all who visited the city whose land this now was.

The Pulan might have named this the Unclaimed Land; and the name, once applied, had, indeed, stuck. But it was the Shakar and not the Pulan who had clearly demonstrated the necessary engineering skill to carve out numerous canals, thus draining the marshy fens to make life bearable and the land, consequently, more habitable. And only Shakar had the requisite talent to create such a city as this.

In that instant the sight was enough to steal breath.

Having had his passing fill of such magnificence Varoi continued on his way, leaving Borit to marvel alone. He had duties to uphold, tasks to fulfil and, since he was assigned here for the foreseeable future, there would be opportunities to gaze awestruck again.

Hours later, having absolved himself of all further responsibility regarding the prisoners, and with his dismissal of their escort arranged, Varoi set out for the High Citadel, where he was due to enrol for Konicci training.

The city hummed with bustling industry. Any other time Varoi might have felt tempted to explore, but not now. Now he focused his attention on his long-held ambition of becoming Konicci. An ambition, he did not need reminding, it would be incredibly difficult to attain.

And it seemed he was not the only one intent on enrolling that day. Three others had arrived before him. They loitered in the guardroom cooling their heels. This was not quite the reception Varoi had anticipated.

He introduced himself to the others by name rather than rank, determined they would, at least, start on an equal footing. Likewise, it seemed the three males were named Danova com 'Nominni, Bevis com 'Marai and Noltoi com 'Devericci.

As they completed their introductions an armour-clad female strolled in. If not for her warrior's garb and military bearing Varoi might have thought she had strayed into their presence by mistake. The error, he discovered, was his in assuming a mere female to be barred from such select company.

"Colvair com 'Severicci, here to enrol for Konicci training," she announced, to all and sundry, before anyone present dared to dispute her right to remain. Hardly had they told Colvair their names than a servant appeared, announcing he was deputized to escort them to their induction interview.

They followed close on the servant's heels as he led them through vaulted vestibules and along echoing corridors into the hallowed interior of the High Citadel.

They followed without conversation, their attention fixed on the way ahead.

Varoi observed that the servant's purple livery consisted of a tight-fitting tunic and hose, cinched at the waist with a scarlet *sabi* or sash. He recognised this colour of *sabi* as indicating the highest rank attainable among menial staff, which implied a certain deference for those being escorted. He wondered whether his fellow recruits recognised as much. Varoi knew he must get used to wearing a *sabi*. In his case the colour of *sabi* would be lilac, as befitted a warrior engaged in Konicci training.

In due course the servant ushered them into a capacious room furnished with rank upon rank of straight-backed, hardwood chairs. Each chair's seat was highly polished, mayhap due to hard usage, Varoi mused. A raised dais occupied one end of the room, its space lacking any form of comfort, even the benefit of chairs. With a wave of his hand the servant indicated their surroundings.

"Sit wherever you wish," he instructed. And with those few words he withdrew, leaving Varoi and his fellows to consider where best they might take their ease. There was plainly a surfeit of choice.

Varoi considered the situation: the door behind him was closed; the seating was set out in rows; the dais was clearly the focus of this arrangement. He knew full well that a wise commander learnt to judge his warriors by their individual choices and actions and not just in military terms. He wondered, was there a viewing hole? A place discreetly constructed so as to enable the hidden observer to oversee all.

His sideways glance took in his fellow recruits. Who would be first to take potential advantage of this situation? His answer came almost at once.

"There's no point in my hanging about, waiting while you lot make up your collective minds."

With that tart comment, Colvair sauntered to the front of the hall, where she selected a seat located almost dead centre, one where she could not fail to be noticed and, settling down, crossed one shapely leg over the other in an elegant pose.

After that it was simply a matter of each warrior deciding where best to sit.

Varoi selected a position second row back and two seats in. Noltoi and Bevis chose the same row, occupying the two end seats, at opposite ends of the room. Danova opted to arrange himself prominently, selecting a seat in the front row right and at the farthest end. Varoi had no idea what significance each decision revealed in strategic terms. Although, doubtless Colvair's implied an outright refusal to be intimidated or overlooked.

Soon after the last of them had made his choice and settled into position, a small door in the side wall swung open and an imposing figure strode into the room. Varoi watched with interest as the new arrival made his way to the dais, stepped on to the platform and glanced around. He was an impressive figure in every respect. Varoi didn't need the purple *sabi* to inform him: this male would take charge of his training from now on. His aura of supreme assurance sufficed.

Varoi had no doubt: this male *was* the Konicci
weapons master himself.

"Most interesting," said the male confronting them,
studying each one of them in turn. "A small contingent this
time around, but interesting enough. My name, in case
you're still wondering, is Shah com 'Savicci, Weapons
Master to the Konicci. You will address me as Weapons
Master at all times; when you have occasion to address me
at all. Starting with the front row right hand seat, each of
you in turn will stand and be recognised, stating only your
name for now. All are assumed to be equal during Konicci
training."

With these words Shah turned towards Danova,
who might well have been wishing he had chosen
differently by now. "Begin," he commanded.

Varoi was relieved to be neither first nor last when
it came to stating his name. At this stage in proceedings he
preferred to remain unostentatious, content, for now, to let
Colvair and Danova become the focus of Shah's attention.
That might well change. But not for some time – a hope
that was vain as it turned out.

"There are certain rules that govern your conduct
while you remain in the High Citadel," the weapons master
informed them. "The first and most important imperative is
this: no running is allowed. You disobey this ruling on
pain of death, quite literally. Now, without more ado, let us
get down to the business for which you have come here."
Shah gestured for them to follow as he descended from the
podium.

Emerging from a wide tunnel, Varoi saw ahead of
him a huge indoor training arena the like of which he had
never before seen. To either side of the tunnel opening
were displayed racks upon racks of weapons. The arena
itself was covered in sawdust and marked out in a series of
circles. Varoi had hoped to see some form of training

session taking place. He was disappointed to find there was none.

The weapons master turned to face them, his expression grim.

"This," he said, "is where all your training will take place. First, though, you will satisfy my curiosity by proving whether or not you are worthy of any efforts I choose to make on your behalf."

Shah glanced about at his audience, fixing each of them in turn with a considering gaze.

"Not all who apply get accepted. Being nominated is only the first hurdle among many you will encounter along the path to being declared Konicci. You will be judged every step of the way. There is no room for complacency here, no time to relax or drop your guard for even a minute. Should you do so you will either fail or be killed. Do not for one moment imagine this to be an easy undertaking."

Varoi had heard those same words before from Commander com 'Dolino. Strangely, they impressed him far more now that he was actually here, facing the first in an endless series of trials and assessments.

"Do not assume," the weapons master said, "that because your names have been put forward you automatically qualify for training. Now ... I want you all to watch what I do. Then each in turn will repeat those actions ... precisely."

They watched as Shah strode a few paces to the nearest circle marked out and reached over his shoulder to draw his sword.

Varoi's eyes widened in surprise. Just for a moment, as Shah reached up to grasp the weapon's black hilt, he thought he had seen something ... unusual, something he had never before witnessed in relation to a sword.

"Ah," said Shah. "I see one among you is *ananaha*. Your name?" he enquired, halting in front of Varoi, a slight smile tilting the corners of his mouth. Varoi realised, as he answered the weapons master with suitable respect, that much as he'd hoped to maintain partial anonymity he had lost whatever small advantage he possessed with that instinctive reaction.

"Now, if you would kindly explain whatever it was you thought you saw."

Varoi had no qualms in complying with that request. For one thing he didn't *think* he had seen something unexpected. He knew. "As you went to set hand to your sword a dazzling flash of green lightening sizzled along the length of its hilt."

"A precise description of what undoubtedly occurred. To explain: the blade was crafted to my requirements. To ensure none other than myself would be tempted to lay claim to the weapon, an exclusivity ward was built into its hilt. Should any among you wish to tempt fortune, now is your chance. You'll not have a better opportunity."

With slow deliberation Shah drew his sword, presenting it, haft first.

None seemed willing to take the risk.

"Tis as well that you refuse," Shah told them. "The remedy is as painful as the curse."

"You begin thus," Shah said, moving to the closest circle of sawdust and setting his sword point down. "And then …"

Without further preamble, Shah swept up his weapon and commenced a series of swift and intricate manoeuvres. Beginning with his right hand, transferring later to his left, he whirled it with life-threatening speed and dexterity. Each move differed slightly from the accepted norm.

Varoi, having developed a few useful variations of his own, could appreciate the subtlety employed: a sly feint followed up by an equally cunning underhand jab, which would serve to incapacitate an opponent for a time; the deft flick that could easily remove an inattentive opponent's ear. Light flickered along the length of the fast-moving blade, further adding to its mesmerizing effect, as Shah, having completed that section, brought both hands into play. The hand-and-a-half sword was designed to enable full pile-driving force to be applied. Shah's abrupt change of tactic was the required prelude to a series of swift powerhouse moves. He demonstrated with admirable skill the weapon's ability to sever head from neck, legs from torso or split an opponent in twain.

The demonstration finished, Shah rested his weapon point down, pinning his pupils in place with a solemn regard.

"That is what I want each one of you to do in turn. You will carry out the exercise in the same order you introduced yourselves."

They nodded. Then Danova stepped forward to begin.

Shah's expression remained stern as he surveyed each in turn once the task was complete.
"You did well. I observed a few minor discrepancies: nothing significant, nothing that cannot be improved upon. You'll be relieved to learn you all passed your first assessment with ease. I would expect nothing less. I warn you: do not confuse congratulations with praise. There is a world of difference between the two. Your training proper is about to begin. Make no mistake it will not be easy."

Sheathing his sword, the weapons master began to pace. "You will train with all manner of weapons, ones familiar and others less so. In order to defeat an opponent it pays to experience first-hand the various disciplines involved in relation to each weapon, thus exposing any

294

weakness you can exploit. One more thing: at least once during the course of training, assuming you last that long, you will encounter an adversary intent on killing you. I trust I make myself clear?"

Being forewarned, Varoi understood. In short: they would leave here changed … or dead.

_Chapter 13: Boundaries

Varoi was relieved when, at the end of a long and exhausting day, he and his fellow recruits were shown to their individual rooms. He was especially relieved to find he was not expected to share his quarters or bed down in a huge dormatorium. He was further relieved to discover the bundle of belongings he'd left in the guardroom had also found its way there.

He had no idea how other members of his group fared. For himself, he was far too exhausted to peer out his window at the view, let alone unpack. All Varoi wanted to do was sleep. But sleep was out of the question, for now. First he had a small task to perform. One not quite as arduous as those others in which he'd engaged this day. But all the more important in his opinion.

All else must wait until he had contacted Ayesha. Ayesha, and the rare solace of *lossa antario*, came first.

He flopped down on an available chair and tugged off his boots. Next he hauled off his clothes, discarding them in an untidy pile on the floor, before crawling gratefully between crisp, linen sheets. He was too worn out from the day's exertions to take advantage of the bowl of warm water and fresh towel thoughtfully provided for his benefit. Maybe tomorrow he would pay attention to such niceties. For now, he had no energy left. Correction: no energy save that required to make contact with his beloved.

Settling back on the pillows and closing his eyes, he allowed one hand to indulge in a casual caress, to feel beneath those questing fingers his firm muscles and taut flesh. The mere though of Ayesha doing likewise sufficed to make his heated body hard and hungry in response. He yearned for a taste of her sweet lips, the touch and texture of smooth, silky skin. Sensations that only the intimate connection of *lossa antario* could provide, when two lovers found themselves so far apart.

296

Varoi strove to conjure up a vision of Ayesha as he had seen her last: long tawny hair mussed from a night's sleep, her nightshift wrinkled and slipped casually awry to bare one shoulder, lips slightly parted in protest as he pushed his way past her, closing the door behind. Such a sultry and evocative image set his heart pounding and hot blood racing through his veins.

Diligently he fought to bring his rampaging libido under control. Ayesha might not appreciate a lustful approach. He had no way of knowing how convenient his timing might be.

Gathering his shamanic powers close, Varoi sent forth a slender thread of enquiry. Determined upon a refined approach, he skimmed her cheek with a touch that was almost graceful in its delicacy. Then, impatiently, he awaited her response.

Ayesha was late arriving for the celebrations. She was not deliberately tardy; rather, she had allowed herself to become sidetracked. Stepping into the huge hall she glanced about, hoping to catch sight of her family who should have arrived en masse and been considerably more prompt than she.

The room was crowded, which did not surprise her one wit. It did, however, pose something of a problem. She had no wish to loiter alone on the periphery of this joyous gathering for any length of time. What she wanted were familiar faces around when next she encountered Schezan.

Spying an exuberant Toku edging his way towards her through the throng, she raised a beckoning hand and started out in his direction. She didn't get far.

To her left a lofty individual dressed in gold-embroidered black brocade peeled away from his group and started towards her. Seconds later Toku froze in his tracks.

Puzzled, Ayesha took another step forward, then stopped, as someone tall and imposing inserted himself between.

"Ayesha," said Schezan. "I was beginning to think you might be avoiding me. I see I was wrong. You merely took your time in order that your appearance should prove a perfect complement to mine."

She glanced up. As so often in the past, she was struck by his exquisite male beauty. Tall, dark and magnificently well built, his amber eyes flashing, he exuded masculine charm. He was a weakness, a fire in her blood; but, even so, there was a flaw in their relationship. One she recognised, even if Schezan did not.

Reaching out, he caught her up in his arms, dragging her close against him, bringing his mouth down to meet hers and rendering her speechless, stifling all her attempts at protest of such rough handling. Schezan seized full advantage, by using the kiss to imprint upon her his full authority, effectively stealing her breath.

Had it been anyone other she might willingly accept such misuse. A similar approach from Varoi would certainly be welcomed. Not so this particular male.

Consumed by anger, she registered her spite by kicking him hard in the shins, bringing both hands up to his chest and thrusting at him with all her might. He stood firm, despite her display of feminine pique. Still she had contrived a reaction of sorts. Leaning back he glanced down, amber eyes ablaze.

"So much fury in so small a package. Tell me, Ayesha, what has got into you? This is hardly the welcome I have come to expect of my Chosen."

Ayesha was livid and did not care that they were not alone. She opened her mouth to give him a piece of her mind. A large slice, complete with embellishments, was what he deserved in her view and she was only too happy to oblige.

Something light and delicate nuzzled her cheek, a decided irritation at this precise moment in time. Without thought, she flicked the small distraction aside and reinforced her rejection with an abrasive mental rebuke. *Not now!*

Varoi gasped in surprise as his slender thread of enquiry snapped back with a stinging recoil. *Not now!* Surely, the delicacy of his touch had not warranted so harsh a rebuke?

He had contrived a subtle approach in case Ayesha was not alone. The vexed thought occurred: was it possible the person with whom she was currently engaged was Schezan? If so, might that not explain her ungracious attitude? And if that *were* the case, might he not be justified in repeating the exercise? Time, he decided, to place a touch more emphasis on shared intimacy, which, when enhanced by an intensity of some magnitude, should ensure that his presence could not be ignored.

Varoi considered such action worth the risk. After all, what had he to lose?

Determined not to be politely sidelined, thereby allowing his arch rival to benefit from his prolonged absence, Varoi dispatched yet another thread of enquiry. This one was considerably more obvious in its approach. Then he settled back on the pillows and awaited results.

Ayesha slammed her fists into Schezan's chest, driving him back a pace, forcing him to allow her more space.

"You assume too much, Schezan com 'Varicci. Mayhap I once declared you Chosen; but, for your information, this is one situation that is prone to change."

"What is that remark supposed to mean?" Schezan queried, his dark brows drawn together in a ferocious scowl. There was a spark of malice in Schezan's golden gaze, a warning glint Ayesha knew well. Dire warning to all in their vicinity: Schezan was not to be taken lightly.

But then, in her opinion, neither was she. She felt she deserved some measure of respect; would have it whatever it took.

"It means exactly what I said it does, Schezan. You have a rival, one who claims that he and I are fated to be soulmates. Surely *that* is something with which you can identify? I wonder. Do you consider us that closely matched?"

"Soulmates?" Schezan snorted with amused disbelief. "I had no idea you believed in such nonsense. If I have a rival then tell me his name. Don't keep me in suspense, I beg. I have a right to confront this insolent challenger forthwith. To ascertain for myself the true merit of his credentials."

Ayesha smiled to herself, pleased, for once, that Varoi *was* conveniently elsewhere. She had no doubt regarding Schezan's determination to confront any such rival the first opportunity he got. He would pierce Varoi through without question or remorse, just for having the temerity to entertain the prospect that he had any hope of winning her hand. It was not a case of petty jealousy, rather one of prior possession. Schezan simply could not bear to be thwarted.

"Alas, Schezan," she began. "Your rival is regrettably absent."

"How tiresome of him. You still have not told me his name? You cannot expect me to take you seriously without proof of this male's existence?"

There was sufficient space between them to ensure she felt safe from his burgeoning ire. Not that he would dare behave inappropriately when there were witnesses present.

"You won't know him, Schezan, I assure you of that. He is but lately arrived on the scene. I have no hesitation, however, in revealing his identity. His name is

Varoi: Lieutenant Varoi com 'Domicci. One of those who
…"

"Varoi com 'Domicci. I might have guessed,"
Schezan sneered. "How distressingly *in*convenient that he
should be absent at this precise time. Almost as though his
departure were contrived."

"You *do* know him?" Ayesha could not conceal her
surprise. If Schezan were aware of Varoi's existence, at
least he had no reason to doubt her word.

"You could say we share a … *certain* relationship."
There was a snide inference behind that comment,
something Schezan, seemingly, preferred to leave unsaid.

Ayesha was not about to be deterred from
uncovering the truth. Not if it had any bearing on her
newly fledged relationship with Varoi. She had a right to
know what it was about Varoi that made Schezan so
patently hostile.

"What kind of relationship would that be?" she
wondered aloud.

"Let's just say it's ancient history and leave it at
that."

"And might this shared past have any effect on your
rivalry?"

"It would seem so. I fear, Ayesha, you have been
made a dupe. Varoi is using you as an excuse to get at me.
Hardly courteous behaviour you must agree."

"Perhaps he considers his behaviour to be justified.
What does he have against you, might I enquire? Is it
something I am permitted to know?"

"Who am I to refuse so polite a request? Let's just
say, Varoi com 'Domicci holds me responsible for his
sister's untimely death. A wholly unfounded accusation, I
can assure you."

"You are both rivals for my favour, Schezan. Do
you expect me to believe such slanderous accusations,
when Varoi has uttered not one word against *you*?"

"Believe what you wish, Ayesha. An unfortunate accident resulted in his sister's death, whereupon Varoi accused me of murder, simple as that. All because I was the only other person present at the time. Varoi laid the burden of blame with me, personally. Perhaps I should have been more forceful in my denial. Had I done so mayhap his accusations would have long since ceased. Whatever he says, I am not responsible."

"Then what *are* you saying, Schezan?"

Schezan gave his shoulders a negligent shrug, assuming a distressed expression, waiting to see how Ayesha would react. It was obvious from her comments that Varoi had told her nothing of their enduring enmity. In that omission he saw a chance he could exploit. Ayesha would not soon forget Varoi's neglect in revealing the fact that he and Schezan were already acquainted. Why *had* his rival not chosen to mention that fact? Varoi was a fool to make such a mistake ... as *he* had been on that fateful night. He recalled the event with stunning clarity. None had seen fit to challenge him about it since ... none save Varoi.

Had it been the dreadful accident he claimed? Could it have been prevented? The answer was yes and *yes*. It *had* happened the way Varoi said: more or less.

He never should have agreed to meet Bayritz for a tryst that night. Had he refused, things would not have turned out as they did. But his own selfish needs pushed him into committing that mistake, one he'd regretted ever since.

Bayritz was just one of a number of females he'd kept in tow at that time, none of whom he considered a potential mate. Of them all, Bayritz was by far the prettiest. She was also the most skilled when it came to providing him with sexual relief, which, for him, at the time, was an important consideration. It did not imply, though, that he had any intention of making theirs a more permanent arrangement.

It was his declared intention to one day choose as mate a female more suited to the elevated station of consort to the High Obajan. It was the position he expected to attain when his father, the present High Obajan, died. Still, Bayritz persisted in her attempts to persuade him otherwise. His constant refusal only served to firm her resolve. In Schezan's view, none of his playmates lived up to his exalted expectations, none were possessed of sufficient wit and intelligence, not to mention a certain pizzazz, such as he had since found in Ayesha. She alone lived up to his requirements. Besides which, she was a princess in her own right. Nor did he intend a minor impediment, such as the one posed by his rival, to prevent him attaining that to which he laid claim.

The truth of what had happened, painful though it was to recall, was that he lost his temper that fateful night. He and Bayritz had started to argue, something they were often wont to do at the time. As tempers flared out of control, she had served him a vigorous shove. Caught off-guard by her attack, he'd shoved back with equal, if not greater vigour. As a result, Bayritz had tumbled backwards over the precipice.

It was a long way down in the dark, with naught but rocks and boulders to cushion her landing. A fatal mistake instantly regretted. All in all, a spectacular way to die.

Would he have behaved differently had he known what would result from his reaction? Having disposed of one tiresome impediment to replace it with another, one far more tenacious and vexing? Perhaps. In fact, almost certainly, yes.

His response to Varoi's follow-up assault had been equally instinctive. Yes, he had tried to dispose of Varoi, seeing him as the sole witness of note. There was no reason to inform Ayesha of that. As matters stood, it was his word against Varoi's.

Too long had Varoi been a thorn in his flesh. One he'd been unable to dig out and dispose of as he would have wished, no matter how hard he tried. And he *had* tried. Varoi was correct in one respect. He *had* tried to kill him that night. The fact he had failed then did not mean he would not try again at some later date.

For the most part their resentment lay dormant, until such time as it came to the fore. Left to fester unchecked it was liable to erupt without warning, verbal confrontation being the usual result. So far, they had not come to blows. So far, although not for much longer, it seemed. Their seething animosity was a living thing that had too long been denied the violent outlet required to expunge the problem once and for all. The chance for that solution would come soon enough, if he had any influence at all.

Carefully he studied Ayesha's expression. It was plain she felt angry and confused. Schezan knew he could put that anger and confusion to good use.

And he would.

Ayesha did not know what to believe. She was angry with Schezan for maligning Varoi when he was not around to explain his actions. But she was angrier still, and inexplicably hurt, that Varoi had not seen fit to entrust her with this information. Such deceitful behaviour was not what she had come to expect of Varoi. What troubled her most was the fact that his wilful duplicity might be the result of erroneous assumption: did he really think she would misunderstand? That suspicion in no wise reduced her increasing sense of betrayal. Then, just as she was coming to terms with the situation, Varoi and *lossa antario* provided yet further cause for offence.

Ayesha had known full well who had brushed against her awareness a few moments ago. The tactful diplomacy of his touch had been clue enough. What she did not expect was that Varoi would respond with a message that was stronger, even more provocative than that which had gone before.

She was unprepared for the pure sensuality of his follow-up approach, which left her weak at the knees and yearning for more. Her eyes grew wide in response to that disturbing touch. It was all she could do to stay in control. As it was, a warm flush tinged her cheeks with a becoming blush and her green eyes sparkled with barely restrained desire.

Her defensive rebuff came equally strong and swift. *What are you doing, Varoi? Can you not take a hint? I said. NOT NOW!*

Like a clap of thunder she sent him a broadside, a ringing slap that made his skin tingle and his head spin.

It took Varoi several heartbeats to recover and recognise from exactly where Ayesha had culled such stunning amounts of power. It seemed she had seized hold of his slender thread of enquiry, innocuous though it appeared to him, and, having inverted its initial potential, had delivered it back from whence it came, *with interest.* Who was it said that female Shakar represented no real threat? He knew different. It was a painful form of rejection. One he was in no haste to repeat any time soon.

Saddened by yet another rebuttal, Varoi rolled over in bed and went to sleep.

It was the end of another long and tiring day when Varoi entered his quarters alone. A black moon had risen over the Unclaimed Land; nothing new or unusual in that. Such nights occurred with monotonous regularity, one in each lunar month. It was an ill-omened night, nonetheless, when the one-eyed Moon goddess Lecristo, she who ruled fate and happenstance, turned her blind eye toward all dark and nefarious deeds.

The black moon reminded Varoi of another such night, one he much preferred to forget. He slammed home the shutters, removing the inauspicious scene and turning his back on the past with a finality he knew to be false.

A vision awoke in his mind's eye: of his sister Bayritz flying backwards over a precipice; of Schezan com 'Varicci standing above her, arms outstretched. Did she fall or was she pushed? Did Schezan strive to hold fast or fend off? Only two knew the answer to that.

And one was dead.

Six years had passed since it happened; still the memories remained fresh, the bitterest and most painful always the last to fade. Perhaps if he'd asked, instead of accusing, the truth concerning Schezan's actions might have been made clear ... or he could have lied.

Varoi flung himself full length on the bed. The blade of bitter memory bit deep; then twisted awry in raw grief. A sob escaped.

Much later, exhaustion released him to sleep.

Varoi stood above a precipice staring down into oblivion, oblivion more deep and drear than any he had hitherto seen. Abruptly the scene changed.

He was standing amidst a snowy landscape, reduced to the soft monochromes of winter. A leaden sky loomed low overhead promising yet more snow to come. He saw a dark and brooding forest ahead and to his left a village of tents. Not tents, Varoi realised, as closer examination revealed their rounded outlines more clearly, but yurts. That meant this land hereabouts belonged to the Pulan, of which there were bound to be significant numbers somewhere close by.

Instinctively Varoi started to back away, wanting to retreat from hostile territory, only to find something large and solid barring his way.

"Come, cousin," said a gravelly voice from behind. "Tis time for the gathering to get under way."

306

Before Varoi could even begin to absorb the import of those words a heavy hand was clamped to his shoulder and he was turned about and steered in the direction of the nearest yurt. It was bigger by far than all the others around.

Biting his tongue for fear of saying the wrong thing, Varoi ducked through the tent flap and then straightened to take a quick look round.

A heavy scent of burning tallow scented the still air; smoke hung spiralling on the atmosphere, adding to the general stuffiness. The air seemed warmer inside than out; but, even so, Varoi experienced a sudden chill. Nor could he ignore a growing sense of alarm.

The structure was huge, bigger inside than he'd first supposed. And it was stuffed to the gunnels with hostile Pulan, all glaring fiercely in his direction.

Refusing to be intimidated, and espying a vacant seat where two long benches had been placed opposite each other leaving a vacant space at the centre of the yurt, Varoi strode to the seat and sat down.

"Budge up, cousin," said the stranger and Varoi obliged. He had no intention of causing offence or starting an argument, not when he was in no position to win.

A bowl was passed along the line. Varoi, receiving it, held it in both hands, studying its contents with baleful suspicion, aware his actions were studied in turn.

"Drink, cousin, so that I too may take my turn. Or do you wish me to perish of thirst?"

Lifting the bowl one-handed, Varoi contrived to slop some of its contents on the ground. He half expected to be cursed for his careless inattention, but no rebuke was offered. Instead, a myriad pairs of eyes followed his every move, followed but made no comment.

Placing the bowl to his lips, he ventured a cautious sip. The liquid was warm, fomented milk, thick and tangy, with just a hint of something added to the brew. A

307

suspicion grew as his tongue savoured the potent distillation ... juniper berries and ... sloe! Varoi downed the draught with one long swallow. Then he passed the bowl back so that it might be refilled.

The powerful concoction was already taking effect by the time the bowl returned. Varoi passed it across to the man alongside, who did not hesitate as Varoi had done. He poured a generous amount on to the ground at his feet, in the form of a libation, before imbibing the rest. So, thought Varoi, mayhap spilling a little was not a mistake on my part but an inspired decision.

While he sat considering this, along with the knowledge that his appearance in the yurt continued to pass unchallenged, an older man rose and began addressing those assembled. As he did, all conversation, subdued or otherwise, ceased.

"We have a problem: one that refuses to go away; one that cannot be solved by the usual methods. We know this because we have already tried. Despite our best efforts to drive them out, still the Shakar remain in the Unclaimed Land. Worse yet, they thrive. What, then, should we do?"

"Eradicate them!" came a shout from behind.

The Pulan who had been speaking rewarded the comment with an indulgent smile. "I would that it were that simple. Yet, one way or another, the Shakar must be persuaded to leave. And soon, before any further damage is sustained by the Land."

There was a general chorus of "Aye" before he went on.

"Once we could rely on the Unclaimed Land itself to ensure an early departure of any would-be colonists: releasing its usual virulent deterrents in the form of parasites, pestilence and plague. Now it is the Shakar who are become a pestilence and plague: boring wells for clean water, digging dykes and canals, anything that serves to drain bogs and marshes and dry out the soil. You've all

seen and noted the change to which I refer, more and more land turned over to the plough.

"Once the Unclaimed Land played host to a rich diversity of life: it sustained, it sheltered, life burgeoned there as nowhere else on Etheria. All that has changed. The change cannot be allowed to continue until all that was vibrant is lost. We must act now, before it's too late. The gods gifted us with the Unclaimed Land, a place of respite from these harsher climes. It is ours to cherish so that in turn it may nourish our souls. With us lies the burden of responsibility for what happens next.

"The Shakar do not falter and fail as we might hope. They thrive! Their numbers are few, but increasing all the while. Dare we delay? Dare we wait till it is too late? Shall we shrug off our burden of care as we did in the past? Consigning the Land to its fate and expecting all to be well at the last?"

There was a pause, quickly filled by stamping of feet and shouts of "Nay!" "Banish the incomers!" "Drive them out!"

Yet another indulgent smile. "I sense your commitment. It gives me hope."

An answering shout rang out. Boots once more began stamping down on the hard-packed earth. Varoi glanced about. This was the first time since taking his seat in the yurt that he had dared do more than remain silent, his first real chance to study those assembled.

He was seated at the centre of the yurt, where two wooden benches had been set out. At his back, lining the walls, stood row upon row of Pulan: of differing ages, mostly young and most of them undoubtedly warrior class and every last one of them male. It was a daunting sight. He was hopelessly outnumbered and yet they paid him no particular heed, as though he were accepted, as though he too were Pulan.

Varoi turned his attention back to the man who had been speaking. He was still on his feet, waiting for the sounds of approval to die down. There was something familiar about his face and demeanour, an air of authority that made him stand out from the rest ... and something else besides. As though this were a man whose face he'd seen across an unsheathed blade.

He was dressed in dark breeches tucked into knee-high boots. The tops of the boots revealed themselves to be fur-lined. His upper body was warmly clad in the furs of wolf and wolverine. He was broad shouldered and barrel chested with a stance that shouted "command." And, in Varoi's opinion, he was also grossly hirsute, his pale hair forming a dense halo about his head, his face hidden behind a bushy beard and moustache. All, save his eyes, was obscured and these last were as chips of ice, especially when, as now, he turned to confront Varoi's curious gaze. A chill travelled the length of Varoi's spine. Still, he refused to become unnerved.

Not all in the yurt were shouting approval, not all those present were stamping their feet. Most of the noise was attributable to those lining the tent walls. Young men mostly, including some not yet old enough to have been bloodied in battle.

Waving his audience to silence, the speaker resumed. "Tis time to act; to cast off our sloth. Past sorties and raids have availed us naught, save passing satisfaction for the irritation thus caused. Tis no longer enough! We must send the Shakar packing. Send them back to whence they came. Tis time we reasserted dominion of the Unclaimed Land."

"And the Fenlanders?" came a shout. "What of them?"

"They are not our enemy. They never were."

"They allowed the Shakar to remain."

"Tis true, but what else could they do? They are not warriors like us. And they benefit from whatever actions the Shakar put in hand. They are not our problem, whereas the Shakar are for so long as we allow them to remain. Tis our apathy that allowed them this chance. Tis up to us to amend the situation as soon as we may. I say it is time to suit action to words. Tis time we did more. Time we restored the Unclaimed Land to what it was before the Shakar began bringing about its ruination."

A significant pause, during which snow could be heard hissing against the skin of the yurt. Then the entire gathering erupted into uproar, leaving only Varoi and the man who had instigated this reaction silent amidst the raging storm. Varoi had his own reasons for not wanting to join in, while the other seemed to revel in the maelstrom he had knowingly created.

Varoi longed to protest, to point out the glaring discrepancies in their information. Far from destroying the land the Shakar had come to think of as theirs, they had improved it, but only where such improvement was justified. The lush grasslands, which formed a buffer zone between the high plateaus of the steppes that were the acknowledged domain of the Pulan and the neighbouring fens, remained as they had always been. Habitat of pronghorn antelope and bear, of bustard and wild cattle, which were preyed upon in turn by the grey collared cat that moved through the long-stemmed grasses like smoke, by wolf and wolverine alike.

The fens had been changed of necessity; there was no point in denying that. Once a wet wasteland where people endured rather than thrived, its fouled pools of water had been the source of pestilence and plague. Before the Shakar's arrival supplies of clean water could seldom be found. Those humans inhabiting the fens left things be. But at what cost to their health and survival? Few children survived their early years and surviving adults were sickly and unsound, seldom living beyond their middle years. The Shakar had changed all that.

Enterprising engineers contrived to dig wells, ensuring ample supplies of sweet water. The land was drained and waterways created so that tradesmen could ply their trade far inland, eradicating some water-borne pests in the process and leaving others for nature to contain: frogs, fingerlings and salamanders gobbled up the larva of biting insects, helping to keep the environment safe for those living in the fens.

Further north, far beyond the city's reach, things remained as they had been: there were still vast tracts of marsh and bog and brackish water where huge flocks of waders and waterfowl might be found.

"You refuse to join in. Does this mean you disapprove?"

Varoi glanced up, meeting the questioner's gaze without flinching. "I've been thinking. You need a strategy."

"Indeed we do," the man facing him agreed. "We'd be fools to think we could again get away with so loose an arrangement as last time. You have a suggestion?"

Varoi shook his head, unwilling to offer his sworn enemy a potential advantage. The speaker did not seem to mind.

"Strategy is important," he went on. "Far better to go in with only half an idea than nothing whatever in mind. And there is time enough in which to plan. Three whole seasons we have at our disposal: winter keeps us trapped here, spring and summer are our busiest times of year, but autumn ... that is a good time to act."

Raising his voice so that all present could hear he called the gathering to order. "If complete agreement has been reached a war council can be formed from those of the Inner Circle here present." With an encompassing

312

gesture he indicated those now seated on benches. "We shall call on others' experience as need dictates. All in favour say 'Aye.'"

There followed a universal shout of assent.

Varoi watched as the ceremonial bowl of brotherhood was once more passed around. When his turn came again he remembered to offer a libation. Then, closing his eyes, he set the bowl to his lips and prayed for deliverance.

The hallway was wide and well lit, with tall, triangular windows admitting ample amounts of light. Dust motes danced in rays of golden sunlight. There were hints of gold on overhead cornices and in the richly coloured tapestries lining the walls between each of those same windows. In truth, though, he paid these details scant heed, save in passing.

What Varoi did notice was the attitudes of those servants he passed. Each, without exception, offered him obeisance. Varoi considered that behaviour to be most strange. Why would anyone, even a liveried servant, pay particular attention to him, a common warrior, unless addressed? Yet they did.

Something else he noticed, as he swept down the corridor: the swish and rustle of robes as he moved. All the servants he saw were dressed in regulation purple tunic and hose, not a robe in sight. Indeed, to his knowledge, few among the Shakar male wore robes, other than council members and, of course, the High Obajan.

All this he noticed and one thing more. Someone was dogging his footsteps. Not quietly, like an assassin or thief, but boldly, making no secret of his presence as he kept pace. Varoi was desperate to know who walked in his shadow. Why was he there? Whoever they were must be male since their pace exactly matched his. He had no way of finding out. For some reason he was compelled to keep *facing forward as he strode along. Perhaps when he reached the corridor's end he would find out.*

The hallway ended at a door; one that was tall and imposing and bracketed by armed guards. Varoi supposed his progress must then come to a halt, while he waited for whoever was inside to grant him admittance. Instead, the guards came to attention at his approach, offering him a brisk salute. Varoi formed a thought and the door swung wide. He was startled and rather perturbed: when had he learnt to do that? Varoi strode forward and the one who was trailing behind followed him through, passing with neither let nor hindrance on the part of either guard, which further alarmed Varoi.

A table and two chairs occupied the centre of the room. A slave with a fan stood to one side, creating a cool breeze. A liveried servant stood poised to attend his every need. Varoi ignored them both.

Skirting the table he spun to face his shadow, to find himself confronting a male of similar age to himself, clad in battered, brown leather body armour, with a sword hilt jutting just above his left shoulder. Varoi frowned at that. When had he last been so lax as to allow a potential assassin at his back? Except ... this male might prove to be his personal bodyguard.

Varoi continued to study the warrior, who seemed noticeably unruffled by such intense scrutiny. He was broad of shoulder and narrow of hip, his brown hair drawn back into a warrior's tail, golden eyes returning Varoi a respectful regard.

It unnerved Varoi to discover his shadow to be an exact replica of himself, right down to the face he saw in the mirror each day.

There was one small difference, though, Varoi was pleased to note: a small nick on his chin where a well-sharpened blade had slipped past his guard. Varoi couldn't resist curling his lip at the sight: not quite perfect then. *He saw wry amusement bloom on his counterpart's face.*

Varoi pulled out a chair and sat down. And was amazed when, without asking permission, his counterpart did likewise. Any advantage he had hoped to gain thereby negated, Varoi opened his mouth to offer a scathing attack, but was, again, pre-empted.

"I know you're angry and you have every right to chastise. If you would just let me explain ..."

Varoi's answer came swift, without thought or effort on his part, as though it had been well rehearsed. "You knew what you attempted to be ill-advised. Why take the chance?"

The servant advanced to set down a tray laden with two cups and a jug of cordial. Varoi helped himself to a measure while awaiting the expected reply.

"I had no choice in the matter."

"You had every choice. You knew cross-species healing to be perilous at best. So, why take the risk?" *Thunder echoed in Varoi's voice and the air around him grew noticeably chill. Ice formed on the outside of his glass. Yet another anomaly with which to contend: only males possessed of superior shamanic ability were required to harness their temper in such a way. Varoi had never considered himself that strong.*

"I beg to differ. I did not lightly assume such responsibility, whatever you think. You should know me better by now. I owed the man a debt of honour, Father. You know as well I what that entails." *The male inclined his head in a questioning pose.*

Varoi could not think, could not form the sentence he wished to speak, had heard nothing beyond that one crucial word: "Father."

I have a son! The thought astounded. The air in the room turned to glass and shattered, piercing his skin,

315

*passing through flesh and bone, stabbing his heart.
Perhaps if I ask I may learn his name.*

*The air around him shimmered, dissolved into tears
... and then he was some place else.*

*The door he faced was constructed of bleached
lyme, a timber seldom put to such humble use, which
implied that this abode belonged to someone of influence.
He felt compelled to satisfy his growing curiosity: what else
was he meant to do? He took firm hold of the handle and
gave it a twist. The door swung inward, silently.*

*Striding across the threshold he found himself in a
bedchamber, a lavishly furnished one. Sweeping the room
with a glance, he took in the pots of cosmetics and had no
need of the figure silhouetted against a tall, canted window
to know that this room belonged to a female of his race.
His gaze lingered awhile on the sumptuously accoutred
bed, before returning to the female form, aware at once
who she was, with her tawny hair falling in silken waves to
her waist. Desire filled him. Grown hungry and greedy
with need, he whispered her name, "Ayesha," and had the
pleasure of seeing her turn to face him.*

*She smiled wistfully and stretched forth a beckoning
hand. Varoi took a pace forward; took two paces closer
and then ... someone else stepped in between.*

*At first the intrusion seemed unreal, but gradually a
shape materialised. Varoi absorbed this information at a
glance: dark, shoulder-length hair, broad shoulders and
chest tapering to narrow hips. Varoi saw all hopes of a
blissful reunion plummet.*

The intruder was not only male ... but unclothed.

*Anger aroused, Varoi reached to thrust the
interloper aside. But, in the interim, his hands had become
invisible ... or else were curiously constrained. For
whatever reason he had no power to prevent this unwanted
male from having his way, which fact in no wise placated*

him. Forced to watch rather than take part, Varoi tried to make sense of unfolding events.

And came to the surprising conclusion: this might well be himself that he was compelled to observe. It was not so displeasing an idea.

Varoi longed to glimpse Ayesha's face, intent on confirming this possibility. All he saw were elegant fingers closely entwined in the male's hair. Then the male swept Ayesha up, setting her down atop the bed, revealing that she, too, was naked.

Seeing his beloved laid out before him, her luscious curves and silken skin a sumptuous feast, sent Varoi's already awakened libido into meltdown. It was all he could do to restrain himself from leaping atop her there and then, to contain those urges too long held in check. He would not be so crude and impatient. She deserved better than that; though that fact did not prepare him for what happened next.

Varoi moved forward, intent on taking advantage of the rich bounty on offer, but his rival proved even quicker to respond. Varoi groaned in frustration as the unknown male, having clambered atop the bed, first kissed Ayesha then nuzzled the soft mounds of her breasts before nudging her knees apart so he could slip inside and begin the deep deliberate strokes that would bring him to climax.

This unwelcome intruder was accorded privileges that should, by rights, have been his. Varoi had no wish to be a mere voyeur on this occasion. He pressed close, anxious to learn what name she uttered whilst caught in the throes of ecstasy ... and heard her cry out "Schezan!"

Varoi started awake, to the sound of rain drumming on the roof, the fierce rattle of hail against his windowpane. Pale light filtered in past gaps in the slatted shutters, warning him that dawn was nigh, a reminder that he was expected to rise early and perform to the best of his ability, much as he had the previous day. And he would be

317

required to do so on each successive day, until his training came to an end.

Sighing, Varoi closed his eyes, seeking the solace he had not found in sleep, trying to make sense of his dreams.

If the dreams he'd just had were predictions of events to come, then, while there was little he could do to affect the eventual outcome concerning two of those episodes, there was much he might do to ensure the last went according to plan. One fundamental fact remained: the gods had revealed Ayesha to be his mate; without her consent there wasn't the remotest possibility of his ever siring a son.

Chapter 14: Risk

The rattle of staves coming together was followed by a resounding crack, which captured Varoi's attention as nothing else had. Then his limbs grew limp as his body subsided into a downward slump.

"Hold," he heard the weapons master shout, and all sound muted or otherwise came to an abrupt halt. Stunned, but still conscious, Varoi fisted his hands and awaited the inevitable scolding he felt sure was his due. As though from a great distance he heard the weapons master ask, "What did you do?"

Varoi tried to focus through the sudden abundance of coloured lights, but found his vision strangely askew.

"Nothing out of the ordinary, Weapons Master," Colvair replied, voicing her opinion as she was entitled to do. "He seemed rather distracted, that's all I can say."

Varoi could not fault her bald assessment of the facts, which was basically true.

"His attention's been off for the past few days, if you ask me," said Danova, adding his viewpoint to the one already expressed.

"I wasn't asking, Danova. So feel safe in keeping your opinions to yourself." And that was the weapons master again, who did not sound altogether pleased. "What happened, Varoi? Can you hear me?"

Varoi tried to answer, but the words got all jumbled up in the process. "Mmmm nah," he mumbled, willing his mouth to form words. A pity his brain was not functioning as it should.

"Look at me, Varoi. Can you see? How many fingers am I holding up?"

"Mmmm manoo."

"Did he say one or two?"

"Hard to tell, Weapons Master. Might I suggest," a whispered conversation ensued, to the essentials of which Varoi was not privy.

Then, "Can you use your fingers to provide an answer, Varoi?"

If only he could. Screwing his eyes tight shut, Varoi concentrated on one clenched fist. And found it *was* possible to respond after all.

"Two. Well, that's promising. His vision can't be too badly impaired and that's something for which to be grateful. You and you, carry him to that bench. We'll let him recover out of the way and see how he is in a little while. Colvair, you need a new partner. Andanta! Come down here."

"He's a class above us, Weapons Master," Colvair reminded, with what Varoi thought was a hint of nerves.

"I am aware of that, Colvair. It is time you stepped up your game. Andanta can help you with that. Now go. Prepare."

Hands grasped Varoi roughly, shoulders and thighs, as the two warriors given charge of removing him went about their task.

Four nights in a row Varoi had sought to make contact with Ayesha and each time his overtures, however tactful, were briskly rebuffed. Four nights in a row he had fallen asleep, wondering what he had done to so displease her, causing her to treat him thus. And each night, after falling asleep, he had dreamt the self-same dreams as he had that first night ... with minor variations to the theme ... but variations too insignificant to alter the overall effect either of the dream itself or on his growing conviction that they were, in fact, prophetic. How could he ignore such predictions? Even the one involving his son revealed untoward aspects.

No wonder, then, that he was somewhat distracted. No wonder he did not give of his best, when facing an opponent who was equal to him in every respect.

And now, the weapons master himself must be well aware how lax his concentration was. Doubtless he would pay the price of his momentary lapse and be thrown out of Konicci training, an opportunity he had worked so hard to attain.

Varoi threw one hand across his face, shielding his eyes, intent on concealing the distress he felt at that failure. He was reluctant to confront the contemptuous expressions he expected to see on those around. Nor could he ignore the fact that he had thrown away his best chance of seeing Bayritz avenged.

Someone sat on the end of bench. Varoi kept his face covered, hoping whoever it was might leave him in peace. He was no coward, but knew well that a rebuke was in order after what had just occurred. Still, he was in no mood to face his accuser just yet.

"Are you ready to look me in the eye and explain?" The weapons master's voice was quiet and unaccusing, not at all what Varoi had come to expect.

Lowering his hand and finding his vision had returned to normal, Varoi sat up. Turning to confront Shah he looked him straight in the eye and said, "The fact is, Weapons Master, Colvair is more than competent when it comes to handling a weapon."

"And that's your excuse? Come on, Varoi. Our acquaintance may be only short, but I think I know you better than that."

"I have no excuse, Weapons Master. Colvair is good. I could have done better. Had I been paying proper attention she would not have taken me off-guard."

"But?"

"There are no buts. The error was entirely mine and I accept the penalty."

"You don't plan to argue or plead? Will not ask for lenience?"

"What would be the point? We both know I made a mistake." Varoi lifted his chin, prepared to be called to account. Whatever the punishment he would accept it with good grace. He could see no benefit in making an even bigger fool of himself.

"I'm delighted to discover you're not fool enough to think you can disguise the truth. There *are* some who would try. Consider yourself reprieved. One more lapse of concentration on your part, though, and you'll be out on your ear or carried out in a cart. You're lucky it was a staff that rattled your brains and not a more lethal weapon. Consider this your first and final warning; you won't receive more. Now, if you're quite recovered from your enforced spell of rest, come with me."

The weapons master strode a few paces distant and looked up at the group of warriors now gazing down from the gallery, intent on assessing their opposition. "You!" he pointed a finger directly.

One of those assembled tilted his head in a questioning pose, pointing at his chest as if to ask, "Who me?"

"Yes, you, Barate. Come down here. I have an opponent you might like to try."

Varoi watched with misgivings as the well-built warrior, with tawny, shoulder-length hair that swung loose about broad shoulders and who stood almost a head taller than his fellows, strode to the back of the gallery and started downstairs. Varoi could hear him galloping down the steps and guessed he was unwilling to risk the weapons master's ire by delaying. Varoi knew of Barate by reputation and had hoped to avoid him, for a while, at least. He was considered the most proficient warrior in his group.

322

"Choose your weapon," the weapons master urged, as the young warrior strode into the arena through the tunnel entrance, binding his hair back as he came.

Barate snatched a staff from the rack of weapons left ready to hand. His attitude was ebullient, his fierce grin showing an uncivil glimpse of white teeth. There was something perilous, almost predatory about the way he moved. Varoi felt his hackles rise in response. Colvair was good at what she did. This warrior represented something entirely different, a more dangerous proposition by far. And, from what little Varoi knew, Barate was justified in being this self-assured.

"Well, Varoi," said Shah, unable to pretend any regret for what he was about to do. "Since Colvair is now otherwise engaged, let me introduce your next opponent. I might point out: I expect you to do better than you have so far."

Varoi said not one word in response. If the weapons master planned to test his metal, who was he to complain? Instead, he backed up until he found himself at the edge of the nearest circle and, skirting it, took up a stance. Not once did he take his eyes off Barate. This was one adversary he would not take for granted. And maybe that was the point. If so, he could not fault Shah for providing such a challenge.

"You both know the rules," Shah instructed. "When ready you may begi ..."   Barate barrelled the distance between himself and Varoi at astonishing speed, directing a series of stunning blows at his opponent's unprotected head in an obvious attempt to bring the contest to a swift close.

Varoi was not so easily caught out. Not only had he seen Barate in action, but these were exactly the tactics he preferred to use himself when given the chance. Not one of the head-splitting strikes got past his guard. To begin with he allowed Barate to have his way, concentrating his efforts instead on maintaining a defensive action. But then, without warning, Varoi changed strategy, taking the fight to his adversary and gaining a significant measure of satisfaction in the process. Barate, it seemed, was not invincible.

Unaware that he, too, now wore a manic grin, Varoi settled down to the kind of contest he most enjoyed. The kind normally provided by the Pulan. The kind that might see his head lopped from his shoulders should he relax his guard for even half a second. Shah watched the action with growing interest, aware that he was seeing Varoi's hidden potential for the first time. He was surprised it had taken so aggressive an opponent to produce this effect.

The battering ram that was Barate's attack continued at full force with no sign of slackening in pace. Varoi parried every clout and wallop of Barate's quarterstaff with equal ferocity then dealt out his own stinging attack. To Shah, watching, it was obvious: for the first time since his enrolment, Varoi's attention was fully engaged.

Ayesha cursed herself for her shoddy behaviour and unfair treatment of Varoi and Schezan both. They did not deserve her constant refusal to communicate.

Today she would begin making amends. She would speak to Schezan first, in an overdue effort to put matters right between them. Mayhap then they could start afresh from where they had left off, although Schezan must be made to understand that Varoi's challenge would still stand. They were rivals for her affection, as simple as that. How they conducted themselves in that respect was up to them. Either way, one or the other would win her outright.

Schezan first, then Varoi; when Varoi reached for her next she would be waiting. She had kept him at arm's length long enough, but not any more. In truth Ayesha was unsure which of them had suffered the most from her

324

persistent reticence. One way or the other she fully intended finding out.

She caught up with Schezan soon after he came off duty. At sight of her a quizzical expression crossed his face and was gone, instantly replaced by one of distance and disdain.

If she chose to ignore him, it seemed to imply, let her not think I care one wit.

Ayesha stopped square in his path, waiting for Schezan to come close enough that she could speak to him without raising her voice. A small spark of anger remained: it was well damped down, submerged now by simmering regret. Now was not the time for recriminations. Now was the time for making amends; to make peace so the situation in which they found themselves might be reasonably resolved.

Provided she did not provoke him and he in turn failed to provoke her, there was every reason to suppose her honest approach would work.

He halted a few paces distant, his gaze shuttered, giving nothing away.

"Ayesha?"

"Schezan." She took a breath. "I wish to apologise."

"About what, precisely? About your unjust accusations regarding my not seeking you out immediately upon my return?"

"Amongst other things."

"And does that mean I can safely forget my potential rival?"

"Rather, I was hoping I might make amends."

Schezan moved closer. "I know of one way that might be achieved."

He stood above her looking down, the heat of his gaze accelerating her pulse to a prodigious degree. Ayesha had a fair idea what Schezan had in mind and felt unable to raise a reasonable objection to any such proposal. Without waiting for her response Schezan swooped and scooped her up in his arms. There was a small stand of trees nearby he appeared intent on making good use of, one that offered ample privacy. If Ayesha felt any misgivings at his behaviour he seemed not to care.

Secure in his arrogance and male beauty Schezan never bothered to question further Ayesha's unforeseen change in attitude. She was female and, therefore, prone to such complexities. This talk of a rival was a mere ploy, a means of unsettling him. That she had made the mistake of naming Varoi in that context simply implied a degree of desperation. He knew better than most what it took to satisfy her needs.

Setting her back on her feet in a leafy arbour Schezan dipped his head and pressed his lips to hers, one hand cupping the back of her head while the other slyly lifted the hem of her skirt. Passion roused, Ayesha relaxed into the kiss, giving back more in a determined attempt to assuage Schezan's growing ardour, oblivious, at first, of the danger she might now be in.

Schezan's hand slithered slowly up her inner thigh then stopped: brought to a halt by an unforeseen anomaly.

"What is this?" he growled through clenched teeth, leaning back to watch her expression; appearing angry, yet curious at the same time.

Ayesha's eyes were heavy lidded as she viewed him from beneath a thick fan of lashes. "What's what?" she queried, equally bemused.

Schezan let go of her head, but did not step back. One finger continued its sensual exploration. "You know full well to what I refer." There was no doubting the warning implicit in his tone. His amber eyes resembled those of a cat, slitted and glaring in their malevolence.

Ayesha grew tense. "I know nothing of what you infer."

"I think you do. I think you know perfectly well. Something is different; something about you has recently changed."

"I cannot imagine what you mean," Ayesha was desperate, playing for time, reminded now, by his attitude, of one specific thing he might find that was different.

"Someone," and now Schezan's voice assumed a distinctly menacing tone, "has seen fit to interfere. There is a way of finding out who."

Ayesha gasped in surprise as Schezan's one questing finger slipped inside. "Oh, you must mean ..." she haltingly began and got no further. But then, nor did Schezan.

He growled in frustration, seeking to penetrate her secret. "There is always a signature energy present in such irregularities. And now I see to whom it belongs. You said that I had a rival. You said nothing about his having concealed a ward against penetration within your person. When were you going to explain?"

Ayesha felt her temper glow red hot at his unjust accusation. What Schezan implied was not what had actually occurred. Varoi had sought to offer protection. There was nothing improper about that. Nor had he taken advantage of the situation, however tempting that had been.

"You weren't here," she reminded him brusquely. "Varoi was. The Pulan were camped on our doorstep posing all manner of threat."

"So you allowed this, even encouraged him? If you think I'm being unreasonable, consider this." A pulsating glow passed through her groin and into her body, continuing to radiate outward till every particle of her being was involved. Nor could Ayesha escape his unwelcome attention even had she tried. At first the sensation was almost pleasurable, but soon it assumed a more sinister quality, until she was close to screaming aloud her fear and revulsion. She would *not* award him the gratification of

327

knowing this unique form of chastisement worked. When he, at last, removed his hand it was all she could do not to slump forward against the hard muscles of his chest. Willpower alone ensured that she did not.

"Was there a need for that?" she asked, gritting her teeth against the resonance still echoing within.

"I thought there was," Schezan replied. Releasing her he stepped back, a look of grim satisfaction shadowing his handsome face. If she dared to doubt his shamanic ability she would not do so again. And there was no way his rival, Varoi, would ever learn what had been done, no way he could seek to interfere. The bruises would fade in a matter of days. His brutal chastisement would live on in her memory.

"I'll leave you to think on this." Schezan studied Ayesha a moment longer; then gave a quick satisfied nod, before turning on his heel and striding away.

Ayesha waited to be sure he was gone and then began the long, agonising walk home. She ached in every bone and muscle; not the healthy ache of hard, physical labour, but a different kind, the kind that made her want to break down and weep.

She had made the mistake of thinking Schezan would not discover the shared intimacy she had enjoyed with Varoi during his absence. It was none of his business after all. If he expected an apology, he could forget it. The time for such an apology was past. She refused to grant him even that small satisfaction.

Ayesha forced herself to lie very still when Varoi came to her that same night, courtesy of *lossa antario*. She would not reject him as she'd recently done. Nor would she flinch aside from his touch, though it cost her dearly when she could not respond in suitable fashion, as his strong, capable hands began to gently caress every available inch of her sensitised flesh.

Ayesha had been privy to his touch only when first they had sought the sensual benefits that *lossa antario* allowed. Now, she heard his voice in her mind. The distress it conveyed nigh broke her heart.

Ayesha. Please, tell me. What is wrong?

Why should anything be wrong Varoi? I was merely distracted the last few days. I had rather a lot on my mind.

I don't mean that. You have a right to refuse my attentions should you so choose. I would never force myself upon you. But something else is definitely amiss. You take no pleasure in my caress, however gentle or circumspect, as though you fear what I might attempt. Almost, you shy away. If what I do displeases you, please say. I'm aware something is different, but cannot tell what. It troubles me more than words can express.

Despite her evasion, Varoi knew something was very wrong. Intent on resolving the problem his hands first slowed and then stilled, coming to rest either side of her hips. Something about her felt different but he wasn't sure what. Always, before, Ayesha had welcomed his touch. Now the slightest brush, while not openly rebuffed, created a tension. Nor was it the response he had come to expect, the heightened excitement of roused lust. Rather, it resembled an underlying unease, which appeared to radiate outward from every pore of her being.

Another male might think her frigid. Varoi knew better than that, having previously tasted the true extent of her passion. Nor was she prone to reluctance when it came to voicing her opinions aloud. Varoi decided to approach the difficulty head on. *Whatever the problem, you know you can safely share it with me. Once you welcomed my touch. But that, it seems, is no longer true. Share your concerns that I may behave accordingly.*

Ayesha could not withhold the softest of sighs. *Why must he insist?* Unaware that even these passing thoughts were open to him, she strove for a simple explanation, hoping that would satisfy him. *If you must know I took a tumble coming downstairs. As a result, I am covered in bruises, top to toe. Does that satisfy your curiosity?*

Ah, and these bruises then are everywhere?

Yes, Varoi; as I just said.

Varoi allowed his hands to idly wander the length of her body. A scrupulous investigation would seem to be in order. Beginning with her arms he allowed his deft fingers to walk along their smooth, silken flesh. *Here?* he whispered. Refusing her the chance to raise protest, he next traversed the narrow breadth of her ribcage. *Here?* he softly enquired, before travelling the soft skin of her upper thigh. *Here too?*

Yes, Varoi; there, there and *there! As I just said, bruises everywhere.*

Surely not quite *everywhere?* he responded. *Why has no one seen fit to offer you healing if that is the case and these injuries are visible?*

Because they are not ... visible that is. Nor have I asked them to.

I see. Well, not literally, of course, else I should have known better than to ask. But I do understand.

Really? Ayesha could not keep a small hint of exasperation out of her voice.

And, providing you've no intention of again banishing me from your presence, I have a solution I might try. Before Ayesha could offer a suitable response, Varoi took her face in his hands and brought his mouth down to meet hers.

It was not the solution she had anticipated. Still, it had the desired effect.

The kiss they shared was warm and tender, tender enough to steal her breath. She'd almost forgotten how gentle a lover Varoi could be. Desperate to deepen the kiss, Ayesha reached to tangle her fingers in the glorious confusion of Varoi's hair.

Taking this as his cue, Varoi applied the slightest pressure of his mouth in an attempt to prise her lips apart; sweeping his tongue inside, intent on commencing a full and thorough investigation. Ayesha tightened her grip on his hair as his exploration got under way, then moaned in appreciation of his gratifying efforts to please. Too long had she waited for this.

Varoi sensed there was more to the problem than Ayesha had chosen to reveal. How he would react on discovering the truth he had no idea. For now he favoured a different objective, one they could both enjoy.

Ayesha felt her body come alive. Heat radiated outwards from the source, a gentle warmth, not destructive and corrosive as Schezan's had been. A touch she found soothing and sensual at the same time, it sent pulses of pleasure to her core, initiating the most loving, most natural response of all. Her lowered lashes sparkled with unshed tears of gratitude.

Varoi grew very still, encouraging his senses to expand, allowing his *ananaha* abilities full rein, as he gently cruised the inside of Ayesha's mouth, noting her texture and taste at his leisure. Something strange drew his attention, a worrying discordance, a seriously disturbing anomaly. It took a mere fraction of his concentration to trace its source and discover the truth of what had been done. Lifting his mouth from hers he posed the inevitable question. *It wasn't a fall that caused those bruises, Ayesha, was it? It was something, or should I say someone, else.*

Ayesha despaired. Why, oh why, could he not leave the matter alone? *I don't know what you mean?* Still, she could not keep the tremor from her voice.

I won't pressure you by enquiring who is responsible. I believe I already know. Nor will I ask by what means the punishment was dealt out. Suffice it to say,

I can guess. You forget one important thing, Ayesha. I possess an innate ability that allows me to scan for discrepancies. I sense what has been done. I must add: I do not approve. No male should treat any female thus. Whatever his grievance, real or imagined, it is a gross breach of trust.

Ayesha felt compelled to offer a tart reminder. *Twas you who put the shield in place. You might have guessed it would cause trouble.*

I had no way of knowing if the spell actually worked. And ... while tis true ... I arranged things in my favour, still the spell can be overruled: with your consent.

Now he tells me. Why did you not think to mention this before?

Varoi paused before offering a reply. *Because I hoped, foolishly I will admit, that there would be no such need. Because, I dared cherish the prospect such rare privilege might be reserved to me.*

Ayesha wavered in the face of his honesty. While she did, Varoi seized the advantage, touching his mouth to hers in a slow, sensual kiss that brought every part of her body to swift and needy arousal.

The next instant he was gone.

Sensing his departure Ayesha reached to take hold of him again. *Varoi?*

He was already gone and only silence and a sense of yearning remained. His absence created a burgeoning ache that had naught to do with bruises or pain.

Varoi had no idea what lay in store as he teased Ayesha's lips apart and swept his tongue inside the warm, moist cavern of her mouth in an erotic gesture designed primarily to arouse: certainly not what he had actually found. This was the first time he'd attempted such an enquiry with the unique aid of *lossa antario*.

The snap and fizz of destructive magic took him completely by surprise. The spell was waning even as he strove to latch hold and tease its owner's signature free in an attempt to hold it up to close inspection. Still, evidence remained, revealing what had been done, enough to provide information concerning how the construct had been deployed. To marvel at its unscrupulous owner's nerve. He continued his study of the spell's construction while striving to negate its harsh effect.

Assuming its mechanics to have been indirectly applied, which act would obviate any need for Ayesha's complicity, Varoi was distressed to discover this was not the case. Learning that it was not just attached but interwoven with his protective construct filled Varoi with disgust and dismay. The protective shield he had arranged was meant to support Ayesha, not aid his rival in perpetrating so brutal a crime. Because his original weaving touched every cell, this pernicious formula contrived to do likewise, ensuring its effect involved each individual muscle and nerve.

No wonder Ayesha grew tense when subjected to the slightest touch. Each muscular action, every small change in facial expression would jangle her nerves to the point of pain. The ache she endured must be exquisite, since that was how this construct had been arranged. It was the exact reverse of what he had intended.

The question remained: how had such a vicious punishment been contrived?

Varoi knew he couldn't continue pretending a detachment he did not feel. He had done his best, under the guise of sensual stimulation, to dispel the results of this cruel weaving. It was time to disengage from the sublime benefits of *lossa antario*, to allow Ayesha a full recovery. What she needed now was time and rest. So, without more ado, he contrived an immediate withdrawal from her presence.

333

Leaving Ayesha to her own devices was one thing. The question persisted even then: how had this thing been managed and by whom? Although, as he'd taken pains to tell Ayesha, he felt sure he already knew. And what Ayesha had asserted in return seemed to confirm his suspicions as true. Still, Varoi sat on his bed, resting his chin on his hand, trying to fathom the answer.

Schezan! It must be Schezan. Who else would feel justified in taking such aggressive action? Who else would be in any position to contrive an opportunity? None save Schezan, Ayesha's Chosen, the same male to whom she was pledged.

And for what purpose?

Surely his rival had no objection to his conferring such protection on the one female to whom they both sought to lay claim? Then again, perhaps he did.

Which begged the unanswered question: how?

Such a gross act required internal contact, which, in turn, implied Ayesha's willing consent. Not with a kiss, please Goddess, not like that. Not while engaged in the most innocent form of pleasure an ardent lover might devise.

It came to him then and the brazen effrontery involved hit Varoi hardest of all. The one sure means that denied Ayesha any chance of escape from such unwelcome attention. Stabbed by a wicked spike of jealousy, Varoi held firm, his pain far less than anything Ayesha had been forced to endure. There was one known means an aggrieved lover might select.

It was obvious Ayesha had trusted Schezan if she permitted such intimacy, although whether she still did was a moot point. In violating her trust had Schezan not placed his role as Chosen at risk? Surely, so vile an act would alienate him? In Varoi's opinion, it seemed to have done so. What could Schezan hope to gain?

An unforeseen probability occurred. Since Ayesha had already declared Schezan to be her Chosen his agreement was, inevitably, required in order for her to obtain a release from completing her vows. Without such a release her ordeal might not be at an end. And while Ayesha and Schezan continued to live in close proximity, the risk of his subjecting her to further reprisals remained a distinct probability.

With the siege over, the battle won and their victory celebrations done, the townsfolk of Tenbay began putting matters to rights. They had plenty to occupy them. Among their immediate concerns was a determination to become more involved in Tenbay's defence. That particular resolve did not sit well with Schezan as garrison commander.

"They'll be wanting the place to themselves ere long," he fumed. "Mark my words. Arm the fen men and you'll soon see your mistake. Instead of guarding our backs, like an ally, they'll be stabbing us from behind and claiming the land as theirs." Schezan's tone was bitter with resentment as he went on. "Give them an inch and they'll seize an ell. I'm damned if they'll gain my support in the doing."

"I'm sure they intend nothing of the kind," Commander com 'Dolino sought to maintain a reasonable tone. He had no wish to antagonise Tenbay's garrison commander. "They have a right to some means of defence in order to keep their women and children safe, don't you think?"

"I disagree." Schezan's tart response served to further emphasise his dissent regarding the matter under discussion. "Furthermore, if they persist in this ridiculous scheme, they'll receive no encouragement from me."

"I'm willing to undertake some preliminary training. Once a few of them have learnt the basics I'll leave it up to them how they choose to manage their affairs."

"Fine. You do that. Just don't expect any assistance from me."

At that Schezan rose to his feet, pushed back his chair, spun on his heel and marched out the door, bringing the meeting to an abrupt and disagreeable close.

Schezan was often in a foul mood. But of late his grim humour had escalated beyond normal limits and, those who could, stayed well out of his way.

Ayesha was diligent in her efforts to do just that. Others were less fortunate. These last were reduced to hoping matters would shortly improve. Schezan in a vile temper was akin to a she Saarcat in heat: a hissing, snarling fury clad in a fur coat; inclined to take umbrage at the least insult and respond with excessive hostility.

The trouble was that Schezan felt obliged to deal firmly with any who posed a threat to his ambitions. As sole surviving son of the present High Obajan he held a status he was keen to maintain. Nothing made him more bad tempered and dangerous than a threat to those cherished aims. Past challenges had been removed with singular ease. Present ones posed a more substantial threat. Nothing that could not be dealt with, providing adequate means and opportunity could be arranged.

And one could always be contrived, once he set his mind to the problem.

He'd had a brother once, older than him by several moons. A tragic boating accident, when Schezan was twelve and his brother thirteen, had left his brother dead and Schezan, apparently, half drowned, following a mishap involving the local weir. It was a wonder any remains of Schezan's brother had actually been found; considering the grisly mess made of his body by predatory blue-fin eels.

That event had seen Schezan elevated to the status of heir assumptive to the High Obajan, a significant promotion in rank.

He recalled a comment overheard at the time. "Sons are like cuckoos, Magia. There can be only one heir to a nest. Sooner or later it comes down to this. I can sire more males should the need arise." His mother had been less than impressed by his father's pragmatic acceptance of what was, presumably, an accident.

His interfering rival Varoi com 'Domicci was one problem Schezan could well do without. And while Ayesha might think it was she who had done the choosing when it came to claiming him as a potential mate, Schezan knew different. She had been given no more choice than his brother had. The instant his father took pains to inform him that a princess was living in Tenbay's settlement, Schezan had determined that, should she prove a suitable match, she *would* be his mate. *Lossa antario* played no part in that. Only a fool left important details to a mere game of chance. Schezan took no such risks. Now Varoi threatened to interfere in the complex working of his strategy. Something would definitely have to be done about Varoi com 'Domicci.

First he must make sure to fully acquaint Ayesha with her situation: there could be no release from her pledge. The promise naming him as Chosen had been taken in good faith. And, barring accidents, it would continue to stand, inviolate.

It was obvious why Varoi dared to demand Ayesha as his prize. Too bad, his rival had come too late to the feast; the best morsels had already been claimed. Besides which, he was not in a benevolent frame of mind.

Ayesha found plenty to occupy her: long days at the infirmary tending those injured in defence of the town, her off-duty hours spent putting the herb garden back in order. The Pulan had trampled some plants to oblivion and defoliated others entirely. At least they'd left the hive and its resident bees alone. Perhaps the colony itself had formed a defensive army. If so, it was not to be wondered at.

Varoi had gone beyond reach just when she needed him most, which annoyed Ayesha more than she would have dreamt possible. Of course, it could only be a matter of time before he made contact with her again. Meanwhile, no matter how she fretted and struggled to attract his attention, all her efforts were patently doomed.

Why was that? In truth, the answer was obvious. Not that her mood improved with the knowing. In shamanic ability, as in everything else relating to the Shakar, it was the male of the species who was noticeably strongest. Which fact explained why Ayesha could only complete their connection when Varoi's ability was unfurled. When, as now, it had been shut down tight, any attempt to open communications was doomed. It annoyed her immensely, especially since she'd forgotten to ask Varoi about his previous acquaintance with Schezan. Whether it should prove to be truth or falsehood she felt entitled to find out.

While Varoi had been present in the flesh it had taken no more than a raised eyebrow or sulky pout to gain his attention and bring him to heel. Now, when she most longed for his comforting strength and calm assurance, he was unavailable. The long nights she'd spent in his arms seemed no more substantial than a pleasant dream.

Varoi thought it best to leave Ayesha alone for the time being. If she were as sore as she had seemed she deserved a chance for healing to take place, though he knew for a fact what he'd done would speed the process along. Still, he had plenty on which to focus his attention. As it was, three days later he lay atop his bed, opening his mind and sensibilities to the possibility that *lossa antario* might be deployed. The tenuous thread of interest lay unfurled about him. All it required for contact to commence was that Ayesha should choose to reach out for him.

When, at last, she did, he welcomed her advances with patent relief. And he was instantly swamped by thrilling sensation, like tiny flames flickering over his skin, bringing him to instant and fierce arousal. How could he not respond in kind? He reached for her in the darkness, felt their awareness combine and succumbed to her sensual allure, lost in the all-consuming passion that *lossa antario* allowed.

She was his and he was hers. They belonged to each other. Nothing and no one must come between.

Varoi's kiss, so incredibly tender, so blissfully sweet, made Ayesha want to weep. After the way Schezan had treated her she had begun to think all males the same: callous and cruel and not worth the bother. Varoi was nothing like Schezan. They were in no way alike in her estimation. She could not begin to imagine Schezan even thinking to provide her with protection in the way Varoi most assuredly had; could not imagine herself requesting any such favour of him. But there was still something more she required of Varoi. And she would have an answer.

Tell me about your sister, Varoi.

You mean Bayritz?

Yes. Tell me about your sister Bayritz. Schezan claims that is how you first met, through her, through the tragedy that led to her death. At first I was angry with you for not telling me that. Now, I just want to know.

Know what, Ayesha? What is it you want to know?

The truth – or at least your version of what supposedly happened. I think I'm owed some sort of an explanation, don't you?

Varoi's abrupt descent into silence made Ayesha wonder whether an account would be forthcoming. After a while, Varoi started to explain. As she listened to the tale unfold, Ayesha could sense the wealth of sadness and regret this poignant recollection brought in train.

Varoi visualized that fateful night with distressing clarity, recalling Bayritz as she had been when alive: vibrant, vivacious and full of mischief. He preferred picturing her thus. Not until he ceased speaking did he become aware of Ayesha stroking his hair. Gently he covered her hand with his, caught it up and brought it to the warmth of his mouth, to place soft little kisses against her palm. The better he came to know her, the more determined he was to make her his.

I'm so sorry, Varoi. I had no idea. You should have told me; then I might not have been angry. Instead, it was Schezan who related the details.

Angry, Ayesha? I don't understand. Why would you be angry with me?

It hurts to know you don't trust me enough to share such confidences with me.

It wasn't that.

Then what was it, precisely?

I trust you, Ayesha. I'm just not sure I trust myself when you're around. And, I felt you might misunderstand my reason for bringing the matter up when first we met.

Ayesha thought about that for a moment, pondered a while longer upon it, then felt compelled to ask. *And why would I do that?*

Varoi baulked at revealing his suspicions. If Schezan had admitted to nothing where did that leave him? But, Ayesha was silent, patiently awaiting his reply. He must offer some explanation. *Because I hold Schezan at fault for my sister's death, while he denies all responsibility in this matter. Such an accusation is bound to seem an act of pure spite where you're concerned. I want you to love me for who and what I am, not out of misguided sympathy. I cannot change the past. Nor do I intend that it should interfere in your affections where I am concerned.*

340

You must miss your sister terribly.

We were kindred spirits, Ayesha. What more can I say?

Schezan implied as much. Yet he insists her death was accidental. He also said you had no proof of guilt and no credible witness to back those accusations.

Well then, he would say that.

And, since there was no credible witness, it's your word against his.

Don't trust what he says, Ayesha. That's not entirely true.

You have proof?

Only the proof of my own eyes, which counts for naught.

No witness then?

The witness I have saw only part of what took place and nothing concerning Bayritz's death.

I believe you.

What are you saying?

That I believe you, for whatever that's worth. Surely something can be done?

Leave it, Ayesha. I know not to trust Schezan and that is enough, nor do I expect him to go unpunished forever. Changing the subject: what of you? How do you fare? Has my esteemed rival been pestering you?

I avoid him as much as possible. When that cannot be managed, I ensure we are never alone.

I am sorry for your difficulty. I wish there was some way I could help.

Your presence now, however ethereal, is comfort enough. Enough of my problems. How goes your training. Is Konicci training all that it's claimed?

It's everything I hoped for and more besides. We are on the go from dawn till dusk. You would not believe how physically strenuous and mentally stimulating it is.

I envy you the chance to develop your skills to their fullest potential. If only I had been born male.

If you had we would not be having this conversation or meeting in this way. Ayesha, promise me this. If you need respite or seek an escape from Schezan's odious attentions, be sure and pay a visit to my sire, Maderan com 'Domicci. He lives in the settlement on Greenbeg Fen. My friend Borit lives nearby. Between them I'm certain they'll avert Schezan from his torment of you.

He doesn't torment me, Varoi. I refuse to allow him that satisfaction.

He could have groaned aloud at her stubbornness. *You know what I mean.*

Indeed I do and it's sweet of you to be so concerned.

It isn't sweet. I'm doing my best to take good care of you.

I know. And, believe me, I appreciate that. Varoi felt gentle fingers laid soft against his cheek. He couldn't help but turn his face, leaning in to savour her caress. He craved her affection so much it hurt, physically. How *had* he survived before they met?

It wasn't that he'd avoided female company. But he had never experienced close intimacy and would not attempt the joining for which he yearned until the official ceremony had been performed. He could wait … had waited what seemed a lifetime already. A little longer was not so bad, provided it led to claiming Ayesha as mate.

Chapter 15: Attitude

When it came to keeping Schezan at arm's length Ayesha was amazed at her own ingenuity. She knew her luck was bound to run out eventually. But not *too* soon. And not without warning, she hoped.

There was one important matter outstanding between them. And the more she thought of it the more determined she became.

Without Schezan agreeing to release her from the pledge, when she'd named him her Chosen and soon to be mate, there was no way she could ever be with Varoi. If the problem were to be satisfactorily resolved, she must act soon.

But not yet, she told herself, not just yet. She was in no fit state to face him now.

"Go home, Ayesha, you're dead on your feet. You've done quite enough for today. Leave early. Take a well-earned rest. You deserve it." Soleil set down the tray she was holding and pushed back a stray lock of hair. She looked tired, Ayesha realised. Perhaps she ought to try taking her own advice.

"Are you sure it isn't you who's most in need of respite? I can stay if you need me to."

"Go. No more arguments, please. I'll leave before long, so stop fretting about me. Take care of yourself, before you end up in one of my cots suffering the results of extreme exhaustion. Now go!" There was exasperation apparent in Soleil's tone, which she made no attempt to conceal. Ayesha knew when she was overruled.

Dragging her stained smock over her head, she draped it across a convenient chair and left the infirmary. As she trudged her way home across the drawbridge she couldn't help but acknowledge the truth. Working from sun up to sun down at the infirmary was a gruelling affair. It took all her reserves of willpower to place one foot before the other on the path. She couldn't wait to get home and put her feet up. Perhaps she would take a long and relaxing bath, if she could find the strength to arrange that as well.

Ayesha had almost reached the outskirts of the forest, where it surrounded the settlement itself, when a deep voice hailed her from behind. Reluctantly, she half turned, already aware it was Schezan who addressed her. Upon viewing his long striding approach she felt an instinctive urge to avoid spending time with him alone.

Returning to Tenbay was out of the question; Schezan already had that means of retreat covered. Best to ignore his shouted intervention and reach the settlement first. There were bound to be others about, ensuring Schezan's unwelcome advances could not get horribly out of hand. She had not forgotten his last unwarranted assault

With three swift strides he overtook her, placing himself in her path. "Not so fast, Ayesha. You and I have important matters to discuss."

"Indeed we do, Schezan. But I'm hungry and tired and in sore need of a bath. I don't think this a good time. If you'll excuse me. We can do this some other time."

She put into the statement as much conviction as she reasonably dare. Short of antagonising Schezan there was little else she could do. *Please Goddess let him leave me alone.* If she hoped for a morsel of pity her optimism was unfounded, it seemed.

"I believe this occasion an excellent opportunity. You may, indeed, feel tired and hungry, but I find hunger serves to whet the appetite, while weariness suggests a subtle hint of languor, which visual aspect I find appealing. So, you'll forgive me if I choose to deny you the chance to avoid our discussion. And, in case it escaped your notice, I believe you'll find I have the upper hand."

A tart reply was on the tip of her tongue. Ayesha throttled the impulse to give her temper full rein. It could only serve to exacerbate the situation. If Schezan wanted to talk, they would talk. She reserved the right to voice her concerns just the same. There was no way she would allow him to browbeat her again.

Seeing a chance to escape she tried to step round him, but he was having none of that.

"Time's up, Ayesha, in case you hadn't noticed. The promise you gave me, the solemn pledge you made before witnesses, tis time we completed our vows."

Hands fisted on hips, she took a defiant stance. "Sorry to disappoint you, but I've changed my mind."

"You can't."

"Oh, but I can. It is my prerogative, as well you know. Both our prerogatives, in fact, but mine most of all. There has to be some advantage to being born female after all. I want your agreement to release me, Schezan."

"And if I refuse?"

"You cannot."

"I can and I will. Like you, Ayesha, I, too, have made up my mind."

"And you expect me to lie at your feet and meekly accept your decision?"

"Not meek, Ayesha. If you imagine I want you meek in my bed you are grievously mistaken. I shall greatly enjoy the fire and passion you bring to our joining. But you *will* do as I say, live by *my* rules and learn to obey."

"If you believe that you are an even bigger fool than I took you for." She saw his jaw clench with anger at her insult and knew she had pushed him too far.

Intuitively, Ayesha froze in place. She'd known Schezan for quite a while, long enough to identify certain idiosyncrasies, to recognise the early warning signs: the slight tic that ran the length of his well-defined jaw, the way in which he narrowed his focus on her, all told her one thing. He was about to succumb to a monumental rage.

Reacting on instinct she shrugged aside the restraining hand he'd set on her shoulder. And, when that same hand rose, balled into a chastising fist, she knew at once that magical retribution was about to be unleashed. Instinctively, she did the only thing she could.

Seeing the strike about to be released, she ducked beneath his upraised arm and ran.

"You cannot escape, Ayesha," he called after, while aiming a small but excruciatingly painful whip of light at her fleeing feet. *Perhaps not, but I can try.* She let out a squeal that was prompted by sheer fright more than pain. His low chuckle informed Ayesha that her reaction pleased him immensely.

She be damned if she'd afford him such satisfaction again.

And where was help when she needed it most? Where had all the settlement's inhabitants gone? Ayesha wondered in desperation as she dashed through the trees and out into the wide sunlit area beyond. But she found naught save empty streets lined with houses whose vacant windows stared back at her with uncaring aplomb.

A second strike lashed at her heels as she burst out of the small stand of trees. His aim was improving. The streets of the settlement beckoned her on in a straight line. Time, she thought, for evasive action.

Ayesha wavered; then made up her mind. She cut left down a side street, heading away from the open spaces that seemed to abound. Never had she seen the streets so deserted, save when she had come here with Varoi, before the Pulan army arrived to lay siege. Never had she noticed how broad the streets were nor how abundant was the open space. Or perhaps she had, but had never found such to her disadvantage before.

Where was everyone? The answer came to her in a trice. Schezan must have known that the Elders had arranged a meeting and that most adult Shakar would be

346

likewise engaged. He'd known that the settlement would be deserted before deciding to confront her thus. *Foolish Ayesha to even think you could outwit someone as clever and cunning as Schezan.*

She scrambled over a low boundary wall and took swift advantage of its leeward shelter to run. She must get home ahead of Schezan. She would not risk his spiteful form of retaliation a second time. Somehow she must escape.

So she took chances where she could: dodged across open ground, wove around low growing shrubs, scuttled along the outside of buildings in a desperate bid to avoid Schezan. Twice more he sent spiteful lashes of power winging in her wake. Where they hit the ground, ahead or behind, they sent up small clouds of dust and spurts of wild magic that stung almost as much as a direct strike. Somehow she managed to evade the worst.

She was panting and out of breath, heart pounding like a drum, as she flung wide the door of her home and shot inside. Throwing the bolts across, she took a moment to appreciate where she was. Then, whirling about, she sped full pelt to the rear of the house. Slamming that door shut she hammered home the bolts without once stopping to register the significance: *if the house was empty why was that door not locked?*

With the first part of her mission accomplished, Ayesha raced through the lower half of the house, slamming home shutters across windows, barring them in place. She was partway through the process before she received her first intimation that she wasn't, in fact, alone.

"What are you doing, Ayesha?" Heart pounding like a trip hammer, she spun. It was that same deep, mellifluous voice she had so dreaded hearing again.

Ayesha stared in mute incomprehension and awe as the unexpected apparition stepped forth, emerging from the darkened recess in which he'd been hid.

347

In a mere matter of days her brother Toku had been transformed, his voice having gone from high and piping to the same rich timbre as Schezan.

"What is it, Ayesha?" he asked. "What's wrong?"

Ayesha let out her breath in one long, heartfelt gasp of relief. "Toku. I didn't expect to find you here?"

He grinned. "Well, that much is obvious. I could say the same about you. Except, it wouldn't be true. I had a feeling you might have need of me. And so you find me here. Are you going to let me in on the secret?"

"Secret? What secret?"

"Well, plainly something untoward is going on. Care to explain?"

Flustered though she was, Ayesha continued with her original aim, resolutely slamming shutters closed. "Help me, Toku. Then I'll explain."

Her sense of urgency was highly contagious. Without hesitation Toku aided his sister in her frantic efforts to secure the house. As the last latch slid into place a thunderous knocking came at the door. Toku's quizzical expression was comical, a fact Ayesha was in no mood to appreciate just then. Toku opened his mouth to exclaim, but fell silent as a fearful Ayesha pressed a warning finger to her lips.

"Open up, Ayesha. I know you're in there. It's time we dealt with this matter once and for all. This stupid nonsense has got to stop, immediately."

Toku mouthed the word: *Schezan*. Ayesha hesitated. She was exhausted. Her legs felt like jelly. It required her last remaining dregs of energy to stand. On top of which she was scared witless: of what Schezan might actually do if he succeeded in forcing his way in. She prayed Toku would cooperate, just this once. Then, steeling her nerve, she planted her feet and raised her voice in reply. "We have nothing left I wish to discuss, Schezan. I told you before. I have made up my mind."

348

"Then unmake it. I'm not asking, Ayesha. I'm demanding that you comply with my wishes, as previously arranged."

"Demand all you want, it changes naught. I have the right and I fully intend exercising that same privilege."

Silence descended for a time, during which Ayesha dared to hope that Schezan had given up and gone away. But then there came another loud hammering of clenched fists. This time the door at the rear bore the brunt of Schezan's irate attack. Ayesha felt a shiver of fear glide remorselessly down her spine as the door began to shudder under the pounding.

"Open the door, Ayesha. I know you're alone in there." There was a grim purpose in his tone. For a moment, all Ayesha could do was stare as the door trembled on its hinges and the frame threatened to give way.

"You're wrong if you think Ayesha alone and unprotected." The male voice that responded to Schezan's determined assault evoked a strong image of obstinacy and resolve. This time, the ensuing silence held.

Toku folded both arms across his chest and assumed a resolute stance before the door, prepared to confront the older male should necessity require. The door would not withstand another such pounding.

"Who is with you, Ayesha?" Schezan demanded to know. "Don't tell me you have yet more suitors in tow." There was a hint of sarcasm evident in his tone.

"I already have more suitors than I require, as you well know. You'll not gain entry without permission, I promise you. Why not accept the fact you've been outmanoeuvred and leave matters at that."

She had no idea whether Schezan would so readily accept defeat. But then.

"You've not heard the last of this, Ayesha. I refuse to release you from your pledge."

She waited for the hammering to begin anew, certain the stressed timbers would finally give way. Seconds stretched, and still the oppressive silence held. Then she heard what she yearned to hear: the measured pace of Schezan's departing tread skirting the rear of the house. Cracking a nearby shutter ajar, she risked a swift peek, to spy Schezan striding away down the path. Intense irritation was evident in the way he stalked; as though his rage was bottled up tight, stored against future confrontation. Ayesha had no wish to be around when that day came.

Upon reaching the gate, he paused to look back. And, though she quickly stepped aside to avoid his attention, the voice in her head could not be denied.

You are mine, Ayesha, and I will *have you. There's no point in denying what we both know is true. One of these nights, when you're alone in your bed, you'll awake to find me already there. Lying beside you. Waiting to claim what I consider my due.*

As the measured tread of Schezan's footsteps diminished, Ayesha sank into a convenient chair, her courage and calm composure shattered by the conflict that had just now occurred. A solitary tear escaped as Toku unfolded his arms and relaxed his stance, stepping forward to stroke aside a silken strand of hair.

"You look exhausted, Ayesha, and more than a little scared. Mind telling me what that was about?"

Ayesha let out a shaky laugh. Scared? That was putting it mildly. She held out her hand, watching it tremble. Her heartbeat sounded loud in her ears. "Schezan is displeased that he has a rival. His displeasure has been further compounded by my desire to seek release from our pledge." She sucked in a steadying breath and sank deeper into the chair's plump upholstery as she prepared to provide an unsavoury revelation. "But there's more to it than that. I used *lossa antario* for the first time, fully

350

expecting the male I encountered to be Schezan. I was wrong. The male in question now claims me as his soulmate."

Toku held up a restraining hand. "No. Don't tell me. Let me guess. The male in question just happens to be Varoi com 'Domicci. Am I correct?"

Ayesha gave a negligent shrug. "Do you enjoy being right all the time? Yes, it is Varoi. Though how you could tell I cannot imagine. For your information I had no idea things would turn out thus. To be honest, I thought *lossa antario* nothing more than a myth. How was I to know it actually existed?"

"You obviously don't listen to what you're told."

"And you, of course, do. Tis easy to be wise after the event; now I must deal with the problems arising. Sometimes I wish I could have remained ignorant."

"Do you? Truly?"

"No." Much as it grieved Ayesha to admit, without her use of *lossa antario* she never would have known Varoi. "I thought Schezan an excellent choice of mate."

"When first you met him all you saw was his tall, handsome exterior, his aura of strength, not to mention his position as heir to the High Obajan. You were blind to all possible vices, as you were to his less obvious attributes. You made up your mind he was what you wanted and wasted no time in seeking to gain his attention."

"You make me sound cold-blooded, calculating and ambitious. It was nothing like that. I thought Schezan the perfect mate. Now I know different.

"I sense there is something you're not saying. You *can* trust me, you know."

"Perhaps."

"There is no perhaps about it."

Ayesha tilted her head askance to study Toku. She saw changes in his demeanour that had not previously been evident. It wasn't just that his voice had deepened or that he had grown taller. The ebullient Toku remained, but now merged with a calmer, more confident mien. The siege had proved a sobering experience for some. Now she saw that Toku, too, could be counted among that number.

"Very well, I'll take you at your word. But I expect you to keep what I reveal strictly to yourself."

"Don't tell me you've lain with Varoi. That *would* be asking for serious trouble."

"We shared a bed, but that was all we shared. Nothing happened. He took no liberties. That is not the cause of contention between myself and Schezan. During the siege I became fearful the Pulan would rape me should the fortress be overrun. Varoi provided me with a magical shield. One that could not be penetrated without my consent. In the end his efforts proved unnecessary. He wasn't to know at the time, neither of us knew what might happen. He offered me peace of mind. Schezan took strong exception to the method used in applying that protection."

Toku hissed under his breath, "I'll bet he did."

"I knew Schezan had a temper. In some strange way that was part of his appeal. I just didn't realise he could be so vindictive."

"But you do now?"

"I do, yes. Nor had I any idea he would be averse to relinquishing his claim on me as Chosen. Considering the situation as it stands, I thought he'd be pleased."

"Schezan wants a partner appropriate to his position and rank. You could call it cold-blooded politics, since that's what it is. Like you, it seems, he eschewed the subtle benefits that *lossa antario* affords. Your beauty and rank mattered more than finding a soulmate who would remain faithful no matter what."

"Toku. I'm shocked."

"That I can say it? Or because it is true?"

"A little of both, I think. You saw past the surface veneer to what lay beneath. How could I have been so blind, so egotistically inclined?"

"Don't punish yourself, Ayesha. Just thank the Goddess you saw through the façade before it was too late."

"What I wouldn't give for a modest amount of your innate intuition. I might have trusted *lossa antario* sooner then, I think."

"Might being the operative word. You saw arrogant male beauty and much vaunted pride and little else besides to recommend him. An easy mistake to make."

"And now I must pay the price. I have to leave. I cannot risk another such encounter. I'll not outwit him so easily again."

"What of the difficulty involved in gaining your release? And where can you go that you'll be safe? Or is that something else you'd rather not reveal?"

"Perhaps you can help me with that, later. First I must speak with father, see if he cannot arrange my release. He is chief and elder after all, who knows what can be managed at a pinch."

Ayesha pushed herself up from the chair, which was proving rather too comfy now that the effects of her trauma had begun to wear off. "I need to wash away the stink of sweat and fear, and to put on some clean clothes."

Toku leant close, set a hand to her cheek and brushed a gentle kiss across her brow. He'd grown tall, taller than she'd realised over the past few days. He'd be preparing for the Quickening ere long. And she would miss the entire ceremony, which grieved Ayesha more than words could say. "You don't smell so bad to me," he ventured with a shy grin.

Ayesha smiled up at her brother, what a thoughtful thing for him to say. She had a possible destination in mind. Perhaps Toku could help with arranging her departure. "When I've made myself presentable we'll talk some more."

She had lived a rather sheltered life, Ayesha realised, at least until recently. Sitting here on a dilapidated porch swing, overlooking the garden and livings belonging to Varoi's sire and gazing out toward the fens beyond, made her aware of how little she understood the reality of fen life as it touched on the lives of most adult Shakar. This, she thought, is what Varoi and others like him fight to preserve.

With a flash of malachite feathers a kingfisher flew low overhead. A shrill whistle and whirr of its wings could be heard as it dived into the reeds.

"It's hunting froglets and fingerlings," a deep voice behind her informed, "which are rife at this time of year."

Ayesha glanced over her shoulder and smiled at the tall male with his loosely bound braid of brown and silver hair. His face had a weathered appearance that spoke of respectable age, but his back was as straight as a blade and his amber eyes were as clear and lucent as those of a child. She smiled up at him as he placed a tray laden with pottery plates and mugs on the rough-hewn table set alongside.

"I had no idea there was water this close at hand."

Maderan com 'Domicci smiled back. "There is always water hereabouts, in the heart of the fens. The Shakar did an excellent job of digging ditches and dykes to drain the worst bogs and marshland, creating inland waterways suited to commerce and sailing craft, making rich land available to the plough. But we were never tempted to completely destroy the wondrous variety of habitat that abounds. Had we done so, there would not be the prolific abundance of natural resources we still enjoy. Not all that was here before our arrival was hostile to life."

"And yet you still suffer the occasional outbreak of pestilence and plague."

"Not nearly as much and not so often as when first we arrived. Conditions have improved over the years. Tis best we don't rush things. To do so might alienate our neighbours and, since they were here first, that would not be wise. So. You still find ponds and marshy places well stocked with fish where herons stalk the reedy shallows. Along with small streamlets and rushy rills that are home to otters, mallards and migrant warblers. Most with their livings here would not wish things otherwise."

Ayesha accepted the cup he offered, raising it to her lips as she considered the land to which he had just referred. The garden itself was neatly laid out with an abundance of herbs and sweet-scented flowers, all of which were alive with the buzz of insects and bees. A solitary hive occupied one corner, its industrious inhabitants well provided for. Beyond the garden lay the livings themselves, an area of land that could be ploughed for crops or grazed according to its owner's choice.

Maderan com 'Domicci put most of his to the plough. There were rows of root vegetables along with bushes laden with late season fruits, fallow areas where crops had been harvested or seed was just beginning to sprout.

"You work all this land yourself?"

"I have help when it's needed, but mostly I manage it alone."

"It seems an austere way of life, though I suspect it offers its own rewards."

"Hard labour agrees with me. It keeps me active. Once I had help. Now I manage alone. The flower garden and bees remain; a poignant reminder of my mate."

"You must miss her very much. I miss my two brothers Toku and Sami a great deal, almost as much as I miss Varoi, but I know I'll being seeing them all again, sometime soon. Whereas you ..."

Her voice tailed off, overcome by an acute sense of embarrassment. Intent on offering him sympathy she found herself highlighting their differences instead. Shamed by her inability to find appropriate words, Ayesha buried her nose in her cup, lowering her lashes as she peered at Varoi's sire over its rim.

Still handsome despite his advanced age, she was acutely aware of his virility. He was old enough to be her sire and deserved a fair measure of respect.

As though understanding her dilemma, Maderan proffered a sly wink, which caused Ayesha to blush furiously. What was it about older males that she found so attractive? Dangerously so in the case of Schezan.

Patting her lightly upon her arm Maderan passed Ayesha a plate then offered her some of the food he had prepared. He was not averse to a little female flattery and Ayesha's confused blush pleased him immensely. He was well aware he must be the cause.

"Varoi is lucky to have found you, Ayesha. Some males search years without ever finding their intended mate. It is pleasing to learn you have a close relationship with those siblings of yours. Varoi and his sister Bayritz were equally close; not just in age but in shared affection as well.

"I know Varoi blames himself for the tragedy that befell her. And that he vowed revenge upon the male he holds responsible. There is a custom still upheld in the fens: births, deaths and all other important news must be shared with the bees. Varoi took it upon himself to inform the hive concerning the details surrounding that sad event. He believes me to be unaware of his oath to avenge. I found out by chance and would not want him to think I had been spying on him.

"I lost my wife because of what occurred. I'm not prepared to lose my son as well. Vengeance was the only thing keeping Varoi sane at that time. Best that he remain

ignorant of what I overheard, until such time as he decides
to share that information. I would be grateful if you did not
enlighten him."

Ayesha frowned. She didn't like keeping secrets
from Varoi, especially not when she had just upbraided him
for doing the self-same thing.

"Can you keep my secret?" Maderan's earnest
expression decided for her.

"I can and will. Although I hope I shall not be
required to lie in order to achieve that aim."

"I hope not as well." If Maderan had any further
thoughts on the matter he chose not to express them just
then.

"So, you're Borit. Varoi told me about you but didn't
mention you were ..."

"Human?" Borit supplied. "A lot of us are who live
in the fens." Borit didn't sound the least bit annoyed,
though his comment implied that he might be.

"You didn't let me finish. I was going to say tall
and remarkably well built. Seldom have I seen such
powerful muscles on a human." She reached out a hand to
skim it down his arm with an admiring grin. "And it's all
real!"

Borit laughed, highly amused by her attempted
flattery. "Well, of course it's real. I'm a blacksmith,
Ayesha. Didn't Varoi tell you? Working all day at the
forge, pumping the bellows or swinging a hammer, is
bound to develop good muscular tone. Not all men of the
fens are short and puny."

"I didn't mean to suggest otherwise."

"I know you didn't. I was just teasing. I'm pleased
to make your acquaintance at last."

"And I likewise. Shall we become friends do you
think? I rather hope so."

"I'd like that too. Can I ask you a question?"

"If you wish."

"Did Varoi explain how his sister Bayritz died?"

"Varoi did, eventually. It was Schezan who took pains to inform me first."

"And what did Schezan have to say?"

"That it was an accident. That there was a misunderstanding on Varoi's part. That Bayritz pushed him first and he pushed her back. That she was too close to the edge of the cliff when it happened."

"And what did Varoi say about that?"

"He doesn't believe it *was* accidental. But he has no proof and it was dark. Still, perhaps Varoi is right."

"You sound as though you know something Varoi does not."

"Because I was there. I had reason to be in the forest that night. But I didn't see Bayritz fall. I heard a shout and went to find out what was going on. To satisfy my curiosity, that's all. I saw Varoi fighting Schezan. It was obvious to me he didn't stand a chance of winning any such contest."

"What do you mean?"

Schezan already was what you would term a full-blooded male. Whereas Varoi, at seventeen summers old, was slighter in build than Schezan. Schezan could have kept Varoi at arm's length, waited for his temper to cool. Instead, he met Varoi head on. They grappled. Varoi threw a few punches, to no apparent effect. Then Schezan made a move that made my blood run cold."

"What do you mean?"

"Schezan grabbed ahold of Varoi, swung him about, forcing him backwards, until Varoi's feet all but dangled over the edge of the precipice. One second Varoi was solely intent on avenging his sister, next minute he was fighting for his life. I did what I could to provide a distraction."

"I'm sure you did."

358

"And I helped Varoi to escape."

"For which he owes you his life."

"I don't see things that way. If you wish, I can show you where the drama all took place?"

"I've heard enough about what happened. Perhaps it *is* time I saw for myself."

"It isn't so scary in daylight. Though it will provide you with some idea of the scale of things. I have a free day tomorrow. We could go then."

"If it's no trouble."

Borit, smiling, shook his head. "I shall call for you just after first light."

Ayesha stared down into the steep-sided gorge, which was aptly named the Demon's Throat, nodded once and then found herself unable to retreat, held in thrall by the mesmerizing rush of rough water swirling round the rocks far below.

It was a perilous place, with a long fall on to the unforgiving rocks far below. A risk Varoi had happily embraced, both on his descent into the gorge and during the climb back up. He must have acquired some kind of proof for this to count towards his trials of passage. "And did he?" she wondered aloud. "Did Varoi complete the challenge?"

"Oh yes," Borit replied. "He showed me evidence of that. But he found no joy in his achievement, not after what befell Bayritz."

Just standing this close to the edge was frightening enough. She thought of Varoi, held teetering on the brink by Schezan, expecting that any moment might be his last. But worse than that was the image she had of his sister, crying out as she plummeted down toward the rocks far below.

An overwhelming urge to jump took hold, until Borit, as though made aware of her predicament, placed a strong, restraining hand on her arm. Released from an inexplicable impulse, Ayesha stepped back. Retreating to a safe distance, she gave Borit a sideways glance.

"I had no idea how long the drop was, nor how steep the crumbling nature of the cliff, not to mention the huge boulders that lie at its feet." A sudden thought occurred. "How did you know? That Varoi was in need of rescue, I mean?"

"I didn't. Hearing shouts, I became curious to know what was going on. When I got here I couldn't believe my own eyes."

"How much did you see?"

"Not as much as you might suppose, but enough to know he was in danger."

"So you helped him? Without even knowing who he was?"

"That's about how it happened; how I became involved."

"And you've stayed friends with him ever since?"

"It's no hardship, being friends with Varoi?"

Ayesha looked at him then, surprised at how revealing a statement that was. "You really mean that?"

"Would I say it if it wasn't true?"

"No," she said. "I don't suppose you would."

Borit's next comment was equally thoughtful. "Still, it amazes me how Varoi managed to survive Schezan's assault. Had I not happened along when I did, who knows what dire outcome might have been the result. They were both committed to seeing the matter brought to a definitive conclusion."

He was stating the facts aloud, trying to make sense of them. There was no attempt at implied criticism.

"I'm sure Varoi was glad you intervened when you did."

Borit began walking away, as if anxious to distance himself from the scene of a tragedy with which he had somehow been involved. "I can show you where we hid, if you wish."

Ayesha was curious about that. It was one detail Varoi had not seen fit to explain. Schezan had also avoided the issue. "If it isn't too far."

"Not far at all; in fact, it's on our way back. Although, unlike this section of river, the forest hereabouts is Common Land. The land on which we presently stand belongs to Varoi's father."

"Which implies Schezan was trespassing that night."

"As I understand it, Bayritz invited him along to keep her company." That statement was also revealing. *So, this would have been a romantic tryst,* Ayesha reasoned. *With Varoi's task reduced to a mere distraction.* Now, at last, she felt she understood. A test of courage for which Varoi was permitted one witness. No need, then, to state the obvious: that witness was never meant to be Schezan.

Supposing Bayritz had pushed Schezan too far that fateful night? Might not his reaction be prompted by sheer spite? She knew from personal experience exactly how ruthless Schezan could be when thwarted. Ayesha recalled his comment regarding the incident that had led to Bayritz's death: "she pushed me; I pushed her back; mayhap a little harder than was meant." Those words, if true, were revealing enough.

Which, in turn, begged the inevitable question: how far might he go in order to remove any who dare stand in his way? And there was an impediment in regards to his plans: her declared intent to join with Varoi.

Might Schezan be willing to risk all, including his reputation, in order to remove Varoi, once and for all? Thereby solving all his problems with one fell stroke. Ayesha had a sudden and nasty suspicion he might be tempted to do just that.

She leant against a nearby tree, watching Borit prowl about the gnarled trunk of an old ironbark oak. He was looking a mite miffed as he scuffed about in the leaf litter with the toe of his boot.

"Some scallywag has been here of late. I had a rope ladder secreted here that would have supplied us an easy ascent. As it is …"

He let that thought hang as he took yet another disgruntled turn about the tree. Ayesha did her best to hide her amusement at his obviously dented male pride, considering it a rather endearing aspect of the blacksmith's nature. She could see why he and Varoi had become firm friends.

Glancing up after yet another disconsolate circuit he caught her stifling a wry grin and she was pleased to see his eyes twinkle with like amusement.

"I confess: the joke appears to be on me. Still, it's disappointing that I'm unable to offer you a tour of my humble establishment." She tilted her head in a quizzical pose as he went on to explain. "I built the treehouse some years back. And, while I may have outgrown it since, it still takes my weight. I would have enjoyed showing you around." He tilted his chin to peer aloft, into the cool and leafy canopy. "You can see a little from down here, but it's not the same. Still, it should give you some idea of how effective a hiding place it proved at the time. Far enough out of reach that Schezan could not discover our whereabouts."

Ayesha took her cue from Borit's upward glance and saw a ceiling composed of broad boughs and leafy twigs. And, sure enough, the base of a treehouse high in the canopy. Not that she could see much else. But that, after all, was the point.

"Ah well," said Borit waving that problem aside. "Still, at least you can see why this proved the ideal refuge at the time."

"I do indeed." She fell silent, considering what she knew and what she'd just learnt regarding Schezan's penchant for dealing, in hostile fashion, with any who dare try to thwart his long-held ambitions.

"You can tell me to mind my own business, Ayesha," Borit went on, "but you seem a mite distracted. Is something wrong?"

"I have things on my mind. And yes, I believe something may be wrong."

"Is it anything with which I can help?"

"If you must know, I'm worried Schezan may see fit to call on Varoi."

"With dishonourable intentions you mean?"

"Something like that. I'm probably fretting unnecessarily. Best that you ignore me, I think."

Borit stopped prowling, coming to stand before her. He reminded her of a shaggy-haired hound, all doleful concern. "Whatever the problem, you can share it with me." And that, she thought, was what she needed to hear.

Ayesha decided to take him at his word. "Right. Here it is, then. You can tell me I'm foolish and I'll not take offence." Choosing her words with especial care she began to explain, seeing no point to embellish the truth.

"Varoi advised me, if ever I felt the need to escape Schezan's attentions, I would be welcome here. That you and his father, Maderan, would provide respite. So, when things got a mite too intense, I did as he advised. I'm no longer sure that choice was wise. I think, mayhap, it is Varoi that will prove the most likely target of Schezan's malicious intent. And, since I've become well versed in my Chosen's particular style of venomous rancour, I've become vastly worried on Varoi's behalf."

"You think it prudent to warn him? If so, I'll leave for the city right away."

"In which case, I shall accompany you."

"No, Ayesha. That would be a mistake." But, while Borit remained adamant, Ayesha had not the slightest intention of being left behind.

"I don't see why. Have you ever ventured inside the High Citadel? Have you any notion what rules apply. Or do you assume you can just stroll through the gates with impunity, without anyone paying you heed. Because, I assure you, that would not be the case. There are rules and customs of which you are ignorant. Any one of which could get you arrested or even killed. Face it, Borit. You need my help."

Ayesha lifted her chin in blatant defiance, feet planted, hands fisted on hips.

While she plagued him with her sweetness and reason, Borit was not blind to her subterfuge. If anything, he was more widely travelled than she. But Borit knew if he insisted on her remaining behind she would most likely find some other means of pursuing her sworn objective. Better, he thought, to keep her safely under his watchful eye than leave her traipsing the byways of the capital unchaperoned. Varoi would have his entrails for bootlaces if she came to any harm. That thought alone sufficed to decide matters in her favour.

"If you come, you must do as I say." Ayesha opened her mouth to voice a protest, but Borit would not be gainsaid. "And you'll pose as my sister for so long as I deem it necessary. Provided you don't smile you could pass for human at a pinch. You must wear your hair differently as well. The ruse should work, provided you're careful," he enthused.

Ayesha glared. If he thought her that easy to manipulate he could think again. Then she resorted to an angelic smile, one she guessed should set Borit's nerves on edge. "I have a cousin in the city. She will help us find a place to stay."

"Oh well," said Borit, wisely giving in. "In that case, what choice do I have?"

Varoi settled back, resting his head against a smooth slab of stone, sprawling his arms out to the side so he could drape his forearms along the edges of the bath. He enjoying the indolent lap of water, so hot it might scald if he moved too fast. Closing his eyes, he revelled in the soothing sensation as limbs grown stiff from vigorous exertion began to relax. Bruises gained at the expense of another's attempt at overcoming his hard-fought defence likewise started to ease. The welcome knowledge that those same hurts were similar in proportion to the ones inflicted by him proved some consolation.

Varoi cracked one eye open to study his erstwhile opponent, and noted, with grim satisfaction, the purpling bruise that marked a large area of Andanta's collarbone.

As his eyes drifted shut Varoi garnered in his last remaining dregs of energy. He paid no heed as the thread of *lossa antario* drifted unnoticed overhead.

Until, that is, he was made aware of another's lustful intentions.

The cooling waters were a soothing balm to his various aches and pains. But they were no defence against Ayesha's sensual ministrations.

Varoi's lax body grew tense. His nipples become pert and other, once limp, parts of his anatomy sprang to instant attention. Damn, but she chose the most inopportune times to remind him of her continuing affection.

Slowly, he opened his eyes, settling his gaze upon the male sprawled opposite. He was pleased to discover his opponent was unaware of his increasing state of arousal. Now if he could just persuade Ayesha to leave him alone for a while …

Ayesha. Now is not a good time. She silenced his protest with a kiss that was both tender and passionate. Varoi closed his eyes, gave himself up to the exotic bliss of pure physical pleasure. And felt the tension within him climb, felt a part of him that required scant encouragement jerk in response.

There was something supremely erotic about making love in a bath of warm water, Varoi discovered, as though all sensation were concentrated in those regions of the body most amenable to stimulation. It impelled his libidinous imagination in all manner of exciting ways.

But then he recalled, again, where he was.

Ayesha. Bayshir. Your timing is most inconvenient.

How so? He tried to capture her wandering hands with his, but failed.

Because: not only am I in the bath; I am not alone.

Who shares your ablutions then, Varoi? Her tone was sharp with suspicion and he envisaged her accompanying scowl.

Do not fret, Bayshir. My two companions are male. I would not dream of betraying you with another, but even so.

If they are male then what is your problem?

My problem is ... Varoi abruptly fell silent, as Ayesha discovered for herself the true extent of his arousal.

He threw back his head and, with difficulty, stifled a growl as Ayesha slid supple fingers along his length. Slowly, he opened his eyes ... finding to his consternation that he was now being watched by the one male whose attentions he least wanted to provoke.

"Don't mind me," said Andanta with an amused smile, as Varoi clapped both hands over the offending part of his anatomy. "Go right ahead with whatever it is you have in mind." He cocked his head to one side and added. "I've always rather fancied the idea of being a voyeur."

Varoi slid lower in the water, acutely aware that its lucid quality hid nothing he wanted to conceal. Relieved to find his other companion had fallen fast asleep, he ventured a sickly smile. "*Lossa antario* has occasional disadvantages in my humble opinion," he tried to explain. His eyes grew hooded, their pupils huge and dark, even as he sought to deny the intensely sensual satisfaction Ayesha supplied.

Unable to deter her by other means, he gave short warning of what he was about. *Ayesha. Now is not a good time!* Then he cut communication at a stroke.

He's gone, Ayesha thought, abruptly realising she not yet issued the warning she had specifically wanted to provide.

The morning was fair and Toku whistled merrily as he strode along. He was halfway across the drawbridge when a hand descended upon his shoulder.

Acting on instinct, he spun.

"Schezan! What is it you want?" Toku was mortified when the very first word he uttered came out in a high-pitched shriek. The mere fact that the rest of his sentence emerged in deeper, more mature tones failed to compensate him one bit.

Schezan raised one dark, sardonic brow in silent comment, causing Toku to flush an unbecoming shade of red. "Then twas to you that Ayesha fled like a frightened child, when I sought her out with the express intention of discussing the formalizing of our vows."

Schezan's hand weighed heavy on Toku's shoulder, and the urge to thrust it aside grew. Yet Toku knew better than to succumb to rash temptation where Schezan was concerned. One day Tenbay's garrison commander might wield command over him. He would offer no provocation; lest Schezan should choose, at some later date, to exercise his authority in belated retaliation. But that did *not* mean he was prepared to ignore Schezan's inference that his sister's behaviour was cowardly in any way.

Toku stiffened his stance as he made reply. "Twas not the formalization of your pledge that set Ayesha to flight; rather it was the prospect of a lifetime's union with a male who no longer represents her ultimate choice."

"Do you wish to annoy me, Toku? Be assured, such action would be unwise."

"That was not my intent. I simply stated the facts as Ayesha explained them."

"And where is Ayesha, my soon to be wife? She seems determined to avoid me of late. Foolishly, in my view, since it would take but a brief consultation to put her concerns to rest."

"I know not where Ayesha is. Our hours of relaxation seldom coincide of late. She has her duties and I have mine."

Schezan's face had darkened with irritation as Toku spoke, leaving him in no doubt that Schezan considered his subtle evasion a ploy. Wanting to escape such hostile attention, Toku retreated a step. "I have duties I must attend. Is there a message I can deliver on your behalf?"

Schezan's hand, denied a resting place, fell to his side. "You might tell her that *I* have every intention of honouring our pledge and I expect her to do likewise. Where can I find your sire? Or does he seek to avoid me as well?"

Toku clamped a tight lid on his irritation, supplying a polite answer instead. Eager to flee Schezan's presence he proffered the required information and left.

Schezan wore a thoughtful expression as he watched Toku striding away. His tactics were plainly not working as they should: not with Ayesha, nor with Toku. Perhaps their sire would prove more amenable to his request.

When Schezan arrived at the barbican he was not in the best of moods. Twice thwarted in his endeavours was a position that did not sit well with him. And, while he might be compelled to control his temper where members of Ayesha's family were involved, he felt no such obligation where members of his garrison were concerned.

One glance at his thunderous expression served warning enough. It was the luck of the duty guard commander to be first to suffer the brunt of Schezan's sour disposition as he offered a respectful salute. "Commander."

"Have you nothing better to do than hang about here getting under foot?" Schezan demanded to know, his voice heavy with sarcasm. Bigli responded as he thought fit. "Commander com 'Varicci, I await your pleasure."

"My pleasure, Guard Commander, is best served by seeing you attend to your appointed task."

Summarily dismissed, the guard commander mounted the barbican stairs, feet pounding out a brisk rhythm as he went. He knew better than to argue when faced with such a surly countenance.

"Ho, Bigli," said the lieutenant he found slouched at ease in the topmost entry. "What has you moving in such disagreeable haste?"

"It's Guard Commander to you, Lieutenant," Bigli retorted with sharp contempt. "And a smart salute would not go amiss."

The young lieutenant made a face but, straightening his stance, offered the required salute. "Who's got you in such a snit?" he unwisely asked.

From below came a shout of disapproval. "Guard Commander," Schezan bellowed in his rear. "Attend to your duties. And, when you've quite finished tearing that one off a strip, send the insolent oaf down here. Let's see how he dares address me!"

Bigli grimaced. "I tried to warn you," he remarked softly as he turned away.

Che started down the stairs. Boot-heels rapping out a steady rhythm, he made his descent, fully prepared to face his garrison commander's wrath. If he survived this day in one piece, he'd know better next time not to ignore the warning signs.

Having dealt ruthlessly with his insubordinate lieutenant, Schezan went in search of Ayesha's father, Chief lo 'Savoi. A more tactful approach was required in this case. Neither one of them held precedence in terms of rank or overall authority. If he could persuade Ayesha's sire to accept his point of view, the ceremony could go ahead without further delay. Even Ayesha would not dare defy her sire. His most immediate concern then would be to locate Ayesha, prior to implementing the necessary formalities. After that nothing would stand in his way.

To his chagrin, all efforts at reasonable argument availed him naught. "I can give you nothing without my daughter's consent. Since she is not here to speak for herself it would be presumptuous of me to effect an arrangement not to her liking."

"What do you mean? Where is she if not in the settlement?"

"I'm told that she visits with friends. That she is safe in their care satisfies me. I would not presume to re-order her life on a whim. Though some of my acquaintance would consider acting otherwise, that is not my way."

The words stung. Schezan perceived the implied criticism. Whether or not he could amend matters to his satisfaction remained to be seen.

"You must know by now that you have a rival," Ayesha's father continued.

Schezan growled. "A mere inconvenience in my view."

"As I understand it, Varoi and Ayesha contacted each other through *lossa antario*, which presumably means they are soulmates. 'Those whom the gods bring together shall not be sundered.' You should be familiar with that phrase."

Schezan bared his teeth in a menacing snarl. "That means nothing to me."

"You would defy the gods?"

"I would defy any and all who attempt to tamper with our given pledge."

"Then I'm sorry for you. There is nothing I can add. Ayesha is away visiting friends. I suggest you take time during her absence to rethink your decision."

"If that is your last word on the subject, you'll appreciate why I cannot agree."

"Perhaps you would be wise to exercise a little patience, Schezan."

"Perhaps I shall consider your words." With that Schezan whirled about and strode away, leaving Chief lo 'Savoi to stare at his departing back. *There goes a male with neither the wit nor patience to handle my strong-willed daughter. I always knew they were not a good match.* With a profound sigh he returned to his work.

Much though the chief's attitude annoyed him there was little Schezan could do ... which wasn't to say he could do nothing whatever. There was one course of action he might pursue. He couldn't locate Ayesha and apply pressure there. That was a nuisance.

But there *was* one other impediment to his ambitions, one obstacle that *could* be removed. And there was more than one way of dealing with the problem. Thanks to enquires he knew where Varoi might be found. He had the perfect excuse to visit the capital. All he needed now was the right opportunity.

Chapter 16: Convergence

Shah considered the assembled trainees with a practised air. Both Colvair and Andanta's groups had now been combined, giving him a total of twelve. Even numbers were an important consideration, bearing in mind the final contest during which some would pass whilst others among them died.

Such disparities as once existed between them had now been nullified by means of judicious pruning of those too incompetent to survive and the occasional disability. All those who remained were relatively equal: relative being the appropriate term.

Shah studied each warrior in turn, checking their turnout, the state of their armour and their apparent readiness for action, along with the keen demeanour he'd come to expect of all who were Konicci trained. No sloppy dressers or braggarts succeeded here.

Certain he had their undivided attention, Shah proceeded to explain. "Having become reasonably competent in various new techniques, the time has come for you to apply these same in a more testing environment. To this end, half of you will be wearing one of these." Shah held up a bundle of what looked like black scarves. "Being blindfolded ensures that your primary sense of sight is denied its customary usage. This will refine your other instincts, all of which should help you stay alive in certain adverse conditions, such as fighting an opponent in the dark or when blinded by any means, including injury.

"Those who possess the *ananaha* gift, and you know who I mean, are denied its application here, with sound reason: firstly, it provides an unfair advantage against others not similarly blessed; secondly, should your gift be disabled you will be wholly reliant upon minimal ability, something others rely on constantly; and thirdly, since this exercise is managed to ensure you suffer no threat of death or dismemberment, you have no reason to deploy the *ananaha* gift. It will do all of you good to hone those attributes you casually choose to forget.

"Learn to put your other senses to use. They will serve you better in the long run. Step forward those I name."

Hearing his name called, Varoi took a step closer and waited to see what would transpire. Each day brought fresh challenges. He was amazed by the variety of new skills he'd so far acquired.

Slipping one of the blindfolds over Varoi's head, Shah tied it in place, set one hand to Varoi's head and recited a short incantation. "You will be unable to remove the blindfold until the cantrip is released. It ensures that no cheating occurs, since the blindfold cannot come loose or slip. Be assured, you will benefit from this exercise."

Varoi locked his *ananaha* gift down tight, determined he would not be the one caught cheating. A quarterstaff was placed in his hands and he was led to one of the circles marked out in sawdust on the floor. He had no way of knowing who his opponent would be and could only hope he would be equal to the task. He heard Shah instruct those not obliged to wear blindfolds. Whatever the advice given he had no idea.

The sound of approaching footsteps warned that his opponent drew near. Varoi was forced to admit his disadvantage. For one thing, he had no notion whom his adversary was. He knew who he or she wasn't. That had been made clear on seeing whose names had been called. It left Andanta, Danova and Colvair, none of whom would offer him quarter and any one of whom would derive immense pleasure from making him suffer or laying him out cold. If only he'd taken better note of each one's distinctive approach. They all had one. He'd noticed often enough. Now, with the blindfold in place, he lacked the ability to identify the individual clues that sight had hitherto provided. He began to appreciate what the weapons master meant. He would close his eyes more often in future with luck, and the benefit of hindsight, thereby ensuring he was not so disadvantaged again.

"When you're ready, you may begin. Prepare!"

At Shah's command, Varoi thumped his staff on the floor ... then raised it into a defensive position ... in time to deflect the first blow. After that he concentrated all his efforts on defence. And, as air whistled or whooshed past his ears or a solid crack to his staff sent shivers spiralling along his arm, he was glad he'd made that choice.

As suspected, his selected opponent was well qualified to split his skull and make his ears ring. It was dark inside the blindfold. Never had he been more acutely aware of how much he relied on the faculty of sight. He worked to secure an advantage despite the predicament he found himself in.

Time passed, relentlessly, predictably, as time has a habit of doing. The world spun. Varoi found his second wind.

He learnt to keep his tread light, the better to hear his opposition, which was not easy in a room full of sound. The tap of toe or rap of boot-heel revealed much: a slight change in the angle of attack; a determined lunge, meant to drive past his guard. Balanced upon the balls of his feet he listened intently, filtering out all distracting clamour, focused entirely on surviving this round and, if possible, cutting loose with a few well-directed blows of his own.

The first part of the exercise had been a salutary lesson in deflecting blows. Of accepting, with sanguine equanimity, those smacks and wallops that invariably found their way through. The casual belabouring he had been dealt served to underline his present shortcomings. Still, he would learn what he could and value whatever benefits were forthcoming as a result.

Restricting himself to defensive action was not his normal style. Hampered like this he was hardly a respectable foe. That was, until he honed his senses to better effect and learnt to interpret the relevant information being received. Perhaps then he could turn this situation on its head.

All around him quarterstaffs clattered and clacked together. The occasional "oof" as a blow thumped home relieved the overall theme. Varoi had expelled enough explosive comments of his own. Time he went on the attack.

A sideways shift in his opponent's stance provided both incentive and ripe opportunity. Varoi fielded a blow with casual dexterity ... then swung his staff back.

The gratifying smack of wood against flesh was promptly followed by a yelp of startlement. Below his blindfold, Varoi grinned in grim satisfaction. He was starting to enjoy this particular mode of strenuous activity.

"You might," said Borit, in peevish tones, "have thought to mention the fact that the cousin of whom you spoke was related, through marriage, to another whose sphere of influence encompassed certain aspects of what goes on inside the High Citadel. You might, though you did not, have seen fit to relieve me of the worry regarding the exact means by which we were supposed to gain entry to so well-guarded a domain." He seemed remarkably put out, Ayesha thought. They were standing just inside the entrance to the guardroom of the aforementioned High Citadel, waiting for one of Ayesha's distant relatives to put in an appearance, which event was scheduled to happen any time soon.

"Hush your complaining," Ayesha hissed behind her hand.

"I would not *be* complaining had you not given me cause," Borit replied.

Ayesha rolled her eyes. *Males!* They were all the same, human or otherwise. How they loved being in control. To be fair, she'd had no more idea than Borit how, exactly, they could get inside the High Citadel. Yet here they were. Proof, if proof were needed, that a few discreetly posed queries could get you whatever you required. Well, almost anything; they were only partway inside.

"I wish you would cease complaining. Do you honestly imagine I would have allowed you to do *this* with my hair had I any choice?"

"What's wrong with your hair? It looks pretty to me."

"Tell me," Ayesha swivelled on her chair so she could glare up into Borit's face. "Does your sister really wear her hair like this? If so, I'd be most surprised." She patted the coil of tawny hair piled atop her head. It was held in place with a fistful of pins and felt heavy and tight. "It's *so* damned uncomfortable."

"I have no sister," Borit replied. "I had a brother, once. He died of ague when he was five and I was eight. My mother died too, but my father survived."

"And you, Borit. You also survived."

"The plague never touched me. Father said I must be one of the gods' Chosen and had not yet performed the task for which I was born."

"Then you have a father."

"Had, Ayesha. My father died five years later. A freak accident took his life. He was mending a wagon when the shaft split apart, one half piercing his chest."

"Then I'm sorry for you. But still, it must have been a quick death."

Borit turned aside, hiding his face from Ayesha's scrutiny. "Not really, he lived on for almost an hour, much of it spent in complete agony."

376

Ayesha couldn't imagine how that must be, could think of nothing suitable to say. Instead, she placed a sympathetic arm about Borit's shoulder and they sat in silence for a while. Borit, she realised, would have been thirteen summers old when the mishap occurred: old enough to live alone; too young to witness such tragedy."

An elderly man in servant's livery was approaching. He had a vast stomach and spindly limbs.

"Is this the male to whom your distant cousin is wed?" asked Borit, sniggering.

Ayesha rolled her eyes in exasperation, but said not one word. A sharp retort was on the tip of her tongue, but she refused to be drawn. Instead she whispered a sharp reminder. "Don't forget, leave the talking to me."

"So, you're the new recruits," the liveried servant exclaimed, looking them up and down with a jaundiced eye. "Seems we're scraping the bottom of the barrel these days." He wagged a warning finger. "Mind your manners and don't talk back is my advice." They nodded agreeably. "Best mind my words or you'll not last long."

Borit gave Ayesha a speculative glance. Raising her chin she assumed a dignified pose. "Follow me." She said and stepped out smartly in the servant's wake.

They were led a short distance down the corridor to where another servant, one with charge of the linen stores, waited with quiet patience. Where the first man had been ancient and spindly, this one was young and physically well-made. His purple livery clung with surprising elegance to every sleek and supple line. Ayesha took time to appreciate the view.

"Barret will see you both suitably clothed, after which he'll introduce you to Lieutenant com 'Calovanni."

Ayesha gave Borit a sly dig in the ribs. Calovanni was the officer who had promised to help. Borit made no obvious response. He recalled well enough the arrangements they had made.

377

"He's a rather pompous old bod, but he means well," Barret observed, nodding his head in the general direction of his departing superior before leading them into the linen closet and closing the door. "I received explicit instructions from Lieutenant com 'Calovanni. Seems he expects your tenure to be brief. Quite what he means by that I'm not at liberty to divulge. But I'll see you suitably kitted out just the same. Behave yourselves and keep your collective noses out of trouble and who knows how long your employment might last. Now, let's see."

Barret scanned them up and down, taking astute note of individual build and proportions. Borit squirmed under that intense scrutiny. He was used to women studying him thus, but men doing so made him distinctly embarrassed, no matter how necessary the inspection might be.

"'Tis just as well," Barret observed, "that the livery provided comes in two parts, namely tunic and hose. It provides adequate allowance for variations in stature and size; which isn't to say this is going to be easy by any means."

Behind his back Borit scowled and Ayesha smirked.

"Ah well. All in a day's work." Barret rifled through stacks of garments, emerging with two separate piles.

"Yours and yours," he said, handing them out. "Changing rooms are through there. Let me know how you get on. I'll be right here should you need assistance."

Unlike Borit, who dressed quickly, Ayesha took her time trying the outfit on. She wanted to look her best. After all, she *was* hoping to find Varoi. The last thing she wanted was for him to see her looking anything but her best. So she primped, smoothed and straightened, adjusting the garments until she was satisfied.

Ayesha sauntered back out into the linen store and enquired of Barret, "Well, what do you think?" It was

378

asking a lot that he compliment her, but perhaps he would deign to pass an opinion of sorts.

Barret gave her a quick once-over. "You'll pass," was his sole comment. Ayesha realised she would have to be content with that. "Now, let's find Lieutenant com 'Calovanni."

Having introduced them to the lieutenant, Barret departed.

"Tis pleasant to see you again, Ayesha," Lieutenant com 'Calovanni gave them both a friendly smile. "I know you're anxious to locate a certain individual, who shall remain nameless as far as I'm concerned. Nevertheless, I feel compelled to impress upon you the importance of our more stringent rules. Break them and you'll find yourselves in trouble. And so shall I for providing your means of access. Bear with me while I explain."

Borit shuffled his feet, anxious to proceed with the task in hand. Noticing this, Calovanni added, "It won't take long. I'm concerned for your safety, that's all. Besides, my wife will be displeased should you happen to come to harm."

They left the lieutenant's office with ample amounts of pertinent advice. Lieutenant com 'Calovanni's instructions had been most clear. All they needed to do now was find Varoi.

"We had best split up," suggested Ayesha, as they stepped into the corridor. "From what my cousin's cousin's mate implies, Varoi could be in more than one place. And, judging by the map he showed us, all likely locations are set well apart."

Borit felt inclined to agree. Splitting their resources might be risky, but if it improved their chance of finding Varoi ...

"He could be anywhere, anywhere at all."

"Perhaps. Then again, certain locations sound more promising, you must admit. I suggest we try those first."

Borit had no argument with that.

Schezan was halfway along the darkened tunnel leading to the practice arena when he espied a tall male clad in servant's livery striding purposely ahead. Smiling, he drew the knife from his belt.

It was the perfect opportunity. Servants were not normally allowed in this vicinity. To be caught skulking here was tantamount to treason.

As though made aware of imminent danger, the liveried servant spun and, in the time it took Schezan to slip the knife betwixt his ribs, recognised his assailant.

"Schezan!" Borit gasped out the word as Schezan thrust the blade home, twisting it unmercifully as he glared into the blacksmith's eyes, adding increased pressure with a vehemence he very much enjoyed.

Better and better, thought Schezan, as Borit's hand fumbled with the blade's haft. His eyes were glazing even as he slumped to the ground. I wanted a worthwhile diversion. What could *be* more appropriate than this?

Aiming a vicious kick at the dying man's ribs, Schezan made his way to the tunnel's exit and took a quick peek at the arena beyond. *Joy, oh joy!* If he was in luck, which it seemed that he was, he was about to put paid to the menace that was Varoi com 'Domicci.

Through the rejoinder of clashing staves, the continual flurry of parry and riposte, one singular truth penetrated the fog of Varoi's difficulty: Konicci were never meant to only defend or simply survive; it was their purpose to succeed; to triumph where less determined combatants failed; to smite and lay low their sworn enemy. Therefore, it was imperative he now bear that truth in mind. Doing so, he launched himself forward with renewed vigour, resolute in attack, and was arrested by the single word. "Hold!"

Stretching forth a hand, intent on releasing the blindfold swathing Varoi's head, Shah declared, "Varoi com 'Domicci you learn your lesson well. Tis not enough, in any case, merely to persist."

Even as his reaching fingers drew close, a commotion broke out in the tunnel behind. Waylaid in the act the same hand instinctively flew up, intent on unsheathing its sword. Half a dozen heads abruptly swivelled in the tunnel's direction; twice as many eyes narrowed their acute perspective on the dark mouth of the tunnel itself.

A racketing din of bumps and thuds, of grunts and groans and extraordinarily fluent curses, issued forth from that gloomy maw. Moments later, all went ominously quiet. Then ...

"Treacherous scum, you'll skulk no more." The speaker's voice could clearly be heard.

Varoi felt every hair on his body prickle erect. There was something horribly familiar about those convincing tones; something that put him instantly on guard.

Next minute a warning shout rang out, "Weapons Master, if you would question this man you'd best be quick. He's fading fast."

The passing indecisiveness that had momentarily gripped Varoi and his fellow trainees was replaced by bristling vigilance as the weapons master summoned three of their number to accompany him. Their booted feet converged on the tunnel as another's came forward to intercept.

Shah studied the approaching male. Garbed in Konicci armour, his normally immaculate attire was in serious disarray and splattered with gore.

Shah knew who he was at a glance. Who could not? Living and breathing the same air as the High Obajan gave Shah a unique insight of what went on within the

High Citadel. It was, after all, where the ruling male of all Shakar had his home. Knowing did not equate to liking and Shah reserved judgement on this particular male's character, for now. Yet he knew better than to question his actions or appear in any way impolite. Shah hoped that those pupils with him were equally discreet.

"I found him lurking near the exit," Schezan began, by way of explanation. "He has an accomplice, I suspect. One of the guards, perhaps, or another recently joined with your number. One among the trainees will likely know who he is."

Shah moved forward into the tunnel, anxious to question the man, who, he now saw, was dressed in servant's livery. "Was he armed?"

"A knife; I disarmed him during the struggle." Schezan glanced back towards the arena. "Your pupils: shall I see how they fare?"

Shah was far too concerned by the apparent anomaly of a spy finding his way into their midst, to pay this comment any particular heed. "As you wish."

As Schezan moved past him unobserved, Shah strode forward into the dark and gloomy tunnel, every nerve and sinew tense. This was the perfect place to arrange an ambush. Was this male he was about to confront lying in wait for his quarry or had he another, more sinister purpose in mind? And if he had an accomplice amongst Shah's pupils, who might that be?

Shah found Borit sprawled on his side, one hand wrapped about the dagger's hilt. There was just enough light available to see he was still alive. His breathing was shallow and his eyes were shut. Shah laid a hand to his breast, felt the slow rise and fall of his ribs, the ebbing tide of a life almost quenched. Uncaring what suffering he caused, Shah shook the Fenlander. He wanted answers and he wanted them quick. While there was still a chance they might be obtained.

382

Borit's eyes fluttered open on a rising spiral of pain. Anguish tracked its passage across his face; then fled.

"Who are you? Why are you here?"

Borit blinked, but said naught. Had the man even heard? Shah wondered.

"Tell me!" Shah demanded, raising his voice, adding a touch of compulsion to his words.

To his relief the ploy worked, albeit not as expected. "Varoi ..." the man's voice was faint, barely audible, but Shah heard.

"What about Varoi? Is he your accomplice? Is Varoi the traitor in our midst?"

Borit's eyes drifted closed, "...ware Schezan."

Shah froze with shock at those words. Seconds later he was galvanized into action. "Stay with this man," he commanded. "Let no one near without my express permission." With those few words he hastened away.

Varoi listened in grim silence to the advancing tread of a large and confident male, certain he had only to hear the male speak to confirm his identity. Every instinct he owned was on high alert.

The weapons master had taken pains to inform his trainees that those blessed with the *ananaha* gift should not deploy it here, especially not during this exercise. *"Not unless your life is endangered should you rely on those benefits."* Those had been his explicit instructions from day one. Varoi had adhered to that command faultlessly.

Now he prepared to set those instructions aside. If the approaching male turned out to be who he suspected, he would need every asset he possessed just to stay alive. This Varoi firmly believed.

Every instinct, every iota of self-preservation warned: this male was Schezan.

Varoi dare not waste time wondering who the innocent victim of Schezan's duplicity might be. Whatever Schezan's lethal intent Varoi felt certain he featured largely

383

in the execution of that scheme. Perhaps, in this case, execution would prove the definitive term.

Two paces distant the footsteps stopped. Varoi, hearing a movement alongside, was momentarily distracted. Who might that someone might be? Andanta or Colvair? Both were equally adept.

"Having caused this untoward disruption I feel obliged to keep you suitably amused. So, I thought: a practice bout! A chance to demonstrate Konicci skills. But for this I need an opponent. Who among you shall I choose?"

There followed the sound of footsteps pacing to and fro. Varoi knew this to be a charade. Muffled in darkness he waited for the predator to pounce: to reveal its deadly intent, not with tooth and claw, but with other lethal instruments.

"There is one among you, I hear, who suits my purpose admirably. One who has solved the secret to winning this game. Come now, don't be modest, you know who I mean. Varoi com 'Domicci step forward; let's find out how good you are."

Varoi waited to see whether one of his fellows would point him out. When none did he took the requisite pace forward.

"So there you are," exclaimed Schezan, with false cheerfulness. "Not trying to hide behind a female's skirts, I trust?"

Varoi ignored the artful jibe. No doubt there would be more and worse to come. Instead, he assumed a confident pose, prepared to deliver as solid an assault as his hampered faculties allowed. He would have preferred to see Schezan's face but there was no likelihood of that. The blindfold had been magically bound in place. Schezan was unlikely to countenance any immediate change in that situation.

As though in answer to his unspoken wish he heard a query voiced, "Should not the blindfold first be removed?"

"Why? How can I demonstrate the sundry benefits of this form of training if the essential element is removed? You others had best give us room."

As Schezan snatched a weapon from the rack, Varoi moved. This was no time to consider his position, time only to act. Varoi flung himself into headlong attack.

Swinging his quarterstaff overhead he brought it across in a slashing arc, to have it batted nonchalantly aside.

"How shall we arrange this, do you suppose?" Schezan took time to ask.

Varoi wasted no breath on useless prose. Assuming himself at a disadvantage, Varoi managed his attack as though on the battlefield itself, where each stroke mattered and every blow that connected was sure to count. Like a whirling image of demonic fury, he attacked, organising his assault with surprisingly lethal accuracy.

Incoming blows whistled past him with terminal ferocity. Despite his visual incapacity, few attacks got past his guard. Those that did he accepted with stoic aplomb.

Varoi leapt and kicked, jabbed and whirled, feinted and ducked and spun, administering blows with punishing precision. His assault was a tribute to daring tenacity. He was reckless, ruthless, fearless and formidable. In truth, he fought as though he had nothing to lose. If Schezan had thought he gained an advantage in being able to see his adversary, Varoi made sure he was rudely apprised of his mistake.

There were, Varoi discovered, certain benefits in being unaware how well his opponent fared. He danced a deadly fandango with a partner whose image was Death. And seemed to care not one wit how the contest might end.

Schezan had planned a display of potent ability. Varoi was happy to oblige.

If Schezan came off worse, so be it. In Varoi's view the punishment was apt.

Then his legs were swept from under and he crashed. Rolling away from the point of impact Varoi brought his staff up, intent on deflecting the follow-up strike.

Shah emerged from the tunnel ... and halted mid-stride; brought up short by a bizarre series of kaleidoscopic images.

The light in the arena was cool and bright. Stray glints of luminescence glanced from buckles and iron-shod staffs alike. Stark reminders, if such were required, that the business of this location related to weapons and mortal combat and little else. Dust motes whirled a merry dance amidst soft rays of downward slanting light, stirred to frantic activity by what transpired.

Against the far wall stood all save one of the blindfolded trainees currently in Shah's charge. In front of these was arranged a defensive barrier consisting of the three warriors he had left behind. At the centre of the arena, the main focus of Shah's rapt attention stood and fought Schezan com 'Varicci, an acknowledged Konicci elite, and his one remaining blindfolded trainee. It didn't require too many guesses on the part of Shah to discover which one.

The dying intruder's words had filled him with wary unease. But, as he stood for a moment to observe, he could not fail to be impressed by the deft display with which Varoi kept his opponent at bay, despite the occasional thwack he received. He could not help but admire such skilled artistry.

Until Schezan's weapon swung wide and homed in, that is, sweeping Varoi's tired legs from under.

As the blindfold warrior landed and rolled, deploying his weapon in a defensive pose, so Schezan stabbed his staff down on a destructive trajectory. Varoi had seriously misjudged his opponent's intent. In his effort to avoid the follow-on attack he had provided Schezan with the perfect opportunity.

A thrill of alarm shot through Shah's frame, as he instantly divined Schezan's malign intent, and sparked an instinctive reaction.

"Hold!" bellowed the weapons master, caught indolent in the breach. Deft fingers moved in a frantic flick.

The blindfold dissolved and Varoi, seeing his peril, rolled out from under attack. An unassailable force that rendered him powerless to react seized Schezan.

"Drop your weapons," bawled Shah, desperate to avert a catastrophe. If Schezan knew a way to negate this spell he might yet foil its effect.

In his mind Shah heard again the words uttered by a dying man. *"... ware Schezan."* And understood, at last, where the real danger lay.

Varoi's staff clattered noisily to the ground. But Schezan steadfastly refused the command, despite the strong directive involving compulsion that was attached. Shah strode two paces forward and wrenched the quarterstaff from out his grasp.

But, if Schezan was unable to move, still he could speak. And he did so with utmost hostility. "How dare you seek to interfere?"

Shah eyed him with unconcealed disgust. "I dare because I must. Whatever argument you have with this male must wait for a more opportune time."

"Argument? Who mentioned any argument? I merely thought to demonstrate the lessons that might be learnt by this form of exercise."

"So you say. What kind of fool do you think I am? That last attack was potentially lethal, as well you know."

Schezan laughed, a terrible sound that froze the blood and sent chills racing along the spine.

Varoi started to move away then stopped. "Let's finish this, then, if that is your wish, but on equal terms. Unless, that is, you volunteer to be the one made blind."

Shah growled his displeasure at such a suggestion. "There will be no contest between you. Not while you are my concern, Varoi. This dispute must wait for another time. Colvair, Danova, Noltoi, escort this male to the guardroom. Keep him there till I arrive. I wish a private word with Varoi. You others, continue to practise."

Shah turned to move a few paces distant before explaining his actions in more muted tones. "I cannot afford such disruptions. For that reason I shall in future ensure that Commander com 'Varicci is denied access to this area. I dare not refuse him entry to all parts of the High Citadel since this is his sire's formal abode."

Varoi nodded, understanding the situation only too well. A thought occurred, which he felt obliged to voice, no matter whether it caused more trouble; since, no doubt, the weapons master already considered him a serious liability. "Can I ask what became of the injured man?"

But, as the weapons master opened his mouth to reply, Schezan could not resist a final taunt as he was led away. "Say farewell to the blacksmith for me, Varoi. Such a shame I won't be around to watch your tears fall."

Suspecting yet another attempt to provoke, Varoi could not resist the urge to rise to the bait. His head swivelled in Schezan's direction. "What do you mean?"

"Did I not say? How very remiss of me, that I fail to take full advantage of a heaven-sent opportunity. Your friend Borit proved the perfect diversion. Ah well, must fly, my escort seems most anxious to dispose of me."

Varoi stared after Schezan, horrified by the likelihood, however remote, that Schezan had somehow contrived to use Borit as a means to an end. "Weapons Master, may I request permission to attend the injured man?"

"Be my guest, but you'll do no good. He's dying. There's no doubt of that."

"But, if he's my friend, I owe him my life." Shah gave a dismissive wave that sent Varoi hurrying into the tunnel after Schezan. A sense of foreboding had settled heavy on his heart. Ahead he saw three of his fellow trainees standing guard over a downed man. As Schezan and his escort strode past the guards offered a salute, as much in respect of the Konicci uniform as anything else, Varoi suspected. Nor could he help but bristle with righteous indignation that Schezan should receive any such respect.

As Varoi glanced down at the lax form he found his worst fears confirmed. Yet, as he bent to inspect Borit's wound, he was restrained. Angry, Varoi shook off the arresting hand. "He's my friend, Andanta. Get out of my way," he growled.

"I can't do that, Varoi. I have my orders. *"Let no one near."* I stand by ..." "Let him pass," said a voice of command. And suddenly the way was clear.

"How can we help?" Andanta ventured, at sight of Varoi's obvious concern. Mute with grief Varoi refrained from offering any reply. Borit's face was childlike in repose; he was alive, but only just. "If there were a healer available I would fetch him. I know of none that treats humans, I'm afraid."

"Then healing him shall be my task," Varoi avowed and, ignoring all protests, directed that Borit be moved to the chamber set aside for that purpose.

"What do you want us to do now?" Andanta said, as they laid Borit down.

"Leave us alone, but keep watch on the door," Varoi replied.

Once the door closed behind him Varoi ran his fingers around the frame, sealing the room against intrusion. As far as he knew, cross-species healing had never been attempted before. Yet he owed Borit his life, twice over. One way or another, the debt would be paid.

Moving across to the pallet he knelt behind Borit's head. No healing could occur whilst the instrument of destruction remained in place. With one comforting hand to Borit's face, Varoi took hold of the dagger's hilt and attempted to draw the offending weapon forth. And discovered how vicious a wounding Borit had been dealt. The blade was not just driven deep, but skewed at an impossibly adverse angle.

It took both hands, applied with main force, to wrench the blade out. With it came a crimson tide of gore; gushing forth at an alarming rate to pool on the floor. This was no time for social niceties. Closing his eyes and setting both hands to Borit's brow, Varoi centred his concentration on the task in hand.

Murmuring the required declaration of intent, Varoi plunged ahead, confident that nothing could deter him now. And was confronted by a solid wall of resistance, so dark, so formidable it almost made him quail.

Made of sterner stuff than the average Shakar male, Varoi persisted. Applying shamanic power like a battering ram he strove to force his way through. But the barrier proved too strong, too resilient and equipped with unimaginable power. Borit's spirit, his very life force, fought the sole agency intent on keeping him alive.

Caught in a destructive backlash, Varoi lurched into recoil, and knew instant dismay at what appeared an insoluble quandary. Lashed by the swollen tides of turbulence, he struggled against the undertow, determined to succeed whatever the cost. So strong a will to live should not be denied.

With retreat came brief respite and a chance to regroup and review his chosen course of action. A subtle approach might work where force had failed.

Changing tactics he again requested the necessary permission to proceed. Then, light and insubstantial as a feather, he drifted through Borit's subconscious, seeking the route to healing he required. Trust, he saw, was the indefinable clue; the one matchless element that might result in victory. Despite the increased risk, determination remained a solid counterpoint.

He saw, at last, what was required and how it might be obtained. His own survival provided the pivotal link. Unless he assumed the solid burden of trust imposed, there was no hope. Part of him was still attached to the central core of his existence. If that failed the consequences would be dire. He had no choice.

Offering up his ethereal self, Varoi took one last chance, and felt the febrile cord of his existence snag. Stretched to infinity and beyond, feeling his strength failing, he fought … and felt himself fade to non-existence. If Borit lived, as he believed he would, the debt was paid. Darkness swallowed him whole.

Ayesha doubled back. She was more than a little put-out, having just learnt that the two groups she and Borit were seeking had recently combined. How come Lieutenant Calovanni hadn't seen fit to inform them thus? Perhaps he'd considered it fun to send them on a wild goose chase. She would have a few choice words for him once her mission was done.

There was one place left she had not yet tried. No doubt Borit would get there first but … what the hell!

Spying a group of warriors heading in her direction she pressed her body up against an adjacent wall in a vain attempt to be overlooked ... until she caught sight of the male striding along in their midst. Then her primary instincts flared into full alert and, stepping forward to block their path, she brought the group to an abrupt halt.

"Why are you here, Schezan?" Her worst suspicions aroused, Ayesha was in no mood to be subtle.

Schezan came to a precipitate halt, forcing his escort to do likewise. "It's nice seeing you too, Ayesha." Schezan assumed a considering pose, head tilted to one side. "So, to what do I owe the pleasure of your company? Shall I guess? I warrant I have a fair idea."

Ayesha, bristling at his condescending attitude, drew breath to respond. But one among the three warriors who accompanied him spoke first. "Who is this servant that sees fit to address you with such familiarity?"

Ayesha could not help but cringe as a soft rosy blush suffused her cheeks. Thanks to an overriding impatience to confront Schezan, she had quite forgotten she was clad in servant's livery.

Schezan's reply was sly and teasing in tone, born of malicious spite and gleeful malevolence. "Come now, don't be deceived. She is no servant, despite her attire. She is Shakar, just like you and I; one whose sire has far-reaching influence. Furthermore she is sworn as Chosen to me."

"Not for much longer, Schezan." Ayesha bridled at his insulting tone. "I have found my soulmate and he isn't you. Nothing and no one can come between."

"Are you sure about that?"

"What do you mean?"

"Death, Ayesha. Death, itself, can intervene."

An icy finger of doubt probed at her vitals. "What have you done, Schezan? If you have killed Varoi, then I warn you ..."

"If only I had. Twas not for lack of trying, I can assure you. The obstinate bastard refused to stay down.

And then, as success was within my grasp, I was interrupted, most inconveniently."

At last Ayesha thought she understood. This was no guard of honour that surrounded Schezan, as she'd first assumed, but an altogether different form of escort. As a sense of relief flooded her veins, Schezan took pains to see her further informed.

"Varoi may have survived, but his human friend was less fortunate."

A nasty suspicion started to form, as a new source of concern reared its head. "What do you mean? What foul deed have you visited on Borit?"

"Was that his name? Twas the face I found familiar. He was a trifling inconvenience of which I disposed. Too late to rue his passing, I fear."

This news was not good. The urge to hasten took hold. Ayesha spun, prepared to take flight.

"Hold!" The warning shout stopped her in her tracks, but not for long.

Colvair said, "Take care of him. I'll see she comes to no harm." With these few words she hastened away. Catching Ayesha in three swift strides she seized hold of her arm, bringing her to an abrupt halt. "Running in this place can get you killed."

"I'm willing to take that risk."

"Well, I'm not. Varoi will be most displeased if I'm the one who sees you cut down. I know where to go and you don't. I suspect you could use a guide."

Ayesha had no further arguments to offer. Having introduced herself, Colvair set off at a ground-covering gait. Despite the fact they weren't running Ayesha had trouble keeping up.

"So you're the cause of all this trouble," Colvair began. "I might have known. Any unauthorised conflict meant to inflict fatal wounds usually gets laid at the feet of some female."

Ayesha bristled. A tart retort was on the tip of her tongue.

As they started away Schezan could not resist a final jibe. "Foolish Ayesha, to choose for her mate a male untried in the Konicci arts."

"What does he mean?" she asked Colvair.

"Did no one tell you? You must be aware that all who train as Konicci are required to undergo the ultimate challenge of trial by combat, during which one or the other opponent must die."

"Is there no alternative to death during this trial?"

"None whatsoever." Before Ayesha could summon a suitable query, Colvair added with bitter regret. "If only we could leash that one's tongue as well as his limbs, escort duty would not seem quite so tiresome."

Curiosity aroused, Ayesha perceived it was Schezan to whom Colvair referred. The inevitable prompt emerged. "What do you mean?"

"Did you not see? The weapons master placed a spell of restraint upon the male who claims you as Chosen. Silencing him would have proved profitable as well. Twould have granted us respite from his constant carping. He has a tongue like a lash, which he applies with continuous asperity."

"I couldn't agree more." Ayesha was pleased to find a like-minded ally. Still, she continued to fret. Her first concern was for Borit, who had willingly accompanied her here. What chance his survival if Schezan had left him for dead?

Ayesha found consolation in a constantly murmured refrain. Varoi, at least, is safe … or so she thought.

Chapter 17: Conclusion

Shadows within the tunnel's mouth started to curl and curdle, to coagulate; forming a mass, a shape so dark it appeared to be part of the shadows themselves … which it was not. Shah knew this long before the black clad figure emerged.

This was a phenomenon he had witnessed once or twice before. Always it left him speechless with awe. Not a condition associated with the weapons master as a rule.

How was it done? He wished he knew; wished he had access to the secret.

Magic. No other answer served. Yet this was a magic seldom observed, available to only a chosen few, those who had been created High Obajan. And there was never more than one at any time.

Shah studied the swirling shadows; the soft shimmer and sly glint where the air seemed to thicken. While he waited he idly fingered the hilt of his sword, a worthy weapon should the need arise, which he felt sure it would not.

He cast an inquisitive glance towards where his trainees were absorbed by the latest round of martial activity. Their individual focus was intent upon whichever fellow trainee opposed them, relieved to find none aware of his mysterious visitor's arrival.

He crossed to the tunnel's mouth with a ground-covering stride, dropping a spell of coverture between his goal and his trainees. It allowed him to follow their every altercation, while providing his black-clad visitor total anonymity

"What has he been up to this time?" his visitor growled by way of greeting, his demeanour one of long-suffering pique.

Shah saluted and dipped his head in a show of obeisance. "Eminence. How did you know?"

"I always know when Schezan has been causing chaos. He is my flesh and blood, after all." Which wasn't the full explanation, Shah knew. "He possesses a temper. Seldom does he bother to rein it in, which creates a backlash alerting me to whatever mischief he may be about. It lights up like a beacon inside my head and lands me with a punishing headache till I can track him down. Sometimes the situation is such that I cannot intervene. Meanwhile, I'm forced to endure till the tantrum passes its peak. What is it this time? Nothing too disruptive I trust?"

"I'll tell what little I know and all that I've seen; then leave your good self to pass judgement on what has occurred."

The High Obajan nodded his understanding. "That's always the best."

"How to begin ..." Shah drew in a breath and proceeded to explain.

"Anything else I should know at this time?" his black-clad visitor enquired as Shah's narrative drew to an end.

"If you want my opinion, which I'm sure you could well do without, there's a female at the heart of this dispute. "I've heard rumours of a soulmate being involved during an earlier incident concerning Varoi."

"And you think this may be relevant?"

Shah could offer no other clues. "He's your son, Eminence. Sounding him out might be useful, although how you handle him is not for me to say. It would be remiss of me should I fail to point out: he is a danger to himself and others, in particular the male involved in this altercation. If he were to be excluded it might eliminate future risk." Shah felt he'd said enough.

"I shall consider your comments," was all the acknowledgement he received. Shah dipped his head in a solemn show of respect as the High Obajan turned and slipped away, melting into the background shadows as though he was composed of naught but mist. When Shah looked up his black-clad visitor had vanished as though he had never been.

Schezan paced. The guardroom was small, too small to contain a large and powerful male in a towering rage. His clicking boot-heels seemed to fill the echoing space.

"How long must I be detained? I have important matters to which I wish to attend." His sour tone was a clear indication of his growing frustration.

The guard commander applied his most placating manner as he made reply. "I *can* understand your problem, but getting upset won't help." The atmosphere in the guardroom may have been oppressive before; now it stepped up a notch to downright dangerous.

Schezan whirled. "Now see here."

But his unwitting tormentor wasn't listening. Instead, he came to attention, offering a brisk salute as the door flew wide and, with a crisp rustle of robes, the High Obajan swept in. A brisk nod of his head saw the duty guard commander dismissed, as an angry Schezan spun to confront a sire only marginally less irate.

"I know what you're going to say," Schezan began.

"No, you don't. Not yet. Why don't you explain what's been going on? I'll draw my own conclusions as we go along."

Schezan gave his father a wary glance, sucked in a fraught breath and offered his version of recent events, from first to last, ending with, "Ayesha is the perfect choice as consort for a future High Obajan: witty, pretty, urbane."

"And is she your soulmate?"

Schezan gave a scornful laugh. "Who cares? She *is* what I want."

The air between them briefly shimmered. Schezan experienced a sudden chill. For the first time since they'd started their conversation he had a nagging suspicion he might have said something wrong.

His father pointed out his son's errors with evident contempt. "First, you fatally wounded a civilian. Following that, you attempted to eliminate one of the Konicci trainees. Who were, I might add, under instruction at the time, meaning, of course, that your efforts were duly witnessed by this male's fellow trainees."

"I explained all that. The civilian is a Fenlander, a man of low birth. He means nothing to me; he simply got in my way. That is all. Varoi com 'Domicci, however, deserves to die for coming between Ayesha and me."

"You cannot run around killing off anyone who just happens to upset you or stands in the way of your vaunted ambitions, whatever the provocation may be. It cannot be allowed for one thing. Besides which, your reckless behaviour reflects badly on me."

"When *I* am High Obajan all shall answer to me," Schezan snarled.

"*If!* There is one certainty in life and that is death. And *I* am not yet dead."

There was a fire roaring in the grate and it was hardly cold outside, yet the air in the guardroom was now so frigid it could have been glass. They stood glaring at each other, father and son, and Schezan thought: *If it gets any colder there will be icicles hanging from the rafters in here. My father certainly knows how to make his displeasure felt.*

"You should return to Tenbay and resume your duties as garrison commander. That *is* where you rightly belong."

Schezan persisted. "I am your recognised son and heir."

"A son who has become an inconvenience. A son who seeks to interfere with those in authority.

"This is my home."

"Correction: was. Now you are become no better than an embarrassing guest. One I would rid myself of with dignified haste."

"You're banishing me?"

"Temporarily. For a little while only, so that tempers may cool. There is a swift vessel due to depart on the incoming tide. You will be on it. To make things even more convenient, an escort's arranged. They, along with your bag and baggage, are waiting outside."

"And this matter we have just discussed? This outstanding dispute with Varoi com 'Domicci?"

"All record of this appalling incident will be erased."

"That wasn't what I meant."

"Deal with your dispute at some other time, once Varoi com 'Domicci's training has come to an end. Do not forget, he may not survive to become Konicci."

"And what if he does?"

"I shall keep you informed. Meanwhile, you'll do as I say. And you'll not return until I see fit to say that you may."

It was most annoying. But this was his father, the High Obajan, and Schezan knew better than to disobey. "You seem to have thought of everything." Without another word he turned on his heel and strode out the door.

Varoi awoke to a sense of unreality ... and an indigo sky shot through with silvery, luminescent streaks. He struggled to comprehend: why was he now outside when he should have been in?

As awareness returned full pelt, the strangeness of his predicament was finally brought home to him. Not only was he no longer on the floor of the treatment room, he was not even in Nai Hai du Veral. Nowhere in that great city had horizons the equal of this. For now his attention was drawn to his immediate surroundings, which were distinctive and definitely surreal.

Unfolding his limbs Varoi rose to his feet and looked around. First he took in the black nothingness that flowed like a river at his feet. Yet, unlike any river he knew, it was not bordered with flaxen reeds or rushes, nor randomly bedecked with the flowers of lilies or flags, nor did it chuckle as a river did. It was still and eerie and deathly silent.

Nor did it resemble a road. He'd seen enough paths and highways in his travels to notice the difference and compare.

This was a nothing: a rift in space, save that it lay at his feet; this was an absence of matter, a something *other* … it broadcast the sour flavour of death. And it raised the hairs on his head to attention. Varoi took a swift step back.

Beyond the black chasm that divided this land, the horizon was draped in a filmy gauze of vapour, which drifted and swirled with a strangely hypnotic pulse. It beckoned him close and, the chasm at his feet notwithstanding, Varoi felt compelled to investigate more closely its irresistible terminus.

Resisting the urge to move forward, to risk that ominous gulf, Varoi took another pace back and half turned. Over his shoulder he spied yet another phenomenon: a rainbow, a phosphorescence more beauteous, more vibrant, more ethereal than any rainbow he'd hitherto seen. This too had the power to enthral, to call forth his spirit with compulsive urgency.

Torn between forces of unimaginable potency, Varoi trembled on the brink.

"There you are, Varoi. Somehow I knew I would find you here." The male voice was rich and mellifluous, wonderfully reassuring in tone and, at the same time, strangely familiar. Relieved to have found an ally where he least expected one to be, Varoi turned back and stood tall.

Slowly, before his disbelieving gaze, a male form materialized. Maderan smiled and stepped forward, emerging from transparent luminescence to solid substantiality within the blink of an eye. Varoi returned his father's smile with barely a hint of the lingering astonishment he felt.

"Tis good to see you again, father. And if I knew where *here* was I would welcome you in a more appropriate manner. As it is ..." a casual wave of Varoi's hands encompassed his immediate surroundings, "... welcome, to wherever I happen to be."

"And you have no idea where you are or how you came here?" There was a hint of disbelief apparent in Maderan's tone.

"No more than I understand your presence at this precise time. If you know then enlighten me, I beg."

"I am a facilitator, Varoi. It is my role in life to ease the passage of those who have passed on."

Varoi could not resist a shudder as the icy finger of fate travelled the length of his spine. "Then I am dead. And this treacherous gulf that lies before me is none other than Death's Divide. Tis fitting, I suppose: a life for a life, always assuming that Borit still lives."

"Do you spy him standing anywhere abouts?" Maderan asked in acerbic tones. "If not, I think we may safely assume your sacrifice worked."

"Then I am content."

"Are you? Truly? Have you no unfinished business, Varoi?"

At that Varoi's eyes filled with tears. An unaccustomed regret seized hold of his heart and squeezed for all it was worth.

"Mayhap I have, but what difference does it make. I am here and so are you. The die has already been cast. I may as well accept this as my fate: to end things here and now. It could be worse."

Maderan tilted his head in a quizzical pose. "Then tell me, son. Would you not wish to return if you could?"

"Of course I would. I grieve that the question should need to be asked." Varoi's voice rose with exasperation and residual remorse. "But I have no further choice in the matter. I took a risk. It brought me here. What more can I say?"

At these words Maderan gave a satisfied nod. "You made your choice and I am a facilitator, Varoi. This *is* why I'm here. Just close your eyes and take my hand then say the word."

Understanding crashed in on Varoi with the resounding impact of a thunderbolt. Softly he spoke a word, then closed his eyes and reached out his hand, trusting his father to lead him home.

At the gloomy exit of the tunnel mouth Colvair came to a halt. Ayesha, peering past her shoulder, viewed the practice arena beyond but saw no sign of Varoi and wondered: was he injured after all? Her pulse stammered at the thought.

"We must wait here until practice is suspended or until our presence is made manifest to the weapons master himself."

"How long?"

"As long as it takes. Be patient, Ayesha. There's nothing you can do save wait." That, Ayesha thought, was the hardest thing of all.

Time passed at a disagreeable rate. Minutes rushed by. Conversely, hours seemed to drag, while they waited for the weapons master to notice their presence. If he noticed them at all, he dismissed them as inconsequential and not worth the effort of paying them heed.

Ayesha felt her patience sorely tried by Shah's attitude, which reminded her too much of Schezan.

402

When, at last, Shah deigned to pay them attention his attitude towards Ayesha seemed disparaging to say the least.

"So, Colvair, I see you've returned. I cannot say I approve your choice of companion. You leave here in company with warriors and a Konicci trained commander and return with a servant in tow. Something of a comedown, wouldn't you say?"

If the weapons master intended an insult he amply succeeded in his attempt. Ayesha felt her hackles rise in response to his barbed remark, while Colvair drew herself up to full height and prepared to inform her superior of Ayesha's nationality and rank. As Ayesha drew breath to offer a tart retort, Colvair set a restraining hand on her arm. With a smart salute she offered the required explanation then awaited the weapons master's response.

A glimmer of interest showed in Shah's golden gaze, but he kept any comment regarding Ayesha's interest in Varoi to himself, restricting his verbal response to the niceties required, ending with, "Take our esteemed visitor to the observation gallery. She can wait there. I must warn you, Princess lo 'Savoi. Varoi has embarked on a hazardous undertaking. He is engaged in healing the man who suffered a mortal wounding at the hand of Commander com 'Varicci. Any chance of success is in serious doubt, notwithstanding the fact that cross-species healing has never, to my knowledge, been attempted before."

With a dismissive wave he dispatched them from his thoughts, leaving Colvair to escort Ayesha to the viewing gallery that overlooked the practice arena itself.

Left alone with her thoughts, Ayesha started to pace. She had thought Varoi safe. Now she suspected him to be anything but.

There was only one answer to her present predicament. Regardless of the weapons master's determination to keep her away from the practice arena *that* was where she wanted to be, since *that* was where Varoi would surely next appear.

Stopping by the door that led from the gallery, she listened for footsteps. Hearing none, she lifted the latch and stepped through. With wary stealth she retraced her steps to the tunnel mouth. And, when none noticed her reappearance, she waited until the weapons master's back was turned before making her way to a convenient bench.

Varoi awoke to a cramped tangle of limbs, to find loose strands of his hair soaked with gore, which pooled in ruby luminescence on the treatment room floor. One hand still reached, half clasped, as though another held it in his grasp.

A hoarse sob rose in Varoi's throat, of mixed grief and relief, of knowledge and regret. Almost he'd rejoined his dead mother and Bayritz, almost they'd been reunited. But their existence was presently past reach, beyond that monstrous chasm that was Death's Divide. Knowing how close he had stood to that dreadful abyss he could never doubt nor fear its terrible reality again.

Slowly, he unravelled his limbs and stood, gazing down in mute concern at the lax form of Borit whose pale features were no longer ashen in hue. A slight tinge of colour transfused his previously wan cheeks.

Carefully, Varoi turned Borit's body on its side, used his knife to slit the purple tunic from shoulder to hem and viewed with relief the livid scar where Schezan's blade had recently plunged in.

Borit was healing. Borit still breathed. Borit would live. All this he knew. The evidence was plainly visible. Varoi let out his pent-up breath with a gusty sigh. He had done all he could; time and repose would accomplish the rest.

From her new vantage point, Ayesha commanded a clear view of the tunnel mouth while remaining mostly hidden from those occupying the practice arena.

Unconcerned by the likely extent of the weapons master's wrath should she be discovered, Ayesha settled herself atop the bench, legs drawn up to her chest, arms folded, head resting upon her arms. There she sat in self-absorbed, mournful reverie while the din of the practice arena faded to insignificance and misery took firm hold.

"Why so downcast?" a male questioner posed, causing Ayesha to glance up.

"Varoi!" At sight of him Ayesha thought her heart would burst.

The distance between them was not so great. She hastened to bridge that gap.

Reaching him she leapt into his arms, wrapping her legs about his waist, locking her ankles in place, ensuring she could not be easily dislodged. He allowed her to inspect him closely, twining her arms about his neck, holding his gaze, breathless with joy that he was safe and whole, as she had feared he might not be.

Varoi was overcome by her appearance, by the sudden rush of blood to his loins, the urgent desire to hold her near, closer than close, and check every inch of her body. To reassure himself that she was well and unharmed. The unexpected manner of her greeting pleased him most of all, confirming that she remained, unequivocally and unashamedly, his.

He feathered soft little kisses across her face: from temple to cheek, and from cheek to chin, before latching his mouth to hers and kissing her breathless. His large, capable hands explored, stroking her head, shoulders and back; restlessly spanning the silky length of her thigh, where it nestled close against his flank. All the while he was emitting a soft resonant growl that was more like a purr.

"Did he hurt you, Ayesha?" he asked her at last. "Did Schezan harm you in any way?" To Varoi she looked perfect but he had to know. Had his rival's unprovoked assault caused Ayesha unwonted distress he would take out his anger on Schezan's worthless flesh.

Unclasping her legs from about his flanks, Ayesha lowered her feet to the floor, allowing her thighs to slide seductively against his.

"Do you wish to inspect me minutely, Varoi?" she invited him with a sly smile, fluttering her lashes demurely.

Varoi felt the heat that invaded his body, heard his heart pound to the wild coursing of blood through his veins. Seizing Ayesha by the shoulders he took a step back, holding her out at arm's length, looking her up and down, as he studied her appearance.

"I can explain the clothes," she said.

"I don't think an explanation is required, Ayesha. It's obvious. You and Borit dressed yourselves up in servant's livery in order to gain access to forbidden parts of the High Citadel."

Varoi could not help but approve her choice of outfit. It suited her admirably, especially the tight-fitting hose.

"Borit said I would never get past the guards otherwise." She had no need to say more. "Although," she went on after a moment's pause, "since it seems you allow female warriors to train as Konicci, I could have worn armour instead."

"That would have been most unwise. Had you appeared in the practice arena clad in armour it would have been assumed that you were here to train. You would not have fared well."

"Oh, I don't know," she cast a considering glance at the warriors watching them. "They seem friendly enough. I notice they're all smiling."

"They're not smiling, Ayesha, they're baring their teeth. There is a vast difference, I'll have you know."

She tilted her head, a mischievous gleam in her eye. "I can do that too, Varoi."

To prove her point, Ayesha bared her teeth. As her delectable canines came into view Varoi's heart did a curious flip. It was most disconcerting, he discovered, standing there in front of all his comrades while Ayesha openly flirted with him.

Ayesha stood, studying Varoi's face. The intensity of his gaze was a poignant reminder of how much she'd missed having him around and how close she'd come to losing him completely. That thought, in turn, raised a question she had avoided broaching, until now.

"Are you going to tell me what happened? I know Borit was seriously wounded. I know you've been tending him, healing him so I was told. Dare I ask? How does he fare?"

An exultant grin lit up Varoi's face, as he recalled how close he had come to losing his friend; the risks he had gladly assumed on Borit's behalf.

"Borit lives to fight another day," he gleefully cried. "Despite unforeseen repercussions the results I achieved were worth it in the end."

"And his injuries?" Ayesha enquired.

"All healing ... healed," Varoi corrected. A jubilant gleam apparent in his eye told Ayesha all she really needed to know.

"Then I am glad. For I never would forgive myself had things turned out differently."

Varoi's laughter was infectious, and without realizing it she was soon joining in.

A growl of disapproval failed to dampen their elated spirits even temporarily.

"If you've quite finished chatting, I would prefer that you remove yourselves to somewhere safe. Others present require room to train with no distraction from the business in hand." Shah's voice was a soft rumble alongside Varoi's ear.

Varoi's attention remained fixed on Ayesha as he made polite reply. "Yes, Weapons Master, anything you say."

"Take the rest of the day for your leisure. Be on time when the morrow comes."

"Certainly, Weapons Master," was Varoi's automatic response.

Still Varoi held her close, sliding strong hands over her body, refusing to let her go. A fierce yearning seeped into his soul, reflected in his lucent amber gaze.

Ayesha's green eyes glistened with tears. One tear escaped. Gently, Varoi brushed it away, using the flat of his thumb, placing a soft kiss where it had lain. Then he kissed her mouth soundly, lovingly, languidly, savouring her sweetness.

"It's been too long, Bayshir," he sighed.

And then, because Shah's hot, angry gaze continued burning holes betwixt his shoulder blades, he swept her up in his arms and carried her away.

www.ingramcontent.com/pod-product-compliance
Lightning Source LLC
Chambersburg PA
CBHW030351030726
47497CB00002B/291